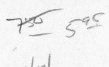

"One of the funniest, most socially exact, heart-rending, and thoroughly enjoyable writers alive."

—Jonathan Raban
The Sunday Times (London)

"When the religion in question is Roman Catholicism and the practitioners in question are the American clergy, no eye has been sharper, no ear finer than that of J. F. Powers. . . . His mastery of our middle-class speech and the elegant economy of his storyteller's gift have long been valued by readers. . . ."

—*The New York Times Book Review*

J. F. Powers is "one of America's most distinguished novelists."

—*Chicago Sun-Times*

"As a Catholic, Powers criticizes from within: with precision and high accuracy and high seriousness, but always with a gentle touch and with charity in the true meaning of that word. . . . What a delight to read the work of an author who believes that there is a difference, after all, between right and wrong. And works hard to define that difference and to hold on to it. . . . Over a period of some 40 years, Powers has established himself as a major author."

—*Minneapolis Star Tribune*

"J. F. Powers is a comic writer of genius, and there is no one like him."

—Mary Gordon
The New York Review of Books

Also by J. F. Powers

Prince of Darkness and Other Stories
The Presence of Grace
Look How the Fish Live
Wheat That Springeth Green*

* Also published by WASHINGTON SQUARE PRESS

J.F. POWERS

Morte D'Urban

Introduction by Mary Gordon

WASHINGTON SQUARE PRESS
PUBLISHED BY POCKET BOOKS

New York   London   Toronto   Sydney   Tokyo   Singapore

A Washington Square Press Publication of
POCKET BOOKS, a division of Simon & Schuster Inc.
1230 Avenue of the Americas, New York, NY 10020

For my mother and father

INTRODUCTION

J. F. Powers is one of those master writers whose genius expresses itself in the description of a small area perfectly understood. Such writers seem to inspire a passionate and loyal following whose position in regard to the objects of their devotion is rather like that of a cadre of militant nurses – reverential, but armed to the teeth. We resent the limited attention paid to our writers, and we think of them as ours, for we appropriate them in a way we would never dream of appropriating another type of writer whose appeal is more broad: Bellow, say, or Doris Lessing. With a hortatory zeal we keep urging our writer upon anyone of our acquaintance who might stay still long enough to hold a book.

It appears that the fate of such writers include periods of eclipse and revelation; one thinks of Barbara Pym, whose territory, like Powers's, includes the demesnes of clerical life. Unlike Barbara Pym, J. F. Powers has never been forgotten in the world of letters, but he has never had the audience he deserves. Despite winning the National Book Award in 1963 for *Morte D'Urban*, he has not been widely taken up. His output has been small: one novel and three collections of stories, *Prince of Darkness* (1947), *The Presence of Grace* (1956), and *Look How The Fish Live* (1975). And he has one subject: priests. But even the rubric priests is too inclusive to describe his speciality. For to understand Powers, one must understand that he is writing about a specific locale: the Middle West.

The Church he writes about has its centre in Chicago, not New York. Chicago is a thousand miles west of New York, a thousand miles further from Rome. It opens onto those large, incomprehensible prairies settled, unlike the East, by people without much Irish or Italian blood. Much earlier than Easterners, Midwesterners believed they could be Catholics and real Americans at the same time. Even now, Eastern Catholics have a sense of themselves as part of an immigrant Church – even the Kennedys, with their good teeth and their Harvard degrees, changed things only slightly.

The Midwestern Church early on lost its Mediterranean tone. The Irish were in charge, particularly in Chicago, but moving further west the Germans grew in power, and the comfort of the ghetto as an imaginative construct was a quickly forgotten temptation. In the middle of the continent, these farmers, businessmen and their sons held to the faith, but the stuff of their dreams was manufactured in the New World. The self-made man, hearty, well heeled, at home in first-class trains, in suites at the Palmer House, was the man they wanted their sons to be. They did not dream of those boys taking New York or Boston – to say nothing of Paris or Rome. Chicago was the focus of ambition and mythology. In Chicago, these Catholics could be at the centre of the things the Protestants felt too high-minded to want, but moving west they could never have access to real power.

They never believed it, though; they never accepted their differentness. For, dress as they might, play golf, vote Republican, send their children to college, they were still led by men who wore black dresses, stayed unmarried, listened to their secrets in dark boxes, owed allegiance to a foreign power to whom they wrote in a foreign tongue. The success of Catholics at assimilating was undeniably connected to the ability of their priests to *pass*, to seem only slightly and interestingly different from Protestant ministers, to be as welcome as they at businessmen's lunches, while secretly praying for the conversion of the Chamber of Commerce and dreaming of a Monsignor being named White House Advisor.

Father Urban Roche, the central character of *Morte D'Urban*, is a product of the Midwest's most treasured image of itself. In this novel, we can see the extended use Powers makes of the priesthood as a kind of metonymic device to explore the themes of community, America, the spiritual/moral life. Urban is an American success; a Midwestern success. His success in the pulpit stems from his mastery of the Midwestern conception of Madison Avenue lingo. His particular linguistic speciality is the recycled dead metaphor. God is 'The Good Thief of Time, accosting us wherever we go, along the highways and byways of life'. In priests' retreats, Urban refers to parish priests as 'those heroic family doctors of the soul', and to himself as 'this poor specialist'. And yet he is a member of a foreign organization, the Catholic Church, and, even more suspicious, within that body he is a member of a religious order, the Clementine Fathers. Urban's reasons for joining the priesthood and the Clementines are revealing: the boy Harvey Roche became the man Father Urban because he perceived at a young age that the best of America was reserved for Protestants:

You felt it was their country, handed down to them by the Pilgrims, George Washington, and others, and that they were taking a risk in letting you live in it. . . He knew, too, that Catholics were mostly Irish and Portuguese, and that their religion, poverty and appearance. . . were all against them.

The one man Harvey meets who seems to have it made like the Protestants is the visiting Father Placidus, a Clementine who spurns rectory hospitality to 'put up at the Merchants's Hotel, where bootblacks, bellboys, and waiters who'd never seen him before seemed to welcome him back'. So Harvey becomes Urban, not because he is called to serve God but because he sees the priesthood as the easiest way to stay in the best hotels, to meet the best people, to live like a Protestant.

But the glamorous Father Placidus is an anomaly within his Order. The Clementines are almost to a man third-raters. Urban is their one star, and they resent him even as they take advantage of his talents. He has perfected the skills of the successful executive, and adapted them to the service of the Church. In creating Urban-at-work, Powers unfolds a world to us, of toastmasters and nightcaps, and priests as good at pleasing as the businessmen they preach to. When we watch Powers's comic treatment of Urban and his clientele, the complicated tone he is capable of sustaining is at once apparent. Self-satisfaction oozes from the well-oiled pores of these priests and businessmen as it does from Malvolio or Tartuffe. Yet no great evil is done by these fat bankers aching to be non-sectarian; nor is it done by the priests. They swim, all of them, in a warm, prosperous ocean of bonhomie and belief in their own broad-mindedness, which they mistake for culture. Powers records them, sticking them, like shining beetles, on a pin.

But in the comic world of *Morte D'Urban* genuine evil has its place. It arrives in the presence of the benefactors, Mrs Thwaites and Billy Cosgrove. Both of these are catches of Father Urban's, for his most important function in the Order is the procuring of rich benefactors for it. Urban sees his vocation as the maker of friends with the Mammon of Wickedness. In a revealing passage, Powers allows us to glimpse Urban's thoughts on that most difficult of Gospel parables:

Our Lord, in Father Urban's opinion, had been dealing with some pretty rough customers out there in the Middle East, the kind of people who wouldn't have been at all distressed by the steward's conduct – either that or people had been a whole lot brighter in biblical times, able to grasp a distinction then. It had even entered Father Urban's mind that Our Lord who, after all, knew what people were like, may have been a little tired on the day he spoke this parable. Sometimes, too, when you were trying to get through to a cold congregation, it was a case of any port in a storm. You'd say things that wouldn't stand up very well in print.

Urban cannot tolerate mystery, paradox, irony – the ingredients of Christ's lesson; therefore he is no match against the evil of Mrs Thwaites and, particularly, Billy Cosgrove. It is in itself ironic that the moment Father Urban begins to act like a real priest he begins to encounter worldly failure. This chilling scene, one of the most memorable and quietly horrible in modern fiction, brings with it a new spiritual awareness, and on it the novel turns.

Morte D'Urban's great distinction is that it is a conversion story told in comic terms. Urban's *peripeteia* takes place in the context of a virtuoso display of Powers's talent for recording American kitsch. His change of life happens at a fishing lodge named Henn's Haven where 'the stuffed birds and fur-bearing animals on the walls wore cellophane slipcovers', and where the proprietor draws Father Urban's attention to a sign that says: 'WE DON'T KNOW WHERE MOTHER IS, BUT WE HAVE POP ON ICE!' And instead of being knocked off his horse on the road to Damascus, he is knocked out by a bishop's golf ball.

Morte D'Urban is indeed satire, and of a very delicious sort, but it is not satire pure and thorough-going. At the end of the novel, Urban is a sobered and perhaps a broken man. He has lost his executive ability, his desire to see the Church 'The best-run company. . . second only to Standard Oil', just when his Order needs his energies most. He finds his soul, but at a cost.

J. F. Powers is a religious writer, but his religious view is less accessible to the modern reader than others might be because its faith shares the stage with satiric comedy. And he has no predecessors, English scenes of comical/clerical life in Sterne or Trollope or Goldsmith do not do; the English tone is sweeter, for those clergymen never have to worry if the community wants someone like them around. In the English novels, if the clerics themselves do not represent personal power, they represent an institution whose power is unquestioned. The furtive, hot desire for assimilation so common to the American Catholics Powers writes about is impossible to imagine in the rural towns where those parsons christen, marry, bury. And the high drama circling round the priests of Bernanos and Graham Greene flies nowhere near the carefully barbered head of Father Urban or Powers's other priests. Powers is a genuine original. Read him, then, for the pleasures he bestows of ear and eye, but read him too for the supreme trustworthiness of his vision, a trust earned by impeccable craft, and by a balance perfectly struck between a cutting irony and a beleaguered faith.

Mary Gordon, New Paltz 1984

Author's Note

I thank the librarians at the St Cloud (Minnesota) Public Library for their help, as I do a few unworldly friends (who shall be nameless) for theirs. I also thank past benefactors: Mr Henry Allen Moe and the John Simon Guggenheim Foundation; the National Institute of Arts and Letters; Mrs Elizabeth Ames and Yaddo (Saratoga Springs, N. Y.); the Rockefeller Foundation; the University of Iowa Writers' Workshop; and the *Kenyon Review*. Parts of this novel first appeared, in a different form, in *The Critic, Esquire*, the *Kenyon Review*, and the *New Yorker*. Needless to say, all characters in the book are fictitious, the views expressed by some of them are not necessarily those of the Catholic Church or the author, and any resemblance to actual persons, living or dead, is coincidental. I myself am the founder of the Order of St Clement and likewise may be held responsible for the Dalmatians and the Dolomites, to say nothing of the dioceses of Great Plains and Ostergothenburg. The noble lines in the ceremony near the end of the book come from St Bernard of Clairvaux.

J.F.P.

Contents

The life of every man is a diary in which he means to write one story, and writes another. . . .

J. M. BARRIE

First I have to tell you something about our Father Provincial. In the Chicago province of the Order of St Clement there are well over a hundred priests and brothers—all accountable to him. Yes, including yours truly. And he in turn is accountable to somebody else, and so it goes, right on up to the Holy Father, who, of course, is accountable to Somebody Else. Now about our Father Provincial. One man may have a weakness for new cars, another for old cars, and so on. You all know what I mean. Well, our Father Provincial's weakness, it seems, is for bees. We've always had chickens and ducks and geese at the Novitiate, sheep, cattle, and pigs. We may even have a horse or two— just about everything you could think of at the Novitiate, except bees. "But Father," I said to our Father Provincial the other day, "do you mean to tell me I'm to go out and say to these good people: 'For nineteen cents a day, my friends, you can clothe, feed, and educate a young man for the priesthood'?" "That is so, Father Urban," he said. "We have the figures to prove it." How do we do it? you ask. My words exactly to our Father Provincial. "Well, Father Urban," he said, "you know we now have our own bees." No, go right ahead and laugh, good people. I felt like laughing myself at the time. But the fact is we can do it. And if we can do it, you can do it. For nineteen cents a day, my friends. Tax deductible. By the way, should you want them later, you'll find pledge cards and pencils in the pew beside you.

Overture

It had been a lucky day for the Order of St Clement the day Mr Billy Cosgrove entered the sacristy of a suburban church after Mass and shook the hand of Father Urban. Billy, a powerful-looking man in his late fifties, hairy of wrist and sunburned (from golf and sailing, Father Urban would discover), had warmly praised the sermon—in which Father Urban had roared and whispered and crooned about Francis of Assisi and Ignatius of Loyola and Clement of Blois and Louis of France and Edward of England and Charles of the Holy Roman Empire—it was he who, you might say, owned and operated Europe but who, in the end, desired only the society of monks—it was he who rehearsed his own funeral, lay down in his coffin, joined in the prayers for the repose of his soul, mingled his tears with those of his attendants—it was he who rose from his coffin in good health, retired to his chambers, and was seized by a fever from which he very soon died . . . and the wonder was that Father Urban could go on in this high he-who manner without minimizing in the least the importance of becoming a penny-ante benefactor of the Order of St Clement.

Billy, however, left the sacristy without saying anything about a contribution, no pledge card bore his name, and the collection baskets produced no surprises. Father Urban might easily have forgotten him. But on the following Saturday, at South Bend,

after the Southern Cal–Notre Dame game, Billy turned up
again—it was he who hailed Father Urban from a grey Rolls-
Royce limousine. Father Urban left his companions, a couple of
novices of the better sort, and rode back to Chicago with Billy
and his companions, two men of Billy's age (and Father Urban's),
with the look of executives about them. They were not drunk,
but they had been drinking, and Father Urban, riding up in
front with the chauffeur, found it difficult to enter into the conversation. About all he could learn of Billy was that he lived on
the North Shore and was having trouble with the wood he was
burning in his fireplaces. This was enough, though.

A few days later, Billy dropped in at the old Loop offices of
the Order. Father Urban had been hoping to see him again, but
he was sorry that it had to happen there. The old building occupied by the Clementines had been in receivership for years
and looked it—looked condemned, in fact. The Clementines were
on the fifth floor. The previous tenant, a publisher of "sexual-
science" books, had prospered and moved, but the frosted glass
doors still bore the words President, Sales, Editorial, Legal, and
Dr Jass. That nothing had been done about these words, and that
nothing like painting or washing had been done in all the time of
their tenancy, was now a matter of pride with some of his col-
leagues, Father Urban told Billy. "But frankly, Mr Cosgrove, I
think we're overstating the case for poverty."

Billy thanked Father Urban for the load of wood, saying it
had come as a great surprise to him, and suggested a ride in the
country. They went down to the car he'd just bought, a flaming
red convertible, motor running and double-parked, but with a
friendly policeman watching over it. Billy, paying more attention
to the car than to Father Urban, drove east, then north, and onto
the Outer Drive. Weaving from lane to lane in defiance of the
law and safety, and without a word of explanation to Father
Urban, who had fallen silent, he passed everything in sight, and

when a squad car zoomed out of ambush and came into con-
tention, he smiled at the officers and—pointed to Father Urban
in his clericals. The squad car dropped away and the red convertible went on for a while as before. "I hope you didn't mind
that," Billy said presently. He was now driving at a reduced
speed, and Father Urban took this into consideration. "Oh, I
guess not," he replied, with a laugh. He had minded, though,
and still did. When they had passed Evanston, and seemed to be
heading for nowhere in particular, though again at a very brisk
clip, Father Urban suggested a visit to the Novitiate, which lay a
few miles to the east of them. "Why not?" said Billy.

The Novitiate was a major and minor seminary, a home for
aged and invalid Clementines, a haven for missioners between engagements ("We're primarily a preaching order, Mr Cosgrove,
preaching and teaching, you might say"), and the headquarters
of the Chicago province ("I've always thought this one should
be known as the Western, or the other one as the New York or
Boston instead of the Eastern province, as it is. One way or the
other, Mr Cosgrove, don't you think? Just the two provinces, yes.
Separate but equal. No, actually, we're the stronger. Iron Curtain? I suppose you could say it's something like that, yes—
administratively, that is—but in recent years I've traveled all over
the country. No, at the moment, I'm about the only one who
does that as a regular thing. Yes, I realize you meant that as a
compliment, but I don't think unfair competition is quite the
term, or even competition. There's a fine, open spirit between
our two provinces, just as there is between provinces in other
orders, and likewise between our order and others. We're all in
this thing together—one big happy army, you might say.").

The Novitiate was also the source of the split oak logs that
had gone to Billy Cosgrove's house on the North Shore, but only
after a struggle, for although there was an abundance of wood at
the Novitiate, and no shortage of slave labor, the farm and the

woodpile were in the hands of hairsplitters. It would have been much easier to get a cord of books out of the library. Oh no, Father Urban had been told, the wood might not be missed, but this didn't mean that outsiders were entitled to it, and Father Provincial was the only one who could dispense largesse on such a grand scale, and so on. Father Urban had offered to pay for the wood out of his own pocket, and might have done so. As a Clementine, he possessed nothing, and the cassock he wore around the Novitiate was pocketless—St Clement of Blois, the Holy Founder of the Order, having regarded pockets rather than money as the root of evil—but Father Urban was away from the Novitiate most of the time, and while he was away his pockets filled up. Nevertheless, he was true to his vow of poverty—to the spirit, though, rather than the letter. For someone in his position, it could not very well be otherwise. Always, after an accounting at the Novitiate, there would be a surplus: *not* Mass stipends, which had to be turned in and processed, but personal gifts from grateful laymen and understanding pastors, fives, tens, and twenties literally forgotten among Father Urban's effects or prudently held out because traveling first-class cost so much more than a tight-fisted bursar could be expected to make allowances for without losing respect for himself and his job.

Father Urban got the wood, however, after he said, "I happen to know that the Dalmatians are making a play for this man."

Showing Billy around the grounds, he met two of his late antagonists, now all smiles, and said, "Yes, Mr Cosgrove, when they found out the wood was going to you, they were afraid it wouldn't be good enough."

"We have more than we can use," said one.

"You're welcome to more," said the other.

Father Urban, moving on, guided Billy to Our Lady's Grotto. They knelt for a moment in prayer. Then they drank from the spring.

"You ought to bottle it," Billy said.

"Think it would pay?"

"*No.*"

Father Urban laughed. "I see our good friends the Dalmatian Fathers are now selling hams."

"*They* should."

Father Urban laughed again. "Good enough," he said. Although more and more orders were finding it necessary to go into business, there were still laymen, and not all of them crackpots, who took a dim view of this development. Billy Cosgrove, it seemed, was one of them.

Father Urban returned to Chicago with Billy, dined at L'Aiglon with him, and then caught a sleeper for Cincinnati— still not knowing what to make of the man. Their talk had turned to trains, on which Billy was an expert, and there it had stayed. Father Urban had expected something of a delicate nature to come up when he was invited to go for a ride, and again when he was invited to dinner, but Billy, a widower and childless, didn't seem to have a problem in the world. In a way— because so many problems were simply insoluble—Father Urban was glad.

Toward the end of October, when Father Urban was back in Chicago for a few days, Billy had taken him to lunch in the Pump Room. Afterward, they walked to an address near by, a half-timbered store front with a mullioned bow window. "No questions?" Billy asked.

"Lead on," said Father Urban.

Billy took him inside, into a display room which, to judge by a couple of cardboard signs, had been vacated by a manufacturer or distributor of longhair phonograph records—"¡Panache Ltd!" Father Urban followed Billy down a corridor to the rear where there was a stockroom. On the way back, Billy threw open doors to the rooms that led off the corridor, three on each side—offices.

Leaving the display room by a side door, they were in the lobby of an apartment building of the better class. They went up in a self-operating elevator, and presently they were strolling around on the roof. Father Urban asked no questions, and Billy, who was obviously enjoying the pantomime, offered no explanations.

They were gazing down upon Chicago and Lake Michigan when, at last, Billy spoke, saying that the roof could be put to some use, perhaps recreation. Then, after a pause, he said, "This would be a prestige address for *any* concern." Father Urban looked far out across the water, where a sail was coming in, and thought that this was the longest buildup to nothing in his experience. He was disappointed that Billy's intentions, so long a mystery, had come to this, for, of course, Billy was wasting his time if he hoped to rent the property to the poor Clementines. He might have the right man in Father Urban, but he had the wrong order. Father Urban wondered if he himself weren't partly responsible. He had painted a pretty rosy picture of the Order of St Clement, and Billy might have taken, say, "far-flung," one of Father Urban's favorite terms, to mean, say, "flourishing," and so on, right down the line. Just as Father Urban was opening his mouth to tell Billy that he'd talk it over with the fathers (*Don't call us, we'll call you*), he heard Billy say, "I'll let you have it for a song—for a prayer, Father."

Billy had meant exactly what he said.

At the next chapter meeting, which was preceded by an inspection tour of the property, the Clementines voted to accept Billy's rather medieval terms. He was to receive three cords of oak firewood annually from the Clementines and to share, as many lay people did, in the spiritual fruits of their work.

It was to be expected that Father Boniface, the Provincial, would want everything in writing, but he harped on this point until he spoiled an otherwise happy occasion for Father Urban.

Not long after they'd left their old quarters in the Loop, Billy showed Father Urban around an apartment on the top floor of the new location. That apartment, with its easy access to the roof and its wonderful view, was now occupied by the Clementines—by the office staff during the week, by men in town for the day, or between trains. Unfortunately for Father Urban, he was usually out of town on weekends, when the apartment was empty, and, when it wasn't, when he was there with the office staff, well—even at the Novitiate, where there were several kindred souls, he had found in recent years that a little bit of community life went a long way with him. And still the apartment was fulfilling its purpose. It wasn't the apartment that had disappointed Father Urban at the new location.

He had wanted the handsome room facing the street to be a showplace—mellow prints, illuminated manuscripts, old maps, calf-bound volumes, Persian carpets, easy chairs, and so on—everything in keeping with the oak-paneled walls, the bow window, and the fireplace. He had wanted the room to be a rendezvous where passers-by would always be welcome to drop in and chat, to peruse the latest in worth-while books and periodicals. Famous visitors to Chicago might be induced to show themselves there, and talks might be given too, not all on religious subjects and none on narrow, controversial lines. A surprising amount of good might be accomplished in that way, indirectly. Of course, it would always be possible for anyone so desiring to sit down with one of the fathers. If converts were made in such surroundings, they would probably be of a type badly needed and generally neglected—the higher type.

But Father Boniface had said no to all this—the idea of such a nook was associated in his mind with Christian Science—and the room was furnished with junk trucked in from the Novitiate: claw-footed tables and chairs, inhumanly high and hard, and large, pious oils (copies of Renaissance masterpieces, executed by a now departed Clementine) in which everybody seemed to be going blind. The room could have been a nuns' parlor at the turn of the century. And lying about in the noble bow window were poisonous pamphlets ("Who, Me? A Heretic?"), issues of the *Clementine* (that wholesome monthly devoted to the entire family and therefore of interest to nobody in particular), and a number of unpopular popular histories and biographies from the Millstone Press (a millstone having been the means of St Clement's death at the hands of Huguenots).

In Father Urban's opinion, these products had only a limited appeal in the vestibules of churches, and none at all in that neighborhood. Doubtless Divine Providence played a big part in what success they had, and the same might be said of the radio program ("God Is Our Sponsor"), but there, on the near North Side, more would depend on the Clementines themselves, Father Urban felt. Failure would be noticeable there. Not only should the window and the room be made attractive but men assigned to this location should be attractive too—picked men, men able to get through to the kind of people residing or working in the district: worldly executives who liked it for its atmosphere, neurotics engaged in the lively arts, retired crooks and politicians, and the womenfolk belonging to all these—not exactly a family audience. Perhaps it *was* a job for the Jesuits, as Father Boniface said, but the Clementines were there on the spot, weren't they? Why should it always be left to the Jesuits to be all things to all men? So Father Urban had argued, but he had got nowhere.

It seemed to him that the Order of St Clement labored under the curse of mediocrity, and had done so almost from the beginning. In Europe, the Clementines hadn't (it was always said) recovered from the French Revolution. It was certain that they hadn't ever really got going in the New World. Their history revealed little to brag about—one saint (the Holy Founder) and a few bishops of missionary sees, no theologians worthy of the name, no original thinkers, not even a scientist. The Clementines were unique in that they were noted for nothing at all. They were in bad shape all over the world. The Chicago province was probably better off than the others, but that wasn't saying much. Their college was failing, their high schools were a break-even proposition at best, and their parishes, except for a few, were in unsettled parts of Texas and New Mexico where no order in its right mind would go. The latest white elephant was an abandoned sanitarium in rural Minnesota! But that was typical of Father Boniface and the rest of them. They just didn't know a bad thing when they saw it—or a good one.

Father Urban was annoyed that so few of the men seemed to appreciate the new location, except for its nearness to the lake. They went out for their interminable walks just as if they were at the Novitiate. Among themselves they jeered at the neighborhood's smart shops, at its restaurants with foreign names, at the little galleries where, of course, there were pictures of the sort one had to expect to see nowadays. Father Urban was annoyed and hurt, yes, but not surprised. The Order did little scouting, being content with the material that came its way—mostly graduates of its high schools and readers of its advertisements ("Be a Priest!") in the *Clementine* and similar magazines. Men like Father Boniface talked of "beefing up" the Order, but Father Urban had another idea—to raise the *tone* by packing the Novitiate with exceptional men. He had overshot the mark on occasion—two of his recruits had proved to be homosexual and one homicidal—and most of them, of course, simply came and went. But there were three or four lads out at the Novitiate, superior lads hanging on for dear life in difficult surroundings. What hope Father Urban had for the Order was in them, and in a few others younger than himself but safely ordained, and in himself.

Father Urban knew (none better) that the Order wasn't up to the job of being an effective influence for good on the near

North Side, or anywhere else in the fast-changing world of today, and it never would be, he knew, with men of Father Boniface's stamp calling the shots. There had to be a new approach. Ideally, it should be their own, recognizably theirs. Otherwise, it was only a matter of time before the Order died on its feet. Possibly the end would be sudden, by decree—a coup de grâce from Rome—for it was rumored that there might be a re-evaluation of religious orders, a culling out of the herd. If this ever happened, it was Father Urban's fear that the Clementines would be among the first to go.

If this ever happened, though, it wouldn't be Father Urban's fault. While others talked of *more*—more time on the air, more publications, more schools, ever more activity of the kind that had already overextended their lines—Father Urban stumped the country, preaching retreats and parish missions, and did the work of a dozen men. And still he found the time and energy to make friends, as enjoined by Scripture, with the mammon of iniquity.

1

The Green Banana

Father Urban, fifty-four, tall and handsome but a trifle loose in
the jowls and red of eye, smiled and put out his hand. He
wondered, though, if he shouldn't discontinue the practice of
shaking hands with Billy Cosgrove's chauffeur. It had begun as
a democratic gesture on Father Urban's part, but for some time
he had felt that it was being wasted on Paul, a tough little Sicilian.

"The Boss, he'd be here, Fahdah, only he had to go out East.
Put him on the New England States Monday. Back tomorrow."

Father Urban relinquished his traveling bag. "No, I'll carry
this one," he said, keeping the attaché case. "How was he feeling, Paul?" Billy had had a cold.

"Good. Too goddamn good, if you ask me. Tried to give me a
raise. You know what I told him, Fahdah?"

"No," said Father Urban, but he thought he did. It had happened once in his presence—Billy threatening Paul with more
money and Paul threatening to hand in his resignation because
he had enough income tax to pay as it was, and so on.

They were descending to the lower level of the LaSalle Street
Station. "I told him I wouldn't change places with him for a
million bucks."

Father Urban deliberately missed his cue but let it appear that
he was concentrating on the steps.

"That's what I told him."

"What'd he say to that, Paul?"

"I *meant* it, Fahdah."

"I'm sure you did, Paul. Was anyone with him at the time?"

"Some guy. I don't know."

Father Urban had thought so. He had an idea there was always somebody else present when Billy and Paul put on their little show.

The grey Rolls was parked under a "No Parking" sign. Paul opened the rear door for Father Urban and pushed the bag in after him. When Paul was seated behind the wheel, Father Urban leaned forward, opened the glass partition, and stuck a Dunhill Monte Cristo Colorado Maduro No. 1 in the slot between the chauffeur's head and ear. As usual, Paul made too much of it. He was accustomed to Billy, though, and Billy was a stickler for gratitude. Of course, where Billy was concerned, there was much to be grateful for.

"Tell me, Paul. Have you seen anything of Father Gabriel?"

"Naw," Paul said, as if Father Urban and the Clementines had nothing to fear from Father Gabriel and the Dalmatians.

"Nice man," said Father Urban, trying to throw Paul off the scent.

For a few minutes in the Loop, Paul was quiet, fencing with traffic. At one corner, at the last possible moment, he gave way to a truck driver who called his bluff, but at the next corner he was himself again, cutting the Rolls through a soft surf of pedestrians. On Michigan Avenue, he relaxed and said to Father Urban, "Hey, the Chief ran into the Super Chief. It was awful."

"Too bad." Paul was only talking about Billy's electric trains, but it did seem a shame to Father Urban that wrecks were so frequent on Billy's railroad. (The ballroom of his big house was given over to it.) It made Father Urban nervous to watch Billy perform split-second maneuvers with the little trains. It was almost as if he expected them to save themselves.

"So I put 'em in the basket."

"Too bad." Father Urban had seen the basket—a large laundry basket filling up with damaged equipment to be taken out to the veterans' hospital for repairs.

"I don't know," Paul said. "Those boys make out all right."

"I know." Father Urban knew that Billy supplied the vets with the tools and materials they needed to rehabilitate the little trains for him, and that he was always thinking of things to brighten their days—color TV sets, for instance—and still. . . .

Paul, waiting for a light to change, raced his motor at a pedestrian. Instead of hurrying across the street, the pedestrian, an elderly, well-dressed man, stopped directly in front of the Rolls just as the light turned green and, with gestures, appeared to be inviting Paul to run over him. "I wouldn't give you the satisfaction!" Paul yelled out the window. The old pedestrian smiled and held his position. Cars in the next lane proceeded while those behind Paul were honking. Then the light changed to red again, and the pedestrian continued on his way, leaving Paul to sit through another light.

"How do you like that?" he said.

Father Urban said nothing. He rather admired the pedestrian for standing up to Paul and the Rolls—after all, *they* had started it.

"Ever see anything like that, Fahdah?"

"Oh well," said Father Urban, and fell silent. Billy made just such demands on him—demands that couldn't quite be met in conscience. In restaurants, when Billy made a disturbance and sent back the steak, Father Urban would say, "Oh well," and try to smile. He was reluctant to admonish Billy and hoped that the day would come when he'd know how to bring out the best in the man. Some of the most powerful figures in history had been

spoiled children like Billy, but humble monks had brought them
to their knees and turned their bloody hands to the service of
God. Not running off the mouth at every opportunity, but knowing when to cast one's pearls, and how—that, in the best sense
of the word, was priestcraft. So, until Billy was *ready*, it was important not to antagonize him. As for Paul, he was only an aspect
of Billy, and would come later, as Constantine's legions had come
later. Nevertheless, Father Urban wished that he could exercise
more power over Paul. The obscene noises the chauffeur made
when he saw a pretty girl were disturbing (after all, Paul was a
husband and a father) and hard to ignore. Father Urban was
always pleased when Billy said something, as he did now and
then: "Grow up, Greaseball," or "Why don't you check yourself
into a nice, quiet institution, friend?"

There was a parking place near the new location, but Father
Urban was firm about being let out in the street. He was afraid
that Paul, if he got the car parked, would recall his first impres-
sions of the firetrap formerly occupied by the Clementines. "In
there?" Paul had said to himself when he saw the building, "In
that?" when he saw the old bird-cage elevator, and "Down
there?" when he saw the dim corridor at the end of which the
Clementines had their offices. Father Urban hadn't minded
hearing it the first couple of times but would hold still for it
now only when Billy was present. Father Boniface, along on
one such occasion (the first and last for him), had left in the
middle of it, which must have looked like ingratitude to Billy.

"Not like the old days, huh, Fahdah?"

"Thanks a lot, Paul," said Father Urban, and made off with
his attaché case and bag. Paul hadn't reminisced under such circumstances before—he was blocking traffic—but apparently he
had been about to try.

In the reception room, Father Urban met Father John, an older man for whom, in a way, he had a lot of respect. "How's it going, Jack?"

"Not so good, Urban."

"I don't believe it." Father Urban did, though. Jack should have been taken off the road long ago—put to teaching, or encouraged to write again, as he had in his youth. Now and then Father Urban threw him an engagement, but he didn't like to do it. Jack didn't generate much heat from the pulpit, and a number of pastors who had booked him for a mission were never heard from again.

Jack had removed his bifocals and was polishing them on his not too clean handkerchief. Without them he was almost blind, and that part of his face ordinarily under glass looked indecently exposed. "In town long, Urban?"

"Leaving tomorrow. St Paul."

Jack was staring at Father Urban, pretending that he could see. He had been about to say something, it seemed, but had changed his mind.

Father Urban laid a hand on his arm, rather startling him, for he hadn't seen it coming. "I'll be seeing you," Father Urban said. As he was leaving the room, he glanced back and thought how well poor Jack, with his glasses off, went with the pictures.

Father Urban picked up his mail from Father Boniface's secretary. "How's everything with you, Brother?"

"Fine, thank you, Father," said Brother Henry.

"Good, good," said Father Urban, looking through his mail. He was about to leave when he spotted an envelope in the outgoing basket, an envelope addressed to him. "I might as well take this," he said. He removed the envelope from the basket.

"It was my understanding," Brother Henry was saying, "that Father Provincial wanted you to get that in St Paul." Brother Henry had addressed these words more to his typewriter than to Father Urban, and now, with his fingers trembling on the keys, he seemed to be waiting for Father Urban to return the envelope.

"I wouldn't worry about it, Brother, if I were you," said Father Urban, coldly smiling. He was thinking how much more he used to enjoy his days in Chicago, before Father Boniface came to power. Respect for Father Urban was still there, but something negative had been added, or was showing itself. In Brother Henry's case, it was probably only envy—the ground crewman's envy for the man who actually did the flying—and what might be called puritanism. Father Urban had tried to interest Brother Henry in pipe-smoking, saying that it would help his digestion. "Take it easy, Brother," he said now, and went and stuck his head into Father Boniface's office.

The Provincial, a lean, pale, damp-looking Pole with a hairline winding up and around like the endless seam on a baseball, sat at his desk cleaning his fingernails with a letter opener. On the wall behind him, just as in their old quarters, hung a crucifix and part of the propeller from the airplane in which his brother, a chaplain in the First War, had perished. Father Boniface had been a chaplain himself in the Second War. "How's it going, Father?" he asked, and went right on with his nails.

"I can't complain."

"Good."

"I'll be seeing you," said Father Urban, withdrawing his head. He wouldn't be seeing Father Boniface, though, if he could help it, until he stuck his head into the office again, after his next trip. He reported not to the man but to the authority vested in him, but this, too, was hard for Father Urban. He felt that the authority might have been his if the members of the Order had only known that by electing him Provincial they would not be losing him in the field. He would have carried on as always, as a fighting general, you might say. Unfortunately, there was no precedent for such an arrangement, and there hadn't been a discreet way to suggest it. At least none had occurred to Father

Urban at the time. Before the next election rolled around, however, he meant to go into the whole matter with Father August,
his old confessor, who, though rather inclined to take everything
with a grain of salt, including the future of the Order, was popular with the younger element at the Novitiate and wasn't partial
to the present administration. Father August, if he so desired,
could talk up the idea in a quiet way. It would be up to the
others then.

On his way back to the stockroom, Father Urban met Brother
Henry in the corridor, smiled, and said, "This way, you see, you
save a stamp."

"Yes, Father."

In the stockroom, Brother Lawrence, who had found his vocation late in life, got up from his chair by the window and came
to the counter, asking, "Where you off to this time, Father?"
He had been a brakeman in the world and took a lively interest
in Father Urban's travels.

"St Paul."

They discussed the merits of the railroads running between
Chicago and the Twin Cities, and the possibility of a merger
between two of them that Brother Lawrence had heard of, and
then Father Urban checked off the pamphlet titles he'd need on
his next trip.

"You don't take this any more, Father." Brother Lawrence
held up a copy of a pamphlet written years ago.

Father Urban knew that Brother Lawrence was trying to help
Jack—who had figured in his vocation, the two of them having
enjoyed many quiet talks between Galesburg and Quincy,
Brother Lawrence's old run on the C.B. & Q.—but this was asking too much. Even elderly pastors pathologically sympathetic to
Jack's message (temperance) complained about the outdated language, words like "flapper" and "sheik" and "applesauce" (as
an oath), and about the art work on the cover, where a coal-

burning train and a touring car were engaged in what was obviously going to be a photo finish at the crossing. The young people in the touring car, one of whom sat on the tonneau and kicked up a pretty leg, held champagne glasses out of which bubbled the words of the title, "Danger Ahead!" Father Urban shook his head. "I wish he'd revise."

"This just came in," said Brother Lawrence, having done what he could for Jack. He reached under the counter and came up with a pamphlet on mercy killing by Father Clem, a nom de plume in general use in the Order. In this instance, the author was Father Boniface himself. For many years, "Help, Murder!" had disintegrated in vestibules and then it had entirely disappeared, but now here it was again. Father Urban wasn't fooled by the flashy new cover, nor, he thought, would the big dealers, the priests and nuns who could make or break a pamphlet, be fooled by it. Brother Lawrence didn't seem to realize that this was the second time around for "Help."

"Is it moving at all, Brother?"

"It just came in, Father."

Father Urban nodded. Loyal, he thought—all of 'em loyal to Father Boniface. "I'll think about it," he said, going back to the chair by the window. After removing Brother Lawrence's reading matter—a paperback by Erle Stanley Gardner—he sat down to his mail. He re-read Billy's postcard (a view of Faneuil Hall, Boston): "N. E. States on time. Merchants to N. Y. tomorrow. Back on Friday, Century. Lunch with you? Just—Billy." Father Urban's cards to Billy came to much the same thing, even to the self-effacing "Just," which Billy had appropriated. Father Urban then discarded the second-class stuff unopened and got down to the usual requests for his services in the future, several of them from pastors who'd had him before. Remembering the food and accommodations at one place, inexcusable for such a well-to-do parish, he resolved what would have been a conflict of dates. Then he opened the envelope lifted from Brother Henry's basket, and groaned, wadded up the letter, and groaned again.

Brother Lawrence, at the counter, turned and stared—as if to see whether Father Urban was all right, or was having a heart attack.

Father Urban gave him a discouraging look. Then he uncrumpled the letter, laid it on his knee, and ironed it with the palm of his hand. He had opened the envelope, expecting to read that he was asked to pray for this or that, for somebody dead or dying, or was asked to call on some friend of the Order in the Twin Cities, for such was the stuff of Father Boniface's correspondence with Father Urban. But here was a letter saying that Father Urban's engagement in St Paul would be his last on the road, that "someone" would take his itinerary from there. Here was a letter ordering him to report to the newest white elephant, the new foundation, as it was called in the letter, near Duesterhaus, Minnesota. No, it didn't make sense, even by Clementine standards, which had been hard enough to fathom before but which had now become positively inscrutable, and why had the matter been handled in this manner, by letter? Because Father Boniface was afraid of him! Or at least was afraid of a scene. Go and see him then! Have it out! And be asked how he came into possession of the letter? Or not be asked, and have his little transgression hanging over him, detracting from whatever he might say?

Father Urban restored the letter to its envelope, and put the envelope in his pocket. As he saw it, the letter had been coming for a long time, from the moment Father Boniface came to power. It had been on the way for two years, and now, finally, it had arrived. *How did a man like Father Boniface ever get elected?* Simple. Nature might abhor a vacuum, but the Order of St Clement didn't. It was as simple as that.

But Father Boniface would regret this. When the word got around that Father Urban was unavailable, and his long-standing engagements were assigned to another, to Jack, say, and the cancellations rolled in, then Father Boniface would know what he'd done when he gave his best man the green banana.

Jack, who had entered the stockroom, and was talking trains with Brother Lawrence, suddenly caught sight of Father Urban and came back to him. "I don't know why I didn't tell you this before, Urban," Jack said. "But I've been transferred."

"Oh?"

"Yes. To this new place in Minnesota."

Father Urban gazed out the window at a row of garbage cans in the alley—all the ground-floor windows in the neighborhood had steel bars over them, another sign of the times, he thought —and felt that he should say something encouraging, but he wasn't up to it. "Will you be in charge up there?" he asked. Anything was possible.

"Oh no. Nothing like that." Jack said he understood that Father Wilfrid, the man now in charge, was staying on. The other two men there, though, were being sent elsewhere—where, Jack didn't know, nor did he know who would be replacing him on the road. "Maybe nobody," he said, as if he had no illusions about himself.

"Well, I'm sorry to hear it," Father Urban said. In the circumstances, Jack's transfer was almost as much of a blow to him as his own. Why did it have to happen this way? Why did it have to happen to them both at the same time? Why did they have to go off together like two men sentenced by the same judge, on the same day, to the same institution? "But I can't say I'm surprised," said Father Urban, again gazing through the bars at the garbage cans in the alley. "As soon as a man's any good to himself and the Order, you can be sure he'll be given something else to do. I've seen it happen too often. That's one reason we're where we are today—nowhere."

Jack glanced around. He probably meant that Brother Lawrence shouldn't be hearing such talk.

"Well, you know, in a thing like this, Urban. . . ."

"Ours not to reason why? Is that it?"

Jack, it seemed, had something to say, but didn't care to say it and was giving the world every possible chance to end first. "No, Urban, it's *not* for us to say, and you know it. Not in a thing like this." Jack had spoken with surprising firmness for him and now appeared anxious to leave.

"Have it your way," Father Urban said, releasing him. He watched Jack depart and noted that his rubber heels were worn down to the leather. Jack's attitude was the right one, of course, but it must come easier for someone like him. What did *he* have to lose?

Father Urban knew that he'd have to do better with Billy. We go where the Lord willeth, and all that, but could he do it? Wouldn't it be easier to phone Billy's office and call off their next day's luncheon date? If they met, and it came out how Father Urban really felt about the transfer, Billy might take it as an act of ingratitude to him, which in a way it was, and try to throw his weight around with Father Boniface. Nothing good could come of that. It would be much easier to give Billy the bad news, and show the right attitude, in a letter. So there was really nothing to keep Father Urban from leaving for St Paul on the Zephyr that afternoon. If he hurried, he could catch the North Coast Limited. And if he left that afternoon, he'd be well out of an evening at the apartment or at the Novitiate, an evening of pretending that all was well with the world.

But then Jack entered the stockroom again, and came back to him again, and, for several moments, just stood there looking down at him in a benign manner, which Father Urban found nerve-wracking. He was afraid that Jack had somehow found out what he obviously hadn't known before: that he wasn't the only one ticketed for Minnesota. For reasons of pride, Father Urban hadn't told Jack before, and for the same reasons, and also because he hadn't told him before, he didn't wish to now. Yes, he knew that he was making it harder for himself later. "Well, Jack?"

"I've been thinking about what you said before," Jack said. "I just want to say that in a thing like this I don't much care what happens to me, but it's nice to know somebody else does."

"Oh?" said Father Urban, but he nodded—as if to say yes, he had spoken as he had not out of a mean spirit of criticism, which ill became one under a vow of obedience to his superiors, but out of an excess of brotherly love. What the hell else could he do? Tell the truth? *Now?* The truth, if it came out now, would hurt Jack more than it would Father Urban, which was saying a great deal, and that was why Father Urban allowed the misunderstanding to go on. It meant a lot to a poor soul like Jack. You could even say it was serving a very good purpose. Going a step further, Father Urban said, "Jack, if you don't have another engagement, I'd like to take you out to lunch."

As it happened, Jack didn't have another engagement.

They were sitting in the Pump Room, dining on champagne and shish kebab, one of Billy Cosgrove's favorite combinations, and the spirit of Billy, powerful if not all-protecting (it couldn't be invoked against unjust superiors), seemed to watch over them there. At the next table, coffee was being served by a colored boy got up in turban, white breeches, and green hose, the first of his brilliant kind to come within range of Jack's limited vision. Jack aimed a finger, from what he seemed to think was a concealed position on the table, in the boy's direction.

Father Urban nodded. "Yes, I know. I've been here once or twice before." In fact, he had been there many times, and was known there even before he met Billy, who, however, was the only one of his hosts ever to urge him to make use of his account. Father Urban had done so on occasion, but this was the first time he had brought along a guest. The idea had been to give Jack something to remember in their exile. Father Urban was beginning to wonder, though, if his guest wouldn't have been happier in a cafeteria.

Jack flinched and drew back when a Turk passed with a piece of meat on a flaming sword. "You'd think they'd do that in the kitchen."

"Oh, that's all part of coming here," said Father Urban. He drained his glass, and the waiter was there to fill it up.

"Maybe you could pay us a little visit when you're through in St Paul," Jack said. "At Duesterhaus."

Father Urban hesitated. No, he wasn't ready to go into that. "I might," he said. "Drink up."

Jack raised his full glass and downed it all. He seemed to forget all about his glass until the waiter came to fill Father Urban's. "Save you a trip," he said to the waiter.

"You shouldn't bolt your food," said Father Urban.

The waiter filled Jack's glass and moved away.

Before they finished the lamb, they were working on a second bottle of champagne, and Father Urban was passing into another phase. He was almost ready to be delivered of his secret. It could be a minor operation, only a few painful moments, and these under a light anesthesia of wine. Jack took people at their best and would see that Father Urban had been in a state of shock when the misunderstanding arose. Jack might not be hurt at all. In any event, he had to be told. Otherwise, their first meeting at Duesterhaus would be an ordeal. Jack would recall to the end of his days how the two of them had sat in the Pump Room enjoying what they'd thought was a farewell party, when all the time. . . .

"Lamb," Jack said, going deeper into a matter that hadn't interested Father Urban earlier. "We know Our Lord ate lamb."

Father Urban gazed around the handsome room. A man nodded to him. Father Urban nodded back and murmured, "Hello."

"Friend?" said Jack.

"Apparently."

"If what we're eating now. . . ."

"Shish kebab."

"If *this* has always been considered a great delicacy throughout the Middle East, as you say, I think it's quite possible Our Lord could have eaten it at some time. We know Our Lord participated in at least one wedding feast, that of the poor couple who ran out of wine. Let's hope they weren't so poor they couldn't afford meat, mutton if not lamb. I daresay lamb wasn't so dear in those days. But there were a number of occasions when Our Lord dined with the rich and well-to-do—Pharisees and the like."

"I didn't say Our Lord hadn't eaten shish kebab. I only said I didn't know," said Father Urban, thinking they'd have some fine evenings together.

The waiter filled Father Urban's glass.

Jack, again confronted by his full one, downed it all. "Save you a trip."

"I wish you wouldn't keep saying that," Father Urban said, regarding Jack with suspicion. "Would you like some coffee?"

"Urban, I would, if you don't mind."

"Shouldn't drink so much."

"No."

"You can't handle it."

"No, and I've never cared for it—not that *this* isn't very good wine. One of the hardest things about the priesthood for me—the wine."

"Why didn't you say so?" Father Urban knew why, though. Jack had been trying to keep his end up.

A little while later Jack said, "Why not pay us a little visit while you're up that way?" Jack had shown signs of drowsiness before, but now, not waiting for Father Urban to reply, he closed his eyes and dropped off. Poor Jack!

Whether Father Urban would have evaded the question again and left Jack with his illusion, or whether he would have sacrificed it to the truth, he didn't know. He did know that the choice was no longer his, and that their next meeting was going to be much harder than it might have been for him. He would have to pay for misleading Jack into thinking too well of him, but not pay too much, perhaps, when one considered the high cost of fellowship to the author of "Danger Ahead!" Jack, as he must have done on a thousand and one nights, sitting up in a day coach to save money, was weaving in sleep, banking as the train took a curve.

Father Urban shook him gently with one hand, and with the other he hailed a blackamoor coffee boy.

2

A Grand Place, This

After the first night of the mission in St Paul, the only question
was whether the floor of the old church would hold up for the
duration, so great were the crowds. Unfortunately, the pastor
wasn't on hand to see them. But the first assistant, who said he
knew the boss's every wish, seriously considered calling him in
Hot Springs to urge him to fly home a few days early, in time
to hear Father Urban. That was how the first assistant felt about
Father Urban. And the second assistant, who belonged to what
the first assistant said was an old St Paul family, kept taking
Father Urban out to eat. They went to the best restaurants in
the Twin Cities, and in the end Father Urban awarded the palm
to the Criterion. As for the people—they gave as good as they
got, and were, as Father Urban told them, wonderful. The first
assistant was wonderful. The second assistant was wonderful. It
was *that* kind of mission, Father Urban's last mission, and he
went out like a champion.

On the final night, after the solemn closing, the assistants threw
a party for Father Urban in the rectory. With plenty to drink,
snacks provided by a caterer of imagination, and with none of
the company much over thirty (except Father Urban), and no
laymen present, it was a pretty lively affair. Father Urban was

very favorably impressed by the quality of the St Paul clergy. Along about midnight, however, somebody turned up the volume on the hi-fi and there were other indications that the party might get rough. Father Urban was asked whether it wasn't possible for preaching, even good preaching, to defeat its own purpose.

"Ah, ha!" he said.

"I'm not talking about Billy Graham, or Fulton Sheen."

"You're talking about me."

"Well, yes, Father."

First Father Urban threw them a curve by putting in a good word for Billy Graham, and then he said, "I'll answer your question by telling you a little story." Somebody groaned. "All right. Then I won't. I'll give it to you straight. The big miracles happen—or they don't—after I'm gone. That's all there is to it. It's up to you."

"It's up to us."

"I'm afraid so."

"After you're gone."

"Yes." That, said Father Urban, was when the real work began, the long haul. That was when they could be thankful they were what they were—priests of the order of Melchisedech, with the sacraments, the wisdom, the power, and the glory of the Church behind them. Oh, the task that Father Urban set them was great, of course it was, but it was not too great—not for *them*. After all, it was not required that they succeed, but only that they do their best. Father Urban said he sometimes thought there were those who considered this too much. "I may be wrong."

By their silence, the young men showed that he might be right. Yes, they seemed to say, they saw what he meant, and it wasn't too much to ask of them. "Sometimes, though"—this from one of them—"don't the people get all hopped up?"

Father Urban let it appear that he was temporarily at a loss for words, which was not the case, for he had been over this ground before, on many such occasions. The trick was in making it seem that each time was the first time. "Hopped up? Has anything ever been achieved in this world *except* by people hopped up? Salvation least of all! Our Lord said, 'Go, and teach ye all nations.' He did not say, 'Go, and have ye a beer.' Oh, I know what you're driving at, but I think anybody who's ever seen me work will tell you I preach a pretty clean mission. I keep the razzmatazz to a minimum."

"That's true," said the second assistant.

"Yes, and that's why I can't understand it," said the first assistant.

"But you know," said Father Urban, easing up and smiling, "I sometimes wonder if I shouldn't preach and conduct myself in such a criminal manner that the local clergy would seem like living saints to their parishioners! Maybe *that's* the answer to your question! If so, it opens up a whole new field!"

In one way or another, the young men applauded Father Urban, and he, thinking he wouldn't do much better than that, got up and bade them all good night. They wouldn't let him retire, however, until he'd given them each his blessing, and then three of them followed him to the foot of the stairs, one asking where he was off to next. For Father Urban this was the hardest question of the evening. Early in the week, with everything going so well, in church and out, he had decided to say nothing about his next stop. He had met a lot of people in St Paul, and yet not one of them, though they all knew he was a Clementine, had so much as mentioned the foundation at Duesterhaus. This had shown him how much of a splash the Order was making in Minnesota and had made what was happening to him seem even more of a comedown. So he just smiled now and said, in the words of St Paul, "God knows," and got the hell upstairs.

The next morning, after saying the early Mass, he took a taxi to the station and boarded one of the few passenger trains still in operation on the Minnesota Central, the Voyageur, or Voyager, as it was called.

The country beyond Minneapolis seemed awfully empty to him, flat and treeless, Illinois without people. It didn't attract, it didn't repel. He saw more streams than he'd see in Illinois, but they weren't working. November was winter here. Too many white frame farmhouses, not new and not old, not at all what Father Urban would care to come home to for Thanksgiving or Christmas. Rusty implements. Brown dirt. Grey skies. Ice. No snow. A great deal of talk about this on the train. Father Urban dropped entirely out of it after an hour or so.

The Voyageur arrived in Duesterhaus a few minutes before eleven that morning, and Father Urban was the only passenger to get off. Since the Order's new foundation was not in but near the town, he went into the station to ask about a taxi, rather doubting that there would be one in such a place as Duesterhaus appeared to be. The station agent, writing at his desk, seemed unaware of him. An old dog lying behind the counter woke up and gave him a look that said, Can't you see he's working on his report?

"I'd like to call a taxi, if I may," said Father Urban, giving the town the benefit of a doubt, and then he waited.

Presently the agent got up and came to the counter. He pushed the telephone at Father Urban and tossed him a thin directory. "Cost you a dime to call," he said.

The dog opened its eyes, as if it wanted to see how Father Urban would take the bad news.

Father Urban put a dime on the counter.

The dog closed its eyes.

"Under Herman," said the agent, going back to his desk.

The directory was for Olympe, the nearest town of any size, but Father Urban discovered the Duesterhaus numbers in the back pages. "Herman's Hardware is all I find here."

"Yeah, well, that's it."

A woman answered the phone at Herman's and said he'd have to wait awhile. He told her who he was and where he wished to go, thinking this might help, but it didn't. (The woman had to mind the store, and her husband, besides being in the hardware and taxi business, was also an undertaker, she said, and as such would be occupied for the next hour.) Father Urban put another dime on the counter and called the Order of St Clement—the foundation was so listed in the directory. He hadn't done this before because he preferred to arrive under his own power. There was no answer. He picked up the dime.

"How far is it out to the Order of St Clement?" he asked the agent.

"The Home? About a mile."

Father Urban felt that they were talking about the same place, but that the agent was trying to be difficult. "Like to leave my luggage and call for it later."

"We can't be responsible."

"I understand." Father Urban went over to his traveling bag and attaché case, intending to carry them back to the agent for safekeeping.

"Leave 'em there. As safe there as anywhere."

Father Urban moved the pieces away from the door. Then he decided to take the attaché case with him, remembering that a dog had once wet on it in Pittsburgh. He asked the way to his destination, this time referring to it simply as "St Clement's."

"The Home?"

"Have it your way."

"To the stoplight, and turn right."

"Much obliged," said Father Urban, wondering what ailed the man and thinking that if this was how the town welcomed a priest there was plenty of work to do there.

Duesterhaus was a one-stoplight town. New and old yellow

lines ran at cross purposes on the pavement, marking a recent change from diagonal to parallel parking. The main street was a state highway. The drugstore was the bus station.

Father Urban came to the stoplight and was in no doubt that he should turn right. Here, however, an old yokel in overalls stared with such curiosity that Father Urban, as a favor to him, asked the way out to the Order of St Clement's place.

"Better ask inside, Reverend."

Father Urban nodded and kept going. He wasn't—whatever the old fool might think—afraid to enter a tavern, but he didn't have to prove it to himself or anyone else. Dear God, the situations you could find yourself in! What he needed was a peg or two from the silver flask in his attaché case. On second thought, that was not what he needed. Many a good city man had gone down that drain. Yes, and even worse fates, it was said, could overtake a city man in desolation—women, insanity, decay.

He passed a cemetery, Protestant. Farther along the road, he saw a rabbit take off into the cornstalks. It would be something, he thought, if he could learn the ways and habits of animals, could read their tracks in the snow, could tell the flowers and trees by their leaves, the birds by their eggs—"So you thought this was an owl egg, did you, Johnny?"—and could take more of an interest in the weather, too. He had read that there were subtle pleasures to be had from all this. Perhaps. Too bad he couldn't begin then by enjoying his hike. The wind was getting to him, though. He wasn't dressed for the great outdoors, and to walk faster, he felt, might be an invitation to the invisible dogs barking the news of his coming from farm to farm. What if he had to run for it? Wouldn't it be better to stand his ground and beat them off with his attaché case until help arrived? Too late. Hounds. Mastiffs. Dead, perhaps eaten. Anything could happen here.

What if, when he reached the summit of the long rise he was

climbing, there was still nothing? What if the station agent had lied to him? That would be going pretty far, yes, but from what he'd seen of the agent, it wasn't out of the question, and later the man would simply deny everything. You turned right? I said left. The joke would be on the stranger. The dog would laugh. No other witnesses. No recourse. Father Urban trudged on, almost resigned to the idea that he'd been betrayed by the first man he'd met in Duesterhaus.

And then he was standing still on top of the long hill, looking down, seeing what he had finally come to. About fifty yards up from the shore line of a frozen lake (the other end of which he had seen in Duesterhaus and then lost sight of and forgotten) stood two sizable structures, one an ornate old mansion of grey stones, mansard roof, and a heavy brown beard of vines, the other a long, low red-brick affair, the obvious product of fairly recent times. They were as different in their architecture as a steam packet and an ore boat. Sheds and cribs and coops seemed to stir at their moorings whenever the wind blew hard, and perhaps some of them did. Chickens and pigs might have figured in the economy of the place at one time. There was no telling what did now. There was no sign of life.

A board bore the legend ORDER OF SAINT CLEMENT in green paint. The lettering was sharp and elegant, worthy of a tombstone, but the colors, green on cream, didn't do much for each other, and the sign, besides being nailed to a tree, had been peppered with shot, so that the over-all effect was rather like FRESH EGGS FOR SALE.

He left the blacktop road for the dirt one leading down. Under closer scrutiny, the low red-brick building appeared to be unoccupied. He heard a cracking noise—the first suggestion of life about the place—and went in the direction of it. In a field, at some distance from him, a muffled figure was moving slowly through the dead grass and weeds, through the haze. Father Urban coughed. The figure, that of a man, rounded on him. When Father Urban saw the gun, a rifle, he feared for his life, thinking this was some half-witted yokel—who, having been given hunting privileges, and having killed a stranger, would get off scot-free at the inquest.

"Never do that," the man called out.

"Hello, Wilf. I wouldn't have known you."

"Game make a noise like that sometimes," said Father Wilfrid, who, on account of his broad nose and padded cheeks, had been called Bunny in the Novitiate. Bunny Bestudik. He wore a very long coat of rich devil's-food brown, with a collar of pearly nylon fleece. His headpiece, though, was soft and black with an olive cast to it, genuine fur, which, in places, looked as though it had just been licked by a cat. He was a few years younger than Father Urban and had a sandy look.

"What kind of game?"

"Well, deer do."

Father Urban doubted that any deer in its right mind would show itself in broad daylight in such an open area.

"Gophers," Wilf said, patting the rifle. "That's what *I'm* after."

"For a moment, I was afraid it might be people," Father Urban said, smiling, remembering the big rabbit who shot the hunter in *Struwwelpeter*.

"It's no laughing matter. They're here in great numbers. See."

Father Urban observed a small, smooth hole in the ground. "They can play hell with a golf course. Or is that something else?"

"That's your pocket gopher, or ground squirrel, but they're all the same."

"Must be hard for you to shoot with mittens on."

"Think so?" Wilf aimed the rifle at a tree stump in the distance, fired, and missed. He had released the trigger by a little pressure. "Pretty sensitive instrument. That's why it's best to keep the safety on."

"Gun empty now?"

"No, she's good for a few more."

"Where's the safety?"

"Right here," Wilf said, snapping it on without comment. He put out his hand. "Long time no see."

Father Urban shook the mitten. He hadn't seen Wilf for several years—the last time in a forest preserve near Chicago, at a Serbian national picnic, or had it been Croatian? "I Am an American Day," anyway, with Father Urban, in a major address, welcoming the foreign-born in the name of all the discoverers of America, St Brendan, Leif Ericsson, and Christopher Columbus, all Catholics, lest we forget. . . .

"You drive up, Urban?"

"Drive, hell."

"I thought maybe somebody drove you up from St Paul."

"I came by train and after that by foot," said Father Urban. He explained about the taxi.

"Should've given us a ring here. We're in the book now." Wilf sounded rather proud of this. "I could've met you."

"I didn't know but what you'd be busy."

"Not so much doing in the morning."

Father Urban asked about the red-brick building.

"Not in use at present," Wilf said.

"Looks the more habitable of the two."

"More about that anon," Wilf said and pointed to a battered pickup truck parked behind the old stone mansion. He had found it in one of the fields, he said, and seemed to think that this would be hard for anyone to believe. "Quite a break, wouldn't you say?"

"Still runs, huh?"

"Does now. Needed a bit of work. Quite a bit, in fact. But a lot less than some people imagined."

Father Urban guessed that "some people" referred to his immediate predecessors, particularly Father Louis, a capable man, one of the few Clementines about whom that statement could be made.

"If I'd listened to some people, the old bus would be rusting away in some dump now," Wilf said. "Oh, I know it's not much for looks."

"No," said Father Urban.

"But we needed *some* means of transportation, and it came down to this or nothing."

"A hard choice."

Wilf stiffened. "Urban, you know how the Order's run. I don't have to tell you we're on our own here. Sink or swim."

Father Urban nodded slightly. The members of the Order did have to support themselves wherever they were, but indigence, Father Urban felt, was too often a cloak for imcompetence. And wasn't it bad enough for the Order to own and operate such a vehicle without advertising the fact? On the door of the old wreck, in green paint, for everybody to see, were the words: ORDER OF SAINT CLEMENT.

Wilf kicked one of the tires. "New rubber all around," he said.

Father Urban grunted and moved on, drifting around to the front door of the old mansion. "The man at the station kept calling this 'the Home.'"

"We're lucky it isn't called worse, considering all that's gone on here."

"Like what?"

Wilf said that the old house had been built for a lumber baron who had murdered his wife and a servant and killed himself—not in the house itself but in a barn that had long since disappeared. Quite a scandal in its day, and this probably accounted for the use to which the property had been put subsequently, for it had then been purchased by the county and turned into an old-people's home, really a poorhouse. Fortunately, all that was very much in the past—all but the name "the Home." In the thirties, the place had been operated as a sanitarium specializing in alcoholics. The red-brick building dated from that period. The place had continued as a sanitarium until World War II. The federal government had been interested in it then, but had backed out at the last minute. "Backed out *only* because the war ended. If the war hadn't ended, I doubt that we'd be here today."

"What *is* the story on that?"

"I'll go into all that later, Father, if you don't mind."

"Not a-tall." Father Urban hadn't noticed the wrought iron-work around the porch of the old house before, because of the heavy growth of vines. "A little bit of old New Orleans," he said.

"You might say that," Wilf replied, as though he didn't know whether Father Urban meant to be critical or not.

"Been doing some painting, I see." On the porch there was quite a gathering of rocking chairs, freshly painted, green.

"Sometimes it's what you don't see," Wilf said. "Funny thing about these chairs. For a long time, I knew something was wrong, but I didn't know what. Then one day it dawned on me—too many chairs. Too many of these rockers. So some I painted, some I threw out—those beyond repair—and the rest I put up in the attic, for the future. Another man might have seen what was wrong right away."

"Oh, I don't know about that."

Wilf took one of the chairs by the ear and lined it up with the others. "You know, the evenings here can be very nice sometimes."

"Is that so?"

"Just sitting here, watching the sun go down in all its glory. The house faces west, you know."

For a moment, Father Urban saw the two of them as others might someday see them—in a snapshot: "Frs Wilfrid and Urban in their favorite rockers."

"A grand place, this," said Wilf, looking out at the grounds.

"Yes," said Father Urban, looking at the bare trees and bushes, the dead fields, the trees in the distance like black whiskers on the winter horizon.

"You cold?" said Wilf.

"Just numb is all."

They passed through a vestibule, through a door the upper half of which was frosted glass, with the letter "T" on it, and were in the house proper, at the foot of a wide, open stairway, and the juncture of two dark corridors. Immediately to the right there was a door with a sign on it saying, in green paint, OFFICE, and here Wilf left the rifle. Then saying, "First things first," he opened the door across the corridor. "Originally this was the music room, I understand."

The chapel was about what Father Urban had expected. The altar at the other end was one of those old marbleized wooden jobs, and on the floor around it lay the green carpeting that had probably been thrown out at the same time. There were eight or nine old-fashioned mahogany pews, rather nice in their way. There were also a number of folding chairs, old church-supper specials, varnished wood, all slats and rattles. On the walls, the Stations of the Cross, dark pictures, were set about six feet apart. That was about it. Father Urban genuflected, and left Wilf kneeling in his wake, but as he did so he reminded himself to spend more time before the Blessed Sacrament. It was all too easy to neglect prayer if you lived at the pace he had in the world.

Next Father Urban was shown into the refectory, which was

comfortably warm, and might have been a very pleasant room. The high wainscoting need not be varnished like old office furniture, and the view from the alcove could be improved by setting out a few evergreens—and by replacing a pane of glass now cracked and fitted with a metal disc such as Father Urban had last seen on the bottom of a pot when he was young. There were two tables. Father Urban put clergy at the round one in the alcove, laity at the long one on the windowless side of the room. Both tables were covered with plastic, white becoming ivory, not very appetizing. Against one wall there was an old console radio, a "Majestic," he saw when he went over to it, and remembered the once famous words, "mighty monarch of the air." In the center of the room were three of the green rockers, the seats of these fitted with chunks of foam rubber; an overloaded magazine rack; and a heavy-duty stainless-steel smoking stand—a hotel-lobby or club-car model, with a trap-door top and a deep tank that seldom if ever needed emptying. There was a tray for glasses around the top of the smoking stand, and on the tray a dish of horehound drops. Father Urban helped himself to one.

Wilf, who had gone into the kitchen, now returned with a corpulent young man clad in khaki coveralls and introduced him to Father Urban. "Brother Harold, Father. My good right hand."

Father Urban couldn't recall Brother Harold from anywhere. He looked quite intelligent, though, and this wasn't always the case with lay brothers in the Order of St Clement.

"As a rule, we have our principal meal in the evening," Wilf said, "but Brother, here, wants to depart from the usual today."

"Not on my account, I hope."

"Come, see," said Brother Harold.

Intelligent, yes, and light on his feet for a fat man but perhaps a bit feminine. Father Urban followed Wilf and Brother Harold into the kitchen. In the sink lay a big frozen fish, a vicious-looking thing marked like a snake. "Sturgeon?"

"No, that's your northern pike," Wilf said.

"Won't it be quite a job?" Father Urban said to Brother Harold who only smiled.

"Brother, here, is used to it."

"I mean—won't it take a while?" Father Urban had breakfasted early.

"Yes, but it'll be worth it," Wilf said. "We'll just leave everything to Brother."

In the refectory, Father Urban had another horehound drop. "Where's Jack?" he asked Wilf.

"Not here at the moment. I sent him out the same day he arrived. Place about sixty miles from here. Pastor I hadn't heard from before. With things the way they are, I try to be accommodating."

"How *are* things?"

"Pretty good, on the whole."

"I suppose you told Jack I was coming."

"Did I? No, I don't think so. We didn't have a minute together. I sent him right out."

It did seem to Father Urban that Wilf might have found time to tell Jack. "And when's he coming back?"

"I'm expecting him back on the evening train—in time for a little powwow."

Wilf took Father Urban to the office then. "You might care to familiarize yourself with that," he said, and waved Father Urban away from the desk, over to the wall where there was a crude plan of the house. Then he covered the clutter of papers and photographs on the desk with a newspaper. "Find your room yet? Your name's on it. Here you are. Southern exposure."

"How's the place to heat?"

"Oh, it all depends. Of course, I'm not heating the whole house at present."

"Coal or oil?"

"Oil. Furnace converted before I came. *That* was one thing I didn't have to do." Wilf moved over to a bookcase, one shelf of which had been partitioned off into cubbyholes. "Where you get your mail. See—your box has your name on it." Wilf felt inside the box. "Nothing in it yet," he said. From one of the other cubbyholes—one labeled PASSES—he removed a card in a clear plastic protector and handed it to Father Urban.

"How'd you manage this?"

"President of the railroad is a friend of ours."

"Is that so?"

"Father Louis knew him. At least he once rode with him."

"Good man, Louis."

Wilf didn't pick up on this. "It'd be nice if we could get another pass," he said. "We just have the two at present. They don't like it down at the station, of course. Loss of revenue for them. But with us here, attracting visitors from all over, they'll be the winners in the end."

"I sensed something today."

"Was something said?"

"Oh no. I just got the impression I wasn't very welcome."

"Wacker. He's the worst. But be that as it may. Telephone, typewriter, stationery, both paper and envelopes—all here, and feel free to use 'em."

Leaving the office, they went down the corridor that ran straight back from the front door, on their right the chapel, on their left a series of rooms. "Parlor," Wilf said, rapping the first door and passing on. "Not heated at present. Another," he said, rapping on the next door. Signs on these doors said PARLOR A and PARLOR B. The next door, which was the last, said LIBRARY, and this they entered. Here, too, it was cold enough for Father

Urban to see his breath before him. On the walls were pictures of popes, Cardinal Newman and Cardinal Spellman, Archbishop Ireland of St Paul (who had been jobbed out of the red hat in Rome), St Clement of Blois (as he may have appeared), and several bishops. Father Urban recognized all but one of these and asked Wilf about that one. Bishop Dullinger, of the neighboring diocese of Ostergothenburg, Wilf said. "Over here, our bishop."

"Yes, I know," said Father Urban. The face of Monsignor Conor, now, and for many years, bishop of Great Plains, had once been a feature of the diocesan press in Chicago.

"It badly needs cataloguing," Wilf said, with a flourish of his hand, taking in perhaps a thousand volumes.

"Nothing very recent, is there?"

"No money for books, Father. What you see here was given to us."

Father Urban could believe it. He didn't know which he found harder to take, the whining or the bragging. Why talk of cataloguing this rubbish? Why call the thing parked outside transportation? Wilf, it seemed, was trying to do it all with words and signs, and, yes, even in the library—rocking chairs.

Leaving the library, they went up the back stairway and emerged into a large space ("not being heated at the moment") that Wilf called the Rec Room: ping-pong table with a dirty piece of canvas over it ("drop cloth"), paper half off the walls ("be surprised how hard it is to get off"), tools lying around on the floor. "Formerly two rooms. Quite a job taking that wall out."

Father Urban looked up at the ceiling. The wall had been yanked out like a tooth, the gap crudely plastered over, and now, presumably, was expected to heal itself. Letters from Father Louis, and rumor, had prepared Father Urban for such sights.

"More than we bargained for," said Wilf.

"I daresay."

"But well worth it. Now retreatants will have a place to go in their free time. (We don't try to enforce total silence here.) And in the event of an overflow crowd, why, we'll just bring in some folding chairs and pipe the conferences up from downstairs—you realize we're standing right over the chapel, don't you?"

"Own a public-address system, do you?"

"Not at present, no."

Father Urban had suspected as much. "A good one costs like hell, you know, and there's no use having any other kind."

"Wonder if we couldn't pick up a good one secondhand?"

"I really couldn't say," said Father Urban. He went over to the window and gazed out at the frozen lake.

Wilf came and stood beside him and, after a moment, said, "Think you'll be happy here?"

After meditating several replies, Father Urban said, "I don't know why not—do you?"

"No, there's a lot to be done here. You may not think so, but there is."

"What makes you say that?"

"Well, I know this isn't what you're used to. Maybe it's a lot less than you expected. Maybe you didn't expect much. I don't know."

Father Urban felt that Wilf was asking for his support—for more support than should be expected from a man who had been treated so shabbily. "What are those trees that keep their leaves?" he asked.

"That's your red oak."

Father Urban moved away from the window. "Have you had many overflow crowds?"

"Can't say as we have, as yet."

"Any?"

"No."

They left the Rec Room, going out by another door. In the corridor, there were more signs: TOILET, TUB, UTILITY CLOSET, FR WILFRID.

"Where do you get your signs?"

"Brother Harold's taking a course by mail. Show-card lettering."

"Oh?"

"His ultimate goal is sacred art."

"Oh."

"I want retreatants to feel at home here, but I don't want 'em barging in where they've no business. That's just one of the problems here."

"I'd say you've got that one pretty well licked."

"My room," Wilf said, throwing open the door. Wilf had an antique bed with a high carved headboard. "It was in the attic. Otherwise, I can assure you, I wouldn't be sleeping in such a fancy bed."

"Don't tell me that's a feather mattress."

"Somebody who was here on retreat sent it to me. It belonged to his grandmother who had just passed away—in a hospital, he said."

Wilf, who seemed a little nervous about his bed, went over to an old roll-top desk. "I do without a dresser, you see." He opened and shut one of the drawers. He had his black socks in it. "No rug," he said, pawing the floor. "But you'll want to see your room."

Father Urban's bed was narrow and steel, monastic indeed compared with Wilf's, but there were two throw rugs, a dresser with a spotty mirror, a floor lamp, a green rocker, and an easy chair upholstered in glistening red imitation leather. Wilf had only a couple of the green rockers in his room. Father Urban felt that Wilf had made an effort for him. But it did seem a bit chilly in the room to Father Urban, even though he was still wearing his overcoat. "Is the heat on in here?" he asked.

Wilf went over to the register. "Closed," he said, and opened the shutters. "But maybe I'd better check to see that this isn't one I've got turned off in the basement."

"I wish you would," said Father Urban. He laid his attaché case on the bed and, as he did so, pressed down on the mattress— actually, he *preferred* a firm mattress.

"This new chair really belongs in the Rec Room," Wilf said, "but I don't see why you shouldn't have the use of it until such time as we need it there. Before too long, I hope to get more chairs of this type. Nice, isn't it? I got a pretty good deal on these. Just the two at present, and I gave the other one to Father John."

"How about the rugs? Are they here to stay?"

Wilf stiffened. "I don't see why not," he said.

They looked into the little room next door to Father Urban's. It was empty except for a rocking chair and a smoking stand and had a stairway leading up to a trap door in the ceiling. "No heat or electricity in here," Wilf said, "but when the weather warms up this could become your study, if you like."

"Thanks, but I don't think so," said Father Urban.

"That could easily be changed," Wilf said, referring to the sign on the door, a sign saying TO ATTIC.

"No, I don't think so."

"I'll ask Father John then," Wilf said. "Well, no need to show you the rooms on the north side of the house. They're not being heated at present."

So, going down by the front stairway, a rather grand old affair that had stood the years very well, they returned to the first floor. They were still wearing their overcoats, and Father Urban was none too warm in his. "You must save a lot on heat," he said.

3

Anon

In the evening, they drove to town. No one was in attendance at the station, not even the dog. Father Urban strolled in, picked up his bag, and strolled out. What if he'd been a thief?

When the train came, Jack wasn't on it. "He got a ride," Wilf said. "We'll go back to the house, and he'll be there." Jack wasn't there, though. "He'll be here any minute," Wilf said and got ready for the powwow he'd mentioned earlier.

Father Urban looked through some issues of *Life*, while Brother Harold, at the long table, worked at his show-card lettering, and Wilf, after putting pencils and scratch pads around at the other table, stared out at the night, fooled with the radio, which had a bad hum, and rocked himself.

About nine o'clock, Wilf left the room, saying, "Have to call him, I guess. Maybe he's taken ill." When Wilf returned, however, it seemed that he'd only inquired about the long-distance rates. These he discussed at great length with Brother Harold. Whether to call station-to-station or person-to-person—that was the question. There was a difference of thirty cents, which wasn't much, but why throw it away? Since Father Urban wasn't asked for an opinion, he said nothing and read on. (*Life* seemed to feel that money should be no object when it came to national de-

45

fense.) In the end, Brother Harold more or less prevailed, and
Wilf went off again. He returned, however, saying, "Good thing
I *didn't* call person-to-person. He answered the phone himself."
The pastor for whom Jack was filling in had been delayed, but
Jack would be back on the following evening. "So I guess we'll
have to postpone it until then," Wilf said, removing the pencils
and scratch pads from the round table.

Father Urban wasn't sorry about the postponement, and not
only because he wasn't anxious to see Jack. No, he had seen and
heard enough of Wilf for one day.

Except for Brother Harold's cooking—the fat young man had
performed miracles with the big fish, serving it first baked, and
then again, in the evening, as a chowder—the picture looked
pretty dark at Duesterhaus. After lunch, they had visited the
red-brick building. Minor, as Wilf called it, hadn't been used
because the number of retreatants in residence at one time had
never exceeded the accommodations in Major—the old mansion.
Major was being occupied by the staff because Minor could better stand to be left unheated in the winter. Major, left unheated,
would go completely to pieces, Wilf said. This struck Father
Urban as a typically Clementine arrangement, eating the stale
bread because the fresh would keep. It hurt him to see Minor
sitting there cold and empty, with its screens rusting away in
the windows, bird nests in its gutters, with a layer of grit everywhere inside, and the toilet bowls dry, each with its rust-line.
"Lots of iron in the water." This didn't explain why the bowls
hadn't been scoured, though. Everywhere it was the same story.
The dock was buckled up in the lake, and the boat, an old flat-
bottomed scow shaped like a coffin, was also in the grip of ice.
"Winter snuck up on us." Of the summerhouse, though the
screens were gone in places as big as your hand, Wilf said:
"Here's the spot to read your office in the summertime, away from
the mosquitoes." Asked about the mosquitoes, whether they were

very bad, he said: "It all depends." There was a hole in the root-cellar door: "See what the gophers did." A birdhouse and a long pole had parted company: "See what the wind did." And when a black dog, the property of a neighboring farmer, came bounding up to Wilf, he thumped its head and said, "If this dog ever has pups, I mean to have one," to which Father Urban drily replied, "You may have to wait a long time," for it was obviously a male dog. "Well, you know what I mean," Wilf said—and coming from him just then, after all Father Urban had seen and heard, these were mighty reassuring words. They were standing on the front porch of the house, the tour having ended, when a flight of geese rowed by, high in the sky. "Canadian honkers!" Wilf cried. "Hello! Good-by! See how they follow the leader!" And this, when Father Urban thought about it, as he did that night in bed, was the most disturbing thing Wilf had said all day.

Father Urban spent the next morning in his room, reading his office, cutting his fingernails, gazing out the window at the frozen lake, and listening to the small life around him: Brother Harold singing and running water in the kitchen, Wilf singing and typing in the office, and, close by, in the wall, what sounded like a mouse bowling acorns. During the night, heavier game had passed that way.

"How's it going?" Wilf said at lunch.

"All right, I guess."

"You'll soon get into the swing of things."

After lunch (fish patties), Father Urban returned to his room, but the sun, which had warmed it in the morning, had gone. Soon he was cold. He found that he could get his hands up his sleeves—what he needed was a muff—but that he couldn't do as much for his feet. Presently he removed his shoes and got into bed.

Later that afternoon, he pulled himself together and took a

walk around the grounds, keeping an eye out for wildlife (and seeing none), and trying to get interested in the trees, which were numerous. They could be broken down into three main groups, red oaks, evergreens, and trees. Here his investigation ended, on account of the cold. He visited the chapel, but didn't stay long, on account of the cold and Wilf (who was there reading his office and wearing his devil's-food coat). Then he went to the refectory, where it was warm, and looked at *Life* for a while. (*Life* seemed to feel that money was no object when it came to national defense.) When he heard Wilf approaching the refectory, he retired to his room. Presently he was in bed again, this time between two blankets, with his shoes on. He had his rosary with him, and began the Glorious Mysteries, but somewhere along the line he forgot what he was doing, and just lay there, watching it get dark in his room.

That evening he came to the table sneezing.

"Oh, oh, I was afraid of that," Wilf said. "And I'll bet you're not wearing long underwear."

"No, as a matter of fact, I'm not."

"I knew it. I was the same way once." Wilf said that he'd got over his pride, or whatever it was that kept people from wearing long underwear, and so had Brother Harold. "I'll bet you wore it when you were a kid."

Father Urban granted that he had.

"Well, there you are. You'd be surprised how many people wear long underwear, and not just old people, and not just farmers around here. What would you say if I told you lots of people in Chicago and New York, quite young people, wear long underwear?"

"You may be right."

"That's what I mean. Who's to know?"

Father Urban had run across dedicated wearers of long underwear before. They were very sensitive people who were best humored in their cause, but this wasn't easy to do without seeming to give in to them and it.

Wilf glanced toward the kitchen where Brother Harold, preparing dessert, was using an electric mixer, and said, "I wonder if we couldn't fix you up with a set between us."

Father Urban shook his head. "Maybe I'll get some of my own."

"If you do—and I really think you should—take my advice and get the two-piece kind. Then, when the weather warms up, you can shed the top or bottom, as you see fit. That's what I do."

"I'll remember that," said Father Urban, and there they left it. No, they didn't.

"And you'd better get some before that cold gets any worse," Wilf said when Brother Harold brought in the dessert. They'd dined on baked fish—another one, though, the beginning of another cycle—and Father Urban had left some on his plate, which did not escape Wilf's eye. "Now you take your Eskimos. They never catch cold, you'll notice"—as if you could see them right out the window—"and I'll tell you why. They can't afford to. Even the dumbest Eskimo knows he's got to take care of himself. So what does he do? He eats plenty of fish."

When it was time to drive to the station, Wilf came into the refectory wearing his fur hat and devil's-food coat. "How you feelin' now?" Perhaps five minutes had elapsed since he'd asked about Father Urban's health.

"Better."

"Good. I don't want to postpone it again."

"Be sure and give Jack my regards," said Father Urban.

Wilf had advised him to give up any notion he might have of going to the station, and Father Urban had done so—willingly. He didn't want Jack to assume, as he naturally would if he saw him at the station, that he had responded to the invitation extended to him in the Pump Room, and was only visiting. Oh, much better that Jack get it all straight from the outset, from Wilf.

When the pickup truck, one bright headlight, one dim, turned into the driveway, Father Urban moved away from the window, sat down, and took up a copy of *Life*. He was studying it when Wilf and Jack entered the refectory. "Oh," he said, rising. "Glad to see you."

"Glad to see *you*," said Jack.

They shook hands, and then Jack removed his glasses, which had misted over in the warm refectory, and got out his handkerchief. "Cold," he said.

And thus passed the dreaded moment of meeting, with Jack polishing his glasses, and Father Urban feeling grateful to him for saying nothing about the matter that must have been uppermost in his mind.

And if this *wasn't* the case, if Jack wasn't trying to make it easy on him, but was having trouble finding the right words, he would have to wait until later, for the pencils and scratchpads were out now, and Wilf and Brother Harold were taking their places at the round table. Father Urban and Jack joined them.

POWWOW

Present were the Rev. Fathers Wilfrid (Bestudik), John (Kelleher), and Urban (Roche), with Brother Harold (Peters) recording.

The Rector, after calling upon Father John for an invocation, which was offered, stated that he would deal with the past, present, and future, but before doing so he said he thought those present should join together and give the foundation a name that would be in keeping with its present purpose and would identify it in the minds of others. "The Order of St Clement" as a name hadn't caught on. People in the area were still referring to the place by other names.

RECTOR: Now I was thinking of Mount St Clement. Or St Clement's Hill, if you like. There aren't too many possibilities, actually. At least I haven't thought of many. Of course, if any of you here can come up with something better, fine.

FR JOHN: I can't.

RECTOR: I've given the matter quite a lot of thought, and I don't believe we can do much better than Mount St Clement.

FR URBAN: I haven't given the matter any thought at all, but St Clement's Hill strikes me as better than Mount St Clement—if only because what we have here is only a hill.

RECTOR: I realize that, of course, but liberties are frequently taken in things like this. I could give you several examples. However, I don't think it makes too much difference.

FR URBAN: In my opinion, we'd do well to call a hill a hill here.

RECTOR: Good enough. St Clement's Hill then—unless, of course, Chicago takes exception.

FR JOHN: Yes.

The Rector said that St Clement's Hill had been the residence of a rich man, a public institution, and a sanitarium before passing into the hands of the Order. Perhaps it should be mentioned that the grounds had been the scene of a domestic tragedy years ago, the original owner and his wife and another having died by violent means. The son of the original owner had married a Catholic, and she, now a widow and a woman of advanced age, had regained possession of the property and had presented it to the Order. Under the terms of the deed, she and her deceased husband were commemorated daily at the Rector's Mass. The Rec-

tor, shortly after he arrived at St Clement's Hill, had gone to see her, to pay his respects. He had found her not easy to talk to. In fact, she had the television going all the time he was there. He hadn't been sure that she understood who he was.

FR URBAN: When was this?

RECTOR: About a year ago.

FR URBAN: And you haven't been back to see her?

RECTOR: No.

FR URBAN: Bum's rush?

RECTOR: No, but she didn't ask me to come back, and didn't pay much attention to me while I was there. She's an old woman.

FR URBAN: Any idea why she should wish this place off on us?

RECTOR: I wouldn't say that. I daresay there are plenty of other orders that would be glad to have it.

FR URBAN: Who closed the deal?

RECTOR: Chicago. She wrote to us.

FR URBAN: But somebody must have looked at it first.

RECTOR: Father Provincial made a special trip up here.

FR URBAN: I see. What's the old woman's name?

RECTOR: Thwaites. Mrs Andrew Thwaites.

FR URBAN: I take it she lives near by?

RECTOR: Lake Lucille. That's near Great Plains.

FR URBAN: That a town—Lake Lucille?

RECTOR: No, just a lake—a very nice lake. She has a house there, a big place, more room than she needs.

FR URBAN: Any surviving heirs?

RECTOR: Yes, but they don't live with her.

FR URBAN: And you don't feel that Mrs Thwaites is interested in doing any more for us here?

RECTOR: No, I don't—but of course we can't complain. Now then.

St Clement's Hill had presented numerous problems at first, and still did. The Rector had arrived on the scene about a year ago—one year ago yesterday, to be precise. In the meantime, many of the problems either had been or were being solved. For example, there had been no means of transportation in the beginning, but this problem had been solved—not to everyone's satisfaction, perhaps—but in the best possible way. Many of the achievements of the past year could be seen. There were others, though, that could not be seen. For example, it had been necessary to sink a deeper well, an operation requiring skilled professional labor and therefore a costly one. It had been money well spent, however, since there was now a plentiful supply of water. For drinking purposes, the water was excellent. Visitors praised it.

RECTOR: In my opinion, our water is something that could be—well, talked up.

FR URBAN: You don't mean it's therapeutic, do you?

RECTOR: For all I know it is. But I was talking about the way it tastes. Our water *tastes* good.

FR URBAN: Has it been tested for purity?

RECTOR: Yes, and it's right up there. The iron content is very low—for this part of the country. The main thing, though, is that it tastes so good. I don't know but what I prefer it to the water at the Novitiate. But be that as it may.

Sewage disposal could become troublesome in the future, and a new system would be expensive unless they did the work themselves. The digging they could do, but the rest of it—laying out a drainage field and putting down pipes—this, if not done by professionals, had to be carried out under expert supervision, since there was always the danger of polluting the fresh water supply. Unfortunately, such co-operative arrangements weren't always too successful.

FR URBAN: No?

RECTOR: No. Brother Harold and I did a little work in Parlor B while Parlor A was being papered. After the men went home at night, we used their steamer—I don't know whether you've ever seen one or not. Steams the old paper right off the wall. Really does the job. We were just trying to help. The men didn't like it. Something about the union. As a result, I changed my mind about letting them finish Parlor B. I'm afraid they didn't take it very well.

FR JOHN: Too bad.

RECTOR: Yes, but it couldn't be helped.

FR URBAN: Assuming you had an estimate beforehand, as I imagine you did, what was your reason for trying to help? You weren't paying them by the hour, were you?

RECTOR: No, but I had an estimate in round numbers, and I was trying to keep the cost down to the minimum. In fact, I was hoping to bring it down below that. I thought I was dealing with a Catholic concern.

FR URBAN: Sometimes that can be a mistake.

Perhaps the walls of Parlor B, now stripped of paper, should just be painted. Wallpapering was a tricky business, especially in an old house with high ceilings. The plan was to paint the walls of the Recreation Room, for which new furniture had already been purchased, and pictures of past Provincials would be hung there, as was the custom.

FR URBAN: In seminaries. As I understand it, this is to be a room for retreatants—for laymen—and I think they should be given every consideration.

RECTOR: I hadn't thought of it in that light. Thank you, Father.

There wasn't much wrong with the new building (Minor) that a little elbow grease wouldn't put right when the time came, but the old house (Major) was in some need of repairs and altera-

tions. Something would have to be done about a sacristy for the chapel. Just to erect a plywood cubicle, such as had been done for a confessional, was not the answer. Otherwise, though, the chapel facilities were adequate. If, in the future, it became necessary to heat the house throughout (not all rooms were being heated at the moment), insulation should be installed in the attic. The walls were insulated with sawdust, an acceptable material even by modern standards. Sawdust when wet, however, was worse than no insulation at all, and the roof leaked slightly in the northwest corner, which, unfortunately, caught the prevailing winter winds. Major could badly use a "pointing" job, but this, in itself a large and costly undertaking, would mean doing away with the vines, and this might lead to serious trouble. Therefore, at least for the time being, the Rector was in favor of leaving well enough alone. If this, perhaps, sounded strange to some of those present, he asked them to remember that he had to consider not merely what was desirable but what was desirable and possible. Somewhere the Rector had seen politics defined as the art of the possible. This, it seemed to him, might also be said to define the art of administration. Not that the Rector regarded himself as a great administrator. To this day, he didn't know why he had been placed in his present position. It had come as a very great surprise to him at the time.

"Go up there," Father Provincial had told him. "Go up there and see what can best be done." The Rector had gone, taking Brother Harold with him. During the early part of the first winter they had barely subsisted on what the Rector earned doing weekend work. Cold they often were, and sometimes hungry.

Now, as to food production, it was felt that the surface hadn't been scratched at St Clement's Hill. To say that the presence there of a priest or brother with an agricultural background

*would make a world of difference was in no sense a criticism of
the Rector or Brother Harold. They had put in a garden last
spring, and the results, though they might have been better, had
been good, and very likely would be better in the coming year.
To this end, a compost heap was now maturing. It should be
borne in mind that there was a lot more to gardening than looking through seed catalogues and ordering what took one's fancy.
No attempt had been made to raise chickens, ducks, geese, or
turkeys, due, of course, to the shortage of labor. There were
three apple and two plum trees which evidently ought to be
sprayed for worms. Raspberries, both red and black, were abun-
dant, but so were birds. There were colonies of gophers on the
property. Gophers did untold damage.*

FR URBAN: Any rats?
RECTOR: No problem with rats, probably due to the fact that we
have the use of a dog. Eventually, we may have a dog of our own.
FR URBAN: Wouldn't a cat be better?
RECTOR: If we had rats, I daresay a cat would be better. But
just having a good dog around keeps them away. Personally, I've
never cared for cats.

*Fishing, with a catch of well over five hundred pounds in the
freezer at the end of summer, was the brightest spot in the
economy. At one point during the previous winter, the Rector
and Brother Harold had almost gone into ice fishing, but they
had been under pressure from concerns even greater than hunger. Never, for a moment, had the Rector forgotten why he
was there. Always, as he reconnoitered, spying out the land, he
had kept in mind the words: what can best be done. These
were the words of Father Provincial, and the more the Rector
had meditated on them, the more it had seemed to him that they
could mean but one thing.*

FR JOHN: A retreat house for laymen.

RECTOR: Yes, and I've never looked back since then—not that I'm entirely satisfied with everything here.

FR URBAN: What, in particular, aren't you entirely satisfied with?

RECTOR: I was coming to that, but I might as well tell you now. The fact is we haven't had too much help from the local clergy. What it comes down to is this: *we* have to make ourselves better known.

FR URBAN: How?

RECTOR: This is just a dummy, of course.

The Rector produced a dummy copy of a brochure designed to show the prospective retreatant what he could expect at St Clement's Hill. It took him through a typical day. There were photographs of retreatants hearing Mass in the chapel, making use of the library, bathing in the lake, and strolling under the trees—"just talking things over." Clementines were shown going about their business. A lot of hard work had gone into the brochure.

RECTOR: And now I'd like to have your frank opinion.

FR JOHN: It's a splendid idea, Father.

RECTOR: Thanks, Father. But what I want to know is this: is there anything that you take exception to, anything at all, or that you think could be improved? If there is, I wish you'd please say so. We want this brochure to be the best thing of its kind.

FR JOHN: I'm sure it's all right as it is. Of course, I haven't read it.

RECTOR: I want you to, Father. I want you to take it up to your room and go over it with a blue pencil. Would you do that?

FR JOHN: I'll be glad to, Father, but I'm sure it's fine as it is.

RECTOR: I don't have to tell you that I value your opinion more than I do my own in something like this. I'm not a writer. All I could do was try and put myself in the place of a layman with half a mind to make a retreat. For all I know, I may have failed in what I set out to do.

FR JOHN: I wouldn't say that, Father. Not at all.

RECTOR: Father Urban?

FR URBAN: Like Jack, I haven't read it.

RECTOR: I want you to, Father. Even though you're not a writer, I have a high regard for your opinion in a matter like this— and in other matters, I might add.

FR URBAN: Well, since you've asked for my frank opinion, I will say the title and some of the captions. . . .

RECTOR: Go ahead, Father. I can take it.

FR URBAN: "Oh, Come All Ye Faithful!"—isn't that too closely associated with Christmas?

RECTOR: That thought did occur to me. *Too* closely, you think?

FR URBAN: And you really don't mean *all*, do you? We aren't trying to attract women and children, are we?

RECTOR: Not at the moment, no.

FR URBAN: The title strikes me as sounding a little urgent, too, if you know what I mean.

FR JOHN: I wouldn't say that, Urban.

RECTOR: No, this is what I asked for—constructive criticism. Go ahead.

FR URBAN: This caption here, this "Oh, My God. . . ."—I think you can do better than that.

FR JOHN: Where's that?

RECTOR: Where you see retreatants at Mass.

FR URBAN: If you want something ejaculatory, why not look for it in the Mass itself? "I will go unto the altar of God," for instance.

RECTOR: Right you are, Father. We can't do better than that. Anything else?

FR URBAN: Offhand, no, though there is one thing I'm curious about. Holy Spirit Lake.

FR JOHN: Where's that?

RECTOR: Where you see the man in the boat. "A Quiet Hour on Holy Spirit Lake." As a matter of fact, that's me in the boat. You don't see it very well, I guess, but I'm reading my office.

FR URBAN: Out of focus, isn't it?

FR JOHN: Looks fine to me.

RECTOR: To be perfectly frank, I didn't want to get a good picture of the boat.

FR URBAN: I saw a sign at the other end of the lake, in town. It said Pickle Lake.

RECTOR: The lake has a couple of names.

FR URBAN: That's not its real name?

RECTOR: Well, it's a matter of historical record that the Chippewas called it Spirit Lake. For a long time, even after the white man came, it was called that. Then it got the name of Pickle Lake.

FR JOHN: That's odd.

RECTOR: On account of its shape. But I don't see why we can't go back to the original name, if we like.

FR URBAN: Don't misunderstand me, Father. I much prefer Holy Spirit, if that's what the Indians called it.

RECTOR: As a matter of fact, they called it Spirit Lake. Unfortunately, from what I've been able to find out, "spirit" could have meant "devil" to the Indians, and probably did.

FR JOHN: Better call it Holy Spirit Lake.

RECTOR: Yes.

The Rector wished to include a view of the Recreation Room in the brochure, and so an effort would be made to complete the work there soon. The photograph of Father Louis in the garden was very unsatisfactory, and since the point was to show the same man worshiping and working (to bring out the ora and labora idea, which laymen found so attractive), the Rector wished to photograph Father Urban in the chapel and in the garden.

FR URBAN: Why me? What's wrong with you? Or Jack, for that matter?

RECTOR: I just thought you'd take the best picture. However, if that's the way you feel. . . . I wish now I hadn't tried to use Father Louis.

FR URBAN: All right. I'm game.

RECTOR: Thank you, Father. Tomorrow morning, if you don't mind, before the ground's covered with snow.

Although retreatants would always be welcome at St Clement's Hill, more emphasis was going to be put on the warmer months there. St Clement's Hill could be operating at full capacity through summer and into autumn. In fact, it might be necessary to keep Minor open during the cold months in years to come, but perhaps they shouldn't cross that bridge until they came to it. The immediate target was Lent. It was hoped that the brochure would be printed and distributed by then.

FR URBAN: What do we do in the meantime?

RECTOR: What we've been doing. During the week we've been working around the place, improving the facilities—getting ready for the future—and on weekends we've been helping out in parishes. Two of us go to Olympe, and one to Great Plains.

FR URBAN: No weekend retreats then?

RECTOR: Not at present. When cold weather came, the demand for retreats fell way off. So now we all go out on weekends. Except Brother, of course.

FR URBAN: In other words, there wouldn't be anybody here now to give retreats even if we had retreatants?

RECTOR: Look at it like this. We don't have retreatants now, and we do have to eat. We'll just have to go on doing this until we can afford *not* to—until we can make a *clean* break. A difficult situation, but not a permanent one, I trust. As I say, I'm hoping to change it by Lent.

FR URBAN: And you're counting on a brochure to do it?

RECTOR: Not entirely, although I will say I have great hope for *this* brochure.

FR JOHN: It should be very helpful.

FR URBAN: How do you stand with the Bishop?

RECTOR: I think we can say he's behind us.

FR URBAN: What kind of a send-off did he give you?

RECTOR: How do you mean?

FR URBAN: Well, didn't he write a letter or something?

RECTOR: No. To tell you the truth, Father, I think the Bishop had other plans for us here—in case we didn't make a go of this, I mean. When I saw him last spring—

FR URBAN: You haven't seen him since then?

RECTOR: Father Provincial saw him, and then, some months later, I saw him. He spoke then of the need for a seminary—diocesan, of course. He only mentioned it in passing, and I'm glad he didn't make it any stronger than that. As you know, our experience in co-operative ventures hasn't always been good.

FR JOHN: Bolivar Springs.

RECTOR: With the clergy shortage there is in this diocese, it might be some time before the Bishop would be in a position to operate his own seminary, but it wouldn't be long before he'd want a man or two on the staff. We all know that's the beginning of the end.

FR JOHN: Bolivar Springs.

FR URBAN: Well, I must say it's no mystery to me—why you aren't getting local support.

RECTOR: I've never thought of it as much of a mystery. Even

the Jesuits had their troubles before they got established in Minnesota. Frankly, I wish they'd had a few more. They're drawing from our territory, and the Benedictines are almost as bad.

FR URBAN: You have to expect that.

RECTOR: Look at it like this. In cities we have boundaries to keep people from attending the church of their choice. Well, I say we need boundaries to keep them from making retreats outside their own diocese—unless, of course, proper facilities are lacking within it. Otherwise, the little fella gets squeezed out. He might as well close up shop.

FR URBAN: Unless the Bishop's behind you in any diocese, you might as well close up shop.

RECTOR: I think we can say that Bishop Conor's behind us.

FR URBAN: Dragging his feet.

RECTOR: No, watching and waiting. If we really make a go of it here, you'll see a big change in him. After all, if he weren't behind us, we wouldn't be here. You mustn't forget that. We're still in the making-friends stage. That's all. The Bishop's well aware of the work we're doing in parishes.

FR URBAN: He should be.

RECTOR: We've had our largest groups from parishes where we help out on weekends. So, you see, it works both ways. Once off the ground, we should be self-supporting.

FR URBAN: We've been here a year and we still aren't fulfilling our real purpose.

This was a source of great regret to the Rector. The situation at St Clement's Hill did indeed leave much to be desired, but it was not hopeless. Nothing was, with God's help. And whatever one might personally think of the present course—the Rector, for his part, regarded it only as the best one possible—it had received the approval of Father Provincial, and therefore it would be followed out.

RECTOR: Any questions? If not, maybe we should all try and get a good night's sleep.

FR URBAN: I was kept awake last night by noises in the wall. Whatever it was, it sounded too heavy for a mouse. *Do* we have rats? I'd appreciate a straight answer.

RECTOR: Probably a squirrel.

FR URBAN: A squirrel?

RECTOR: Your little red squirrel.

FR URBAN: I don't get it.

RECTOR: Wherever you have oak trees, you have nuts, and wherever you have nuts, you have squirrels. They don't hurt anything. I'm talking about the cute little fella with the white belly. Your *great* red squirrel, sometimes called the fox squirrel, is something else again. I wouldn't want *him* in the house.

FR URBAN: I shouldn't think you'd want *any* of 'em in the house.

RECTOR: They're not in the house proper.

FR URBAN: Well, can't we get rid of 'em?

RECTOR: That's easier said than done. Generations of red squirrels have stored their nuts in this old house.

FR URBAN: Stop up their holes.

RECTOR: That's been tried. It doesn't work.

FR URBAN: It has to, if you get all the holes.

RECTOR: Have you taken a good look at the eaves, Father?

FR URBAN: I can't say I have. No.

RECTOR: Take a good look at the eaves. For many years they weren't painted, and now they're beyond painting. The way the wood is now, a squirrel can eat his way in or out in a matter of minutes. I've watched 'em do it. To cover the holes with tin, as Father Louis did, is just a waste of time, and it ruins the appearance of the house. The squirrels are always one hole ahead of you. Father Louis found that out. Shoot 'em or trap 'em, and more just take their place.

FR URBAN: We need new eaves then.

RECTOR: Have any idea what *they'd* set us back?

FR URBAN: I have no idea.

RECTOR: Well, *I* do. I've had several estimates. No, the time to replace your eaves is when you replace your roof. One thing leads to another. It took years of neglect to get this house in the shape it's in now, and there's no use trying to reverse the process overnight—unless you're prepared to go all the way, which we're not, at the moment. You may not believe it, and maybe I shouldn't say it, but there's more to running a place like this than meets the eye.

FR JOHN: I don't think Father Urban means to criticize you, Father.

FR URBAN: Not a-tall.

RECTOR: And there's this to be said for red squirrels—*little* red squirrels. They keep rats, gophers, chipmunks (which I'm rather fond of, by the way), and *other* squirrels out of a house. They're a very courageous little animal. I'm told a little red squirrel, given the chance, will castrate a grey squirrel, though I don't know how much truth there is in that. I do know I've often seen red squirrels chasing grey squirrels. I've often wondered what would happen if a *great* red squirrel came around the house. I don't know but what I'd put my money on the little fella.

Father Urban and Jack left the refectory together, Jack carrying the dummy copy of the brochure. At the top of the stairs, they said good night to each other—"good night" seemed to be all there was to say—and they said it again at Father Urban's door.

"I didn't realize *you'd* been transferred," Jack said then. "Not until he started talking about taking your picture for the brochure."

"You mean he didn't tell you?"

"He just told me you were here—just on a visit, I thought."

"I see."

"I believe you did say you might pay us a visit."

"Believe I did, yes."

"Yes. Well, good night, Urban."

"Good night, Jack."

4

Grey Days

Harvey Roche (later Father Urban) was born in that part of
Illinois which more and more identifies itself with Abraham Lincoln but has its taproot in the South. Protestants were very sure
of themselves there. If you were a Catholic boy like Harvey
Roche, you felt that it was their country, handed down to them
by the Pilgrims, George Washington, and others, and that they
were taking a risk in letting you live in it. It wasn't that they
remembered what tyrants (not *all* of them Catholics) had done
to non-conformists in the past. They did not see themselves as
descendants of the poor and oppressed. No, although that might
be history, that was not it. What troubled them was the hocus-
pocus that went on in Catholic churches. And Harvey Roche, as
a boy, didn't blame them. *Wasn't* it all very strange there, in
that place, at that time, the fancy vestments, the Latin, the wine?
What if Catholics were Protestants, and Protestants were Catholics, and *they* worshiped in such a manner? What would Catholics think? Could you see Dr Bradshaw, of Grace Church, burning incense and throwing holy water around? Could you see the
best people in town, who attended Grace Church, or the First
Baptist, going to Mass? You could not. And what if you knew
that *none* of the best people did? Harvey Roche knew this when

he was twelve. (As a caddy at the country club, where his father was greenskeeper, he also knew that the best people, though Protestants, didn't always use the best language, or the best balls.) He knew, too, that Catholics were mostly Irish and Portuguese, and that their religion, poverty, and appearance (especially in the case of the Portuguese) were all against them. He knew that they moved away from the Patch, the weedy edge of town, when they could. When he was a little older, he was told that some Catholics changed their religion, or lapsed, after they moved from the Patch, hoping to improve themselves still further. Apostasy, though, without going into the matter of eternal damnation at all, just wasn't worth it there, he was told by Monsignor Morez who was the first to suggest to him that there might be better places. "There are those who feel Rome is wrong to go on thinking of this as a missionary country, but I am not one of them." This was the sort of thing that antagonized just about everybody who could understand it: preachers who had never, in the brief history of their sect, had it so good; enlightened ministers who, whatever they might think of popery, would have been willing to make an exception of *him;* and even priests of the diocese who preferred the Church's situation there, difficult as it was, to what it was in certain non-missionary countries that need not be named. Monsignor Morez had come from one of the French-speaking cantons of Switzerland as a babe in arms, had grown up in Boston, and attended a seminary in Ohio. Nobody had lived longer in the town by the time he died, a very old and even tinier man, but the idea persisted that he was a foreigner. His name was strange, and also his dress—his frock coat, homburg, and pince-nez. Then, too, there were his numerous trips "back" to the old country, these financed through selling shares left him by the Bishop who had tempted him into the diocese in his youth. ("I wondered how he could ever make it up to me. Well, he tried.") In the winter, upstairs in the study, before an anthracite fire, and in the summer on the front porch, the long rectangle of well-watered grass and the black iron fence between them and the traffic (the church was right downtown), Harvey read aloud to the old man from the St Louis papers. In return, he received his spending money and lessons in Latin and Greek, philosophy and theology. There were lessons in fortitude, too. Harvey was present one summer night when the old man admonished a hooded mob from the porch, then fired off a shotgun, which did the job as words hadn't, and then broke a bone in his foot kicking over the fiery cross that had been planted on the lawn. Where the cross fell and burned out, spoiling the grass, the old man had a bed of red geraniums blooming the next day. Dr Bradshaw not only called around but preached about it in Grace Church. If this was victory, though, it scarcely made up for the defeats suffered by Rome and the old man, the most galling ones brought on by a succession of thirsty transatlantic curates. The trips to jail to ransom the curates, whom the local authorities loved to lock up, went off in an atmosphere of muffled drums, Harvey at the wheel of the parish Overland, the side curtains crackling, and the old man: "There are those who feel Rome is wrong. . . ." At sixteen, Harvey was in every respect but age and ordination ready for a parish—so Monsignor Morez told the curate of the day, wishing, he said, that he could say as much for him. By that time, however, Harvey knew what an older young man, one fresh from the seminary, or some other remote place, might discover too late about himself there. He knew that the hands and heart of a priest could be occupied anywhere, of course, but he also knew that many were paralyzed by the possibility of scandal there, or, what was the same, were driven to drink by it, or, like Monsignor Morez, were turned in on themselves. Harvey began to entertain doubts about the diocese as a theatre for his future. And then came a man who showed him what could be done even there, a man from

Maynooth by way of Chicago, sixteen stone and every ounce a priest, a man better known than the order he represented, as Harvey himself was to be in time. Father Placidus (Hartigan) had everything, and he had it in spades. Whoever heard of a visiting priest *not* staying at the rectory? Father Placidus put up at the Merchants' Hotel, where bootblacks, bellboys, and waiters who'd never seen him before seemed to welcome him back. Everybody he met during his short stay seemed much better for the experience, including even the chief of police and also the sheriff and the mayor, on all of whom he (attended by Harvey) paid courtesy calls. (Asked to inspect the new car barn and the new reservoir, he gladly consented.) Thus Father Placidus gave Harvey another view of his religion—it need not always be little Tarcisius with the Blessed Sacrament concealed in his breast, pursued by government troops. Five glorious days with Father Placidus! They went for drives in the parish Overland, for Father Placidus was a motoring enthusiast, and they were never without motoring chocolate, as he called it, for these trips. When they stepped out of the machine to stretch their legs, the muddiest ponds sparkled like jewels for Father Placidus, the grass grew greener for him, and nuts of all kinds fell from the trees at the sound of his coming. There were strings and woodwinds in his voice too, and these were heard on their walks. Pope Benedict XV was a saint, Belloc and Chesterton were the writers to watch, and the White Sox (Father Placidus would not call them the Black Sox) would come back stronger than ever some day. And one evening, after benediction, the two of them swiftly repaired to the Opera House, and there, during curtain calls, members of the Chicago company of *Mlle Modiste* recognized the great man in his box and saluted him and his young companion. Five glorious days and nights! Must it all end? How could it? Blacker than the night it came out of, bell tolling, weeping from its boiler plates, the Chicago Express made

an unscheduled stop. "I'm going with you, Father," Harvey
cried, waiting until then to say that he'd talked the matter over
with his folks. "*If* you don't mind." And Father Placidus, who,
though aware of Harvey's doubts about his future there, had not
once suggested that he join the Clementines and see the world,
said, "Mind? It's not for me to mind, my boy. Not a-tall." "My
suitcase is in the station, Father, and I have my ticket." "Not
a-tall, my boy. It's all arranged." That night Harvey slept in a
Pullman berth for the first time in his life, and the next morning
he learned from the porter that Father Placidus had sat up in
the smoker. That act of charity, and others (and prayer, of
course), sustained Harvey in his first months at the Novitiate,
for he soon found out that there was only one Father Placidus
in the Order of St Clement. Actually, there may not have been
another like him in the whole world. Father Placidus was a big
man, with a spirit of bigness about him. His main concern after
his religion was athletics. In this respect, once he became Provincial, as he did later, he accomplished a great deal at the
Novitiate. He himself coached basketball and baseball, though
he'd played neither until rather late in life, and in these the
Novitiate more than held its own against some of the best small
colleges in the Chicago area. He pushed soccer as an intramural
sport, rather than tag, and so far as possible included the faculty.
The truth was he exercised a civilizing influence even in a field
as remote from his own interests as the curriculum, but after
God and Sport came Song with Father Placidus. He loved Victor
Herbert's music—so much that he would sing such ballads as
"Kiss Me Again" and "I'm Falling in Love with Someone" in
mixed company, to say nothing of "Come into the Garden,
Maud," by Balfe, to whom he believed himself to be related, on
his mother's side. He created the Choristers out of the slime of
the earth and took them as far east as Cleveland, as far west as
Kansas City and Omaha. First-string critics attended their con-

certs (Father Placidus saw to that) and wrote rave notices about the director and his bonny boys in black, as he called them. *Oh, Lord Jeffrey Amherst was a soldier of the king!* And then, all too soon (though not for everybody), the great man's three-year term ended, and with it an era. He went back on the road. The basketball team, once a thing of beauty in purple and gold, took the floor in khaki trunks and white underwear tops, and still won, but soon, for obvious reasons, the only schools that would schedule the Mallards were business colleges and seminaries with posts on their courts. The baseball team was plagued by rain and broken bats, and finally had to abandon its schedule. Significantly, perhaps, the man who let these things happen (while he kept late hours with a few favorites who shared his passion for the Dewey decimal system of book classification) died in office. His successor, alas, cared even less for what went on around him, his one desire being to get everybody out of the country as quickly as possible, into the foreign missions. All that remained of the great days and the great teams were photographs and memories. Father Placidus, in his ball cap and sweat shirt, blowing his whistle, Father Placidus, in his choir robe, waving his ivory wand, Father Placidus at the piano, at the pipe organ, at the altar, and in the pulpit at the kill. Father Placidus was a powerful speaker when he was "right." The young Urban had ridden into the dark wood of the parish-mission circuit alongside him and had sat next to him at the "long count" Dempsey-Tunney fight where he suffered and concealed a seizure lest he spoil his young companion's evening. *Requiescat in pace.* Monsignor Morez, too. *His* young companion would always regret whatever sorrow he might have caused the old man by joining the Clementines—more, it seemed than he'd let on. After the old man's funeral, the last and worst of the thirsty transatlantic curates said that it had distressed *him* no end to hear the Clementines, that fine body of men, generally referred to as the Rinky

Dinks by the deceased. Others, besides Monsignor Morez and Father Placidus, seeing the possibilities in Harvey, had helped him along the way, and a few, for the same reason, had tried to hinder him, for there are those who resent excellence of any kind, having none themselves. The twin brothers, caddies like himself at the country club, who one whole summer kept him close to tears, ripping the buttons off his fly and hitting him on the bony parts of his arms, and all because he could outplay them at golf. The Novicemaster who kept his charges copying a touching appeal composed by himself, and rated them—candidates for the priesthood!—solely on their ability to perform this labor (until Father Placidus became Provincial and put an end to it). Mr Gill, the Rhodes scholar and the only layman on the faculty, who sold Father Placidus on the idea of restoring the Drama to the Church, and incidentally himself, and mimicked Harvey's drawl, denied him the best parts in plays, and never stopped trying to cast him as a yokel. Father Oliver who taught "Science" and who had flunked nobody until he flunked Harvey Roche. What had happened to them all? The twins had served jail terms for assault and battery, the Novicemaster had wiped out whatever his appeal might have profited the Order by setting fire to his mattress and burning out a floor at the Novitiate, Mr Gill had succumbed completely to drink and lost his position (in the end he was embarrassingly grateful to a former student for recommending him to some nuns who ran a home for the aged), and Father Oliver, after receiving permission to visit the Century of Progress exposition one day in the summer of 1933, had gone over the hill. And Harvey Roche had become Father Urban. He would not say that life had dealt harshly with these people because of their treatment of him. Not a-tall. "*Revenge is mine.*" And rightly so, for all the crimes of men are crimes against Him, and would be seen as such but for ignorance. Nevertheless, in view of these casualties, it was sobering to think

what might befall Father Boniface now that he'd joined the select
little group of people who'd made life unnecessarily difficult for
Father Urban, and that Wilf, if he didn't watch himself, would
soon be joining that group.

"Just hold it there," Wilf said.

Father Urban held the hoe to the frozen ground. He had been
chopping away in a lifelike manner because he didn't want to
be accused of posing. Earlier that morning, in the chapel, Wilf
had fired away at him all during Mass—except at the elevation.
"You were posing then," Wilf had told him at breakfast. Well,
wasn't he posing now? Wasn't Wilf—"Now you take your *Life*
magazine"—being inconsistent?

"No," Wilf said, shaking his head. He wanted the hoe.

Father Urban held the camera and watched Wilf. Why so sad?
Loved the good earth, was that it?

"That's more what I'm after," Wilf said.

Father Urban took the hoe again. He was cold, miscast, and
his tailored cassock was all wrong, too. "Just trying to keep
warm," he muttered, hacking at the ground. Wilf was warm in
his devil's-food coat. Wilf could shoot him now, or not at all.

"Better. Head up. Too much. There. Ah. Hold it. One more.
Ah. That does it."

"Thank God."

"Know why I kept after you? You were posing. You had to
find your own way—and you did."

A little later that morning, Father Urban reported for work
in the brown coveralls Wilf had issued him, and though they
were all wearing them, Father Urban felt pretty silly in his. In
the Rec Room, Wilf issued him a white cap that advertised a
well-known brand of paint (that wasn't being used on the job,
to judge by the cans on the floor).

"Oh, oh," Wilf said. "I'm afraid you take a medium. I thought sure you'd take a large."

"Oh well," said Father Urban, and still he noticed that everybody else's cap seemed to fit.

"Brother's wearing a large, Father a small, and I take a medium myself," Wilf said. "I'd let you have mine, but I've been wearing it for some time." Wilf removed his cap and showed Father Urban how it was inside.

"Yes. Well, I can do without one."

"You'll get paint and plaster in your hair. You don't want that, do you?"

"No, not particularly."

"We have to get the chipped places, nail holes, and the like," Wilf said. He glanced over at Jack who was sandpapering the woodwork around a window, creating a certain amount of dust. "And if this old paint should contain arsenic, as I'm told a lot of it does—well, you might lose all your hair."

"Now wait a minute," said Father Urban.

"I don't know that it *does*. The chances are it *doesn't*."

"If *I* thought there was *any* chance, *I'd* have it analyzed."

"Don't think *I* wouldn't—if we were going to do more than we're going to do."

"We just have to get the chipped places, nail holes, and the like," said Brother Harold. He was sopping at the wall with a sponge and loosening the paper, layers of it, with a putty knife.

"That's right," Wilf said. "But to be on the safe side we wear these caps."

"What about *breathing* it?" said Father Urban.

"I'm told there isn't as much danger as you might think," Wilf said, "You see, you're pretty well protected by the hair in your nose—same as coal miners. Of course, over a prolonged period. . . ."

"And the hair in your nose—what about *that?*"

"That's where nature comes in. Most of the hair in your nose grows *down*. The dust can't settle and reach the roots. What would happen if you just rolled up the sides?"

Father Urban looked down at the cap in his hand.

Wilf took it, rolled up the sides, and gave it back.

Father Urban tried it on.

"I'm sorry about this, Father," Wilf said then. "I'll see if I can get you a medium. I guess your head just *looks* big."

Father Urban was given a window, a block of wood, and a piece of sandpaper, and thus began the most difficult period in his life to date. Wilf showed him how to wrap the sandpaper around the block of wood. "Always sand *with* the grain," Wilf told him at the start, and a couple of times thereafter. Wilf also told him to use *up* the sandpaper he had before taking a fresh piece. After an hour of that, Father Urban and Jack were put to removing wallpaper. "Change jobs, and you never get tired," Wilf said. "Always start at the top with your sponge, and let gravity work for you." He told Father Urban not to use too much water. "We don't want to spot up the ceiling downstairs."

"We're right over the chapel," said Brother Harold.

"Oh, you can use more water than that," Wilf told Jack, and laughed.

That was what got Father Urban down—Wilf's know-it-all attitude. Every few minutes, he'd say, "How's it going?" or "Going all right?" or he'd come over where you were working and just nod and cluck. Pretty hard to take. And he seemed to think that the time would pass easier for everybody if *he* talked. Blah, blah, blah. He addressed himself to Brother Harold, and thus, indirectly, they got the story of his life, which Brother Harold must have heard before and which Father Urban didn't find interesting. There had been a priest somewhere in Wilf's family for over a hundred years, but if Wilf's uncle had died four days sooner, or if Wilf had been ordained four days later, the chain would have been broken. Wilf was the only priest in the family at the moment, but two nephews were on the way. That was about what it came down to, Wilf's life story, that and the time Wilf had spent a week on retreat with the late Father Flanagan of Boys' Town, that and attending a funeral at which Al Capone had been among the mourners, that and bringing in a Greyhound bus whose driver had taken ill on one of those hairpin curves in the Ozarks. "I guess I've always been something of a 'take charge' guy, Brother."

Yes, there were many times when Father Urban was moved to cry out—to hoot—but he kept remembering a movie he'd seen just after the war. Londoners caught in the blitz—taxi drivers, young lovers, old drunks, old tea drinkers, nurses, surgeons, *everybody*—went right on with whatever they happened to be doing, and each time there was an explosion, they seemed to have the best of it, to have the last word, by saying nothing. In the same way, Father Urban maintained a secret ascendancy over the life around him—up to a point, for he muttered some to himself.

Most of the time, Wilf talked shop with Brother Harold, and this, of course, enabled him to show off. Sandpaper was production paper, sticks for stirring paint were spatulas, turpentine was turp, the tarpaulin was a tarp, and so on. Oh, Wilf's command of the language was impressive, but this didn't necessarily mean that he knew what he was doing. It was Father Urban's feeling that the Rec Room was going to look like hell.

Jack was reluctant to talk about it. "It may turn out all right in the end," he'd say if Father Urban raised the subject in the evening, when they were alone in the refectory. "Are they in or out?"

"In," Father Urban would say if Wilf and Brother Harold were up in the Rec Room—where they went not to work but to commune with the job. They stood, and sat, and squatted, and stood again. They smoked and talked. They doodled with tools —Wilf was very fond of the steel tape measure, fed it in and out by the hour, measuring his shoe, the distance between his toe and his knee, between his nose and the floor. Father Urban, who had looked in on them a couple of times, didn't understand it. ("What *you're* thinking of, Brother, is Rockite. That's not asbestos board. Oh, sure, they *call* it that.")

Father Urban steered clear of the Rec Room after working hours, and so did Jack. Since the lighting in the refectory—two bulbs in a five-bulb chandelier—wasn't ideal for reading, they played checkers. Conversation was incidental. Jack concentrated on the game. This was probably just as well, because he had a way of running any subject that interested him into the ground.

On the evening after Thanksgiving Day (for which Wilf had procured an old hen, very tasty as prepared by Brother Harold, especially after so much fish), Father Urban said, "Ever think of revising 'Danger Ahead!', Jack?"

"Not much demand for it nowadays, Urban."

"There could be," said Father Urban, rising to turn off the radio. Besides the usual hum, there didn't seem to be much on the radio but accident reports and warnings to drive safely. "Bring it up to date, why don't you?"

"Your move, Urban."

"I only mention it because I feel you should be doing *something* while you're here. Don't just let yourself go. A man can go nuts in a place like this."

"I've been thinking of doing some writing, Urban."

"That's what I mean. Otherwise this'll just be a big slice out of your life. My God!"

"It may turn out all right in the end, Urban. Are they in or out?"

"Out," Father Urban said on that evening, and shook his head in sorrow.

When Wilf and Brother Harold were out, they were over in Olympe in connection with a crusade to get people to go to church more and to shop less during the Christmas season. Wilf was not the leader of the crusade, in which Protestants were participating on a separate-but-equal basis, but he was evidently high up in its councils. He called on merchants in their homes and asked them to point up the true meaning of the season in their window displays and advertising, and Brother Harold reported to headquarters (the Catholic high school in Olympe) where he and other artists produced "Put Christ Back into Christmas" signs, which were hung in the windows of stores and homes.

None of this was new to Father Urban. He would grant that there were abuses of the Christmas spirit (he felt that merchants should hold off until after Thanksgiving, or at least until after Halloween), but he also believed that whatever was done, or not done, should be done under the auspices of the hierarchy. If Wilf had hoped for his support, or Jack's, he must have been disappointed, for they had let him see that they were just not interested. Father Urban had gone further than that. "How many are you sending to your brother?" he'd asked, seeing Wilf with a stack of "Put Christ Back into Christmas" signs. "Heh, heh," said Wilf, whose brother, Rudy, ran a variety store in Berwyn, Illinois. And then he came around later, carrying a big brown envelope, saying (in the smarmiest voice you ever heard) that he was sending a supply of signs to Rudy—and saying this not to Father Urban, though he was in the refectory at the time, but to Brother Harold!

It bothered Wilf that Father Urban's cap didn't fit him, but until there was occasion to make another purchase at the lumberyard in Duesterhaus, which was also the source of the spatulas,

Wilf couldn't very well ask for another cap, he said. At one time, he had dealt exclusively with the lumberyard. Of late, though, hardly at all—for the Rec Room job only a pint of turpentine had come from the lumberyard, and on the strength of this purchase he had asked for two caps and a spatula. "Ticklish situation," he said. He was afraid that the people at the lumberyard knew of his recent dealings with a Minneapolis discount house, since the latter shipped by rail. "Wacker at the station—he'd tell 'em. Don't think he wouldn't."

Father Urban didn't mind wearing a cap with the sides turned up, but he did feel that Wilf would do well to patronize local concerns. "There is such a thing, you know, as being penny wise and pound foolish."

"Yes, I know. But those people at the lumberyard are *way* out of line pricewise. Too bad. They've got a little shaker there that really does the job. I wish you could see it. Ugh," he said, for the discount-house paint, which was described in the catalogue as war-surplus stock, was very hard to stir. Wilf attributed the paint's stiffness not to old age but richness. "Plenty of lead in this, Fathers. High government specifications."

Wilf cut the first cans with thinner until the contents took on the consistency of paint, but by going over and over the re-plastered place in the ceiling, he committed them to giving the entire ceiling three coats. Even then, it didn't look right. "She didn't dry the way I thought she would," he said. Suddenly—or so it seemed—he was down to one can of paint. This one he cut and cut until it tinkled like water. The situation got so bad that he didn't really trust anybody else to paint. "*Stretch* it on," he said, bearing down on his roller. "It's that old plaster!" he cried. And finally: "*Nobody* could figure a job like this to the last drop."

"I take it we're out of paint," said Father Urban.

"Well, we needed a little breathing spell anyway."

The little breathing spell proved little indeed. Wilf went downstairs to the typewriter, Brother Harold shot off to the post
office a few minutes later, and, before Father Urban could get
out of his clown suit, Wilf was back up in the Rec Room—saying
he'd changed his mind and they'd begin work on the floor at
once, so as not to lose what he called valuable time. They'd remove what remained of the original varnish and prepare the floor
for refinishing.

"But shouldn't the floor be done last, after the walls?" said
Father Urban.

"It's *usually* done last," Wilf said. "Not always."

So, for the next two days, they messed around with varnish
remover and scrapers, and then came Saturday. That afternoon
and evening, and Sunday morning, the three priests were away
from the Hill, as usual, working in another capacity—as priests.
They returned to the Hill on Sunday afternoon, and on Monday
morning they were back up in the Rec Room, with a fresh supply of paint.

And then once again, with only one wall to go, sentiment began to build up against the old plaster. "I knew it," Wilf said.
"I knew we should've given it a coat of sealer. It would've been
money saved in the end." And a few minutes later, turning on
Brother Harold (of all people), he cried, *"What! No* thinner?"
No, said Brother Harold, there wasn't a drop left in the house.
"Turpentine then!" This didn't last him long, not the way he
used it, and when it was gone, he cried for more. "But there
must be some around the place somewhere!" But there wasn't,
no, not a drop. "Oh, damn the cost!" Wilf cried then and, wearing his coveralls, drove to town for more. He returned with a
bottle, a spatula, and, yes, a cap for Father Urban, a perfect fit.
But he wore a worried look.

"Oh, it's no use!" he said a little while later. "It's as I feared.

She's bleeding. We'll just have to reorder. Brother, this is what we get for trying to call it too close."

"If it hadn't been for that old plaster. . . ." said Brother Harold.

Wilf talked of calling long distance, but in the end he fired off a letter, marking the envelope *Rush-Urgent*, and again Father Urban was wrong in thinking they'd have to stop work until more paint arrived from Minneapolis.

"We can do one of two things," Wilf said. "We can apply the mahogany varnish you see in those cans over there—it's the quick-drying type, three or four hours at the outside. That was my original plan, but I've since been thinking. . . ."

Everybody stood by, waiting to hear the alternative.

"Why not *sand* the floor? And then, after we finish off this wall, we can apply a light stain, and a dressing of some kind—perhaps beeswax. I like *that* idea, and I think Father Boniface would."

At this, Brother Harold nodded.

"If we do that, we'll have a floor we can really be proud of."

"Let me understand you," said Father Urban.

"Yes?" said Wilf, with a laugh—as if he didn't see what was so difficult to understand. "Oh, I can return the varnish for credit, if that's what's bothering you, Father. Or we can keep it and use it elsewhere—where it won't be so noticeable."

"That isn't what bothers me," Father Urban said. "Don't you need a machine of some kind for sanding a floor?"

"Not necessarily."

"Do it by hand, you mean?"

"Why not? It isn't as if there were only one or two of us."

Father Urban had nothing to say to this, and the other two, of course, had nothing to say at all.

"You can rent machines," Wilf said. "But there's more to it

than that. This paint may look dry, but it really isn't. It takes
paint months to dry—to really dry. You bring in a sander, and
kick up a lot of dust, and the walls and ceiling would pick it all
up—and then where would we be?"

"God, I don't know," said Father Urban. "But *I'm* for varnishing the floor."

"You don't see so much varnish nowadays. You take the floors
in your nice new homes, *they're* not varnished. You just have the
natural beauty of the wood."

"Yes, but are you sure we've got the wood for it?"

Wilf stared down at the old floor, as did the others.

"What is this stuff anyway?" said Father Urban. It looked
like the kind of wood he'd seen on back porches.

"It's fir."

"Is that what they're using in these new homes?"

"Mostly they're using oak and maple."

"Not fir?"

"No."

"Well, there you are."

"I was just thinking it would look better some other way."

"You'd soon change your mind if you saw this old floor
treated like something it obviously isn't. It's always been varnished. It wouldn't look right any other way. It'd look—*funny*."

Wilf was silent, staring down at the floor.

Father Urban stole a glance at Brother Harold and decided to
take a chance on him. "What's your opinion, Brother?"

"It's up to Father Wilfrid."

"At one time I was considering asphalt tile," Wilf said. "You
see a lot of that in your new buildings. Pretty expensive, though,
and we don't own a blowtorch."

"Blowtorch?" said Father Urban.

"You heat your tile with a blowtorch as you lay it."

Father Urban shook his head. He didn't feel that Wilf should be trusted with a blowtorch.

"It's really quite simple."

"Yeah? Well, *I'm* for varnishing it. This is an old floor and should be treated as such—in my opinion."

"One thing is certain," Wilf said. "We don't want it to look—*funny*."

"No," said Brother Harold.

"No," said Jack.

"No," said Father Urban.

And so they varnished it.

The following morning, it was dry to the touch, and so they put down the tarpaulin and newspapers and gave the trim around the windows and doors another coat—the original ivory trim no longer peeked through the blue. Finding themselves with time on their hands, and blue paint to spare, they did over a few rocking chairs. ("They'll go in better now.") Then the paint for the wall arrived from Minneapolis—very little time had been lost—and they finished the job. However, when they took up the newspapers, there was a certain amount of adhesion. ("Drying conditions are never ideal in cold weather.") But the newsprint, where it stuck to the floor, was easily removed with thinner—as was the varnish. Wilf, touching up these places, and going beyond them, seemed in danger of repeating the mistake he'd made earlier, in the case of the ceiling, but he caught himself. "We'll leave the rest to the shoes of retreatants," he said, "And with throw rugs. . . ." He stood back, brush in hand, and said, "Well, what d'ya think?" But before anybody could say, he went on. "Of course, these bright lights show up everything." Yes. The salmon pink walls and ceiling spoke to them eloquently of the fat and lean days. "But with proper lighting. . . . Well, what d'ya think?"

"Looks fine to me," said Jack.

"Yes," said Brother Harold.

Father Urban made a suitable noise.

"It's been a long haul," Wilf said, "but we made it."

Made *what?* So many times Father Urban had been tempted to take Wilf aside and say, Look. Why not talk to a few people who make a business of this sort of thing? Get some estimates. Then tell 'em how it is with us at the moment, say we'll take care of 'em as soon as we can put this place on a paying basis, and make 'em feel a part of *that.* Actually, in this kind of an operation, it's unhealthy *not* to be in debt. If you want me to do the talking, I will. The point is we can do better than this. Now how about it? But Father Urban hadn't taken Wilf aside and said this. Father Urban had scarcely complained. Seeing what he saw, and knowing what he knew, and doing nothing about it—it wasn't easy, not for him. In this way, though, if there was any purpose in his present situation, it would be revealed to them all, for better or worse. He was only one of the hands. Let the captain sail the ship. Malice might play a part in such an attitude—a desire to see the ship go down with all aboard, himself included—but wasn't it, except for that, the right attitude for one in his position?

5

A Couple of Nights Before Christmas

And then Father Urban weakened, but not as he'd been afraid he might. No, even though they were ripping up the old linoleum in the kitchen and the bathrooms at Major, and laying tile with a blowtorch (Wilf did find a place in Olympe that would rent him one, and allow him to apply the rent on a new one, should he decide to buy later), Father Urban didn't take him aside, or rebel, or complain. No, Father Urban weakened in another way. He agreed to address the Great Plains Commercial Club at its annual Poinsettia Smorgasbord, and thus he put himself in a position to serve the Order as no other man could.

"I was hoping something like this would happen," said Wilf, tying in the invitation with the interview he'd given the Duesterhaus *Farmer* on the subject of personnel changes and other improvements at the Hill. The *Farmer*, a weekly, had printed quite a lot about Father Urban ("whose presence at St Clement's Hill will come as a pleasant surprise to many in Duesterhaus and surrounding trade area") and very little about Jack ("also well known"), and so perhaps Wilf was right in taking credit for the invitation.

The Poinsettia Smorgasbord, held in the Greenwich Village Room of the General Diggles Hotel, was the only Club event to

which members (professional as well as businessmen) brought
their wives. It certainly lived up to its billing as a very nice
affair. First came the cocktail period (Father Urban, assured that
soft drinks were being served to those who preferred them, said,
"Oh, fine. Well, maybe a little scotch and soda—Johnnie Walker,
Black, if you please"), then came the smorgasbord itself, and then
came Father Urban who, as the toastmaster said afterward, gave
them all a very rich experience. In the course of Father Urban's
talk, which he called "Christmas down through the ages, a trav-
elogue in time," he not only related stories from history and
legend but sang snatches of carols from far-off lands. Never
once did he strike a partisan note. Jews could have heard him,
and perhaps a few did, without taking offense. He closed with
a rousing recitation of "The Night Before Christmas."

Unfortunately, the members of the Club were in the habit
of hearing from atomic scientists and foreign-policy experts, and
so there was a question period. Right away some fool wanted to
know what the speaker thought of "this here campaign to put
Christ in Christmas."

"I'm glad you asked that," Father Urban said. "For my part,
I find Christmas as it's celebrated nowadays still pretty much to
my liking. I will say, though, that I like my Christmas trees
green." He was applauded for his stand. He wanted to leave it
at that, but could see that more was expected of him. Obviously,
the crusade had roused feelings of animosity in many present. He
went on—as though he'd meant to go on. "As I see it, merchants
—to mention only one group—are paying homage in the way
best suited to them and their real talents." This was better, he
could see, but it still wasn't good enough. He tried again,
citing the example, from literature, of the mute tumbler whose
prayer took the form of acrobatics before the altar of Our Lady.
This was an example he'd used many times, but never before in
that connection. Pressed for details, he told the whole story,

adding a few touches of his own—and, if anything, improved the story. They loved it.

That should have ended the matter. But the man who'd asked the original question was still alive and kicking. He wanted to know whether Father Urban's position wasn't different from that held by "some leaders in the Catholic Church—I'm talking about the man in charge out there where you are."

"And I'm glad you asked *that*," Father Urban said. "To begin with, I don't think the man in question, able though he is, can be regarded as one of the leaders in the Catholic Church. He'd tell you that himself, if he were here." And thank God he isn't! "Now what you refer to as my 'position' is hardly that. It's only an opinion, and opinions differ. Let me explain. As you know, I'm a Catholic, and as such I believe in the infallibility of the Pope—in certain matters. In other matters, even those relating to religion, '*Je ne sais*,' as the French say, is sometimes the right answer. *I don't know*. Why, until a few years ago, the doctrine of the Assumption—that is, the ascent of Our Lady into Heaven—was no more than an opinion. Oh, a most trustworthy opinion, to be sure, and held by some of the wisest and holiest men in Christendom, but still only an opinion. Why, the infallibility of the Pope—the doctrine we were just discussing—was just a matter of opinion a hundred years ago. (Actually, you know, the area it covers is quite small.) So, if any of you good people should happen to be in Rome, and you hear the Holy Father say he believes it's going to rain, you don't have to believe it—no, not even if you're a Catholic."

This, coming from a priest, was pretty strong stuff.

The toastmaster called for order.

"Yes?" said Father Urban to an attractive red-haired woman who had her hand up. He was glad to move on to somebody else.

"But we *may* believe—and isn't it *better* if we do?"

"Believe it's going to rain because the Pope says so?" There was always a pious troublemaker or two in any audience, but they usually weren't much to look at.

"*Yes!* Oh, the example you give is ridiculous, of course, but isn't the Holy Father entitled to all the respect we can give him? As Christ's vicar on earth?"

The question was tasteless and irrelevant, but Father Urban smiled. He doubted that anyone who meant well toward him and his predominantly non-Catholic audience would have asked such a question. He had no choice but to shoot the woman down. "As a Catholic—that is, as one who respects *proper* authority— I'm afraid I'd be more inclined to trust the weather bureau in such a matter."

When Father Urban was able to continue, he was again speaking to the audience at large: "Differences of opinion can occur in any organization, human or divine, large or small—yes, even in the best-run families, between husbands and wives, so I've been told anyway." Laughter. People who, perhaps, hadn't entirely trusted the speaker until he dealt with the red head, and then hadn't been far from carrying him around the room on their shoulders, were now in a mood to get cozy with him. "Now don't misunderstand me. I'm not saying that differences of opinion are a good thing in themselves, but I do think there's a lot to be said for taking them for what they often are—healthy manifestations of the democratic process." Clapping here and there, but Father Urban could tell it wasn't going to catch on, and so, quickly, before this would be unnecessary, he raised his hand for silence. "Now that we're on the subject, let me tell you of another difference of opinion in which I was involved recently. For many years, I traveled out of Chicago, but now, as some of you may know, I'm stationed right here in Minnesota—and *very* happy to be here, let me say. Where I am was known, until recently, as the Retreat House of the Order of St Clement. Quite a mouthful, you say, and I agree. There are just four of us there, three priests and a brother, and we got to wondering if we couldn't find another name for the place (which, by the way, I hope you'll all find time to visit—Catholic or not, it makes no difference to *us*. Just stop in and say hello). Well, one of our men (the one in charge, as it happened) was all for calling the place Mount St Clement, whereas I was more for St Clement's Hill, and so we called it that." Here Father Urban did a double-take. "Say, I wonder how *that* happened!" he cried, and drew another fine laugh, and that was it. Waving, and saying, "Good night! Good night!" he sat down—certain that he'd repaired a good part of the damage done by Wilf and the crusade, and also that he'd put the Hill on the map for a lot of people who really mattered in the community. The audience gave him a wonderful hand, almost a standing ovation.

A number of couples came up to him afterward and thanked him for coming, one woman asking if there was any way of obtaining a copy of his talk, and one man saying that, though he was not a Catholic himself, he had always regarded Catholicism as one of the world's top religions and had never felt closer to it than he had that evening. The toastmaster (not a Catholic himself) expressed regret that Father Urban had been questioned so closely along certain lines. "Not a-tall, not a-tall," said Father Urban, and accepted an invitation to have a nightcap with the toastmaster and his wife at their home.

Others followed them there. Unfortunately, a couple of ulcer cases, under the spell of Father Urban's company, seemed to be forgetting themselves. After one drink, Father Urban stood up, saying, "I don't want you, and your better halves, blaming me for your downfall. Besides, I have to get up in the morning."

In the car, on the way back to the Hill, Father Urban spoke to the toastmaster, and to one of the ulcer cases who'd come along for the ride, of the great work the Order was doing all over the world, particularly in the Chicago province, and made it sound important and exciting even to himself. The toastmaster, whose name was George, was reluctant to say good night. "Yes, as a matter of fact, we are pretty busy right now," said Father Urban, but promised to have dinner with both men, separately or together, at his earliest opportunity.

Wilf was still up—up in the Rec Room admiring it in the large mirror which now hung on one wall and added another dimension to the room, in Wilf's opinion, but which, in Father Urban's opinion, only added insult to injury.

"How'd it go?"

"Oh, all right, I guess. By the way, they tried to give me something, but I gave it back to them."

"How much?"

"I couldn't say. It was in an envelope, and I just handed it back. 'Merry Christmas from the Order,' I said."

"Probably wasn't a whole lot anyway."

"Let's hope not," said Father Urban, and wasn't a bit annoyed with Wilf, for a change. A few hours away from Wilf and the Hill—a few hours spent with real people, in real places—had given him a lift.

Father Urban's appearance before the Commercial Club made the front page of the Great Plains *Record*, a paper Wilf read. It was clear from the account that the speaker had been badgered about the crusade—that it had *not* figured in his talk—and yet Wilf, who was interested in making the Hill better known, and might have thanked Father Urban for doing so, said not a word. A few days later, the *Farmer* came out with a rather garbled version of the *Record's* story (the mute tumbler was described as a Clementine "fryer"), and still there was nothing from Wilf, no commendation, no comment.

Father Urban clipped both accounts and sent them to Billy

Cosgrove—just for laughs, he said in his covering letter, although in truth he was rather pleased with his remarks and believed that Billy would be. "Clippings enjoyed here," Billy responded at once, by card, which was the first communication Father Urban had received from him since arriving at the Hill. "And re your transfer, I'll say that's one hell of a way to run a railroad."

Right as Billy was, Father Urban didn't want the exchange to end on that note, and shot off a card: "St Paul tells us, 'We know that to them that love God all things work together unto good.' Just—Fr Urban."

A couple of nights before Christmas, after the evening meal, Father Urban was the first one back in the refectory. Brother Harold was in the kitchen, Wilf was in the office, and Jack was in the chapel. Father Urban turned on the tree (which Wilf, doubtless, had been the one to turn off a few minutes earlier) and plugged in the nativity crib. Slowly, around and around the Holy Family, the oxen, sheep, and shepherds filed by, disappearing and reappearing in the wings, and out front the Three Kings bowed down, straightened up, and bowed down again. The crib had arrived that morning, a gift from Billy. There were many presents under the tree, most of them for Father Urban, and forwarded to him from the Novitiate where he usually spent the holidays, for few of his admirers knew of his new assignment. He hadn't mentioned it on his Christmas cards (which, it would seem he'd mailed from some stopping-off place, as in other years). He might be back on the road where he belonged in another year, back at the Novitiate again, distributing the loot to those who otherwise got nothing at all for Christmas. This would be a bad year for some of the old men at the Novitiate. This year Jack, Wilf, and Brother Harold would all be wearing, eating, smoking, or otherwise using the stuff in the months ahead. Father Urban was grateful for whatever came his way, of course (one year he'd got seven electric razors), but when he thought of Billy he couldn't help thinking that what might have been a mighty river flowing to the whole Order's benefit had, through Father Boniface's folly, been reduced to a trickle. A wicker hamper of food and liquor, and a nativity crib. Maybe the crib was a little like ducks in a shooting gallery, as Jack had said when he saw it work, but Father Urban rather liked it, and would say so. "Dear Billy. . . ."

"Balsam," said Wilf, entering the refectory. "You wouldn't get that nice clean smell with spruce."

"That's right," said Father Urban. He'd been lucky in the woods, it seemed, for he hadn't known balsam from spruce. That morning, when Wilf had got out the little plastic tree he'd used the year before, Father Urban, saying nothing and acting on the old seminary principle of don't-ask-if-you-can't-take-no-for-an-answer, had gone for the ax. He'd returned from the woods with a seven footer. "*Hey, what is this?*" Wilf had admitted, though, that the real tree made the plastic one look sick, had put it away, and surrendered the single cord of lights to Father Urban. Wilf had come off pretty well in the incident, showing that he—at least when he had no choice—could appreciate a right action.

"Cigar, Urban?"

"I've got one here somewhere." Under the tree there was a box of cigars for Wilf—not what Father Urban would choose for himself but several cuts above what Wilf ordinarily smoked, and was now in the act of touching off.

"By rights, it should be in the chapel," Wilf said, watching the crib. "It and the tree."

Father Urban said nothing. He wanted the crib and tree to be where they could be enjoyed in comfort, and he believed that Wilf did, too, and would resolve his scruples without any help.

"One tree, though, wouldn't be enough in the chapel."

This would have been Father Urban's first argument.

"Of course, if we had retreatants here now it would be different. We'd have to do something then."

Retreatants at Christmastime? The trees were safe in the woods, and Wilf knew it.

"Little chilly in the chapel," Wilf said, going over to his rocker. "I guess the good Lord will understand."

Jack, looking as though he'd been outdoors, came in from the chapel and stood by the tree, rubbing his hands.

"All right," said Father Urban, knowing what was expected of him.

Jack pulled the card table away from the wall, and Father Urban brought up two folding chairs, and thus began another evening of checkers.

On the first night, Wilf and Jack had played, but Wilf had lost every game and hadn't played since. Perhaps he thought it looked bad for *him* to lose. If he spent the evening in the refectory, he just sat in his rocker and read the papers. If Father Urban offered him his place at the table, he said, "Thanks, but I have some office to say," and then he'd continue with the papers. Why should it always be Father Urban and Jack? Why couldn't Wilf share the burden? Why couldn't Brother Harold? Even if Father Urban hadn't discovered anything better to do with himself in the evening, he could get tired of checkers, couldn't he? He didn't like the game, and he wasn't much good at it—although this was maybe the fault of the game. He wondered if its complexity might not be an illusion, if, in fact, there was much more to checkers than there was to ticktacktoe. The man who made the first move won the game, and the man who won got to make the first move in the next game. That might be all there was to checkers—that, and not making any mistakes. Jack made very few.

"Hey, take it easy!" said Father Urban when Jack's right leg, which had a tendency to vibrate during play, suddenly shot out of control, jarring the table.

"Sorry," Jack said. Now, though, he was on the move—inching forward on his chair, advancing behind his checkers on the board. Suddenly his respiration dropped to normal, and he sat back. Usually, when Jack did this, it meant that the turning point in the battle had passed. But had it? Father Urban made one of his unorthodox moves, after which it became clear to him that the decisive action had taken place in another sector. They played out the game, though, and once more Father Urban lost— gracefully, as Wilf hadn't. Why not? It was just a game, wasn't it? And what else was Jack good at? It came down to checkers for him. Poor Jack. Of course, his spiritual life was good.

Jack set up the board for another. "What do you know about chess?" he asked.

"I doubt that you'd be so good at chess," said Father Urban, thinking he'd probably be better at that. "I've never played it, though."

"Chess is a very ancient game," Wilf informed them from his rocker.

Father Urban glanced over in Wilf's direction and sniffed. The pity was that a remark like that was actually meant to be instructive. It showed what Wilf thought of them.

"I've never played it either," Jack said to Father Urban. "But I'm surprised you haven't."

"No, I never have—and I don't intend to," said Father Urban, just in case.

"Well, we don't have a board," Jack said, as if to reassure him. Jack seemed to know that he was regarded as a nuisance when it came to checkers, and obviously didn't wish to be, but he couldn't help it. He loved the game.

From the other side of the newspaper, Wilf said, "Your board's the same, but your counters are different."

"Is that *so?*" said Father Urban.

"Altogether different. It's a different game."

That was exactly the kind of thing that made Father Urban gnash his teeth. "I'd say the *principle's* the same," he said.

After a slight delay, Wilf's reply was transmitted over the paper wall: "I'd say the principle's the same in all games."

Father Urban couldn't think of a single exception, try as he might. He moved one of his red checkers and turned toward Wilf—but still couldn't think of anything to say. On the back page of the paper Wilf was reading, there was a very nice picture of Santa Claus—season's greeting from the friendly merchants of Minneapolis. This was the paper that had published a story about the crusade ("PRIEST RAPS SANTA"), and had then printed a letter from the former who, not content with one helping of bad publicity, said that he was far from wishing any person ill, even a mythical person, but believed that constructive criticism was always in good season, and therefore respectfully suggested that merchants in future concentrate their efforts on St Nicholas's Day, which fell early in December and was a day long associated with giving in the old world, so that Christmas, the true meaning of Christmas . . . blah, blah, blah. If the metropolitan press was *really* interested in what people were doing and thinking through-out the state, why hadn't it picked up Father Urban's remarks before the Commercial Club?

Brother Harold entered the refectory, his kitchen chores completed.

"Maybe Brother would like to take my place," said Father Urban.

"No, Brother's got his work to do," said Wilf.

"I thought so," said Father Urban. It was getting pretty bad when it was generally assumed that he, unlike Wilf and Brother

Harold, had nothing better to do with his time than play checkers. He watched Brother Harold go to the long table where he was now working on a commission from Rudy, Wilf's brother, turning out signs that read "Rudy sez 98¢" and "Rudy sez $1.98" and so on. Some of the signs had ears of corn and straw hats drawn on them. The idea in all this was that Rudy was a country-storekeeper type, which, to Wilf's chagrin, Father Urban had professed to believe was the truth. ("What's the matter—can't your brother spell?"—"Oh, that's just a merchandising stunt.")

"If you'd rather not play any more," Jack said, after he'd set up the board for another.

"Not a-tall. I just thought I'd give somebody else a chance. Go ahead."

"*You* go first."

"Why should *I* go first? You won. The one who wins goes first. Come on. Let's play the game," said Father Urban. It was getting pretty bad when Jack could condescend to him. Father Urban wished it were possible to spend the evenings in his room, but the only way to keep warm there was to go to bed, and he didn't want to get into the habit of retiring at 7 P.M. He could so accustom his mind and body to sleep at that early hour that he'd *never* be much good after supper, which could be a serious handicap if he ever returned to the world.

"Oh my," Jack said, clutching his head, after making the first move. "You had a phone call this afternoon, Father," he said to Wilf. "While you and Brother were in town. Long distance."

Wilf let down the wall. "Reporter?"

"I meant to tell you, and then I guess I forgot."

"Say he'd call again?"

"No, he didn't."

"And probably won't now. Probably had to make his deadline."

"I'm sorry, Father."

"Oh, it's all right," Wilf said, and didn't seem so disappointed. Father Urban wondered if his remarks before the Commerical Club could have straightened out Wilf's thinking on the subject of the crusade. Charity toward all, even when a few sharks get in among the swimmers, is always better than holier-than-thou singularity. That, roughly speaking, was the mind of the Church.

"I told the operator you weren't here," Jack said. "But then this fella told her he'd talk to anybody."

"Sounds like the old deadline to me," Wilf said, behind the wall. "News roundup."

"I didn't know what to say," Jack said. "I realize now it was a waste of money, but he said he'd talk to anybody here, and I didn't have anything to say."

Wilf let down the wall. "I hope he didn't take it amiss."

"He didn't seem to. No."

"Let's hope not," Wilf said, and raised the wall again. "You never know when we'll need the press."

Father Urban stirred. "In my opinion," he said, for he felt that Wilf was leaving the impression that if Jack *had* made a statement it would have been in support of the crusade, "you did the right thing, Jack. You had nothing to say, and you said nothing. You can do a lot worse than that."

There wasn't a peep from Wilf.

"Take your time," Father Urban said to Jack.

While Jack was meditating his next move, Father Urban got up and went over to the crib. He squatted down. He peered inside the stable, which was dimly lit by a blue bulb—and yes, something *was* wrong. Not what he'd expected, though. Vibrations hadn't eased the bambino out of bed. The child wasn't there.

Father Urban, hearing the newspaper crackle, sensed that he was under observation and stood up, saying, "If this is somebody's idea of a joke. . . ."

Jack and Brother Harold gave Father Urban their attention.

Wilf, significantly, hid behind the paper.

"I don't think it's very funny," Father Urban said and told Jack that the bambino was missing. "No, it's not there."

But Jack had to see for himself. He got down on all fours and started to feel around inside the stable.

"Look out!" cried Father Urban, as the shepherd with the crook drew nigh to Jack's hand. "You can *see* it's not there—and I want to know why."

Brother Harold bent to his work. Wilf rattled his paper, taking a fresh grip on it, and settled deeper in his chair. Then he dispatched a message over the wall:

"He's not born yet."

Father Urban had anticipated something of the sort and was not amused. Nor, apparently, was Jack. He rose from the floor, slowly until he reached a certain point, then reared up like a horse to more than his full height, and settled down to it painfully. He returned to his chair. He looked worried, as well he might, for he hated trouble.

Father Urban stood his ground, by the tree—his tree, you might say. "All right, Father," he said, his tone threatening, the undisguised, true voice of his feelings—in this matter, and others.

Wilf was silent and invisible.

Father Urban wavered. Should he go back to the game, and say nothing? Or say nothing, and go off to bed? Or make a stand? It's my crib, he could say. He didn't care for the sound of it. He glanced at Jack, who was staring down at the checkers. Why didn't Jack say something? Jack was chicken. And Brother Harold was on Wilf's side—my boss, may he always be in the right, but, right or wrong, my boss.

Father Urban went over and sat down. He knew what he had to do—nothing. He had Wilf where he wanted him. As long as the situation remained unchanged, each passing moment would redound to one man's credit and to the other's shame. It was Wilf's move.

It was Father Urban's move in the other game—the one he was playing with Jack—and he made it: a bad one. Jack, of course, showed him no mercy. Father Urban sniffed. It occurred to him that Jack would have been an entirely different sort of person if he'd handled himself as he did his checkers. Jack could have been a big success in life—and not a very nice person to know. He certainly got back at the world in checkers.

Something was coming over the wall: "Hospital nun I knew in Omaha, she used to take all the baby Jesuses out of the cribs. Every floor had its own tree and crib. She put 'em all back on Christmas morning."

Not good enough, Wilf. They wouldn't be there on Christmas morning. They'd be out in parishes. Brother Harold could put the bambino back on Christmas morning, but it wouldn't be the same thing, and Wilf knew it. Father Urban held to his strategy of silence.

More was coming over the wall: "Thanks to one little nun, everybody's attention was focused on the true meaning of the time before Christmas—on the idea of *waiting*."

Nobody else said anything. Jack, though he appeared apprehensive, was winning another game, and Brother Harold was puddling away at his work—to look at *him*, you'd think nothing was wrong—and Father Urban was *waiting*.

"It's still Advent," Wilf murmured, turning a page.

Father Urban sensed that Wilf had stolen a look at him.

Jack cleared his throat. "I see what you mean, Father," he said, and cleared his throat again. "But I've been wondering if the shepherds should be present yet. Or even Mary and Joseph—in the attitudes we see them in, I mean. And the Magi. The animals, yes, but not running around in circles." Thus spoke Jack to Wilf, who had let down the wall and now sat with it crushed in his lap, and for some moments thereafter both men were silent, each staring into space—while Father Urban asked himself what he was doing there. Why had he been cast into outer darkness, thrown among fools and failures? What star had led him to this?

"I don't know that I ever thought of it like that," Wilf said at last, in a groping voice. "He's right, you know"—this to Father Urban who had taken no position in the matter, and took none now, but was determined to stop Wilf if, on the authority of Jack's doctrine, it was now his intention to leave only the animals, and to immobilize *them.*

Wilf went over to the tree, knelt, and disconnected the crib, stopping the animals and shepherds in their tracks. But then, to Father Urban's surprise, Wilf reached up into the branches of the tree and brought out the bambino and put it back where it belonged—and thus, though it might seem all was well now, they arrived at the moment Father Urban had been waiting for. He let it pass, however.

"*Thanks,*" he'd been going to say at that moment. "*Thanks,*" as he might have said it, would have been quite enough for him. But he had denied himself that pleasure, and if Wilf would just leave it at that, so would he. Wasn't this the *true* meaning of Christmas? Joy to the world and peace to men of *good* will. It was hard, though—oh, very hard—to see someone having it both ways.

Wilf, having plugged in the crib, returned to his rocker. He picked up the paper, and then, boldly meeting Father Urban's gaze, he said: "Just shows how wrong we can be sometimes."

We! As if Father Urban had been wrong about anything! He glared at Jack, and stared him down, his eyes following Jack's down to the checkerboard—where he saw a surprising opportunity. He was not forgetting Wilf, but he would deal with Jack first. With his only king, Father Urban jumped this way and that, taking a dreadful toll of Jack's black men.

"Why didn't I see that?" said Jack. Something in his tone, and, on second thought, the easiness of the conquest on the board, suggested to Father Urban that Jack had indeed seen it, had planned it, had offered himself and his black men for sacrifice. Thereupon, though he didn't like what Jack had done, the desire to deal with Wilf died in Father Urban. In a way, he was sorry.

Father Urban, and perhaps Wilf and Brother Harold, too, sensed the rare peace now reigning among them, but Jack rejoiced in it visibly. Still, a moment later, it was Jack who broke the spell. "You know, Urban, I don't feel right about those animals," he said—not, Father Urban knew, to be critical but just to be saying something. For a moment, they had all been lifted up, and this was Jack's way of letting them down lightly to earth, where they had to live. "I've always understood that what heat there was at Bethlehem came from the animals. By rights, they should be closer to the Holy Family. Of course, I realize that's not possible in this case."

Father Urban looked over at the tree, at the hamper of food and liquor there. "Let's open one of Billy's bottles," he said.

6

Sailing Against the Wind

Early in the afternoon on Christmas, after a good meal with Phil Smith, pastor of St Monica's, Great Plains, Father Urban got on the train for Duesterhaus, tired. There had been a midnight Mass at St Monica's, followed by a series of nightcaps with Phil, so that it was two-thirty before they turned in. Father Urban had risen early, had preached at all Masses, and preached well, but now he was paying. The coach was overheated, as usual, and probably the heavy meal, too, was having a bad effect on him. He would have liked some privacy, but he went to a double seat at the end of the coach because Wilf and Jack would be getting on at Olympe and wouldn't understand if he sat apart from them. He had something to discuss with Wilf, too. After showing the conductor his pass, he must have fallen asleep, for the next thing he knew Wilf and Jack were sitting across from him and the conductor was leaving—having, it seemed, given Wilf a receipt for Jack's fare.

Jack was in trouble. He had lost his wallet. Or at least his wallet—containing miscellaneous slips of paper (nothing, though, that would enable the finder to return the wallet to its owner), money (about $1.25, Jack thought), and one of the two Minnesota Central passes—was missing. Two wallets, in fact, were missing, for Father Chmielewski, the pastor where Jack helped out, had presented him with a new one for Christmas. "I was sorry I didn't have anything for him."

"Be that as it may," said Wilf. *When was the last time Jack had seen his wallet?*

The new wallet Jack had seen the evening before, just as they were sitting down to eat, which was when Father Chmielewski had given it to him. Jack had put it in his left back pocket, he remembered, to distribute the weight, since he kept his old wallet in his *right* back pocket. *Had Jack transferred the contents of the old wallet to the new one?* No, he hadn't. *Then he couldn't say that the old wallet had been in his possession at that time?* No, as a matter of fact, he couldn't. He could only assume that it was in its usual place. *When was the last time Jack had seen his old wallet? Think.* The last time Jack had seen his *old* wallet? Yesterday—yesterday on the train going to Olympe, if memory served him right. *Think.* Well, Jack hadn't intended to mention this, but, well, there had been a little accident at the table the evening before. A cup of coffee had gone into his lap, not very hot coffee, fortunately, but enough (since it had cream in it) to necessitate a change of pants, these kindly lent him by Father Chmielewski, not a bad person, really, when you got to know him. *Yes, yes. Had Jack seen his old wallet at that time?* He had not. *No?* No. Father Chmielewski had turned Jack's pants over to the housekeeper, a fine woman, and she had brought them back later that evening. *Now had Jack seen his wallet—his old wallet—at that time?* No, he hadn't. He hadn't seen either wallet at that time. *Had he looked?* No, he hadn't. *Why hadn't he?* He hadn't thought to look, and even if he had, he would not have looked. The housekeeper was a very fine woman.

"The chances are she took the wallets out when she cleaned his pants," Father Urban said to Wilf.

"I just can't believe they're lost," Jack said.

"We don't have a thing to worry about," Father Urban said, again to Wilf.

"A phone call to Father Chmielewski will tell us that," said Wilf, rather ominously. "I never carry my wallet in my back pocket. There's too much chance of it riding up when you sit down. Lots of wallets are lost that way."

Jack looked miserable. "I always keep my back pocket buttoned," he said, but this didn't count for much coming from him just then, as he must have realized.

"Oh Lord!" Once again, as frequently happened on their little trips, Wilf explored the problem he had with the Minnesota Central. He had written what he considered a very nice letter to the president of the road, requesting another pass, but for some reason he had received no reply—none at all. Six, seven weeks now, had gone by since he had written, and each one of those weeks meant sixty-five cents for a round-trip ticket, which might not seem like very much, but over a long period of time it really mounted up. If they were entitled to two passes, why weren't they entitled to three? They weren't joyriding on them. They were serving the same people—a lot of them anyway —that the Minnesota Central was serving. Naturally, Wilf hadn't put any of this in his letter. He had just written a very nice letter—the kind of letter you'd think would at least be answered. "Oh Lord!"

Father Urban sighed. He had said all he had to say on this subject several weeks ago—that Wilf might drop a line to Father Louis, since he was responsible for the two passes they had— but Wilf hadn't responded to this suggestion at all, perhaps because he thought it reflected on him as a good provider.

The train slowed down and came to rest between two corn fields. Such unscheduled stops were a mysterious feature of travel on the Minnesota Central. Sometimes a fast freight would rattle by, but usually there was no explanation—the engineer who had set traps along the way, and had stopped the train in order to service them, was now retired, Wilf understood.

"Of course, anything can happen during the Christmas rush," he said. "I'm always reading about cards and letters being delivered twenty years or more after they were mailed. Still, this may be the man's way of saying no. I'm not overlooking that possibility."

In Father Urban's opinion, this was more than just a possibility. "You'd be wise not to write again," he said.

"But now I may have to! As things stand now, we're down to one pass!"

Jack looked miserable. "Now we're moving," he said, but he was wrong. They had moved, but they weren't moving.

"I don't think we have a thing to worry about—where Jack's pass is concerned," said Father Urban.

"I hope you're right," Wilf said. "And who knows? We may hear something about the other one pretty soon. Maybe even tomorrow, or the next day."

"Or the day after."

"Yes, that's more like it." Wilf was taking the holidays into consideration.

"*Now* we're moving," Jack said, and this time they really were.

Father Urban, having done what he could for Jack with Wilf, now went to bat for himself. "Phil Smith's talking about Florida. Phil and Monsignor Renton."

"They went last year," Wilf said.

"I understand you let Louis fill in at St Monica's last year. . . ."

"Things are different this year. This year I need every man I've got." Wilf thought this over, and then he went on. "To tell you the truth, I was glad to get rid of Louis for a while. He was cold all the time—or said he was—and he wasn't here for the worst part. I know Louis is a friend of yours, Urban, but I'm afraid he's not much of a team man."

"I thought if I went to St Monica's I might be able to stimulate interest in the Hill, recruit retreatants, accept speaking engagements, make contacts. . . ." Yes, and live and work as a *priest*.

"I don't say you wouldn't be able to help us there, but you're needed where you are—and don't forget the brochure."

"I'm not."

"In fact, you'd better tell Phil not to count on you for weekends after Lent begins. No, don't say anything about that. We'll wait awhile and see how it goes."

"Poor Phil," said Father Urban. Phil, and Phil alone among the diocesan clergy, had given Wilf a hand when he most needed it, the previous winter, and Wilf had said that he'd never forget it. He had since found out, though, that Phil was out of favor at the Chancery. Father Urban tried another angle. "I was more or less under the impression that I'd be able to go there, and so this only came up as an outside possibility, but maybe I'd better mention it—now rather than later."

"What's this?"

"Renton thinks Phil can get somebody else, if need be. Maybe a Jesuit, he said." This was something Monsignor Renton had mentioned in passing, with Wilf in mind, Father Urban suspected, but still it had been said.

"Well, that's a chance I'm willing to take," Wilf said. He was irrational on the subject of Jesuits, but not irrational enough to believe that they'd make the mistake of helping a man in Phil's position.

"I just thought I'd better mention it," Father Urban said, and with that he despaired. He had appealed to Wilf's common sense —*it* should have told him that Father Urban could best serve the interests of the Order and the Hill by going to St Monica's. He had appealed to Wilf's sense of loyalty—*it* should have made him want to help Phil Smith. He had appealed to Wilf's fear of Jesuits—*it* was perhaps his greatest fear. Father Urban couldn't see why these considerations, all together, shouldn't override Wilf's desire to employ him as a common workman. Wilf made so little sense, in fact, that Father Urban wondered if he might not be acting under instructions from Chicago to keep the star of the Order blacked out.

Brother Harold was waiting for them at the station in Duesterhaus. Wilf, Jack, and Father Urban packed themselves into the cab of the pickup truck, with Wilf at the wheel, and Brother Harold climbed into the back end and crouched behind the cab.

"O.K.!" he yelled.

"We'll have to do something about that," Wilf said. It was a cold day, growing colder, with dust blowing in from North Dakota.

"You mean get some straw for him?" said Father Urban, as they pulled away.

"As a matter of fact," Wilf replied, sounding hurt, "I was thinking of canvas. Kind of expensive, though."

For the life of him, Father Urban couldn't see how the Catholic Church (among large corporations) could be rated second only to Standard Oil in efficiency, as *Time* had reported a few years back.

When they got back to the Hill, Father Urban picked up his mail, and a box he'd been expecting, and headed for his room where he meant to lie down and rest. On the stairs, he turned and caught a glimpse of Wilf and Jack in the office—of Wilf handing the telephone to Jack. After delivering the mail and the box (which contained an electric heater) to his room, Father Urban put on the heavy sweater he wore around the house and went downstairs. He was thinking Jack might need someone to defend him.

Wilf was in possession of the telephone, was saying good-by, hanging up. Apparently he hadn't trusted Jack to do the talking,

after all. "I don't know what Father Chmielewski must think of
us here!" he said to Father Urban. "I've never been so embar-
rassed in my life!" And then to Jack: "Both wallets where you
left them! Don't you see what this means?"

Jack obviously didn't.

"*You're still wearing Father Chmielewski's pants!*"

Jack looked down at himself in horror.

"What the hell," said Father Urban, trying to take Jack's part,
but not finding it easy. "Why, a thing like this could happen to
anybody!"

Wilf shook off this remark and put out his arm to ward off
any more of the same. He plopped down in his chair and swiveled
himself around until Jack and Father Urban were out of his
sight. "All right," he said, swiveling back to them. "Sit down,
will you?"

Father Urban and Jack sat down.

"Now this is what we'll do." Jack would give Father Chmielewski's pants to Brother Harold for pressing—and say nothing. No,
Jack would give Father Chmielewski's pants to Wilf, and *he*
would give them to Brother Harold for pressing—and say nothing. Then the following week, Jack would return them to Father
Chmielewski, with apologies. No, Jack would just hang them up
in the closet of the bedroom he occupied at Father Chmielewski's
—and say nothing—and *maybe* nothing would be said to him. "If
Father Chmielewski talks, we'll be the laughing stock of the
diocese!"

Jack looked miserable.

"What the hell," said Father Urban.

"You'll see," Wilf said. He said that when he first spoke to
Father Chmielewski, he had naturally been most concerned about
Jack's wallet (because of the pass), and Father Chmielewski had
said that he'd send it over if it was there. *That* was before Father
Chmielewski had gone upstairs to look for it, though, before

he discovered what was now known to them all. What Father Chmielewski would do now, Wilf didn't know. Father Chmielewski had sounded a little confused. "If he does send over the wallet—wallets—well, I'm hoping he doesn't come himself. I don't think he will. If he does, though, we'll have to say something. And if he brings *your* pants, Father—we'll cross that bridge when we come to it. Oh Lord!"

"You don't think Father Chmielewski thinks we're trying to steal his pants, do you?" said Father Urban. "Because if you do, the fact that Jack left his wallet—wallets——"

Wilf said, "Shhhh!"

Brother Harold appeared in the doorway. "I've made some coffee," he said to Wilf, and then he stood there, waiting for them to come and get it.

So Wilf, though he doubtless had more to say, said no more then. He rose and led them to the refectory.

It wasn't the custom for Brother Harold to serve coffee between meals, but perhaps he was being festive that day. He had put out a plate of graham crackers, too, and he had turned on the tree. Something more, however, awaited them in the refectory.

Wilf said, "Hey, where'd that come from?"

Father Urban said, "That's a color set, isn't it?"

Brother Harold, who seemed a little surprised that Father Urban would know this, said that there had been some question in his mind about accepting the set, since he had no idea where it had come from. All the dealer knew was that he'd been authorized by the manufacturer to deliver the set to the Hill on Christmas morning and to say that Santa Claus had sent it. ("Heh, heh," said Wilf.) The dealer and one of his men had erected an antenna on the roof.

"Funny we didn't notice it," said Wilf.

"If we want one of those big poles in the yard, we can have one, they said, only we'll have to wait until spring."

"Until the ground thaws out, you mean?"

"Yes, Father."

"But who could've sent it?" said Jack.

"Santa Claus."

"A good question, that," said Wilf, passing over Father Urban's remark.

"Yes," said Father Urban, not that he was in any doubt of the answer.

"Who it was we may never know," Wilf said, "but I think it's safe to say it was somebody who was here at some time and liked what he saw."

"How about the man who gave you the mattress, Father," said Brother Harold, and somehow conveyed the impression that Wilf was the likeliest object of anonymous benefactions, although such were unheard of at the Hill until now.

"Maybe," Wilf said, "though I rather doubt it. It could've been anybody."

"It's better that we don't know," said Jack.

Father Urban had been holding back, waiting for the proper moment to enlighten them, but he could feel himself being sealed off. "I think it's safe to say we have Billy Cosgrove to thank for this. I happen to know he's given away color sets before—to orphanages, hospitals, and the like."

"Maybe you'd better drop him a line, Urban, but be circumspect—in case you're wrong. Of course, when and if it's established we have Mr Cosgrove to thank, I'll write him a nice letter."

To Father Urban it was perfectly clear that Wilf believed Billy to be the donor, but couldn't accept the implications, and, by making so much of the letter *he* would write, was trying to carve out more of a part for himself in their good fortune. "We should *phone* him," said Father Urban.

"You can't be *that* sure," Wilf said, taking a cup of coffee from Brother Harold. "Careful, Father," he said, speaking to Jack, whose cup rattled as he started across the room to join them.

"I was never surer of anything in my life," said Father Urban.

"Well, if you really think Mr Cosgrove expects it. . . ."

"Billy Cosgrove expects nothing."

"Then to call him long distance seems a little extravagant. . . ."

"He's been a little extravagant himself, don't you think?"

Wilf looked over at the set, a beautiful console model.

"As I see it," Jack said, "whoever's responsible for this gift doesn't want us to know who he is. He isn't seeking *our* appreciation, if you know what I mean."

Father Urban gave Jack the merest glance. "You mean well, I'm sure." Jack didn't know Billy Cosgrove.

"It might be a *mistake*," Jack said.

"I think *you're* right," Wilf said to Jack. "But *you*," he said to Father Urban, "do what you think best." Then, saying to himself, "Well, I'll be darned," he went over to the set. Unlike Jack, he had some idea of its worth. "And color, you say?"

"Yes, but there's just black and white now," Brother Harold said. "Tonight there'll be color."

"Let's see what's on now," said Wilf.

"Not now," said Father Urban to Brother Harold who was bringing him a cup of coffee, and stalked out of the room. Having said what he'd said—that they ought to phone Billy—what else could he do? He went to the office, sat in Wilf's swivel chair, and put through the call. Presently, the operator informed him that Mr Cosgrove was in Florida—should she try to reach him there? Father Urban said, "Thanks—but that won't be necessary," and hung up. He hadn't wanted to phone Billy. He had been driven to it—by fools.

None of the viewers at the Hill had enjoyed regular access to a TV set before, and so, for a while anyway, they watched the programs with a faith, hope, and charity that must have been rare

at the time. "Let's see what's on now," Wilf would say at the
start of the evening, and read to them from the program resumés
in the *Record:* "When hated gunfighter is wounded, townspeople
bet on the hour he'll be killed by dead man's brother." "In state
institution, four old buddies are reunited for group therapy."
Wilf gave them a choice of programs on the two channels they
could get, but Father Urban and Jack were glad to let Wilf run
the set, and he was fair about it. "If you'd rather have the other
one," he'd say from time to time, or "Let's see what the other
one's like."

Father Urban found himself questioning some words of his
uttered some years earlier, words widely quoted in the Catholic
press. He had said that television, this new medium about which
many seemed to be having doubts, could and would be a great
force for good, and in saying this, he had more than anticipated
the thought of the late pontiff (who was to say "could" but not
"would"). Unlike Bishop Sheen who was to say, "Television is
a blessing," and who perhaps had his own program in mind,
Father Urban hadn't been in a position to know what he was
talking about. His own work had kept him in ignorance of the
new medium, and if he happened to enter a room when a set
was on, the chances were it would be switched off—because he
was rated a greater attraction. Of course, he had watched such
events as the World Series and the Kentucky Derby, but the
regular fare, what he was seeing in the evenings now, no, he
really hadn't known about it.

But whatever one might think of the programs—and Wilf and
Brother Harold seemed to think pretty well of them—there was
no getting around the fact that television had come to stay. The
problem it posed was an old one: how to make what was generally accepted more acceptable, i.e., how to make an honest
woman of a whore. Probably no one man could do it. Obviously,

Bishop Sheen hadn't. Father Urban's own opportunities had been all too few and slight: a prayer for use where it was the custom for a clergyman to sign off the station; a series of three-minute talks especially suitable for Lent, these on defective film to which the Order held residual rights; and two appearances "live," making the Stations of the Cross and participating in a panel discussion of juvenile delinquency, the latter on educational TV. In short, Father Urban hadn't had a decent chance to show what he could do in the new medium. It troubled him that a Billy Graham or an Oral Roberts was seen and heard by more souls in an evening than Our Lord and his disciples had preached to in all their travels—and, to tell the truth, Father Urban wasn't too happy about Bishop Sheen, either. It could be that Father Urban would yet make the new medium his own, perhaps when his days of travel were over, assuming, of course, that they weren't already over. *And now—speaking to you from his study at the Novitiate of the Order of St Clement—Father Urban.*

For the present, however, Father Urban was just another viewer. With Wilf at the controls, they went through the evening, through the prime time, through the news, weather, and sports, and into the old movies, which made it harder to get up in the morning. Perhaps the set's living color left something to be desired, because they were in a fringe area, to say the least of it, but color programs were rare. The set gave them a good, clear picture of what there was to see, and it also threw off heat that even the refectory, the only warm room in the house, could use on those very cold nights right after Christmas. While viewing, they sampled the liqueurs and meats and cheeses from Billy's hamper, and consumed kettles of popcorn fresh from Brother Harold's kitchen. It was, after all, even there, the festive season.

The only light came from the set and the Christmas tree, and so it was no longer possible for Wilf to read the papers, for

Brother Harold to do his homework, or for Father Urban and
Jack to play checkers in the evening. Probably Jack was the only
one to regret the passing of their old way of life. His eyes weren't
up to the strain of prolonged viewing, but fortunately he didn't
have the appetite for it that the others had at first. He'd doze off
and come to saying, "What's this?" And Wilf would say, "Oh,
he's a bush pilot, and he's trying to find this girl's father. She's
a Broadway star. Looks a lot like the country around here,
doesn't it?"

There were moments in the evening, though, when Father
Urban, instead of being carried away on the wings or saddle of
adventure, nodded in his chair, for the days right after Christmas were much like those that had gone before.

On the day after Christmas, early in the morning, Wilf led them
to the rear of the corridor that ran between the parlors and the
library on the one side and the chapel on the other, and revealed
to them his plan for a sacristy. The plan called for the corridor
to become a blind alley except in case of emergency, and for the
back stairway to be abandoned (except in case of emergency),
and for the solid wall between the corridor and the chapel to be
breached for a doorway—all this for a *temporary* sacristy.

"Better no sacristy at all," said Father Urban, when he'd heard
Wilf's plan.

"A religious community is judged by its facilities for worship,"
Wilf replied. "We owe it to ourselves and visiting clergy to have
a sacristy. And to Our Lord."

Jack, by tapping on the wall, by pushing on it, and by shaking his head, had shown where his sympathies lay, but at the mention of Our Lord, Father Urban saw Jack drop his hands and
take leave of his senses.

Wilf, however, wanted everybody on his side—as well he might for such a project. "What we should do, Urban, I agree, is add on."

"Agree? Add on? I don't know what *you're* talking about, Father."

"Add on from the outside, Father. That was the original plan, and then, when winter snuck up on us, I hit upon the present plan—as a temporary solution."

"As such it has its advantages," said Father Urban, feeling that any more discouraging comment from him might drive Wilf back to the original plan, and then where would they be? They'd be working outdoors in the middle of winter, taking on the exterior wall, a wall of stone. Why, if they disturbed the vines, they might even bring the house down.

And so Father Urban went along with the others, and with hammer, scout ax, hacksaw, in a cloud of dust and grit he worked along with them. But he wasn't the team man he'd been on the previous job. During his lunch hour, he took a nap from which he sometimes had to be summoned by Brother Harold ("Father wonders if you're all right, Father"), and sometimes, during working hours, he went up to his room, and made no bones about it, for a snort ("I find it cuts the dust"). A good part of his working day was spent in wandering back and forth between the lavatory and the job. Yes, he knew what he was, a disgruntled employee blowing himself to a bit of company time, but he didn't care, and he didn't give the boss quite enough cause to complain. However, it got so that the employee knew what to expect if, in his journeys to and from the lavatory, he paused too long at a window for a look at the outside world. He knew that the boss would soon come along and offer him a cigarette—there was no use trying to smoke a cigar if you did the kind of work they did—and then a light. There they'd be, then, just a couple of average guys such as they saw in the evening on television, taking their well-earned break, smoking

the right brand of cigarette and married to a couple of average
gals who, at that very moment, on another channel, were washing their husbands' dirty work clothes with the right brand of
detergent. And the chances were that the employee would make
the first move back to the job. Mighty clever people, these Bo-
hunks!

Father Urban worked, when he worked, in a quiet rage. In any
other time and place, it seemed to him, a man like Wilf would
have known better than to enter religion, or, having made that
mistake, would have been required to make the best of it. As it
was, Wilf was doing pretty well as a workman—more than should
be expected of a priest—and as a priest, you might say, he was
doing pretty well for a workman. Even a day laborer, and certainly a carpenter or a painter, had to measure up to the competition—otherwise he'd be out of a job, and his wife and family
would suffer. Why shouldn't Wilf, as priest and rector, be subject to the same law? In a very real sense, Wilf had a family
now, and they *were* suffering. Didn't he know this? Didn't he
care?

"You know it doesn't hurt for the laymen to see us like this,"
he told his dirty charges toward the end of their first day on the
sacristy job. They'd just had a visit from a roofing salesman.
"Too many of 'em think the priesthood's a bed of roses."

On the other hand, when Father Chmielewski appeared, as
he did on the following afternoon, Wilf, forewarned, wore a
cassock, met him at the front door, ushered him into the office,
and kept him there for the duration of the visit. "I thought of
bringing him back here to meet you, Urban, but I didn't want
him to see you like this."

"Thanks," said Father Urban.

"He's definitely a pastor of the old school, and in view of all
that's happened lately, I thought I'd better not risk it. I wanted

to, in a way. Too many of the secular clergy think we have it too easy."

Father Chmielewski had delivered Jack's wallets but not his pants, Wilf was happy to say, and since Father Chmielewski hadn't mentioned them or his own (and certainly Wilf hadn't) it only remained for Jack to return Father Chmielewski's on Saturday. Jack should hang them up neatly when he arrived. Jack should not spill any more coffee. Jack should not get Father Chmielewski's mixed up with his own when he dressed on Sunday morning. Unless Father Chmielewski said something, and this now seemed very unlikely, Jack should say nothing.

In the days right after Christmas, Father Urban received a half-dozen requests for his services as a speaker—and turned them all down. To give Wilf no serious trouble, but also to lay no golden eggs for him, was once again Father Urban's policy. Since Wilf prized the workman in Father Urban above all else, that was what he would get.

Wilf knew what was happening, too, for he made it his business to answer the telephone, and he had a way of loitering in the office when the call was for Father Urban. Maybe he figured that a man who drank on the job might have a girl friend, but probably he was just curious. In any case, there was too much of the house dick about Wilf to suit Father Urban—who, however, spoke freely in his presence. "No, I'm sorry. Maybe one of the other fathers could make it. Oh, you wouldn't? I see. Ill? No, just don't feel up to it. We're taking the house apart here. That's right. Renovations. Why don't you call back in a month or two? Thanks for calling."

"Another minor group with major program problems," he'd say to Wilf, and wouldn't be able to tell him exactly who had called. That was what got Wilf, you could see, really got him, though he tried not to show it. Opportunities to speak (outside of church) were rare in Wilf's experience, and he would've snapped them all up, but he couldn't very well act like it.

The secretary of a Catholic business and professional women's group in Great Plains had the nerve to solicit Father Urban's services on a post card, which was like trying to take a whale on a bent pin. He tossed the card into Wilf's wastebasket. "Hey, that's an important organization!" cried Wilf who, it appeared, had read the card. "Then we'll be hearing from her again," Father Urban said, and he was right. A few days later, the secretary phoned to find out whether Father Urban had received her card.

"Oh, a card," he said, watching Wilf squirm. "Maybe you'd better start from the beginning then. I see. You meet once a month except during the summertime, and the Bishop's your moderator. Did you talk this over with him? Well, you'd better do that. He's asked you not to call him—why's that? Trusts you to carry on your fine program, to check with him only when it's necessary. He hasn't been able to come to the last two meetings? I see. But you're sure there'll be no *objection* from him. Well, now, I'll tell you what to do. You get in touch with your moderator, if possible, and get him to write to the rector here. That's Father Wilfrid. His name is spelled with two *i*'s—two *i*'s as in Ignatius. And try to give us a choice of dates. Of course I know th^ Bishop's busy—he's the busiest priest in the diocese, you might say—but we're pretty busy ourselves. Still, one of us might be able to make it. Me? That'll be for Father Wilfrid to decide. Won't be any trouble about transportation, will there? From Duesterhaus? About a mile from downtown Duesterhaus. That's right. So you get in touch with your moderator, and after we hear from him, if it's at all possible, I'll come. Father Wilfrid. That's right. Two *i*'s. And thanks for calling."

Wilf appeared somewhat shaken by what he'd heard. "But what if the Bishop doesn't write?"

"Frankly, I'll be surprised if he does."

"Just playing hard to get, eh?"

"Not a-tall. Why should I knock myself out for somebody who sends me a post card? How do I know it isn't just this woman's idea to have me come and give a talk? How do I know the Bishop would be there for it? I gather he isn't very good about coming to meetings. The point is, if we're going to oblige this group, the Bishop ought to be the one to invite us. When that happens, why, then, there'll be *some* reason to go. I have no illusions about talking to women's groups."

"And if he doesn't invite us?"

"Then I don't think we should go."

"I see what you mean. Yes."

"I knew you would." Wilf could appreciate the theory, but the practice. frightened him. Wilf's natural tendency was to give up and eat the bait.

He was pleasantly surprised by the number of requests being received at the Hill for speakers, he said that evening at table. In fact, he wondered if they shouldn't give some thought to starting up "a speakers' bureau" at the Hill. "The idea has possibilities," he said, and kicked it around for a while. He suggested, among other things, that Brother Harold might give chalk talks to teenagers. "Well, we'll see," he said, finally shutting up.

Jack had shown no enthusiasm for a speakers' bureau, and Father Urban, when asked for his opinion, had said, "I really wouldn't know. I've always worked alone." Father Urban was annoyed with Wilf for presenting the idea as he had—as if more than one man were in demand at the Hill. Actually, it was a dangerous idea. For who, with Father Urban on the menu, would want Wilf, Jack, or Brother Harold? Wilf, to preserve the fiction of a bureau, would be sending himself or Jack ("also well known") out on Father Urban's bookings. Then hard. feelings would arise between the Order and the groups who had contracted to hear Father Urban, and, yes, between members of the community at the Hill. The idea had possibilities all right—for all kinds of strife.

Perhaps Jack recognized this. "Well. . . ." he said the following evening, after Wilf had raised the matter again.

"I grant it might conflict to some extent," Wilf said, "with our other work."

"I turned down a couple of people today for that very reason," Father Urban said. "I just don't have much left in the evenings."

Wilf, after a slight pause, said, "Father and I were speaking of the work we'll *soon* be doing here, Father."

"Oh," said Father Urban, as if he hadn't known. Perhaps he wasn't playing fair with Wilf, but then Wilf—in this matter and others—wasn't playing fair with him.

The lights went out.

"Did you do something out there?" Wilf called into the kitchen.

"No, Father," Brother Harold called back, and a moment later he came into the refectory carrying a dim flashlight.

"Turn it off," Wilf said, and when this had been done—to save the batteries—he continued the inquiry in total darkness. "You didn't have your mixer on, did you?"

"Not then. I did earlier." Perhaps Brother Harold's only fault, in Wilf's view, was that he used his mixer too much.

"And disconnected it?"

"Yes, Father."

"And the TV wasn't on," Wilf said.

"I may be at fault," said another voice. "I left an electric heater on in my room."

"I didn't know you had an electric heater, Father."

"I left it on to take the chill off my room. I plan to spend the evening there. I've got some letters to write."

From out of the darkness: "*I didn't know you had an electric heater, Father.*"

"Monsignor Renton was kind enough to lend me one. It gets pretty cold in my room, you know."

"I hope you didn't tell *him* that, Father."

"As a matter of fact, I did."

"I wish you hadn't, Father."

"God knows it's the truth."

"If that gets around, it could keep retreatants away. Flashlight, Brother." Wilf ordered Brother Harold to take a candle from the kitchen and to go and stand by the fusebox in the corridor. Then Wilf moved off silently, carrying the dim flashlight, and Father Urban followed him. Jack sat on at the table, in the dark.

Upstairs, Father Urban stood by the door of his room, as ordered, while Wilf went inside and disconnected the heater.

"Tell Brother it's O.K. now."

Father Urban sang out that it was O.K.

Wilf was moving toward the floor lamp when it came on. "Left *that* burning, too."

"*That* I forgot."

Wilf knelt to examine the little plate on the heater. "No wonder! Thirteen hundred and twenty on low and sixteen hundred and fifty on high—and you had it on high! You trying to burn the house down, Father?"

"You know what I was trying to do, Father."

"You only sleep here, Father."

"I'd like to be able to do more. I'd like to able to sit down and read and write in something like comfort."

"Well, you won't wear long underwear," Wilf said, going over to the register. He knew better than to feel it. "What's wrong with downstairs? The refectory's always nice and warm."

"It isn't suitable."

"Well, I don't have to tell you this circuit won't take this heater."

"And wasn't suitable even before we got television."

Wilf looked *old*. "I'll take another look at your duct," he said, and quickly departed.

He could be heard down in the bowels of the house, tampering with the furnace, but when the heat came on again, it was, as usual, not for long, and more ebb than flow. When the temperature dropped to normal in his room, as it soon did, Father Urban put aside his breviary and went to bed. By not going downstairs to television, he hoped to keep the pressure on Wilf. He hadn't meant that they should give up television and turn the one cozy room into a study. That, though, was what Wilf must have concluded—in his guilt, which was the guilt of the hooked but not yet hardened viewer—and on the high ground of that misunderstanding, Father Urban would take his stand, saying nothing, letting his actions speak.

The next evening, however, when he might have been home in bed keeping the pressure on Wilf, Father Urban was out. Early in the afternoon, a Mr Bean had called from St Paul to say that he'd be driving back to Great Plains that day and would like to pick up Father Urban on the way and take him to dinner —it was something he'd been wanting to do for some time. "O.K., if that's how it is," said Father Urban, assuming that they'd met somewhere.

Apparently, though, Mr Bean was just one of those people who had *heard* him—whether at St Monica's on Sundays, or at the Poinsettia Smorgasbord, Father Urban didn't know or bother to ask. They drove on to Great Plains, with Mr Bean, a weedy little man with a bass voice, doing all the talking. He was in outdoor advertising, and, for the last few days, he and his cohorts had been preparing for the battle soon to take place between them and the anti-billboard lobby in the state legislature. Mr Bean was full of it. "I still don't know where you stand, Father," he said, when they pulled into the parking lot of the General Diggles Hotel, where they were to eat. "Nor do I," said Father

Urban, getting out of the car. This was the kind of controversy he liked to steer clear of—he could meet somebody on the other side tomorrow.

Nothing had been said about Mrs Bean, but there she was, waiting for them in the Greenwich Village Room: the attractive redhead who had given Father Urban trouble at the smorgasbord. Father Urban felt trapped, felt that he had been brought there because Mrs Bean wanted another crack at him, and in the same arena, and that her husband had acted as matchmaker. But there was no mention of the earlier encounter—Mrs Bean must have assumed that she wouldn't be remembered—and the conversation went along nicely, with everybody having a second drink and with Father Urban giving an amusing account of the hardships and misadventures of the little community at the Hill. Through it all, even in the matter of the electric heater, he covered up for Wilf ("Actually, he's doing a bang-up job") and was moving gradually from the ridiculous to the sublime aspects of the religious life when Mr Bean interrupted him.

"I've been thinking about what you said in the car, Father."

Father Urban couldn't recall saying anything memorable in the car. "Yes?"

"This may give you a better idea of *us*. The industry's pledged the use of 12,000 highway billboards, for emergency-warning purposes. Within twenty-four hours after the declaration—the declaration that an enemy attack is imminent—we'll have a previously prepared civil defense message up in six hundred key points around the country. Of course, we hope that day never comes, but if it does, we'll be ready."

"Sounds like a large order," said Father Urban, thinking it didn't make any sense in the space age but might throw the enemies of outdoor advertising for a slight loss.

"Oh hell, Ray!" said Mrs Bean, and went off on a tangent of her own—the persecutions taking place behind the Iron Curtain, the sufferings of "the Silent Church." Turning on Father Urban, and referring, presumably, to his Sunday sermons at St Monica's, she cried: "I keep hoping you'll say something about *that!* But you never do!"

"We don't know how lucky we are," Father Urban said, trying to calm her down, but somehow sounding guilty—like the slacker she evidently believed him to be.

"Then say *that!*" cried Mrs Bean. "Oh, say *something!*"

"We follow a regular course of sermons in this diocese. At present we're going through the sacraments, and that's what I have to talk about."

"You could still say *something!* Others *do*, you know."

Obviously, Mrs Bean's mind had been conditioned, if not impaired, by reading the Catholic press, and she may have had one more than was good for her, too. What else? Her husband couldn't handle her—that was all too clear—and there were no children from their union to knock the starch out of her. Father Urban wondered if he could be making a mistake in being gentle with her. He had let her have it at the smorgasbord because there had been no other way, but perhaps it was the only way to handle her. She had asked him earlier if he ever read the *Drover*, and he had evaded the question, but when she asked him again, he said:

"It's too rich for my blood."

"Would you read it if I had it sent to you?"

"No." The *Drover*, a weekly, had begun as a paper for the livestock trade, but it was now—and unfortunately had been for the last thirty years—wandering in the wilderness of religion and politics, keeping the old name, and doubtless a few old subscribers, and adding crooks and crosiers to the masthead where longhorns had been before. In no other paper would you find *everything* that was wrong with the Catholic press. The *Drover* had it all, all the worst features of the bully and the martyr. Why anybody—any educated person, even one who didn't like the way the world was going—would want to read the *Drover*, Father Urban didn't know.

"I'm going to subscribe you anyway."

"Sylvia," said Mr Bean.

"*Don't*," said Father Urban, with a smile, but firmly.

Mr Bean said, "If you don't mind me asking, Father, how cold *does* it get in your room?"

Remembering that his sufferings were as nothing compared with those behind the Iron Curtain, Father Urban said, "Let's just say it gets unbearably cool at times, Mr Bean."

At this point, Mrs Bean got up and left the table. The atmosphere was such that Father Urban was relieved to see that she wasn't taking her fur coat with her.

"Father, have you thought of calling in an electrician?"

"I won't say I haven't thought of it, Mr Bean."

"Ray," said Mr Bean.

"Ray," said Father Urban.

"But you haven't done anything yet, Father?"

"No, Ray, I haven't."

"Then don't."

The next day an electrician who did a lot of work for Ray Bean's firm came to the Hill and did a rewiring job on Father Urban's circuit, and there was heat in Father Urban's room. Wilf, invited in to feel it, shook his head and said: "I knew it. I was watching the meter go around downstairs."

The next morning Wilf said, "Don't have it on any more than you have to, will you?" And that evening, dropping in on Father Urban, he said, "You don't have to run it on high, do you?"

The next day was Saturday. Early that morning, Wilf said, "Better pack. I've decided to send you to St Monica's, after all.

Phil's been good to us, and you'll be able to handle some of those speaking engagements you're turning down now."

"Whatever you say," said Father Urban.

7

The Most a Man Can Do

Phil Smith, pastor of St Monica's, though rather puffy in the face and grey-looking, was still a handsome man. His friend Monsignor Renton, Rector of the Cathedral, was large and pink, with a jug head, splendid white teeth, very blue eyes, and white hair, which, always neatly combed, gave him the look of the good little boy of long ago. Phil and Red were great friends and saw each other two or three evenings a week, usually at St Monica's.

Father Urban, invited to have a nightcap on his first Saturday there, had since become a regular (as Wilf never had when he was going to St Monica's) in the upper room. Here everything was pretty much as it had been when Phil and Monsignor Renton were curates at St Monica's: leather chairs and old books and brown photographs of men and boys dressed for tennis, camping, and touring—these had been the three passions of their pastor, a Philadelphian, who'd not only planned the big brownstone rectory (cherry woodwork throughout, walled-off housekeeper's quarters, five bedrooms, each with its toilet and bath, among other refinements), but paid for it with his own money, believing that he was to become the first bishop of Great Plains. Unfortunately, the friend who'd been running interference for him in Rome had got into trouble over *his* friend in France—of course Gallicanism was always a danger with the French, Monsignor Renton said—and the bishopric had gone to another. Brother clergy, still jealous but no longer afraid of the man, had then hung the nickname "Bathroom" on him, and this had proved harder for him to live with, in his big rectory, than the humiliation of having been left at the church "by those Aztecs in the Curia." So said Monsignor Renton. "Oh yes. He was a convert—from Anglicanism—and believed in fair play. I'd say he died a broken man."

The church he'd planned had never been built. *It* would have been the Cathedral, and that was why the rectory was more impressive than the church at St Monica's.

The effects of that ecclesiastical tragedy were again being felt there, now that the big swamp down the hill was no more, was dry land, now that people were living on it—a surprising number of them young Catholics of rural background, fertile, churchgoing people. *They* were Phil's problems. Most men would have been happy with such a problem, or at least would have dealt with it. Phil wasn't happy with it, and he wasn't dealing with it. Phil, who had put off building a church for years, and was still putting it off when Father Urban arrived on the scene, said he didn't like it that the promoters of Orchard Park had used shots of his church and school as part of the come-on propaganda without a word to him. Phil seemed to think that if he'd been asked for his permission, he might have withheld it, and thus nipped Orchard Park in the bud. Otherwise, he didn't say much about his problem.

And what did Monsignor Renton, who had made such an excellent *first* impression on Father Urban, say? He said, "*I* blame the state—for draining the swamp."

Meanwhile, the poor people were standing in the aisles on Sundays. Saturdays, in their way, were worse. Phil just vanished after hearing a few confessions, and Father Chumley, the curate, besides being something of a spook, was a very slow worker. Father Urban, of course, kept his line moving right along, but after a couple of Saturdays at St Monica's, he had a personal following (this always happened if he stayed long enough in one place), and it didn't help the situation to have more people coming oftener.

Penitents caught in the bottleneck at St Monica's went downtown to the Cathedral. Had they been coming from anywhere but St Monica's, Monsignor Renton would have done something about them, not that he was suffering so much personally. (By custom, he heard confessions only at Christmas and Easter, and yet if the lines did get too long on an ordinary Saturday he might put himself into service for a brief spell, crying "Over here! Over here!" while dusting out his confessional.) Fortunately, the Cathedral curates, two youngsters very much under each other's influence (and consequently out of sympathy with him, Monsignor Renton said), attributed the overflow in great part to their extreme, and yet still growing, popularity with the laity.

Monsignor Renton, though, by the time Father Urban started helping out at St Monica's, was beginning to feel the pressure from Orchard Park. On the occasion of their first meeting, which took place in the upper room, he said, "If you ever get the chance, and I *don't always* myself, and you *never* will as long as you come here, watch this 'All-Star Golf' at five o'clock on Channel 3." But then, having said this, he covered for Phil (who was down in the kitchen for ice cubes): "By the way, I think poor Phil suffers from claustrophobia to a certain extent. Fifteen minutes in the box is all he can take."

Why, though, was Phil so hard to find at other times? Why, Father Urban wondered, was Phil so often out? "Going out for a bit of air," he'd say, or "Have to get the oil changed in the car," or just "Have to go out." When in, he seemed to experience acute pain if the phone or doorbell rang, gave a start, and said, "Oh my!" Then, pretty soon, he'd be gone again. Where did he go? According to Mrs Burns, the housekeeper, he was often seen sitting in the periodical section at the public library, and Father Urban, noting the mileage on Phil's late-model Plymouth, suspected that he just drove around, using the car as he did the library, to escape—but to escape what? His job, himself, what?

It hadn't always been that way at St Monica's, said Mrs Burns, not when Phil's mother was living. Every morning, Phil's mother had presented Phil and Mrs Burns and the curate with a list of things to be done during the day, and they'd done them. St Monica's had been a model parish then.

"Why, I never touched the telephone in those days," said Mrs Burns, who cleared all calls now, since neither Phil nor Father Chumley would pick up the telephone unless buzzed on the intercom by Mrs Burns. "All I want on my tombstone, Father," she told Father Urban, "is 6:30, 8, 9:30, and 11." These were the hours of the Sunday Masses.

So, with Phil out, and with Father Chumley, for all practical purposes, out—over in church, praying—things were in a bad way at St Monica's. No wonder Phil was unpopular at the Chancery. Father Urban asked Monsignor Renton about this. "Is Phil getting any heat?"

"Yes, if that means anything—which I doubt," said Monsignor Renton, who, it seemed, didn't care for Father Udovic, the Chancellor.

"How about the consultors?" Father Urban asked. In any diocese, the bishop's consultors are a comparatively gentle breed of men, older fellows who've received their earthly reward and risen as far as they'll rise, but it is their duty, after all, to keep the diocese on a straight course, with or without the help of the Bishop.

"None of those guys wants an Orchard Park to rise up in *his*

parish," said Monsignor Renton, himself a consultor, "and certainly not I."

And the Bishop—how was he taking it?

"Ah," said Monsignor Renton. Phil was an irremovable pastor,
but if the Bishop cared to get rough, he could avail himself
of the prejudice against Phil that did, unfortunately, exist. The
Bishop would never do this, though, for he had too high a regard for Phil as a person and as a priest. In fact, the Bishop
might even have a secret sympathy for Phil in his present difficulty. Oh yes. For years, until his patron and pen pal Cardinal
Mullenix died, the Bishop—"Dear James," as Monsignor Renton
called him—had sat on his ass, waiting to be translated to a more
important see, and had built nothing. "It's my guess there'll be
no change at St Monica's until Phil dies."

"I don't get it," said Father Urban. Phil, although he did have
a heart condition, could live a long time, and St Monica's couldn't
wait. And with all the fresh parishioners, so many of them young
married people pulling down good dough and, unlike their eld-
ers, in the habit of spending it, there was no reason why St
Monica's shouldn't have a new church at once. Yes, and a wing on
the school. And how about a new convent for the good sisters?
The first step should be a parish census. If the priests of the
parish didn't feel up to taking one, and doubtless Phil didn't,
well, there were always parishioners willing to go into the homes
of other parishioners and ask a few questions. After the census,
Phil would know where he stood, and could plan accordingly.
Three, three and a half, maybe four hundred grand wouldn't be
asking too much of the people for a nice new church. "I still
think he should build," said Father Urban.

"No, the fuss would kill him—it'd be suicide," said Monsignor Renton, and asked Father Urban how he'd like to spend
his last days in consultation with fund-raisers, architects, con-
tractors, and salesmen.

Father Urban hadn't had this experience and could think of worse fates. "Then Phil should let somebody come here who *will* build." There were men unhappy in rural parishes, there were men not doing so well where they were as they might do elsewhere, and there were men on the way up, assistants with their tusks fully grown, ready for parishes of their own. "He's like the dog in the manger now."

"I trust you'll never say anything like that to Phil. Because that's exactly how he feels."

"Then why doesn't he put in for a change?"

"Phil feels it would be for too short a time—and so do I."

Well, Father Urban would be sorry when and if Phil departed this life, and perhaps others besides Monsignor Renton and the Bishop would be sorry, but in an ongoing institution like the Church there was just no place for such a man—or, if there was, it wasn't in a parish like St Monica's.

And was Monsignor Renton's devotion to his friend, so good to see, really so pure and selfless as it appeared?

One Saturday night, in the middle of December, Father Urban was locking up the church when Monsignor Renton appeared, carrying a light bulb and saying that nothing annoyed him so much as burned-out bulbs in public places. They dragged out a ladder and replaced a bulb in one of the gilded sconces that flowered out from the sanctuary wall. The janitor, a cripple, was slow to make repairs requiring a ladder, Monsignor Renton explained, but what they were doing still struck Father Urban as rather odd. "Now that's better. You'd never find fixtures like these today." Monsignor Renton then said that he'd picked them up in Italy, and had had them wired for electricity. Even so, although, as every pastor knows, every donor wants *his* gift to be properly displayed, looked after, and prized over all others, Father Urban was still puzzled. But the changing of the light bulb, and the larger mystery of Monsignor Renton's whole attitude toward building a new church, suddenly made sense to Father Urban as they were going out the door, when Monsignor Renton stopped and looked back at the little red wound of light in the darkness of the sanctuary and said, "I offered my first Mass in this old church."

Phil and Monsignor Renton would be leaving for Florida in the wee hours, catching the North Coast Limited for Chicago at its nearest stop, and so New Year's dinner was served the night before at St Monica's. It was a goose-and-champagne affair, with Monsignor Renton present and Father Chumley leaving the table early to hear confessions (no more penitents than he could accommodate were expected on New Year's Eve). Monsignor Renton and Father Urban did most of the talking. According to Monsignor Renton, there would soon be no oil left in the world, and the railroads would then be able to cash in on the situation that they, by running their passenger business so badly, had more or less created. Yes, the automobile was on the way out. It was just a question of time. The happy few would have their own horses and carriages, but most people would have to ride the streetcars (yes, they'd be back), and would be better for it, too. "If we're careful, we should have enough coal for the railroads and industry, once we stop making cars and beer cans."

"I didn't realize there was such an oil shortage," said Father Urban.

"I don't think it's generally known," Monsignor Renton said. "A few years ago, you may recall, everybody was talking about tranquilizers—no ill effects, they said. I knew there'd be ill effects. Now everybody knows it. Too many people in this country are dedicated to the proposition that what goes up may not come down."

"And now, in the same way, you know there's a world oil shortage?"

"Yes. You can't have as many morons as we have driving cars in this country without ill effects. There just isn't that much oil—or anything—in the world."

"How about atomic energy?"

"A bust, I'd say. No good has come of it yet, and I doubt that any will. When I was a boy, one of the worst things you could do was crap on somebody's front porch. I don't know that I ever heard of it actually happening, but I do know we talked about it a lot. Today it happens every day—to everybody. I'm talking about the fallout, of course. Ah, Mrs Burns, it isn't often I get a chance at goose that hasn't been frozen."

When they finally rose from the table, they put on their coats and went out, Monsignor Renton going over to the church, Phil and Father Urban getting into the car.

They drove to the outskirts of Great Plains, and then on, into the country. Father Urban was to meet an old woman he'd be bringing Holy Communion to daily in Phil's absence.

"I have to let her know when I'm going to be away," Phil said.

Father Urban could see how a change of priests could be an unsettling experience for an old person, but he thought it odd that he was being given this chore. "Any others, Phil?"

"There's one other, but Johnny can handle that one."

Father Urban thought this odder still. Why shouldn't one man make the rounds? "What's the name here?" he asked, when they turned into a private road. The big iron gates were open.

"Thwaites."

"Not our benefactress?"

"Yes."

"Your parishioner?"

"Yes."

"What's she like?"

"You'll see."

When Father Urban saw the house, which was approached through wooded grounds, he thought of Major. They were admitted by a rosy-cheeked girl whom Phil introduced only as Katie. Her heavy grey sweater reminded Father Urban of the one he wore when he was at the Hill, and suggested that the house wasn't being heated all over. They kept their coats on, and went upstairs.

In a room much larger than any bedroom at the Hill, Mrs Thwaites sat in an overstuffed wheelchair, watching television on two sets. The only light in the room came from the sets, a dead light, so that Mrs Thwaites's face showed up like a photographic negative: a little old woman with the face of a baby bird, all eyes and beak, but with a full head of bobbed white hair. One hand was wrapped in black rosary beads the size of cranberries, and the other gripped the remote control. A humidifier steamed at her feet. To one side of her chair there was a table with dominoes stacked on it. Across the room, an elevator, door open, was waiting. In one corner, a big bed, fancier than Wilf's and higher off the floor, was also waiting. The shades were drawn in all the windows, and the temperature was equatorial.

Mrs Thwaites cut the jabber that had been coming from one of the sets, but did not invite them to sit down. The pictures went on—a giveaway program and a panel show, with contestants on both wearing paper hats—while Phil introduced Father Urban to Mrs Thwaites.

"So Father Chumley won't be coming," Phil said.

"No, I don't want *him*."

"That's all taken care of, Mrs Thwaites. Father Urban, here, will be the one."

"That's right," said Father Urban.

Mrs Thwaites, without giving him so much as a look, said, "Nine o'clock sharp."

Well, old people were like that, Father Urban told himself. He did wish, though, that Phil had introduced him to Mrs Thwaites

as a Clementine. That might have meant more to her.
"We'd better be running along," Phil said.

Mrs Thwaites beckoned him over to her then, and asked for
his blessing. She bowed her head slightly for it (but Father Urban could see that she was watching the sets), and, when it was
over, she handed Phil an envelope. "Take care of yourself," she
said.

Father Urban, after opening the door for Phil, smiled at Mrs
Thwaites and cried, "Happy New Year!" But he was too late.

Mrs Thwaites had turned up the sound.

On the way back to St Monica's, Father Urban said, "What's
the wheelchair mean?"

"Old age."

"She can walk then?"

"Yes."

"What's she got against Chumley?"

"The last time I was gone, they didn't get along."

"Oh?"

"No," Phil said, but that was all.

"The girl—Irish, isn't she?" Her "Good evening" had sounded
like it to Father Urban.

"Yes."

"Mrs. Thwaites brought her over?"

"Yes."

"I shouldn't think there'd be much for a girl in a place like
that."

"No."

"But I suppose she's well paid, or thinks she is anyway."

"I suppose."

"The old woman—she likes her television."

"Yes."

Back at St Monica's, in the upper room, while Phil was down
getting ice cubes, Father Urban engaged Monsignor Renton on
the subject of Mrs Thwaites and did better.

"If we had another channel up here, she'd have another set," Monsignor Renton said. "She doesn't want to miss anything. Tonight she'll ring out the old, and ring in the new, in all the time zones. I wonder—do they go on to Honolulu?"

"Not on television. What's she got against Chumley?"

"She worries about the next world, and questions every priest she meets. Johnny Chumley told her, 'You are what you eat' —she was on black molasses at the time—'and will be what you are.' Sound doctrine."

"Yes, but it takes some explaining."

"She was out of the Church for a time, did you know?"

"As a matter of fact, I didn't."

"Oh yes. When she married Andrew she left the Church. That was part of the deal. That was Andrew's great work in life— making apostates. And making money."

"Lumber?"

"While it lasted, and then pumps. Hydraulic pumps. Government contracts. Here and abroad. Foreign capital built the railroads in this part of the country, did you know?"

"I don't know whether I did or not. She came back in when he died?"

"Yes, and she's been making up for lost time ever since. That's where you guys come in. My guess is she wanted to take the curse off the old place. Maybe there was a tax angle, too, a write-off of some kind. That's how her mind works. She hasn't done anything else for you, has she?"

"No." From Wilf, Father Urban had understood that there were surviving heirs, but he preferred to start from scratch with Monsignor Renton. "Any children?"

"A boy and a girl. The boy—hell, he must be almost as old as you are. The boy's been in and out of religious orders for years. As a brother. When he's out, as I believe he is at the moment, he's a professional layman, if you know what I mean."

"And the girl?"

"Sally's out of the Church, but I'd say she's the best of the lot —a bad lot."

"Andrew was the son of the man who did away with his wife. . . ."

"His wife and another, and then himself. The other man—just a lumberjack—was a French Canadian. Catholic. In my opinion, that's what made Andrew such a son-of-a-bitch. Ah, well."

After a moment, Father Urban said, "Still, she is back in the Church."

"I'm told she was a looker in her day. Otherwise, I don't think she's changed much."

"Still, she must have changed some."

"It all goes together. The television sets, the bomb shelter, and the religion."

"Bomb shelter?"

"You saw the elevator?"

Father Urban nodded.

"Takes her down to it."

Father Urban felt that Monsignor Renton was probably right about Mrs Thwaites—up to a point. After that, there was no knowing, and, in any case. . . . "Who are we to judge her?" he said. "What if she is only motivated by old age and fear of the Lord? That's enough, thank God. It takes all kinds to make the Church."

"God is not mocked."

"The woman's a daily communicant. That should count for something."

"God is not mocked."

"No, but. . . ."

No, but and *Yes, but* and *On the other hand* and *Much as I agree with you,* and *Apart from that* and *Far be it from me*— Father Urban, it seemed, was always trying to present the other

side, the balanced view. This kept him busy, for Monsignor
Renton talked like a drunken curate. One moment it was "God is
not mocked" or "Christ, and Christ crucified," and the next moment it was "Your ass is out."

Nevertheless, they were kindred souls, at one on fundamen-
tals, and sharing many preferences and prejudices—until the conversation moved into a certain area. This was a very large area,
easily arrived at, and here they were like the blind men in the
fable who, touching the elephant's body here and there, could
not agree about it. The elephant, in the case of the blind men in
the upper room, was their vocation. Much of the secondary
activity sponsored, and sometimes even participated in, by the
clergy left Father Urban cold, and Monsignor Renton said some
things about the various "movements" within the Church that
badly needed saying. "Yes, but don't throw the baby out with
the bath water," said Father Urban, when he felt the cold current
in Monsignor Renton's thought. Father Urban's good work over
the years, as a preacher and as a person but always as a priest,
would count for little if, as Monsignor Renton said, any time not
spent at the altar, or in administering the sacraments, was just
time wasted for a priest. ("That's why I took up golf.")

Father Urban had encountered others who held this limited
view of the priesthood, but with Monsignor Renton it was a
cause. He carried it into the confessional where, of course, he
had Father Urban at an unfair advantage. "Ah, yes. We're here
today, and gone tomorrow, and while we're here we more or less
run on divine momentum—more, if we happen to be priests.
We'd do well to keep that in mind at all times, and perform those
few sacred offices for which we've been chosen by God, and
forget the rest. Oh, of course, we're entitled to a little harmless
relaxation. And, whatever else we do, let's not put ourselves between God and the people—or let them put us between them
and Him as too often happens nowadays. Ah, yes. Now, for your
penance, pray for the Carmelites. Meditate on the life of those

poor men and women. Let's say a half hour a day for the next week, and you might pray for the Trappists, too, if you get a chance. Now make a good act of contrition, and pray for my intention."

Father Urban had had trouble with confessors in the past. For some reason, men he'd select for their mature outlook, men who'd appear to be well aware of their spiritual and intellectual limitations before and after, wouldn't be able to resist the temptation to show off while they had Father Urban in the confessional. The case of Monsignor Renton was somewhat different. He, too, had changed, but only once. He was now the same in and out of the box. He just wasn't the man Father Urban had asked to be his confessor on the night they'd met—a man chosen not only for his mature outlook but for his availability and status in the diocese. Monsignor Renton had talked less and listened more on that night. He hadn't been the same since.

Father Urban listened in long-suffering silence the next time he went to confession, while the man ground his ax and made points he wouldn't have been able to get away with in the upper room, but when he cited the case of the young pastor— "a fine young fella"—who had driven himself into a mental institution "as a result of overindulgence in spurious activity," and now, during meals, walked around the dining hall saying "hello" to the other patients because life had become a never-ending parish supper to him, Father Urban cut in: "Why are you telling me this?" "Pray for him, Father. That will be your penance this time. Forty years ago, we weren't expected to do so much selling, nagging, and hand-holding. Ah, well. Now make a good act of contrition, and pray for my intention."

Father Urban knew where he was with himself, and Monsignor Renton's effect on him, in or out of the confessional, would be small. For himself, he wasn't worried. But what of the man's effect on Phil? Even before Father Urban discovered what was almost certainly behind Monsignor Renton's opposition to a new church—the old church—Father Urban had regarded the man as a bad influence on Phil, and since then had been trying to counteract that influence. Uphill work. Phil was weak, Monsignor Renton was strong, and Father Urban, though strong, had no desire to come between old friends. Hence his sometimes halting speech, his turning of the other cheek. *"Your ass is out, Father"*—*"And yet, Monsignor. . . ."*

That was how it had gone again, in the upper room, on New Year's Eve, and was still going, much later.

Monsignor Renton, who had an edge on, said: "Frankly, if I had to put up a new church—one of these hatcheries, with silo attached—I think I'd rather cut my throat."

"Fortunately, you don't have to do either," Father Urban said, taking a harder line with the man, and keeping the issue before Phil.

"If I had my way, there'd be a church down in Orchard Park."

"If," said Father Urban.

Phil, sunk in his chair, said, "Has there been any more talk of that, Red?"

All such talk began and ended with Monsignor Renton, Father Urban knew. Phil must have known it, too, but he was hoping. Wasn't it cruel of Monsignor Renton to hold out this hope to Phil?

Monsignor Renton said he wasn't getting anywhere with the other consultors. "They're years behind me in their thinking."

"And drinking," said Father Urban.

"Oh, I don't say the present population warrants it, but give 'em time." Monsignor Renton cited the case of the pastor ("No, *not* in this diocese") who had enlarged his plant, both school

and church, to accommodate a housing development, and then
had been left holding the bag when a new bishop came in and
built right in the development. "I wouldn't like to see that happen
to Phil."

"What *would* you like to see happen to Phil?"

Monsignor Renton, not answering the question, got up and
went to the window facing the street. It was time for one of his
curates to come for him and Phil. It was ninety miles to the
North Coast Limited's nearest stop. "Those two jokers of mine!
Never know where they are! And they want me to pay for the
gas! That's *one* problem you don't have, Phil."

"No," said Father Urban. Phil always knew where Johnny
Chumley was—in church or in bed.

"Should be two kinds of men in every busy parish," Phil said.
"Priest-priests and priest-promoters. Johnny says."

"The boy has a good mind for an ex-athlete," said Monsignor
Renton.

"I take it he wants to be one of the priest-priests?" said Father
Urban.

Phil made no reply, but Father Urban didn't regard his silence
as pointed. Often, in conversation late at night in the upper room,
Phil just conked out. Phil had a big ditch in his personality, and
when he was down in it, as he appeared to be now, he was very
quiet. "I'm neither," he said presently.

"I wouldn't say that," Father Urban said, though he was afraid
Phil was right. "Which one would be the boss? Did he say?"
Father Urban was thinking of the weeks ahead with the curate.

"You'll have to ask him about that," Phil said.

"Has a good mind," said Monsignor Renton.

"He may have a good mind, but I'm not so sure he's right about
this," Father Urban said, addressing himself to Phil. "When
you consider what's at stake"—not only the spiritual welfare of

Phil's people but Phil's own soul was at stake—"I'd say a man *has* to be both. At least a man can try. Sometimes that's the most a man can do." Father Urban paused to give Phil a chance to think it over, and Phil really did appear to be doing this. Phil had drunk more than usual that night, hoping, he said, to rest better on the train, and this may have been a factor in Father Urban's favor. "Phil, a man *can* be both."

"Like Jekyll and Hyde," said Monsignor Renton.

"*Otherwise*, we wouldn't be placed in the position we are, placed under the necessity *to be both*." For a moment there, before, Father Urban had been getting through to Phil, but now Phil was gone—he was down in his ditch. And who had put him there? His best friend, and worst enemy—who now, commenting as he had before on Orchard Park, whose windows, yards, and rooftops were all lit up for Christmas, said: "The fires of hell, and in the summertime, with those barbecue pits going, it smells like Afghanistan. Used to be a great place for ducks, didn't it, Phil? Right on the flyway. Oh well."

"Red, you might as well know it now," Phil said. "I'm building."

Monsignor Renton wheeled around. "*Holy* Paul!"

"Congratulations, Phil," said Father Urban. "Wonderful."

For the moment, Monsignor Renton was silent, again gazing out the window.

But he would have Phil to himself for the next month, and doubtless would do his damnedest to get him to change his mind. Phil had to be shored up against him, strengthened in his great decision, committed to it irrevocably, if possible. "Have you told the Bishop, Phil?" said Father Urban.

"Not exactly. I want to know where I am before I see him."

"Good idea, Phil."

"Maybe take the census first."

"*Very* good idea, Phil. How would it be if we did that while you're gone? Save time."

"I wouldn't wish that on you, Father. It can wait."

"If you want my advice, Phil, don't rush into this thing," said Monsignor Renton, coming away from the window.

For the next few minutes, he did everything he could to disrupt the conversation and to draw attention to himself. He brought up entirely unrelated matters. He predicted strikes and shortages. He stood between them so they couldn't see each other. He ran around in circles looking for his collar (when a car horn tooted below). He followed too closely on the stairs. He fell down on the sidewalk.

And through it all, Father Urban persevered, making the most of his last minutes with Phil. Jogging alongside the moving car, he yelled, "At least we can *start* on the census!" and peered inside to catch Phil's reaction to this, but could not, for Monsignor Renton scooted forward on the back seat and called on the driver for more speed. Father Urban had to let go of the door handle then.

He saw Phil's hand flutter up in the rear window of the big black car, and fall, and though he knew he would not be seen or heard by Phil, he waved and yelled, "'Bye!" Phil must have heard him, though, for the hand fluttered up again. Father Urban's last impression was of a man being taken for a ride. To Father Urban, Phil's hand had cried, "*Help!*"

8

Second Only to Standard Oil

Father Urban had given Mrs Burns a cookbook for Christmas inscribed, "To the last one in the world who needs it, Mrs Burns, from one who knows, yours in Christ, Father Urban." Since then relations between them had become ecstatic on Mrs Burns's side. Relations had been splendid before, though, for Father Urban had a way with housekeepers, and Mrs Burns obviously liked the idea of having a priest around the rectory. "Thank God!" she'd cry when Father Urban arrived for the weekend. "Another mouth to feed, Mrs Burns." "Father, I don't mind *that*." What Mrs Burns, a white-haired, well-made widow, did mind was the telephone.

With Phil out of the picture, Father Urban was able to act. "How about it, Father?" he said to Father Chumley. One man would take all A.M. calls, the other man all P.M. calls, and thus life would be made easier for Mrs Burns, said Father Urban. What he did not say was that Father Chumley, if the plan were adopted, would have to cut down on his time in church and give the diocese more of a return on its investment. "O.K.," said Father Chumley, accepting the new plan, and gracefully at that. Perhaps the curate didn't need a fire-eating pastor to shove him around. Perhaps he only needed a push, a gentle push, from the right sort of older man.

However, on the first night the new plan was in effect, Father Urban, who had the P.M. hours, took a call at three in the morning. Making no attempt to rouse the curate, he went out and anointed a parishioner. He would've said nothing about it. Mrs Burns heard him go out, though, and spoke to Father Chumley in the morning.

"I guess I forgot to turn on my phone," the curate confessed at breakfast.

Father Urban, who had moved into Phil's quarters to be near a phone, said, "I guess I forgot to turn mine off."

Father Chumley looked sad.

"Forget it," said Father Urban. He hadn't intended to suggest that this, perhaps, was the difference between them. "I was happy to go out. I really was. It made me feel like a priest—for a change."

"Why, Father!" cried Mrs Burns. "What a thing to say!"

Father Chumley had smiled, though, at Father Urban's little tribute to the infantry.

"It's the truth, Mrs Burns." Father Urban told them about the old Clementine priest, too long a seminary professor, who had witnessed a street accident and cried out, "For God's sake—call a priest!"

Father Chumley smiled again, and Mrs Burns laughed.

"Anyway, I'm glad to be here—on the firing line."

"And we're glad you're here," said Father Chumley.

"Indeed we are," cried Mrs Burns.

Overnight, it seemed, and without seeking it, Father Urban had gained the ascendancy in the house. There was a better feeling between the priests, although Father Urban felt that he was still regarded as something of a showboat by the curate. Mrs Burns, however, had no reservations about Father Urban. If he

in any way fell short of the ideal (and of course he did), Mrs
Burns didn't know it. His word was law, but she still ran for the
telephone.

"No! No! Mustn't touch!"

Or Johnny, as Father Urban now called the curate, would be
the one to head her off.

And then they'd all have a good laugh.

Suddenly St Monica's was a busy, happy rectory.

Father Urban had been in and out of a thousand rectories, always taking an oar when necessary, always glad to help out (up
to a point), but at St Monica's it was different. His hand was
on the tiller there. He located a map of the parish. He brought
it up to date by incorporating Orchard Park. He began the
census. The shaded area on the map, the area covered by him in
the morning and Johnny in the afternoon, grew, and at night
they got together in the upper room to talk over the day's findings.

They were asking the usual questions. Number of children
in the family, whether baptized, attending what school, religion
of both father and mother, whether all of age had made their
Easter duty, whether all regularly employed had received each
his own box of Sunday envelopes, and so on. Phil, it soon appeared, had really fallen down on the job of distributing Sunday
envelopes, and so the census-takers carried a supply along with
them, one man using his attaché case for this purpose, and the
other his Northwest Airlines bag.

They were also trying to find out how people felt about a
new church at St Monica's. This, too, was Father Urban's idea.
Since Phil had said that his decision to build needn't be kept a
secret, Father Urban didn't see why the people of the parish
shouldn't be let in on it, but he presented it only as a possibility,
for he wanted to learn their true feelings. So that the response

could be easily tabulated, people were given a choice of four
answers: Strongly Favor, Favor, Don't Favor, and No Opinion.
The first thing the survey revealed was that too many people
would vote No Opinion if left entirely to themselves, and so
Johnny was urged to strive for greater accuracy, a closer fit.
Father Urban pointed out that several No Opinions encountered by him hadn't understood the purpose of the survey. It
had to be made crystal clear to some people that their response
if favorable, or even strongly favorable, was in no sense a com-
mitment to contribute. Not a-tall. Once this was made crystal
clear, Don't Favors sometimes became Favors or even Strongly
Favors. This was Father Urban's experience anyway.

The early returns showed the Strongly Favors and Favors well
in the lead. As for die-hard Don't Favors, they were generally
elderly people who attended the uncrowded early Mass on Sunday and said things like, "Wouldn't a new church cost too much?"
and "I just like the old one." Fortunately, there weren't too many
of this sort.

Father Urban wanted Phil to put out of mind all thoughts—
thoughts he'd expressed on the night he left—of bringing in a
professional fund-raising outfit. The professional bleeders, able
as they were, saw life everywhere in terms of Chicago and
Boston, and if Phil hired one, his parishioners would soon be
getting cute little notes asking how much they'd donated to
the horses in the past year. They wouldn't even understand
the question. If Phil conducted his own drive, he could tailor
his approach to local conditions, and there would be less wear
and tear on the parishioners. He'd save a lot, too. It would be
harder on Phil, yes, but it could be the making of him as a
pastor. It was Father Urban's hope that the survey would help
Phil to do the right thing when the time came, and to this end,
the early results were encouraging.

Father Urban and Johnny were alarmed, though, by some of

their other findings. Both men were out of touch with hearth and home, the one because of his years of itinerancy and more or less public life, the other because of his years in the seminary and his reclusive habits since then, and so they really couldn't say whether the squalor in which so many parishioners lived, particularly in Orchard Park, was peculiar to them or was now nationwide, peculiar to the times. It wasn't squalor such as Father Urban had seen in city slums. No, if anything, the Orchard Parkers possessed more than their share of the world's goods. Whether the women were unable to keep house, or were unwilling, or both, wasn't clear to Father Urban, but *that* they didn't was a fact too often encountered to be ignored—and not to be passed off with a laughing reference to little ones. What embarrassment there was lacked conviction. The shoes and socks and pajamas and dirty glasses and cups that had a way of disappearing from the living room during the course of his visit— they'd all be back again, he knew. Who was to blame? When, in recent years, Father Urban had read that the American male had gone soft, he'd always considered the source—another green-eyed European, another G.I. who'd married an Asiatic—but Orchard Park suggested that there might be some truth in the charge.

It wasn't rare for women to return to bed after breakfast, if, indeed, they got up for it. They had no more time sense than Mexicans. "Just say the priest was here," Father Urban would tell the little barefooted creatures who opened the door to him. (In the afternoon, the same thing happened to Johnny. Mama would be taking her nap then.) Sometimes, later in the morning, Father Urban would come upon a gathering of homemakers consuming coffee and pastry. But these easygoing and, for the most part, betrousered queens never guessed what he thought of them, so courtly was his manner. "Ladies, the pleasure was all mine."

A dog nipped him, a hamster wet on him, a piece of fruit-cake played hell with one of his gold inlays, and always he had to watch where he sat down, especially in Orchard Park. It was easy enough to see why Phil, in delicate health, with his rather dismal outlook on life, had excused himself from such activity. Even so, the worst thing about the census was not the taking of it, though at St Monica's this was aggravated by years of neglect, and by the weather in January and February. The worst thing was the follow-up work. This was why otherwise perfect pastors put off the census. Wouldn't enough sad cases come to their attention without going out and looking for them? This might become Father Urban's view if he stayed on the firing line long enough, but this was not his view. A job was being done that badly needed doing at St Monica's, a tough job. There were days when the temperature never rose above twenty below zero, when thigh-freezing winds raked down from Canada, when the census-takers were tempted to turn back to the rectory. But they didn't.

"We won't be crucified," said Johnny, who tended to think too much in such terms. "We'll just wear ourselves out, like bees."

"That's right."

Father Urban was pleased with the change in Johnny. In defense of the curate's past—St Monica's was his first assignment —it could be said that he'd been following his pastor's example, by shirking his obligations, and that of a great many saints, by haunting the church. Father Urban, however, by the power of his example, and, of course, by God's grace, had caused Johnny to question not the lives of the saints but his own life as a parish priest. If Johnny didn't say that Father Urban had done this, Johnny's actions did. Johnny only said he'd been suffering greatly from aridity in his spiritual life—"For months now, I've been lost in the desert, the Sahara, I think"—and perhaps the change in him would have come about anyway, in time. Johnny, a big, strong young fellow whose father owned a creamery, had good stuff in him. It just hadn't been coming out.

Casual conversation in the upper 'room told Father Urban more perhaps than Johnny meant to tell him, more perhaps than Johnny knew. It became pretty clear to Father Urban that Johnny, in his last two years in seminary, had fallen into the clutches of Manichees on the faculty. Unlike them, he had been bold. In fact, he had got so far out of line in his final year— giving up smoking and so on—that he'd come within an ace of not being ordained. For about three years, you might say, Johnny had been in a coma. Johnny had been all right before. In high school, he had been voted all-state in hockey.

Father Urban had learned this from Dave, the crippled janitor, who said that Johnny's bodychecking had been something to see and hear, and that Johnny's slapshot, not easy to demonstrate with a pushbroom, had been absolutely professional—that good. It was Dave's opinion that Johnny might have made the grade as a pro if he'd put his mind to it, and Dave's regret that he hadn't.

"How about it?" inquired Father Urban. Johnny, somewhat surprised by Father Urban's interest in hockey, said it wasn't only his ability to mix it up but his lack of foot that had caused his coach, a Canadian, to use him as a defenseman. "I never could've made it in the big time."

This checked perfectly with Father Urban's estimate of Johnny's character. Hockey was one sport Father Urban hadn't played in his youth—there just wasn't the ice for it in Illinois —but he'd often thought, as he watched NHL games, that, had he played hockey, he would have been used at wing or center. That was the difference between Johnny and him. No, Johnny was no Father Urban, and never would be, but he was doing better now than he'd ever done before as a priest. Father Urban, both amused and gratified to hear himself being imitated on the telephone, couldn't have asked for a better assistant. If Phil wanted to know what had happened to the boy in his absence, Father Urban would tell him the truth, in which there might be something for Phil himself: "Hell, I don't know, Phil. Maybe he decided to join the human race."

Father Urban was familiar with the classic view of the parish as a natural unit of society, second in importance only to the family, but he had seldom found this view held by clergy and laity in the same parish. If the pastor tried to get his people to think of themselves not as Jaycees or trade unionists, not as Republicans or Democrats, but primarily as parishioners, the chances were they'd resist him, and Father Urban didn't really blame them. Such a thesis made small appeal to anybody who'd arrived at a greater, or clearer, station in life than that commonly designated by the term parishioner—and who hadn't? If, on the other hand, the people tried to raise the status of parishioners, the chances were their pastor would resist *them*—and wisely—for wherever you found people trying to make a lot of their parishionership, you'd find agitators at work. Invariably they were the products of higher Catholic education, or converts, whose real object was to assume unto themselves all but the strictly sacerdotal activity and to see that *this* was in accord with their understanding of it and the latest word from Rome. They'd had a field day under Pius XII.

Who now looked to the parish in the old way? A few foreign-language groups in cities and on the land—a few people cut off from society. Oh yes, Father Urban kept hearing about ideal parishes (for some reason, he'd never been asked to work one) where the entire congregation chanted from missals and where everything was "liturgical" down to the blessing of foodstuff and the churching of women. Much time and trouble went into training ordinary people to *perform* in church. The more Father Urban heard of these ideal parishes, the more they smacked of Oberammergau to him. Somewhere in between, between *that* and what St Monica's had been like when Phil was there, would be found the ideal parish, Father Urban believed. The most successful parishes were those where more was going on than met the eye, where, behind the scenes, a gifted pastor or assistant pulled the strings. God, it seemed, ran those parishes, which was as it should be. Wherever parishionership became a full-time occupation, whether it consisted in liturgical practices or selling chances on a new car, the wrong people took over. At St Monica's, though, parishioners had been left *too* much to themselves.

Father Urban wanted to set up a serious program—talks by himself and others (if others worth hearing could be found), classes in the papal encyclicals, the Great Catholic Books, and so on—but there just wasn't the time for it, and perhaps more than time would've been lacking at St Monica's for such a program.

So Father Urban played it safe and engaged the people on their own ground. He gave card parties for "seniors." He put on barn or square dancing (as they preferred to call it) for "young marrieds." He tried a rock-and-roll dance for "teens" —once. No trouble, no, but he found he didn't care for it when he saw what it was like. Sleigh rides and skating parties, these presided over by Johnny, were better. For the children of the parish, and their mothers, there were all-cartoon programs in the best movie house in town. For Men's Club, he sent away for films of Notre Dame football games, and these were studied at smoker sessions. For Altar and Rosary Society, nothing special, but there was always the possibility that he'd pop in and say a few words. The school nuns were not forgotten. He gave them the use of his (Phil's) car, permission to shop at supermarkets, and occasionally he threw the boss a ten-dollar bill—"Buy yourself some cigars, Sister." They all loved him. And he addressed the Home and School Association, the local equivalent of the P.T.A., something Phil had never thought, or cared, to do, and a number of fathers and mothers told him that he'd given them new hope.

Father Urban's object in all this was simply to pump a little life into the parish, without being pretentious about it. He discouraged the notion that church-sponsored recreation is necessarily a means to sanctification—an error into which gambling parishes were forever falling. He said he hoped to see more people at the communion rail oftener, but he also said that nobody should feel that this was expected because of his or her perfect attendance at social affairs. He had to watch it, though, in and out of the parish. The Cathedral curates (Monsignor Renton called them Cox and Box) wangled an invitation to the Saturday-morning theatre parties for the children of their parish, and *then* urged that short subjects of a religious nature be dropped into the all-cartoon programs. Father Urban rejected the proposal, saying it wouldn't be fair to the kids *or* to the exhibitor, a Jew, who was already taking a loss on the deal.

Just as parish life quickened under Father Urban's touch, so did life in the town. At noontime luncheons, at wedding breakfasts, at funeral parlors, wherever and whenever people gathered, in joy or sorrow, there was Father Urban. At least he'd put in an appearance. "Look at that clock!" Off he'd go, and be late at the next stop. "And the worst of it is, I can't stay!" "*OHHHH!*" So he'd relent and say a few words. And then off to the hospital, to the county jail, or back to the rectory for a little talk with an erring soul, who might or might not show up. Yes, there were disappointments, a few anyway, for Father Urban was working with people, after all. Very few disappointments, actually.

Yes, he received an anonymous letter with the curt message, "Drop Dead," and, yes, a woman was offended when he laughed at the idea of serving coffee—*cappuccino*, she said—after the last Mass on Sunday, and, yes, alas, he heard that Cox and Box, doubtless smarting from their setback at his hands, were referring to the current regime at St Monica's as one of bread and circuses.

"Wait'll Lent starts," he said one evening to parishioners thronging about him after a card party. "All this'll have to stop."

"Will you still be here, Father?"

"No, I'm afraid not, Charlie."

"*OHHHH!*"

"That'll be the hardest part about Lent for a lot of us," said a woman—*and that woman was Sylvia Bean.*

In the past weeks, Father Urban had occasionally caught sight of Sylvia in the congregation at Mass on Sundays and at card parties, but he had stayed away from her, thinking he was avoiding trouble. In his first week at St Monica's he'd called at her house in the course of census-taking, and she'd begged him to book the Shrapnel Brothers, the editor and the publisher of the *Drover*, into the parish. (They put on Lincoln-Douglas style debates, one brother getting to take the "conservative" position and the other having to take the "liberal" position, this determined by the toss of a coin, and the audience was left to judge the winner.) Sylvia Bean had offered to underwrite the cost of bringing the act to the parish. No, thanks, Father Urban had said after first asking what the Shrapnels charged for a performance, which in a professional way interested him, but Sylvia had persisted, and finally he'd said, "Over my dead body, Mrs Bean." After that, she'd made him feel as she had when he dined with her and Ray in the Greenwich Village Room—that she was finished with him. Evidently he'd been wrong. *That'll be the hardest part about Lent for a lot of us.* This, considering the source, was perhaps the strongest testimonial to the kind of job Father Urban was doing at St Monica's.

Actually, everything would stop before Lent, for Father Urban was to top off his stay by preaching a mission. This, however, was moved back a week, after Monsignor Renton called from Florida to say that he and Phil were thinking of returning to Minnesota by the way of the Bahamas.

"You're not waiting for warm weather, I hope," said Father Urban.

"Has it been cold up there?" inquired Monsignor Renton—as if he hadn't been reading the papers and subtracting eight or ten degrees from the Minneapolis readings to arrive at the temperatures in Great Plains.

"How's Phil, Monsignor?"

"About the same."

This could mean that Phil hadn't yet been talked out of building a new church. "Is Phil there now? I'd like to say hello to him, if he is."

"No, as a matter of fact, he isn't."

Phil could be in the next room, though, within easy hailing distance. This seemed more than just a possibility to Father Urban. "Did you call Father Udovic about this, Monsignor?" he asked, knowing that it irked Monsignor Renton to have to call Father Udovic about anything, and that he preferred not to hear the man's name.

"I called the Chancery."

"And Cox and Box?"

"It won't hurt if they think I'm coming back earlier."

"Well, O.K. then, as far as I'm concerned. But if I hear from

Father Wilfrid to the contrary, I'll call you back—collect. By
the way, where are you staying now?"

"We're checking out now. So long."

Father Urban phoned the Hill. "I'll be back in time for Lent,
of course," he told Wilf, who, however, seemed totally unin-
terested in the subject of his return. "Anything new?"

The brochure had gone to the Novitiate, Wilf said, but not to
the printer. "Maybe it's just as well. Maybe we should shoot
for Holy Week, or late spring—or early summer. Lucky we
don't have retreatants here now."

"The cold, you mean?"

"Weatherwise, it's much like last year."

"Yes, isn't it?" said Father Urban, though what the weather
had been like there—or anywhere—he didn't know. "But otherwise?"

"Trouble in Parlor A. That north wall. We can't get a bond."

"A *bond?*"

"Paint won't dry. Wall's too cold, and you put heat in that
room, and the wall sweats. It's the roof. It's coming down
through the wall."

"The *roof?*"

"Moisture. Melt and freeze. Melt and freeze. That's
where your roof goes."

"Suppose it does, yes. Well. . . ."

"Suppose it's nice and warm where you are."

"It gets pretty chilly here sometimes," said Father Urban.
This, though untrue, seemed the decent thing to say.

"You're on a hill, don't forget. You're getting the same wind
we are."

"I didn't think of that." Father Urban, not wishing it to be
thought that he'd forgotten them, inquired after the less fortunate ones at home, asked that they be given his best, and then
he said good-by to Wilf.

Later that week Father Urban arranged for Johnny to drive Jack over for the opening night of the mission (not to preach, of course). It was nice for Jack, just being there, away from Wilf and the Hill for a few hours, and he made a third for benediction. Nobody preached on opening night, Johnny announcing that Father Urban begged the people to pray for the success of the mission, since their prayers were much more powerful than any words of his, after which came the rosary led by Jack, who had trouble with the mike, and then benediction by Father Urban wearing a cope by Blaise of Bruges. Attendance was excellent. Even though Father Urban hadn't been heard on the first night, attendance was better on the second. Thereafter, and this was the mark of a mission preached by Father Urban, it got better and better. On Friday night, closing night, there was standing room only in the church. This on a night when the stores stayed open until nine! Jack was on hand again, and somebody in Men's Club had considered it advisable to bring in a tape recorder. The last night of the most successful mission anybody could remember began with the rosary (Johnny), was followed by benediction (Jack), and closed with Father Urban preaching his heart out.

"Each soul, then, a little world of its own, with its peaks and valleys, its prairies, rivers and lakes, and sometimes, yes, alas, its dismal swamps, its lightless deeps. Special, unique, known only to God, for better or worse. Only God knows the true nature of the spiritual universe that is this parish, of the little world that is your soul. God alone, the Great Cartographer, could draw it down to the tiniest detail. And if He did, and perhaps He does, what would we see, you and I? A world where God would care to dwell? Or a world too hot, too cold, too wet, too dry? Next to God, we are the best judges of that, you and I. Yes, for you cannot know my soul, and I, though skilled in this and skilled in nothing else, can only guess at

yours. But as a priest, as one of God's poor surveyors, I beg
you keep your rivers and lakes unpolluted. If swamps there
be, drain them, for God's sake and yours, and do not wait.
Where swamps were before, let there be gardens and orchards.
Gardens and orchards and parks! How does your garden grow?
With the silverbells and cockleshells of faith, hope, and charity?
Rid your gardens of the ragweed of covetousness, the dande-
lions of pride, the crabgrass of indifference! And clear your
orchards of the rusty tin cans and broken glass of avarice, the
old rubber tires of self-indulgence! If necessary, plow up your
gardens and orchards! Plant your gardens and orchards with the
good seed and the green saplings of pious works, attendance at
Holy Mass, regular confession, frequent reception of the Sacrament of Sacraments! Do these things, and leave the rest to God!
Do these things, and the warm sun of God's merciful love will
shine upon you and yours! Do these things, and the gentle rain
of God's loving mercy will fall upon you and yours! Now and
for all time! *Now! Forever! If!*"

Forty-five minutes earlier, Father Urban had begun with those
three little words, treating them, he said, as an etymologist
might—"Now don't let *that* scare you, it only means word-
smith"—and, having made no great demands on the three little
words then, he'd left them, had entirely forgotten them, so it
must have seemed to the congregation, but he hadn't. In the
end, he'd come back to them, and those three little words, two
shouted and one whispered, had gone off like fireworks, like
two bombs and a pinwheel. And thus another mission had ended
—almost.

Still in the pulpit, Father Urban, eloquent in silence, stared
out over the heads of the congregation and saw what nobody
else in the old church could see so well, the clock on the choir
loft, which said eight-forty. Making the sign of the cross, which
rippled through the congregation, he turned and, for a moment,

was invisible to the people. When he next appeared to them, he was down on their level, leaving the pulpit, walking, kneeling before them—for this purpose a *prie-dieu* had been placed in a central position in the sanctuary. After an interval noticeably longer than on previous nights, he rose, genuflected before the main altar, and, head down, made his way slowly to the sacristy. Then, when he was again invisible to them, and only then, did the people begin to stir in the pews.

The mission had ended. Many, however, had risen not to leave but to kneel and pray, Father Urban knew, and were now impeding the progress of others trying to leave and putting them in a bad light for trying to do so. This was the one thing about his missions (and there was always much more of it on closing nights) that troubled him. Why should the very first fruits of his week's sowing be confusion, self-righteousness, and animosity in the pews?

Katie had called during dinner to say that Mrs Thwaites wished to see him as soon as possible, and so, when he'd got out of his surplice and cassock, and Jack had got out of his, they drove out to Lake Lucille. When they arrived at the house, Father Urban suggested that Jack remain in the car. "I don't know what's on her mind, and you'll be warmer here with the heater on. You can listen to the radio while I'm gone."

In Mrs Thwaites's room, the TV sets were off, the lights were on, and Dickie, Mrs Thwaites's son, was present. Father Urban sensed that Dickie, whom he'd met on another occasion, was to be the subject of the conversation—and hoped he wasn't thinking of going into the Clementines. Dickie, who had been in and out of too many orders already, according to Monsignor Renton, was now running a book and church-goods store over in Ostergothenburg, an establishment called the Eight Seasons. When Father Urban had asked why it was called that, Dickie

had replied, "Why, because of the eight seasons, of course."
"*What* eight seasons?" "Why, the eight seasons of the church
year, of course." Father Urban hadn't cared for that, not a-tall,
but even without that, he wouldn't have cared for Dickie. The
boy, as his mother fondly referred to him, was forty-six, fat in
the middle and soft all over, with a bottlenose (from his father,
to judge by photographs in Mrs Thwaites's room), and lots of
hair (this from his mother) swept up in a grey mane that might
have looked all right on the conductor of a symphony orchestra.
No, Father Urban just couldn't see Dickie Thwaites, with his
record and his hair, even as a Clementine brother, and so he was
alarmed when he heard Mrs Thwaites say:

"The boy's giving up the store."

"I'm not so sure," said Dickie.

"It's well to be sure," Father Urban said, in case they were
talking about Dickie's vocation. "Were you, perhaps, thinking
of something else?"

Dickie, who was sitting on a big footstool, with his hands all
but lost in his hair, said, "This is the century of the cad."

Father Urban thought this over for a moment, and then, to
Mrs Thwaites, he said: "I take it this is why you've asked
me here."

"Yes, I thought you might be able to tell the boy what to do."

Father Urban glanced at Dickie.

Dickie looked up from the floor at which he'd been staring.
"Of course, I'd be interested in anything you might have to say,
Father."

Father Urban sat back in his chair, a club chair with an odd
cushion, and was suddenly like a man sitting in a floating inner
tube. "Then suppose," he said, sitting forward, "we begin at
the beginning. Why Ostergothenburg?"

Dickie said that he'd chosen Ostergothenburg, a highly
Catholic community (as Great Plains wasn't), to be near his

mother—it was only an hour's drive home in his little Porsche —and to be near St Ludwig's and St Hedwig's. Among the Dolomites who ran these colleges, one for boys, one for girls, both among the fathers and the sisters, Dickie had friends. He had opened the Eight Seasons in the summer, and had done well enough until late in the fall. Then "Dullinger's young toughs" —Father Urban gathered that Dickie was referring to Bishop Dullinger's young clergy—began to visit the Eight Seasons. They came not to buy and not even to browse. They stood around in their great stormcoats, dropping cigarette *and* cigar butts on the floor and saying whatever came to *their* minds, if you please. They laughed at the stock of sacred art, jeered at the work of such men as Franklinstein, Varian, and Foo. There had been incidents. Yes, Dickie's friends and supporters among the Dolomite fathers and sisters had—at least the sisters had— clashed with Dullinger's young toughs in the Eight Seasons. Unfortunately, it was now off-limits for Dolomites of both sexes, and college students seemed to be avoiding it, too. Here was the heavy hand of Bishop Dullinger. Dickie had been stuck with forty per cent of his imported, and therefore unreturnable, Christmas cards. And now the brute (Bishop Dullinger) was refusing to consecrate a chalice purchased at the Eight Seasons, a chalice executed in the manner of Henry Moore. Back before Christmas, a group of laymen, obviously fronting for the diocese, had made Dickie an offer for the Eight Seasons. He'd rejected it out of hand. Then he'd heard a rumor that the diocese was going to open up a store of its own. And now— that very morning—another offer had come from the first group. This time Dickie had listened, but only because he wanted to discuss the matter with his mother and with his friends among the Dolomites. He had been calling St Ludwig's and St Hedwig's all day, but hadn't been able to reach any of his friends, and well. . . .

"Sell," said Father Urban.

"That's what I say," said Mrs Thwaites. "You can't afford not to."

"I want to stay on and fight," Dickie said to the floor.

"No good—not in your business," Father Urban said. "You're already finding that out. Did they make you a fair offer?"

"For the location and good will, yes, but nothing for my stock. Oh, they did say they'd take the rosaries and the worst of the books at cost."

"Unload the rest wherever you can," Father Urban said. "If the stuff's as good as you say—and I don't say it isn't—that shouldn't be so hard. I really don't know too much about it. The only name that meant anything to me was Thomas More. That shows you how much I know about it."

"Yes, doesn't it?" said Dickie, in that nasty way he had.

After observing a moment of silence, Father Urban said, "Well, I'm afraid I have to run along." He'd had enough of Dickie, and Mrs Thwaites looked as though she wanted her sets on.

"Thank you for coming, Father," she said. "And many thanks for the advice."

"I know it wasn't what he wanted to hear," Father Urban said, though he thought perhaps it was, "but I don't think it ever pays to buck a bishop in his see."

"He can't afford it. Now get up," Mrs Thwaites said to Dickie, "and see Father Urban out."

Dickie removed his hands from his hair, rose from the footstool, and walked. At the door he passed out ahead of Father Urban. The boy seemed deep in thought. He said nothing until they reached the bottom of the stairs. "I'm bringing out a series of paperback books. Spiritual classics, *you* might call 'em," he said, as if *he* wouldn't.

"That sounds very worth-while. You'll publish them your-self?"

"No, I'll just edit them."

Father Urban opened the door, as he had upstairs, and again Dickie passed ahead of him. They went down the steps together, and out to the car, Dickie talking. "There'll be problems, of course, in editing. It won't be easy. Denzinger's *Enchiridion*, 'the lost books' of Tertullian—making such works attractive to a sizable audience, perhaps to a large audience, perhaps to a very large audience. Nobody knows what can be done with such works in cheap editions. It's an experiment that's never been tried."

"Well, I must say it sounds very worth-while," said Father Urban, opening the car door and taking care that Dickie didn't get in. Father Urban turned off the radio and introduced Dickie, since he was still there, to Jack, and Jack to Dickie—as an author, saying, and hoping memory served him right, "Father's doing the life of St Adalbert."

"The apostle to the Slavs?"

"The Bohemian," Jack said.

"Oh, the apostle to Pomerania. A good sort of man, for a bishop—too good, by all accounts."

"But I haven't begun it yet."

"Let me know how it goes."

Father Urban drove Jack to the Hill—"No, I won't come in, thanks"—and then drove himself back to Great Plains, slowly, enjoying the landscape in the moonlight. The hills, under snow, the trees casting shadows, had an enchanted look, the look of night in the north in the movies, and the sky was all broken out with stars. Once, at a bend in the road, the headlights slipped up on some white rabbits playing in a field. Father Urban hadn't realized that rabbits had such fun. The world was

really a beautiful place. He rolled along enjoying it all, oblivious
of himself, until he entered the city limits of Great Plains.
He was sorry that he'd have only two or three more days with
the car, which he'd come to depend on, and he was going to miss
the deep satisfaction there was in doing the work of a parish
priest—his daily Mass meant even more to him at St Monica's.
He had done well there in the last five weeks. Could he have
done better? He did not think so. His record would speak for
itself.

    • Mrs Burns, freed from the telephone, given a new lease
on life.

    • Johnny Chumley rehabilitated.

    • People polled on new church—and pollinated.

    • Parish life now a reality.

    • Attendance at daily Mass up 150 per cent (eight–ten
people now made it).

    • Mission—most successful in history of parish.

    • All-around good work for the Order.

    • Mrs Thwaites.

Here, until that evening, there hadn't been much to cheer
about. At the end of each week, Father Urban received an envelope with a fifty-dollar bill in it, but this, though more than it
might have been—it might easily have been nothing—was probably no more than Phil had been getting. Father Urban had
heard Mrs Thwaites's confession once, and had talked over her
chances in the next world, giving her all the reassurance he
could—which wasn't quite enough, he'd felt. Mrs Thwaites was
pretty much as Monsignor Renton had described her, in that
respect. But it now appeared that Father Urban, without knowing it, had scored somewhere along the line. Otherwise why
would Mrs. Thwaites have tried him out in the role of adviser?
And since this was a role he might be asked to play again,
having played it well once, it probably had to be rated as the

greatest of his achievements while at St Monica's. Much good *could* come from it, for the Order.

It was almost ten when Father Urban arrived back at the rectory, but a young man was waiting for him. The young man was wearing a short coat made of the same material as Wilf's long devil's-food one, but green, and he needed a shave. He said he wasn't a Catholic but was married to "one." He said his children were being brought up as Catholics. He said, "What more do you want?"

It was Father Urban's practice, in census-taking, to express regret when he discovered that children were not attending the parish school—not too much regret, though, since the parish school was overcrowded—and it was this, presumably, this regret expressed by Father Urban, and communicated to the young man by his wife, that had brought him to the rectory. "May I ask your religion, sir?" said Father Urban.

"Don't have any," said the young man.

"I see. Well, we don't want to make one of *that*, do we?"

"How'd you like a bust in the nose?"

At that point, Johnny Chumley entered the office and went over to the file, opened a drawer, and stood looking into it.

After a moment, during which nothing happened, the young man got up and walked out.

"Thanks, Johnny," said Father Urban. "I didn't realize he'd been drinking."

Johnny shut the drawer of the file. "Monsignor Renton called a while ago."

"Oh no!" said Father Urban, thinking Monsignor Renton was asking for still more time to wear Phil down.

"No," Johnny said. "No. The Pastor's dead."

9

Dear Billy:

Long live the Pastor?

Although the Great Plains diocese was hard up for men, no order, and certainly not the Clementines, could expect to walk into an established, going concern like St Monica's. Those good men and true who'd coveted the parish while Phil was alive were still there, and doubtless more had joined them now that he was dead. Nevertheless, Father Urban did ask himself whether there might not be a chance, just an outside chance, for the Order. Always, after asking, he had to reply in the negative, and yet he went right on asking. How could he?

To begin with, he was chosen to say a few words at Phil's funeral. Whether this was the wish of the Bishop (or only the wish of Father Udovic, who did the actual asking), Father Urban didn't know. In any case, it was not an easy assignment. Phil hadn't been popular with laity or clergy. He represented a type of gentleman-priest no longer being produced in seminaries—now thoroughly Americanized and turning out policemen, disc jockeys, and an occasional desert father. And the circumstances of Phil's death (heart attack while golfing in the Bahamas) weren't favorable, for it was a very cold day in Minnesota. The Bishop had liked Phil, however, and that was

about all Father Urban had going for him when he began to
speak. "Most Reverend Bishop, Right Reverend and Very Reverend Monsignors, Reverend Fathers, Venerable Sisters, and Be-
loved Members of the Laity." Although Father Urban knew
that the deepest sympathies of the most important part of his
audience could be readily engaged, he spoke more of death itself than of the death of a priest. But he did say it was not too
much to say that Father Phil Smith, seeking to respond to
every call, had given his life for his people, that he had exercised the common touch without ever becoming common, and
that his greatest earthly desire had been to erect a new church
at St Monica's—for God's sake and the people's. "That *I* can
assure you," said Father Urban.

Only that morning, he said, he'd received a post card from
Father Smith (written before he died), a post card ("Thanks
again. Taking boat and pressed for time. All for now. Phil.")
from which he recalled only the words "All for now." He
dwelt upon the meaning in those three little words, though not
as an etymologist might, saying that only saints and children
could really comprehend them, for only great saints and little
children lived each moment for all it was worth. Those three
little words, rightly understood, were all we needed to know.
Rightly understood, they would—like St Augustine's famous
"Love God, and do what you will"—carry us safely through this
world and into the next.

Father Urban then spoke of God as the Good Thief of Time,
accosting us wherever we go, along the highways and byways
of life. So, in light and darkness, as children, as young people,
as old, we meet Him. And bit by bit we are deprived of our
most precious possessions, so we think, our childhood, our
youth, all our days—which, though, lest we forget, we have
from Him. We try to hold back what we can, have a secret
pocket here, a slit in the lining there, where He won't look,

we think, but in the end we give up everything, every last conceit. "That's all, Lord," we say. "No," saith the Lord. "What else, Lord?" "You," saith the Lord. "Now I want you." Thank God He does! Pray God that he always will! God Almighty wants *you!* That is the biggest, the best, fact of life! That is *the* fact of life! Death! Life and death and life—eternal life! *Who could ask for anything more?*

Afterward, in the sacristy, the Bishop called the sermon "a dazzling performance," this in the hearing of several mastodons who stood high in the diocese, and then asked Father Urban whether he'd be able to stay on a bit at St Monica's.

"That's not for me to say, Your Excellency."

"No?"

"No, Your Excellency. That's up to you and Father Wilfrid."

"Is this the man I'm to write the letter to?"

"Letter, Your Excellency?" It appeared that the woman who'd made the mistake of writing to Father Urban on a post card had managed to get in touch with her group's moderator. Father Urban was tempted to carry his show of forgetfulness further, to the point of making the Bishop explain what he was talking about, but thought better of it. He had only wanted it understood that he had many calls on his time and wasn't to be taken for granted, and this, he believed, was now understood. "Oh yes," he said. "That's right, Your Excellency."

For a moment, the Bishop seemed to be waiting—as if expecting to be dispensed from the necessity of dealing with Wilf. This could not be, according to the rules of the game (any breach of which was a breach of his own authority, as the Bishop should be the first to see), and so Father Urban, though he wished he could help the Bishop, waited him out and said nothing. When they parted, as they did most amiably, it was Father Urban's feeling that he might have distinguished himself even more by his replies in the sacristy than by his sermon.

Wilf phoned that afternoon. "I'd like to have you stay on there for a bit," he said.

"How long?"

"I'm hoping it won't be for too long. The brochure's out. Three big boxes came this morning. Freight. And Wacker at the station just dumped 'em out in the snow. They're all right, though. I put a copy in the mail for you, but it looks like it might be cheaper if we delivered the larger quantities ourself."

"In the truck?"

"That's how it looks. Of course, we'll take what we need when we go out on Saturday, Father John and I, and if you're over this way in a car, you might pick up the bundles labeled St Monica's and Cathedral—and any others you can deliver without too much trouble. Saginaw, Bucklin, Lowell."

"If I get over that way."

"And maybe Webster and Conroyo. They're not so far from you."

"How about Arna?"

"It'd help, if you would."

As a matter of fact, Father Urban wouldn't, but he knew several laymen who'd be glad to do the job for him.

"Oh, and another thing," said Wilf. "Talk to that women's group over there, will you? You know the one."

"Was something said about that?"

"Yes. The Bishop wants it."

"You spoke to him?"

"No."

"Father Udovic?"

"No, the girl in the office."

The next day, as Father Urban was leaving the house for a luncheon engagement, he asked Johnny Chumley to call Father Udovic at the Chancery. "Father Udovic wasn't in," Johnny said later, "but I talked to the girl in the office and she said she'd take care of it."

That evening the secretary of the women's group phoned the rectory, and, after a date was agreed upon, Father Urban inquired: "Will the moderator be there?"

"He can't *always* attend, you know."

"No?"

"He's the busiest priest in the diocese, you know."

"Let's just say he's the busiest bishop."

On the night Father Urban addressed the group, the moderator failed to appear. However, he sent word that it was now his hope to attend the *next* meeting, and the group's president made quite a bit more of this hope than she did of the fact that Father Urban was there.

Father Urban was unhappy about this, and, of course, about the Bishop's failure to show up, but nobody could have guessed it. He gave his subject ("The Hand that Rocks the Cradle Rules the World") everything he had, and then flatly refused to accept the envelope tendered him by the chairman. "Not a-tall, not a-tall." During the refreshment period—just coffee, since Lent had begun—he exchanged a few words with Sylvia Bean. Sylvia, not a member of the group, had come as the guest of an older woman. "And I'm certainly glad I did. Too bad the Bishop couldn't come tonight."

Sylvia's companion, who must have seen many such nights, said, "He's a very busy man, I'm told."

"Just about the busiest priest in the diocese," said Father Urban. He returned to the rectory that night still in a quandary. He had hoped to probe the Bishop about the future of the parish, but gently, gently. The refreshment period would have been the time for it, the two of them going on with a subject scarcely raised, or not going on with it, as the case might be. A word from Father Urban, a word from the Bishop, and they would have known where they were—Order and Diocese—and neither would have suffered any embarrassment. It would have been so much better that way, better than asking for an appointment, and having to state one's business.

"Dear James asked me today how you liked parish work," Monsignor Renton said one night in the upper room, about a week later. Monsignor Renton still called at the rectory, though not so often as when Phil was there.

"What'd you tell him?"

"I said I thought you liked it. Say, what'd you do to Cox and Box? They're really down on you."

"I don't know why they should be, unless. . . ." Father Urban described the attempt made by the curates to spike the all-cartoon programs.

"That sounds like 'em all right. You'd never know it was that, though, to hear 'em talk. They say you've got your eye on St Monica's."

"What *will* happen here—in your opinion, Monsignor?"

"Oh, some hot shot'll get it. I'd put in for it myself, if it weren't for Orchard Park."

"Somebody who'll build?"

Monsignor Renton looked bleak at the thought. "At least Phil was spared that. That would've been the death of him."

"And then you would've blamed me."

"Yes, if I hadn't found out what was behind it all."

"What *was* behind it all?" Father Urban, who had fought squarely and fairly in the battle to influence Phil, and had emerged the winner, was wary of alibis from the loser. If Father Urban wasn't the one most responsible (after God, of course) for Phil's decision to build, then who was?

"Dear James," said Monsignor Renton. "He met Phil on the street a few days before we left. 'Build or else,' he said. Phil told me that in Florida."

Johnny Chumley, who was present when Monsignor Renton revealed this, said, "Yes, that's true. The Pastor told me that before he left."

"So there's your villain," said Monsignor Renton.

The Bishop's ultimatum to Phil, and his asking how Father Urban liked parish work, and what Cox and Box, and possibly others, were saying—all these were considerations that led Father Urban to seek an appointment with the Bishop. Time was another. If the Bishop was in a hurry to build, wouldn't Father Urban be the man to do the job for him? In this connection, it had occurred to Father Urban that Phil could be more useful to the parish dead than alive—the old coach gone but the big game still to be played, and won, for him. And if Father Urban did the job, the Bishop needn't feel that he had to turn the parish over to the Clementines. There would be other ways in which they could be repaid. In time, the Bishop might come to think of the Clementines as his Praetorian Guard, standing between him and his own clergy, always ready to assume the risks and privileges of their special position. In any case, Father Urban would see the Bishop and find out whether there was any point in keeping the parishioners in a state of preparedness. As it was, more and more of them were getting after him to build.

The interview, held in the Bishop's office at the Chancery, got off on the wrong foot—with the Bishop patting a copy of the brochure that lay on his desk and saying, with a smile, "For some reason, I hadn't pictured you as a gardener, Father Urban."

"It came as something of a shock to me, too, Your Excellency, but you know how it is with these things." Somebody at the Novitiate had gone over the brochure with a fine-toothed comb, removing some of Wilf's copy ("Known for its shade and water," for instance, which was to have appeared on the cover, was missing, and the title itself, which had begun as "Oh, Come

All Ye Faithful!" become "Welcome to St Clement's Hill", become "You and St Clement's Hill," had ended up as "St Clement's Hill"), but the photographs had survived, including, unfortunately, the one that had caught the Bishop's eye. That one
had already drawn a gleeful notice from Father Louis. "Strongly
advise you read 'The Man with the Hoe,' " he'd written, and this
Father Urban had done late one night in the upper room—a
recreation he hoped wouldn't become popular at the Novitiate
in connection with the photograph of him in the garden, though
he could see how it might.

"Well, Father?" said the Bishop, after asking that Wilf be
thanked for the brochure.

"This more or less begins as a progress report, Your Excellency, but it ends in a question. That's why I've come to you,"
said Father Urban, wondering, though, if Bishop Conor might
not be repelled by flattery of the usual sort. He was a medium-
sized man, about twelve pounds overweight, with iron grey
hair clipped too short and high at the sides, revealing that he'd
had a bad case of scalp acne at one time. He hadn't distinguished
himself as an athlete or scholar in the seminary, nor even as a
scourge of indecency since rising to the hierarchy. He was another one of those good boys who had known, from about
the third grade on, that his day would come, and indeed it had,
though in a smaller way than he'd once hoped. Disappointment
and acne had marked him. He was restless, and he wasn't doing
quite enough about the conceit that is the occupational hazard
of his office. "Since I've been filling in at St Monica's, we've
been trying, Father Chumley and I, just to hold the line. We
thought we'd have our hands full doing just that, until Father
Smith returned—but that, unfortunately. . . ."

"Unfortunately," said the Bishop.

"Busy as we were, Father Chumley and I, we did manage to
take the parish census. (Father Chumley worked like a dog,

Your Excellency.) Now, along with taking the census, we ran a little survey to find out how people felt about the present church. As you know, we have a standing-room-only situation every Sunday at the late Masses. Well, we found that the great majority of parishioners would favor or strongly favor a new church. They understand what this would mean, too—to them *and* from them. Now, although we didn't question them along any such lines, I think I can say that our parishioners, by and large, are ready and willing to accept the responsibility of building and paying for a new church. They have that responsibility, of course, but the point is that they *want* it. In fact," said Father Urban, talking and smiling at the same time, a thing he'd noticed Protestants did better than Catholics—some of those ministers on TV got in their best licks while smiling—"there's been agitation along that line that I haven't known quite how to handle. So the question *is*, Your Excellency."

The Bishop put up his hand in a mild sort of way, and Father Urban was rather glad that he did, for the atmosphere wasn't right for the question. "I was asking somebody the other day how you liked parish work, Father."

"Well," said Father Urban, talking and smiling at the same time, "I hope whoever it was told you the truth. I must say I like it." Was it possible that he wouldn't have to ask the question?

"A little out of your line, isn't it?"

"As you know, Your Excellency, we're primarily a teaching and preaching order. Me, I've always been in the preaching end—for many years traveling out of Chicago, which I guess I still think of as home." Didn't the Bishop feel the same way? There was no indication that he did. "But the truth is we have parishes here and there throughout the country. One in Chicago. So parish work really isn't out of our line—or even out of my line."

The Bishop smiled. "Oh, I've heard good things about you, Father, since you've been at St Monica's. I understand you've done more than hold the line."

"Oh, I didn't mean that." Father Urban didn't doubt that the Bishop had heard of his work at St Monica's. "I only meant I go where I'm sent—and do the best I can."

There was a knock at the door. Father Udovic, the Chancellor, looked in on them. Father Udovic, who was short and blond, wore what were almost cowboy heels. He said something about a long-distance call and withdrew.

"Father Udovic's from Chicago," said the Bishop.

And aren't you? Father Urban wished to say, but didn't dare, since the Bishop's idea seemed to be that Father Urban could be from Chicago with Father Udovic but not with him. That was the impression that Father Urban got anyway, and he didn't like it.

The Bishop rose from his desk. "The reason I asked"—asked *what?*—"and I know it's not for you to say, Father." The Bishop was walking over to the wall where there was a large map of the diocese.

Father Urban got up and followed him.

"We have these parishes up here, three of them. Actually, they're only missions—Indian missions."

Father Urban looked at the spot where the Bishop's finger had touched the map, at the blue water and hen tracks, these indicating bogs. This, then, was the answer to Father Urban's unasked question, and doubtless the Bishop was congratulating himself on his handling of it.

"One man, with a good car, could take care of all three of 'em," the Bishop said, going back to his desk but not sitting down—a needless precaution.

Father Urban had no desire to continue the interview. "Well, of course, it's not for me to say," he said, moving over to the table where he'd left his hat.

"I realize that, Father."

"If you'd like me to mention it to Father Wilfrid, I will. Of course, he'd have to refer the matter to Chicago."

"Do what you think best, Father. Now—to answer your question about this agitation for a new church at St Monica's—the new man, whoever he is, will be the one to deal with that. And, by the way, I'm sorry I couldn't make it to your talk the other night. Maybe next time."

The Bishop had said no, but the word must have gone out, "Buy Clementine," for suddenly, in the middle of Lent, retreatants descended upon the Hill like manna from heaven. Tools were put away and paint-can lids were tapped down hard. Wilf and Jack preached and preached, and Brother Harold performed greater miracles in the kitchen. Father Urban tightened his schedule at St Monica's and drove over to the Hill oftener, since it was Wilf's desire to give each group of retreatants at least one taste of the best wine the Clementines could serve. Wilf didn't *say* that, of course, and Father Urban, who had long since stopped looking to his superiors for gratitude, would have been very much surprised if he had.

Wilf attributed the great change in their fortunes primarily to the brochure. It was doing the job he'd always known it would do. Next in importance, in his estimation, was the clever covering letter he'd written to pastors, a letter in which he thanked them for their "continued support." And after that came the warmer weather and the fact that he'd had the furnace and ducts vacuum-cleaned. ("Found an old overshoe in your duct, Urban—no wonder you were cold") Thus Wilf accounted for the great change—and began negotiations with his discount house to procure "government surplus" beds and mattresses for Minor. "We're on the move, boys."

If so, why—why now?

They had come into the diocese cold, with no fifth column to soften up the population (no old grads around to say, "I went to school with the Clems"), with nothing but the Bishop's permission to sustain them. The lower clergy, after welcoming them with all the lukewarmness at their command, had closed ranks and hardened at the prospect of being regarded by their own flocks as less traveled, less learned, and less spiritual than the newcomers. This is almost inevitable if the newcomers have a country place and wear a striking habit (which, unfortunately, the Clementines didn't), and the secular clergy know it. They know that among them there are too many men whom too many people remember as something else, as, in Johnny Chumley's case, a hockey player. In short, they know that they suffer from a deficiency of mystery and romance, as the Protestant clergy do, compared with them. But what they'd feared hadn't happened in this instance. Wilf had made nothing of the one advantage he'd had. The Clementines, competitors not so much for the alms and stipends of the faithful as for their hearts, had got nowhere until Father Urban entered the lists. He, unlike Wilf, had taken good care to conquer the profane world before tackling the other one, and, for that reason, was able to deal with the clergy from a sitting, rather than a kneeling, position. They loved a winner. It was as simple as that. That was what was really behind the great change.

Father Urban, however, still wouldn't call it success. They were getting the retreatants, yes, but they weren't getting the revenue. The common practice—the retreatant to leave behind an offering to cover his board and room, and, if he wished, a bit more—just wasn't working out at the Hill.

One afternoon, after a group of retreatants had departed,

Father Urban walked into the office and found Wilf holding his head. "The take's still off, eh?"

"It's not quite what it should be," Wilf said.

Father Urban scrutinized the roster of departed retreatants, sighed, and said what he'd refrained from saying before. "Too many Teutonic and Central European strains, I'm afraid, and these not the best of their kind."

"Aw, now," said Wilf. He was inclined to be touchy on this point. He held that it was only an historical accident that the American hierarchy was so Irish in its make-up. Father Urban, on the other hand, held that the Irish, ecclesiastically speaking, were the master race, and had had the saints, and still had the bishops, to prove it.

"No," said Father Urban. "Let's face it. We're getting the ham-and-sausage-supper types now. The horseshoe pitchers. That's all there is to it. They're the ones who're setting the tone, and it's all wrong."

"Maybe we shouldn't look at it that way," Wilf said. "So materially, I mean."

"Try that on your grocer."

"It *is* sort of discouraging." Wilf said that he'd thought of putting up small signs such as hotels had in their bedrooms, but not setting a minimum rate, just *suggesting* one.

"No good."

"No, I don't like it much myself."

Taking leave of Wilf, Father Urban said, "Let's face it. We have to go after a different breed of retreatant."

A few days later, Father Urban was out strolling among the children in the school playground, talking to one of the sisters, a Chicago girl, when Cal, of Cal's Body Shop, brought Phil's car back. In a way, Father Urban was sorry to see it. For two days, he'd had the use of Sylvia Bean's little English sports

car—a Barracuda S-X 2. He complimented Cal on the fine job
he'd done on the back fender of Phil's Plymouth, and then
said he supposed he ought to return the little Barracuda to its
rightful owner. Cal caught on and said, sure, he'd follow in the
big car.

Sylvia wasn't home, but Father Urban left the little Barracuda
in the driveway and gave the key to the maid. Cal moved
over, and Father Urban drove him to his place of business. Cal,
who knew the circumstances of the accident, said he'd shaved
the bill down as far as he could in case Father Urban had to
pay it. "Mighty white of you, Cal." Father Urban then drove
off to see the party responsible for the accident in which,
fortunately, only Phil's car had suffered, and it only forty-
eight dollars' worth.

The other party's address, given to Father Urban by the cop
summoned to the scene of the accident, was simply R.R.2,
Duesterhaus, and so Father Urban dropped in at the Duesterhaus
post office for more information. He discovered that the other
party was a farmer whose property adjoined that of the Order,
none other than the owner of the black dog, Rex, of whom
Wilf was so fond.

At the time of the accident the farmer, an elderly man, had
been about to deliver a load of firewood—white birch logs that
really looked too nice to burn—to a big house a few doors
away from Ray Bean's. Running his old truck off the steep
driveway on his first attempt, he'd backed out into the street
to try again, and without watching where he was going, when
Father Urban happened by. There was a scum of wet snow.
Father Urban's wheel tracks showed that he'd done all he could.
He was completely in the clear. But the farmer had no insurance.

Father Urban found Mr Hanson and the dog at home. The
dog seemed to recognize him, but Mr Hanson didn't, and so
Father Urban introduced himself. He mentioned his connection

with the Hill ("We're neighbors"), and then presented the bill, saying that Cal had shaved it down as far as he could.

Mr Hanson said, Yar, he guessed he'd have to pay it. He didn't have no insurance, he said, because he'd been delivering his last load. He was giving up farming, going to California where his daughter was. His missis had passed away. Some fellers might buy his place, he said. So far, though, they were holding out, wouldn't give him his price. Father Urban asked what that might be. Mr Hanson had an old frame house, a red barn in very bad shape, and about sixty acres left of what, he said, had once been four hundred. In the distance, Father Urban could see the thin little woods, not many birches left, where the farmer had cut his last load. After finding out what Mr Hanson wanted for his property, which took a bit of doing, Father Urban left. At that point, he really didn't know why he'd bothered to find out.

The following afternoon, he was back, and Monsignor Renton was with him ("I just want to know what you think, Monsignor, and I may need your help later"). They walked over the still-frozen ground with Mr Hanson and Rex. The property included about three hundred yards of barren shore line on Pickle Lake (as Mr Hanson called it). He said the fellers who might buy his property weren't interested in farming it but in selling off lots for summer cottages. Father Urban asked who they were, these fellers, and Mr Hanson mentioned a couple of names. One of them was familiar to Father Urban who said, no, he wasn't thinking of cottages, and, no, he wasn't thinking of farming—for one thing, as Mr Hanson had pointed out, the barn needed too much work. Father Urban, not saying what he was thinking of (Monsignor Renton made this easier by whooping it up with the dog), asked Mr Hanson to do nothing until he heard from him, and wrote down St Monica's telephone number ("Just call collect") in case anything got going with

the fellers ("We're neighbors, after all"). Mr Hanson said, Yar,
O.K.

After that, Father Urban and Monsignor Renton drove over
to the Hill. "Busy, Father?" Wilf was in his office.

"Oh, I guess there's nothing that won't keep. Oh hello, Monsignor. I didn't see you."

Presently, Father Urban told Wilf what was on his mind.

"My God!" cried Wilf, but he wanted to hear more.

Later that afternoon, alone in the upper room at St Monica's,
Father Urban made himself a scotch highball, carried it to the
little secretary desk, sat down, and took out several sheets of
paper. For some time, he fingered the letter opener, which was
like a little sword, and then, suddenly, he put it aside, took pen
in hand, and wrote, "Dear Billy:"

Billy phoned the next day, about noon, from the railroad
station in—*Where? You're kidding!* Father Urban had sent Billy
a very long wire at straight rates, but he hadn't asked, or even
hoped, for anything like this. "O.K., I'll be right down to get
you," he said, and then, before he left the rectory, he rang up
Monsignor Renton. "Great, good news, Monsignor!"

They met at the station, Father Urban, Monsignor Renton,
Billy, and a Mr Robertson. Billy and Mr Robertson had taken
the Blackhawk up from Chicago ("I'm not knocking it, but
it used to be a better train"), and they'd made connections at
St Paul that morning with the Voyageur ("Don't knock it,
Monsignor"). Monsignor Renton took them to lunch in the
Greenwich Village Room ("Best we can do, I'm afraid"—
"Don't knock it, Monsignor"), and after a pretty fair meal,
they drove out to Mr Hanson's, Billy and Father Urban in the
Plymouth, Mr Robertson and Monsignor Renton in the latter's
Imperial.

Mr. Hanson and the truck were elsewhere, but Rex showed

the party around the farm. Most of the time they walked in silence, Mr Robertson occasionally raising small binoculars to his eyes. When they were back where they'd started from a half hour before, Billy said:

"Well?"

Mr Robertson gave the frozen ground, which he'd been eying from all angles, from close up and afar, one last kick, and said: "I don't see why not."

"Let's make it a standout course," said Billy.

As they were getting into the cars, Monsignor Renton now alone in his, Rex spoke to them, and a moment later Mr Hanson and the truck appeared.

Billy, who had been told about Father Urban's accident, said to Mr Hanson: "Paid that bill yet—that collision bill?"

"Yar, I got to pay it," said Mr Hanson.

"Yar," said Rex to Monsignor Renton.

"Don't pay it," Billy said.

"Yar, I got to pay it."

"Don't pay it," Billy said, "and consider this place sold."

"Yar, I got to pay it and I got to get my price," said Mr Hanson.

"Help," said Billy, and walked toward the car.

Father Urban took Mr Hanson aside and explained the nature of the deal to him. "We'll pay your price *and* we'll pay the bill from Cal's Body Shop." When Mr Hanson had got it straight, he was much taken with the idea of not paying the bill, and, of course, he was pleased to know that he'd be getting his price. Father Urban asked Mr Hanson, in a nice way, not to cut any more timber off the land, if he didn't mind, for it seemed to Father Urban that there were fewer birches than he remembered in the thin little woods.

"Yar, O.K.," said Mr Hanson, and, instructed by Father Urban, fetched Cal's bill from the house.

Father Urban started to put the bill in his pocket.

"I'll take that," said Billy, from the car.

Monsignor Renton headed back to Great Plains, and Father Urban drove Billy and Mr Robertson to the Hill where he introduced them to Wilf. "I've heard a lot about you, Mr Cosgrove," said Wilf, and offered to show Billy and Mr Robertson around. "This, of course, is the office." And thus another tour got under way. It moved down the corridor to the refectory ("Mr Cosgrove, you have no idea how much we've enjoyed the set, and I trust you got my letter to that effect") and then to the kitchen ("Electric mixer") and then to the chapel, but there Father Urban remained on his knees and left the tour—recalling the one he'd taken in November.

The place was in better shape than it had been then. At the moment, there were a half-dozen retreatants in residence, not bad for the middle of the week. The absence of retreatants, in days past, had been one of the weak points in Wilf's tours. Physically, too, the place was in better shape now. Still too many rocking chairs around, but the Rec Room now had *four* easy chairs (including the one that had been on loan to Father Urban), Parlors A and B had been redone (and renamed St Thomas Aquinas and SS. Cyril and Methodius), there was color TV in the refectory, there was a sacristy off the chapel, there were fresh new signs posted throughout the house, and the driveway was now designated as "one way." And something, it appeared, was going to happen in the chapel.

Rising from his knees, Father Urban visited with Jack and Brother Harold, who had come in carrying a ladder. They were preparing for the morrow, they told Father Urban. Then, and there, in the chapel, after months of apprenticeship and weeks of planning, Brother Harold was to have his big chance as a sacred artist. Father Urban, glancing at the cartoons the artist had made, was relieved that Billy hadn't seen them.

"They're not representational in the photographic sense," said Brother Harold of some of his figures. "So I see," said Father Urban. And still, he thought, once you accepted the idea that the chapel would be "contemporary" (to the extent that paint could counteract such evidences to the contrary as the pews and the altar), maybe it wouldn't be so bad. "How's it going, Jack?"

"I can't complain," Jack said.

Father Urban went to Wilf's office and made a few telephone calls, mostly to pass the time of day. "No, nothing special, George. I happened to be thinking of you. How's that virus? Good. And Marge? Good. No, I'm at the Hill. At the moment, yes. Nothing much, but I may have something to tell you in a few days. Good. 'Bye, George."

"Say," said Wilf, entering the office when the tour had ended. "If you can get away from St Monica's for a couple of days, I think you'd better go down to Chicago. I'd go myself, but I can't spare the time. Anyway, you're the logical choice to put this thing over with Father Boniface and the others."

"Whatever you say," Father Urban said. "If I'm back for confessions on Saturday, it'll be O.K."

"I'm only sorry our guests won't stay and eat here this evening. I believe it's northern pike."

"Don't tempt us," said Billy. His plan, though, called for them to be on their way. They had to catch the Empire Builder on which he'd reserved a suite (so Father Urban needn't worry about space), and they'd rent a car in Great Plains, or take a taxi to the train.

Billy wasn't kidding, Father Urban realized, though it would be a ninety-mile fare from Great Plains to the Empire Builder's nearest stop. "No, we'll take my car. I'll pick it up on the way back," said Father Urban.

After the guests had sampled the water, they said good-by to

Wilf and the Hill, and Father Urban drove them to St Monica's. There he packed his bag and arranged for Johnny Chumley to borrow a parishioner's second car. The next thing they knew, after a couple of drinks in the upper room, it was time to eat. They decided they couldn't do better than the Greenwich Village Room. During dinner, and for almost two hours afterward, going from Drambuies to scotches again, they talked golf.

The fairways at the Hill would be shaggy for the first year or two, Mr Robertson said, but the soil would be ideal for growing grass. Most of the area to be used was already in acceptable grass. Stump clearance could begin at once, reseeding and rolling very soon. The greens had to be constructed from the bottom up, since they had to retain moisture as well as drain water, and they would be topped from sod. If all went well, they'd be playable by early summer. If Father Urban should ever want to expand the course to eighteen holes, or even to thirty-six, the land would always be there.

They went on to discuss famous courses they'd played. Billy and Mr Robertson had been disappointed by St Andrews, but they were not without reverence for it as a shrine. Mr Robertson, or Chub, as Billy and Father Urban called him, spoke of courses he'd laid out (two of which Father Urban was certain he'd played, and perhaps two more), and then they got onto the subject of famous golfers and famous shots. In the end, as must often happen when good fellows get together, they considered the life and times of the great Walter Hagen. Both Billy and Mr Robertson knew stories that hadn't appeared in the Haig's autobiography. "I read the book, but I'm sorry to say I never saw the man play," said Father Urban. "He was raised in the Church, you know."

At one point during the evening, Father Urban left the table to make a phone call—to Dickie Thwaites. ("And say hello to your mother.")

Finally, they pulled themselves together and hit the road, Father Urban driving, and Billy and Mr Robertson singing themselves to sleep in the back seat. Father Urban didn't disturb them until the Builder, as Billy called it, was actually standing in the station. With the help of a couple of porters, Billy and Mr Robertson got settled for what remained of the night. They all rose late the next morning, had brunch together, and arrived in Chicago at 2 P.M., right on time. "That's the Builder for you, and what a ride!" said Billy.

Paul met them in the Rolls. He dropped Billy and Mr Robertson off on Michigan Avenue, where they both had their offices, and then he drove Father Urban to his destination. Paul had cried out, "Well, look who's here!" when he saw Father Urban, but he didn't get any encouragement to continue along such familiar lines. Father Urban had thought of Paul before he saw him and had decided to straighten out their relationship. Father Urban's new attitude was not so much cool as grave and preoccupied. When the Rolls turned into the Novitiate grounds, into the Avenue of Elms, as it was called, Father Urban looked up from his breviary and murmured, "Ah, here we are," and when the Rolls stopped in front of St Clement's Hall, he murmured, "Ah, thank you, Paul."

Father Boniface was in his room, recovering from a touch of flu. When he learned the purpose of Father Urban's visit, he said, "We won't discuss these matters any further now. These are matters for the chapter to take up in the morning."

Father Urban spent the rest of the day walking and talking with men who could be helpful to him in the morning, but he also said hello--*hello!* to a number of dim bulbs whose existence he'd always tried to overlook in the past. "Great to be back, if only for a little while." In general, he got a warm welcome.

Quite late that night, he smoked a cigar with Father Louis, and the talk turned to Wilf. "Oh, he's not so bad," said Father Urban. "Come off it," said Father Louis—in some ways a man much like Father Urban, another one of Father Placidus's boys, a few years younger, yes, but almost in his flight as a golfer, a man who cut a good figure, who had a mind he could use if the occasion ever warranted it (he was presently employed as a professor of moral theology), and also a man who'd done a stretch at St Clement's Hill. He had spent all but one of his seminary years with the Jesuits, and would be with them yet, he said, but for a run-in with his confessor over the value of St Ignatius's "Exercises" *as* prose. He had been asked to leave. He had met Father Placidus and joined the Clementines on the first bounce, as a divorced man takes up with the first floosie he meets, so he'd once told Father Urban. "Wait'll you have to go back there and live with him," he told Father Urban now, making too much of the fact that Father Urban had been living away from the Hill. "A guy like that wouldn't last two minutes in any other outfit." This landed them on familiar ground. At this point, Father Urban usually said, "*Like*," and Father Louis said, "Yes, *like*," but that night Father Urban, much as he wanted to discourage Father Louis in his "order pride," a peculiar form of order pride in that it wasn't his own order he was proud of, let it pass. He had been everybody's pal that day, and would be the same with the man who was probably his best friend. They went on to discuss the matters to be taken up by the chapter in the morning. "More power to you," Father Louis said. "In any other outfit, they'd kiss your feet."

"Everybody's been very nice, but I doubt that it'll come to that," said Father Urban.

It didn't. The next morning, at the chapter meeting, Father Boniface wore a pained expression while Father Urban spoke in behalf of a golf course at the Hill. Father Urban said it was high time somebody considered the plight of the one man for whom the Church was perhaps doing too little. Probably this man had never made a retreat, he said, and would feel funny about making one at, say, a Trappist monastery. This man just didn't care to get in that deep, as he might express it himself, and still he was up to a bit more than he could get out of a parish mission. This man—so he imagined anyway—wouldn't care for the company he'd find in a monastery or, for that matter, at a parish mission. You might say, "Well, isn't that just too bad?" but that wouldn't change anything for this man. He'd still stay away, and be the loser for it, and so it really was too bad, wasn't it? Not every man of this type would be a golfer, of course. Golf was just one way (a good one, Father Urban thought) to get at the problem. It was the old, old problem of the unchurched, you might say. That was the problem, then, and the challenge. Would the Order of St Clement, with a little extra effort and no monetary outlay, respond to the challenge? That, of course, was not for Father Urban to say. That was for Father Provincial and the others to decide, said Father Urban, and sat down. He hadn't mentioned the slim pickings they'd had from retreatants at the Hill. That could come later, if necessary.

Several men, not known to be partial to Father Urban but men he'd walked and talked with the day before, then spoke in favor of the course. The strongest support came from old Father Excelsior who, when he stood up, head to one side, arms thrust down, fists clenched, seemed to be hanging from a rope. Father Excelsior was director of the Millstone Press, and a revered figure in Catholic publishing circles. Father Siegfried, the new procurator, a man closely associated with the administration in Father Urban's mind, also spoke for the course. Father Urban hadn't walked and talked with him, and wondered if this might not be a power play on Father Siegfried's part. The procurator, with his crewcut, and his open, gushing manner, *and* his bloody claws, was definitely a man to watch.

Finally, Father Boniface rose and suggested that the money would be better spent on pamphlets. At this two or three notorious suckholes (among them Brother Henry) nodded. But Father Boniface said that since this was not the alternative, he would abide by the will of the others and not exercise his veto. Father Urban and his faction, most of them younger men, easily prevailed when the matter was put to a vote. "Permission granted," said Father Boniface, "and now the other matter."

Father Urban rose. He expected less trouble in this matter. "This has to do with the Millstone Press, and if you wonder what that has to do with me, or what I have to do with it, the answer is—nothing," said Father Urban, and drew a smile from just about everybody. "I just happened to be on the scene, you might say, when this thing broke. Father Excelsior has asked me to tell it to you as I told it to him." Father Urban told the chapter that he'd been brought in close contact with their benefactress, Mrs Thwaites, and through her he'd come to know her son. Richard Thwaites, a Harvard man who'd retained his habits of study (there was nothing to be gained by mentioning Dickie's sojourns in religious orders), was now engaged in editing a series of what might be called spiritual classics—leading off with translations of Denzinger's *Enchiridion* and the so-called "lost books" of Tertullian. Mr Thwaites felt confident that there was an audience for such works in inexpensive, paperback editions, perhaps a large audience, perhaps a very large audience. Father Urban really didn't know about this, and, frankly, he was doubtful. Father Excelsior, who knew all there was to know about such things, was also doubtful. Mr Thwaites, however, was fully prepared to subsidize the project—the common procedure where scholarly books were concerned. And so, whether or not Mr Thwaites's faith was justified in a material way was beside the point, fortunately, and need not be discussed. The point was that books of this type weren't easy to come by. They would be a credit to any publisher's list. "Isn't that right, Father?"

Father Excelsior nodded. "These are known as university press books in the trade," he said, "and, under the circumstances, I think we should be very glad to get them. Strong as our list is, it could be stronger."

"Now that's not all," Father Urban said, and explained that it was young Mr Thwaites's hope to bring out a series of what might be called children's classics. Oh, books like *Robin Hood* and *King Arthur and the Knights of the Round Table*—but with a Catholic twist. Father Urban had been astonished to hear of the possibilities in this respect. "I'm told that Sir Lancelot is the real hero of the King Arthur story. Well, in the end Sir Lancelot lays aside his sword and becomes a priest. How many people know that? Now, in the case of Robin Hood, Mr Thwaites plans to move the story up in time, to set it in the so-called Reformation period, keeping it in England, of course. It's all legends, you know, and so you have a pretty free hand. Robin Hood will still steal from the rich and give to the poor—you can't very well get around that—but he'll only steal from the rich who've stolen from the Church. So it really isn't stealing. More emphasis, I understand, will be put on Friar Tuck—whether he'll become the real hero of the book, I don't know—and also on Maid Marian. It's pretty generally known that she was Robin Hood's girl friend, whatever that might mean, but how many people know that Maid Marian ended her days in a nunnery?"

"As a nun?" inquired Father Boniface.

"Yes," said Father Urban, and this, he could see, was very good news to Father Boniface and to others who might have thought that Maid Marian was just doing time in a nunnery.

"Mr Thwaites's real interest, though, is in the spiritual classics. The children's classics he calls his 'bread and butter' books."

Father Excelsior nodded. "That's a term we use in the trade," he said.

"I don't have to tell anybody here that such books could be a real shot in the arm to vocations," said Father Urban.

"Mr Thwaites would like us to act as his publisher," Father Boniface said. "Why us?"

"He wants a Catholic publisher, of course, and a good one," Father Urban said. "Mr Thwaites has connections with the Dolomites, and did approach them, I understand, but now he and his mother—she's a strong influence on him—would rather have us." There was a bit more to it, which Father Urban didn't go into. Dickie demanded that both the children's and spiritual classics bear the name of Richard Lyons Thwaites as general editor. ("Coming from one who'll not only do the work but foot the bill, a perfectly reasonable request, and I'm certainly amenable to it," Father Excelsior had said to Father Urban the day before.) The Dolomites, however, didn't care to be associated in any way with Dickie in Bishop Dullinger's mind. Their big idea in life was keeping in with Dullinger. What would he think? What would he say? What would he do? Dickie also demanded that the spiritual classics, though bearing the imprint of the Millstone Press, be given a pleasing format, go forth into the world as "Eight Seasons Editions," and be so announced and advertised. This, too, Father Excelsior said he'd accept, if necessary. The director of the Millstone Press had been having a hard time of it. He was another who'd be happy when Father Boniface's three years were up. "Thousands for pamphlets, hundreds for the *Clementine*, and pennies for books." Father Urban and Father Excelsior had decided it would be better not to raise the Eight Seasons issue at the chapter meeting, since it was a detail over which men with little interest in the larger concerns of publishing might choose up sides.

Father Excelsior had come prepared, if need be, to speak on the subject of editor and publisher, which subject (like those of writer and reader, writer and publisher, publisher and reader, reader and editor, writer and editor, and bookseller *and* all of these, in all possible combinations) was one he'd always done justice to at conventions and book fairs, but there was no need to hear any more from Father Excelsior that morning. With no more ado, the marriage arranged by him and Father Urban, the marriage between the Millstone Press and Eight Seasons Editions (though not in precisely those terms), was voted, Father Boniface said, "Permission granted," and the meeting ended, as it had begun, with a prayer.

After that, many men, among them some who'd once been indifferent and even hostile, came up to Father Urban. They congratulated him, wished him well, pressed his hand, or just stood and gaped at him. Presently, when the room had cleared, Father Urban and his faction (and Father Siegfried) went off for a cup of coffee—swept off like Robin Hood and his merry men.

That night Father Urban departed from Union Station on the Western Star.

In the afternoon, before leaving the Novitiate, he had visited with his old confessor Father August. In the evening, he had dined with Billy and Father Louis in the Pump Room. Lobster and champagne, and Billy reaching the stage where he asked waiters why there were more horse's asses—"horshes's ashes" —in the world than horses, an old question with Billy, and Father Louis getting off on his favorite topic. Hard as it was for a superior man to keep from going sour in the Order of St Clement—no one knew this better than Father Urban—Father

Louis might have handled himself better than he had in the Pump Room. "Clementines, Dalmatians, Dolomites—all third raters," he'd informed Billy. Father Urban had hotly denied this, where the Clementines were concerned, citing Father Excelsior and one or two others. To this, with a great show of judiciousness, Father Louis had replied, "We have *very* few second-rate men." Here Billy had laughed, and perhaps he hadn't been scandalized (always the danger with laymen), and perhaps he'd believed Father Urban when he said that Father Louis was only joking, but it was still one hell of a thing to tell a benefactor. Wasn't it odd, though? Father Urban, thinking it would be well for the Order if somebody on the spot kept in touch with Billy, had considered Father Louis the best available man for the job and had brought him along to dinner. Billy and Father Louis *were* compatible, but in a negative sort of way, and Father Urban rather hoped they wouldn't be seeing too much of each other in his absence.

When Father Urban arrived back at St Monica's, as he did about 3:30 P.M. the next day, he saw Monsignor Renton's black car parked in front of the rectory and hurried inside. Monsignor Renton wasn't there, though. ("He must be in the church," said Mrs Burns.) When Monsignor Renton entered the rectory, Father Urban was on the phone. "That was the Chancery," he said, after hanging up. "I suppose you've heard the bad news." Father Udovic, come Monday, would be pastor of St Monica's.

Monsignor Renton sighed and said, "It may not be permanent."

"Let's hope not," said Father Urban. Until a moment ago, until he'd asked who the new chancellor of the diocese would be, he'd had no particular reason to dislike Father Udovic. "Nobody," Father Udovic had replied, "I'll have two jobs. It shouldn't be so hard." Father Urban, feeling that the importance of the job that had been his in everything but name for so many weeks was being grossly underestimated, had let the man know what might be regarded as the lesser of his two labors: "No, I suppose not—not in a diocese like this."

"Rather see it go to Cox or Box," said Monsignor Renton, which showed how he felt about the appointment—and perhaps that he did regard it as permanent. "I thought the idea was for you to stay on here until ordinations in June, but something must have happened to that. You didn't ask to be relieved, did you?"

"No," said Father Urban, feeling, though, that he was responsible for Father Udovic's appointment, and would be so judged if Monsignor Renton ever found out about the interview with the Bishop.

"Dear James should have his head examined," said Monsignor Renton.

"By the way, how'd you make out?" Father Urban asked. He was asking about the third horse in his three-horse parlay, Billy and Father Boniface being the first two, and both winners. It had been left to Monsignor Renton to approach the Bishop (whose approval was required for any expansion) in the matter of the golf course.

"It's all set," said Monsignor Renton.

Father Urban phoned Wilf and told him that all was well, and then he said to Monsignor Renton: "How about a drink, Red?"

Monsignor Renton was in a melancholy mood. "No," he said.

"Don't take it so hard, Red. How about a cigar?"

Monsignor Renton felt better after lighting up a Dunhill Monte Cristo Colorado Maduro No. 1—Father Urban had replenished his supply in Chicago. They fell to discussing the course, and got so worked up about it that they just had to have a look at the site. They jumped into the Imperial, Father Urban taking the wheel and racing against darkness. Mr Hanson and Rex were home, and the thin little woods looked the same to Father Urban, but it did seem to him that Mr Hanson and Rex were less friendly than before. "Is something wrong?" Father Urban asked.

"Yar," said Mr Hanson. He said he wanted a few days to think over the deal. "I better talk to the other fellers."

"Now *wait* a minute," said Father Urban. After a bit, after exercising great patience, he got at the trouble. It *wasn't* greed. No, while Father Urban was away in Chicago, Wilf had visited Mr Hanson. Citing the condition of the house and the barn, Wilf had asked Mr Hanson, in effect, to show cause why he shouldn't throw in the dog.

"Then you're taking Rex to California?" said Father Urban, noticing that Rex was following the conversation closely.

Mr Hanson shook his head.

"You're not? Did you tell Father Wilfrid that?"

"I didn't tell him nothing. I got to get my price." Mr Hanson seemed to think that Wilf, by harping on the condition of the barn and house, had been trying to beat down the price.

"*Will* you throw in the dog?"

"Yar."

"It's a deal," said Father Urban. He asked Mr Hanson to meet him at a bank in Great Plains the next morning, and wrote down the name of the bank. "Rex'll have a good home, Mr Hanson."

"Yar, O.K."

That evening Father Urban paid a call on one of the bank's vice presidents, on the George whose virus he'd asked about earlier in the week. Father Urban had a check from Billy—a check for enough to purchase the land, to pay for building and furnishing the course, and more ("While you're at it, why don't you buy yourself a decent rowboat?"), but it was a personal check, made out to Father Urban, and that was where George came in. Father Urban and George worked it all out, while Marge, George's wife, served them coffee. George's bank would stand back of the sum to go to Mr Hanson until Billy's check cleared, and thereafter St Clement's Hill would do business with George's bank. This was a big step up. Until then, there having being nothing much to put in a bank, Wilf had run the whole operation out of his shoe, paying bills by postal money order.

The next morning Father Urban and Mr Hanson met at the bank. Mr Hanson, after signing the necessary documents, was given a certified check, and thus he got his price, and his land and dog became the property of the Order of St Clement. Father Urban called up Wilf to tell him the good news.

"I've always admired that Rex," said Wilf.

"Yes, I know," said Father Urban.

"Guess what?" said Wilf.

"What?"

"Some guys in town, here, were after that property. Wanted it for summer cottages."

"You don't say."

"I just got wind of it. That wouldn't have been so good for us, you know. Loss of privacy. And guess who one of 'em was."

"Who?"

"Wacker at the station."

10

Twenty-Four Hours
in a Strange Diocese

Early in April, as stump removal began, the sound of dynamit-
ing echoed over the land, two farmers who understood such
things doing the job, with Father Urban, Wilf, Rex, and, sometimes, retreatants moving from eminence to eminence, away
from the noise and flying debris. The open craters, some to be
transformed into sand traps, awaited the coming of Mr Robertson. He came with a young assistant, and the two of them spent
three days laying out the course, using only steel tape, stakes
and string, the naked eye, and binoculars. "She'll be a little
jewel in a few years," Mr Robertson said, in departing. "But
always remember a golf course is like a fancy woman—you
have to take care of it." "I'll remember that," said Father Urban,
with a smile. "And don't think you can cheat your course,"
said Mr Robertson. "No," said Father Urban. "Take care of
your course," said Mr Robertson, "and your course will take
care of you." "O.K." "And it'd be nice if those boys I'm sending up"—Mr Robertson was sending up a couple of expert
workmen to do the greens—"could get in some fishing while

they're here." "We'll see what we can do, Chub." "And I'll be up again, maybe in June."

By June, the course was beginning to feel and smell right, sweet and right, especially on warm days after mowing. Two mowers, a big one for the fairways, a small one for the greens, had been purchased out of the fund established from Billy's check in George's bank, and the course was now playable except for the greens. The workmen who'd built these had come and gone long ago, but their craft—it was really an art—lived after them. Father Urban watched over the greens, saw to it that they were given their formula of fertilizer, were gently watered, mowed, and weeded—by young men in bare feet. First Father Urban employed Brother Harold (who'd reached the point in the chapel where he needed to get away from it and think, before going on) and later a few youngsters from among those now arriving in shifts from the Novitiate. By their willing labor, the fairways, too, were kept spick-and-span. When their holiday in the land of sky-blue waters ended, not a few of these lads expressed the hope that they'd be stationed at the Hill someday. Father Urban made a point of walking and talking with them all (they took it as a special treat when he joined their bull sessions), and he was not content with hero worship. He tried to breathe into them a quality that he could only hope and pray would take root and become the mark of them all— as, say, scholarliness is the mark of the Jesuit—for there was no use denying that the Clementines lacked distinction *and* distinctiveness, or *persona*. What Father Urban would have called this special something he was trying to impart to the young, he didn't know, but he felt that he had succeeded here and there, and that the Order, to say nothing of St Clement's Hill, would be a better place for those who'd come after him.

Mr Robertson arrived at the end of June and pronounced the greens playable. "You've done well here," he said to Father

Urban, "but don't get careless. I see signs of nightcrawlers and
pocket gophers."

By the middle of July, the course was more than fulfilling its
threefold purpose: to serve the laity, to serve the secular clergy,
and to serve the Order. To the Hill had come a number of those
better types who had never made a retreat before and whose
support—and not just material support—was required if the
place was to succeed as a spiritual powerhouse or oasis (Father
Urban used both terms), although the less desirable types were
still in the majority. To the Hill, too, had come the diocesan
clergy for their annual retreat, which, due to a cancellation, was
preached by Father Urban, and this convention was really paying off. Pastors who had once been backward were now
sending their parishioners to the Hill and saying that the
Clementines were *trained* to do the job they were doing. In his
conferences, Father Urban often referred to parish priests as
"those heroic family doctors of the soul" and to himself as "this
poor specialist."

And then, working through Monsignor Renton, Father Urban got the Bishop to come out to the Hill for a meal—and
should have left it at that. Urged by Father Urban and Monsignor Renton, the Bishop, who said he'd played before, took
to the course. After four holes, on each of which he'd clearly
demonstrated that he was a poor sport as well as a lousy golfer,
the Bishop quit in a huff. Father Urban was unhappy about
this—happy, though, that it was over, for the contrast between
his play and the Bishop's was excruciating. Moreover, the
Bishop appeared to regard Father Urban's near-professional
game as unseemly and impertinent in a priest. There were people
like that, Father Urban knew, and he was only sorry that the
Bishop had to be one of them. He invited the man to come out
again, and *soon*—"All you need, Your Excellency, is practice"
—but was rather glad to hear that the sorehead was off for
Rome.

Otherwise, Father Urban hadn't made any mistakes—if, indeed, it was a mistake to extend to the bishop of a diocese the hospitality enjoyed by others.

Mistakes had been made, though. The gates had been opened too wide in the spring when Wilf, hoping to cut costs and perhaps realize a profit on the fund set aside for the course, had accepted outside help. The bad effects of this were still to be seen—all kinds of people playing the course who might or might not have helped enough or at all. Low-level patronage had proved to be more bother than it was worth. Why, there were people who'd bring you fifty feet of leaky hose and act as if they owned the course!

Just about all the trouble and confusion at the Hill that summer could be traced to Wilf, and not only where the course was concerned. Saying they had to meet competition elsewhere, and fancying he had a special way with married couples ("Now my brother Rudy and his wife"), Wilf had scheduled and preached two family retreats, which he called "sweethearts' retreats," and, ill attended though they were, there just wasn't enough space for that sort of thing at the Hill. Talk about Pandora's box! Minor, where the sweethearts, when they weren't wandering around in the corridors, were holed up in single rooms ("One of the features of these beds is you can stack one on top of another, like bunk beds"), had reminded Father Urban of a Pullman car in an old *Follies* skit.

In general, though, life became easier and more meaningful that summer at the Hill. The place was actually under new management, but Father Urban let the credit go to Wilf, as rector, and to the brochure, of which there was to be a second edition, with an aerial view of the course and a close-up of the new shrine of Our Lady below No. 5 green. "Yes, we've seen a few changes here" was about all Father Urban would ever say in acknowledgment of his achievements.

Father Urban was being used sparingly as a retreatmaster at the Hill, since Wilf and Jack had to be doing something. In fact, Father Urban had preached only one retreat from beginning to end—the one for the diocesan clergy—and that one because Wilf must have recognized that only the best would do. Wilf didn't say this, of course. No, even though he arranged it so that Father Urban gave a conference to every group that passed through the Hill, Wilf always acted as though this were only a matter of giving retreatants a little variety. "I think they'd like to hear you," he'd say. Father Urban noticed, though, that Wilf always asked Jack, or one of the visitors vacationing from the Novitiate, to give the *next* conference: Wilf, although he wanted retreatants to have the best, a little taste of it anyway, didn't care to *follow* Father Urban.

The Clementines were still serving the parishes where they traditionally helped out on weekends (except St Monica's, where Father Udovic was doing without them), Wilf making good use of visitors for this purpose, but Father Urban was left with a certain amount of time on his hands. (He was limiting himself to eighteen holes a day.) And so, with Wilf's permission, and with Sylvia Bean's little Barracuda, though he sometimes traveled by rail, Father Urban became the Hill's roving ambassador of good will.

He made calls in Olympe, Great Plains, Brainerd, St Cloud, Duluth, and the Twin Cities, and once he went as far south as Rochester. The usual thing was to drop in on executives at their places of business, but to let them know right away that he didn't want anything, and if nothing developed, he'd soon be on his way. "Just wanted you to know where we are. Drop in on *us* sometime." Later, if he ran into somebody he'd met in this fashion, it was like old times. Hello—*hello!* He watched the paper for important funerals, too, and turned up at some of these. Wherever he went, people always seemed glad to see him —and, of course, it was all for the Order.

In St Paul, he dropped in on the president of the Minnesota Central. "I'm just between trains, and thought I'd come in and thank you for those two passes—and let you know we're not misusing them."

"Don't need any more, do you?"

"Well, there *are* three of us."

"What's your name, Father?"

Father Urban told him again, and this time the man wrote it down.

"Not from around here, are you?"

"As much from around here as anywhere else. For many years, I traveled out of Chicago, but I consider Minnesota my home now—and consider myself fortunate."

"Well, that's fine."

"Now I know you're a Catholic, and we do have this retreat-house, and, of course, we'd love to see you up there, but I'm not trying to sell you on that. I know you're a busy man. But why not drop in on us sometime, if you're up that way? Play a round of golf, if you like."

"Say, I've heard about that. Before I forget, should I address the pass to you?"

"It might be better if you sent it to Father Wilfrid."

The man wrote it down.

"Two *i's*," Father Urban said. "But better yet—bring it along when you come."

"I just might do that, Father."

And that was it. The pass arrived two days later, addressed to Wilf. "Well, it finally came," he said.

"You don't say," said Father Urban.

For some reason, he'd never gone to Ostergothenburg.

In the other dioceses around them there was always a demand for his services, but Ostergothenburg, though closest to his seat of operations, hadn't been heard from at all. It almost seemed that the clergy of that diocese were pledged to have nothing to do with the Order of St Clement, and that this embargo applied to one who was so much more than just a Clementine. And so, when, in the middle of July, the call finally came from the backward diocese, Father Urban made no bones about being asked to hear confessions on Saturday as well as preach on Sunday. He whipped over in Sylvia's little Barracuda, pursued by such questions as wouldn't it be nice if this proved to be a turning point, nice if another diocese were opened for spiritual exploitation, nice if the Hill could draw retreatants from *all* adjoining dioceses (as a great university draws students from every state and from abroad)? It seemed highly significant to Father Urban that the call had come from the Cathedral in Ostergothenburg.

He arrived on Saturday afternoon, in time to hear confessions and "heard" again in the evening. The next morning, he preached at three Masses—it was this, his preaching he was wanted for at the Cathedral, so he'd thought, and why not?

He had arrived at the Cathedral, however, to discover first that the Rector wasn't on hand that week, then that he hadn't been there for a month, then that he wouldn't be there for another month, and, finally, that he was in Europe. The curates were having a devil of a time getting a replacement for him each weekend, and *that* was why they'd called the Hill. Unfortunately, Father Urban didn't find this out right away, and so, on Saturday night, after confessions, he'd returned to the rectory expecting a party of some kind, a gathering of the clergy who had been wanting to meet him. There had been nothing—not even hospitality from the curates. One took off for the movies and the other went to bed. So there was Father Urban, at nine o'clock in the evening, alone in a strange diocese, in a spare room, with the only light coming from a frosted glass pot in the ceiling—a maid's room, without TV. He knew then, for sure, that he'd been had.

Nevertheless, he preached beautifully the next morning. Even if the people had come with the idea of hearing not whoever happened to be there that week, but Father Urban, they would not have been disappointed. Everywhere Father Urban saw that look of "Who *is* this?" in their eyes, and yet only one elderly man stayed after Mass to speak to him. Except for that, Father Urban had drawn a blank in Ostergothenburg. That was how matters stood at noon.

Hungry from his labors in the pulpit, he returned to the rectory and found that no preparations were being made to eat. The housekeeper, who hadn't done so badly the night before, seemed to be missing. "Hey, where is everybody?" Upstairs, the curate who'd gone to bed at nine the night before came out of his room. "When the Pastor's gone, she always goes to her daughter's on Sunday," he said of the housekeeper, and of his colleague he said, "He *always* goes to his mother's for dinner on Sunday."

"Well, that's nice," said Father Urban.

"However," said the curate, "I have permission to take the visiting priest out to dinner on Sunday, if need be."

Something told Father Urban to quit Ostergothenburg at once —*Turn back! Turn back!*—but he couldn't, not after that "if need be." After that, he *had* to dine out on the Cathedral.

They ate at a little downtown place, early-American décor and a sizzling neon sign in the window. The sign, flashing off and on behind Father Urban's ear, said EAT AT CLARA's. Father Urban ordered "roast beef au jus." When the waitress left, he asked the curate if the older woman at the cash register could be Clara.

"No, she's off on Sunday," said the curate. When the waitress returned to their booth, he asked, to be sure, "Clara's not here, is she?"

"No, she's off on Sunday," said the waitress.

"That's what I thought," the curate said to Father Urban.

"Oh, she sometimes stops by," the waitress said to Father Urban.

Father Urban nodded. When he saw what the waitress had brought him—grey meat, mashed potatoes in the form of two balls, bread cut diagonally, and brown gravy over it all—he said to the curate: "Is your mother still living?" And after a bit, he asked about the other curate, whom he'd scarcely seen. "What does your friend do on Sunday night?"

"He stays in. That's my night out."

"I see. And where do you go?"

"I go to the movies. The first show."

"You guys must see a lot of movies."

"As a rule, we just go once a week."

"Just once a week."

"As a rule. He goes on Saturday night, the second show, and I go on Sunday night."

"The first show."

"Yes."

Father Urban declined dessert, which wasn't easy, since it was on the dinner, the curate and the waitress both pointing this out. When the curate got his—red jello with watery whipped cream on it, topped off with walnut dust—Father Urban, watching the curate attack the stuff, changed his mind. After the waitress had brought him a dish of it and departed again, feeling better and saying, "After all, it's on the dinner," Father Urban changed his mind again—or so he pretended—and gave his dessert to the curate, who was quite happy with it.

"Know a man by the name of Zimmerman?" said Father Urban.

"Old man?"

"He could be seventy, if that's old."

"Goes to our church."

"All right, but who is he? What's he do?"

"Zim's Beer."

A few moments later, Father Urban lit a cigar. "Where's Mirror Lake?"

"Why, he lives out there!" said the curate. "The man you were asking about!"

The usual thing was to put the brighter boys in cathedral parishes. Could this be the case in the Ostergothenburg diocese?

"Who?" said Father Urban.

"Zimmerman! He used to live in town, but now he lives out there!"

"You don't say," said Father Urban.

The day was about right for his new straw hat with the fish-net band (from which he'd removed the feather and sea-shells). After he dropped the curate at the rectory—he'd driven the two blocks to Clara's so the kid could say he'd ridden in a sports, or, as he called it, racing car—Father Urban pulled over in the shade of the Cathedral. He got out of the car, took off his coat, rabat, and collar, and put them on the other seat. Then he got in, started the motor, which had a plummy sound he loved, shifted himself into a slouch, and, with his head resting easily to one side as if he were dreaming, he—there was no other word for it—tooled toward the outskirts of town.

The little snub-nosed Barracuda was five months old, had wire wheels, leather upholstery, and so on, and it certainly made a man feel good to drive it. At a stoplight, though, when a girl in a white MG paused alongside him, a girl wearing sunglasses and nothing else—so it appeared from where he was sitting—and with a crisp blue dog beside her, Father Urban experienced a heavy moment, a moment of regret and longing. He wished the little Barracuda were black or white instead of bright red, which just wasn't right for him, and he wished he had a crisp blue dog beside him. So he put on his sunglasses. When he hit open country, he threw away his cigar and gave the little thoroughbred its head.

He noted a billboard with interest. "FRESH! ZIM'S BEER!" He wondered, though, who wanted fresh beer. Then he saw another billboard: "SEE MIRROR LAKE—SEE YOURSELF FISHING, BOATING, SWIMMING, HEATED CABINS." Would he find Mr Zimmerman living in one of *them*? (*Turn back! Turn back!*) Such a thought wouldn't have occurred to Father Urban—even a small brewery could be a very worth-while affair—if he hadn't formed such a poor impression of life in the Ostergothenburg diocese.

Some shirtless youths in an old car roared up from behind him. "Drag?" they shouted. Their old tub, lower by several inches in front, seemed to be running downhill. It was painted two shades of green to look like a watermelon, which it did, one of the striped variety, and on the front fender were the words "THE MELLON." "Drag race?" Father Urban shook his head. "Chicken!" The Mellon shot ahead. Father Urban put it out of mind and, enjoying the feel, the roadability, of the little Barracuda, thought of Sylvia.

He was worried about her. After she'd brought the little car out to the Hill the day before, and after he'd driven her home before setting out for Ostergothenburg, she'd asked him to read from a book she happened to have with her, just one verse of a poem, and this Father Urban had been glad to do. When he finished, he said, "Yes."

"Is *that* what you mean?"

"Yes, I suppose it is."

And it was—the poet had put it very well:

An intellectual hatred is the worst,
So let her think opinions are accursed.
Have I not seen the loveliest woman born
Out of the mouth of Plenty's horn,
Because of her opinionated mind
Barter that horn and every good
By quiet natures understood
For an old bellows full of angry wind?

Yes, and so had Father Urban. But Father Urban, with and without benefit of poetry, had been through this sort of thing with too many women—women with husbands like Ray Bean, all business, and women with husbands unlike Ray Bean, to say nothing of women without husbands—and he was afraid Sylvia might be building herself up for a letdown. Sylvia might not know what she had in mind. Or she might. In effect, by asking him to read the poem, she had put words in his mouth, words he might think but would never speak, words which might be said to compromise him, words from which, in the privacy of her imagination, Sylvia might distill pleasure of an illicit nature. And "loveliest woman born" was pushing it some in her case. "Damned attractive redhead" would've been more like it. Experience had shown Father Urban that a handsome priest couldn't be too careful with women. Should he go on using Sylvia's car? Considering that he'd be lost without it—many of his little trips would've been impossible without the car—he guessed he would. Maybe he'd use it less, though.

He found Mr Zimmerman living around on the other side, the "old" side, of the lake. Mr and Mrs Zimmerman were out in front of a five- or six-room cottage, sitting in tubular chairs under some lovely oaks, with the Sunday papers on the grass at their feet, and with the lake, which appeared to have a good sandy beach, just a chip shot away. There was a picnic table, and on it a Scotch-plaid jug and some colored aluminum tankards. Mrs Zimmerman filled and brought one of these to Father Urban.

"It's called Icy-ade," she said. Except for her hair, which was longer, and her dress, Mrs Zimmerman looked exactly like her husband. This was a phenomenon Father Urban had often observed in elderly couples, and could only attribute to their common diet. "You may have seen it advertised on television," she said.

"Grape?" said Father Urban, after a taste, since the stuff was purple. "Good and cold."

"That's the main thing," said Mr Zimmerman.

"Still there's a lot to be said for a good glass of beer," said Father Urban.

"Too gassy," said Mr Zimmerman, getting up.

Father Urban followed him to the water's edge and then out onto the dock to which a big plastic boat was tethered. Father Urban, if he owned a boat of that class, would want to see brass and mahogany. Mr Zimmerman's boat looked like a bath toy. After admiring the boat, they considered the sad state of affairs in what Father Urban believed was called a live box. There were three small fish floating in it, and a few more that appeared to be dying, sipping at the surface of the water.

"Wolftangl, he better watch it," Mr Zimmerman said, gazing out across the water. "I'll shoot 'em on sight—*any*where in this lake."

"How's that?" said Father Urban.

"Joe Wolftangl, fella over on the next lake. Raises turtles for the market. One got in my box last month. Fish don't have a chance."

"You catch these fish, and you put 'em in here, and you eat 'em later—is that it?"

"My wife likes to eat 'em, but she don't like to clean 'em." Mr Zimmerman gazed across the water again, and then he returned to land, Father Urban following, saying, "You're not the Zim's Beer Zimmerman, are you?"

"My son runs that now," Mr Zimmerman said. "We had a skunk pass through here again the night before last. Good thing we don't keep chickens."

Why am I here? Father Urban asked himself. *Turn back!* Mrs Zimmerman was gone when they returned to the chairs. Father Urban was about to sit down—having decided to let his host play it his way—when Mr Zimmerman said, "Like to see my shack?"

Father Urban glanced up at the cottage. "O.K.," he said.

They went up to the cottage, but then on into the woods behind it, until they came to a log cabin of recent construction. "My shack," said Mr Zimmerman.

"And what do you do here?" said Father Urban. The cabin was partitioned off into two sections.

"Just read and write," said Mr Zimmerman, moving out of view. "This is where I do the writing."

Father Urban looked in on an upright typewriter, straightback chair, and library table. The typewriter was old and had a patient look. On the wall, there was a larger-than-life photograph of the late junior senator from Wisconsin. There was also a filing cabinet. "And what do you write?" said Father Urban, retreating to the other section where there were chairs. Lincoln and Washington were in there.

"Wait," said Mr Zimmerman, from the room where he did

the writing. He brought Father Urban a large scrapbook with covers of dark polished wood. In wood of a lemon color, inlaid, were the words: "LETTERS TO THE EDITORS BY CARL P. ZIMMER-MAN."

"One of the boys at the prison made that for me," Mr Zimmerman said. "A former employee. I didn't ask him to, but I wrote and thanked him."

"I should think you would," said Father Urban, wondering if that was all Mr Zimmerman had done. "Minneapolis *Tribune*. St Paul *Pioneer Press*. CHICAGO *Tribune*," said Father Urban, and looked up to see Mr Zimmerman smiling. "J. Edgar Hoover," said Father Urban, coming upon one of his open letters. "How'd he get in here?"

"I thought that one was worth keeping. One of his best. The Shrapnel Brothers were here two weeks ago. Spent the day here."

Father Urban didn't reply at once.

"You know who *they* are?"

"Yes." Yes. Most of Mr Zimmerman's letters had appeared in the *Drover*, with the Ostergothenburg *Times* a close second. Father Urban had reached the point where he didn't know what to say. "I take it," he said, "you write mostly for the newspapers."

"And magazines," said Mr Zimmerman. He went into the room where he did the writing. He returned with a sheet of paper. "Here's one I wrote a month or two ago—no, I see it was longer than that. This went to *Time* magazine," he said, handing a carbon copy to Father Urban.

"But wasn't published?"

"No, it wasn't—at least not yet."

"Has *Time* published anything of yours?"

"No, and I don't have to tell you why."

"No?"

"Pink."

Father Urban didn't reply at once.

"I wouldn't say that to you—a stranger—if you weren't a Catholic priest," said Mr Zimmerman.

Father Urban believed that there was a great deal to be said for the conservative position, but he also believed—since a tree is known by its fruit—that Mr Zimmerman and his sort weren't the ones to say it. He handed back the carbon copy and closed the scrapbook. Wouldn't Mr Zimmerman be happier living in town? There were too many references to turtles and skunks and bears in his letters to the editors—snapping turtles down in Washington, dirty skunks down in Washington, and Russian bears. "You haven't always lived out here, have you?"

"Just since I retired." Mr Zimmerman said he wished now he'd retired sooner, and had started reading and writing sooner. "But I've still got some good years left."

"I'm sure you have."

"Well, we'd better be getting back." Mr Zimmerman carried the carbon copy into the other room.

Father Urban stood up and moved over to a large screened-in window. The trees, with their crisp green needles, were beautiful, and somewhere a bird was singing. "Nice here, Mr Zimmerman."

"I have to have a lot of quiet," said Mr Zimmerman, from the other room. He came out of it with more carbon copies—a great many more. "You may want to take a look at these. And maybe we'd better bring this along, too."

So, with Mr Zimmerman carrying the carbon copies, and Father Urban carrying the heavy scrapbook, they returned to the chairs and the lake. Mrs Zimmerman was there and brought Father Urban, over his good-natured protests, another bumper of Icy-ade.

Before Father Urban had got around to the carbon copies,

which lay on the grass by his chair, two couples arrived who looked a lot like the Zimmermans. They came from cottages near by, and bearing food by which Father Urban later remembered them, since their names didn't register with him. A few minutes later, a man and a dog approached from the other direction—"Oh, oh," said somebody. The man and the dog passed on up the beach, the man waving but not as though he expected much response. There was none. Soon the man and the dog returned, and this time they walked up to the chairs. The man was about Father Urban's age but not in his condition. The dog was an aged Airedale, a breed you seldom saw nowadays, and was the color of dark chocolate that had melted and hardened and lightened. Both man and dog were greeted by the Zimmermans and their friends—Father Urban sensed it was because there was nothing else to do—and the dog came off a little better than the man. When they'd passed by before, Father Urban had felt the man's eye on him, picking him out, and now the man made straight for him. After they were introduced to each other, the man stayed with him.

"St Clement's Hill," he said. His name was Studley and he smelled of beer. "Isn't that where they have this new golf course?"

"Yes, we do."

"You have an air strip, too, don't you?"

Father Urban smiled. "No, I'm afraid not."

"Don't you have some kind of tie-in with Flying Farmers?"

"No."

"No air strip?"

Father Urban just looked at him.

"Somebody said you did," said Mr Studley, not weakening.

Father Urban gazed away for a moment. All around him people were drinking from tinkling tankards, including Mr and Mrs Zimmerman who, it seemed, hadn't wanted to get too early a start. "No," said Father Urban, coming back to Mr Studley, who still appeared skeptical. "Not that *I* know of, and I was there yesterday."

Mr Studley laughed. He could have used a bra under his knit sport shirt. "Well, I'll take your word for it. Say, I hope you won't mind if I don't call you 'Father.'"

Not everybody had been listening before. Now everybody was—and scarcely a tinkle was heard from the tankards.

"That's entirely up to you, Mr Studley," said Father Urban. "I'm not a Catholic myself. I'm not much of anything, as a matter of fact. But you know what it says in the Good Book. 'Call no man thy father.'"

"Yes. Well, it's O.K. with me."

"I like your style, sir. You're not from around here, I'd guess."

"For many years I traveled out of Chicago," Father Urban said. "But I'm proud to call Minnesota my home now, Mr Studley."

This appeared to make little or no difference to Mr Studley, but then Father Urban hadn't been talking to him so much as to the others—and they'd liked it fine.

"I see you don't wear the collar, Mr Urban."

Father Urban could do without the "Father," but that didn't mean he'd take "Mister." Nothing was better than that. "Up in the car," he said slowly, "with my coat."

"How's Myra, Grover?" said the woman who'd brought the shortcake. Her husband had carried the strawberries, still in their boxes.

"Still in Cleveland," said Mr Studley, not paying much attention to the question. He was gazing up toward the cottage. "Say, I'd like to have a look at that," he said.

"The car? Why, yes," said Father Urban. Immediately, he moved off with Mr Studley and the dog, thinking he was doing everybody a favor.

After walking around the car a couple of times, and feeling it here and there, Mr Studley opened the door on the driver's side.

"Go ahead. Get in," said Father Urban. He knew how Mr Studley felt.

"Sure you don't mind?" said Mr Studley, getting in. He settled himself into the leather. "Gee, wish I had a chair like this."

Father Urban smiled. He knew what Mr Studley meant. The leather was very kind to a man.

"Oh, oh," said Mr Studley, looking at the dog. "Now *he* wants in."

Father Urban laughed.

"Would you mind?" said Mr Studley.

Father Urban looked at the dog. It really did want to get in, and so Father Urban removed his coat, rabat, and collar from the other seat.

"Sure you don't mind?" said Mr Studley, reaching over and opening the door for the dog.

"Not a-tall."

Wrong as they were for it, Mr Studley and the dog, whose name was Frank, looked right at home in the car. "What'd it cost you?" said Mr Studley.

"Oh, it's not mine. I'm just using it."

"Do you take a drink?" said Mr Studley.

"Sometimes."

"C'mon over to my place, and I'll make you a real drink. I'm right over here."

"Well, I don't know about that."

"C'mon. I'd like you to see my place," said Mr Studley, as though it were little enough to ask.

"Well, I might do that," said Father Urban. He was thinking he'd be doing everybody a bigger favor if he got Mr Studley back to his place. Probably there were others who wanted to have a look at the car, and perhaps talk to Father Urban, but wouldn't feel free to do so with Mr Studley around. They'd all more or less gone underground when he appeared among them.

"My place," said Mr Studley, when they came to it—a place much like the Zimmermans'—but they went on past it, down to the lake. "Here's what I wanted you to see," Mr Studley said, "and if you're the man I think you are, you won't laugh."

Father Urban didn't laugh when, after some difficulty, Mr Studley opened up a garage-like affair, opened it up to the sky, and said, "My plane."

Mr Studley's plane was a World War I four-winged machine, bright red, with a number of heraldic devices painted on it: dice which had come up seven; the ace of spades; the leg of a female, ending in a high-heeled shoe; and a mustachioed man in a high silk hat on the band of which appeared the words "SIR SATAN."

"You were in the First War?" Father Urban asked.

"I would've been if it'd lasted another month."

Father Urban, inspecting the plane's rear end, noted a Civil Defense sticker. "In working order?"

"It very soon could be."

"You'd push it down to the water—is that it?"

"That's right. Those are the floats you see over there."

"And you'd just attach those?"

"That's right. I know all about it."

"What's your business, Mr Studley?"

"I'm retired, unless, of course. . . ."

"Of course."

Mr Studley climbed into the front cockpit. He put on a helmet and lowered the goggles. "Seems a long time ago," he said. "C'mon up."

"No, that's all right."

"C'mon. I was in yours."

It took Father Urban a moment or two to understand what Mr Studley meant. "All right." When Father Urban started to get into the plane, though, the dog growled.

"Frank!" yelled Mr Studley, and Frank laid off.

Father Urban found another helmet-and-goggles in the rear cockpit, but he didn't put them on. They smelled strongly of Frank, as did the whole rear cockpit, and Father Urban very soon left it.

"Now you have to sign my guest book," said Mr Studley, when he touched down.

Father Urban, tempted to sign himself "Father," wrote "Rev." and hoped *that* was all right.

"Now I'll show you something," said Mr Studley. "Here, here, here," he said, pointing to other names in the guest book. "And over here. And here. All priests like yourself."

"You met them over at Zimmerman's?"

"Not all of 'em. Now how about that drink?"

"No, I don't think so. Thanks."

"Well, you don't mind if I have one, do you?"

"Not a-tall. Go right ahead. But *I* have to get back."

"I'll walk you back."

"No, that's all right. Hadn't you better close that?" The door of the hangar rolled up and back in such a way that the plane was exposed to the sky. "It *could* rain."

"Think so?" Mr Studley gazed up at the sky. "Oh hell, let it go. And I'll walk you back. I took you away from 'em, so I'll take you back to 'em. They all hate me. Even the women. Did anybody say anything?"

"No," said Father Urban.

When he arrived back at the chairs with Mr Studley ("Hell, what's wrong with sitting on the grass?"), conversation dropped off to practically nothing. Once again Mrs Zimmerman tried to bring Father Urban a tankard of Icy-ade (Mr Studley wasn't even approached on the subject), but this time Father Urban was firm with her, in a nice way. Then she brought him the guest book which, however, he didn't sign, since Mrs Zimmerman said, "Maybe you'd like to write more than just your name. Will you stay and eat?" Father Urban had thought eating was included in his invitation, but, seeing a chance to get his schedule back into a fluid state, which was how he preferred it, he said, "Well, I don't know about that." "There's plenty." "Well, we'll see, Mrs Zimmerman."

Despite the presence of Mr Studley, conversation was picking up, continuing, it seemed, on the same lines as earlier. It had to do with that morning's gospel.

The gospel had dealt with the steward who called his master's debtors together, and, writing off fifty barrels of oil here, and twenty quarters of wheat there, since he knew he'd soon be out of work and in need of friends, had, oddly enough, won the praise of his rich master. A difficult text, Luke XVI, 1–9, and for some years now, when the Sunday for it rolled around, Father Urban had read it, yes, but had cut back to I Paralipomenon in the Old Testament where you got substantially the same idea (the advisability of using our present situation as a preparation for our next one) in a much more acceptable form. Father Urban's sermon on the financing of the temple—"And they gave for the works of the house of the Lord: of gold, five thousand talents, and ten thousand solids: of silver, ten thousand talents: and of brass, eighteen thousand talents: and of iron, a hundred thousand talents," and so on—was one of his better jobs.

At first, listening to Mr Zimmerman and the other two men—to whom their wives were listening—Father Urban had thought they were talking about him and his sermon. They were not. Nobody, in fact, had mentioned Father Urban's sermon. The truth was Mr Zimmerman hadn't mentioned it when he issued the invitation to the picnic. There was now some doubt in Father Urban's mind that the one had led to the other. Mr Zimmerman, like many before him, was worried about Luke XVI, 1–9.

"Say you're a rich man," he said to the man whose wife had brought the potato salad, "and I'm just somebody that works for you at the lumberyard, but I'm in your bookkeeping department, and I go around to various people that owe you and your firm money and I discount this bill so much and that one so much—I don't get it."

"Our Lord," said Father Urban, "isn't commending the steward for cooking the books, or even condoning this. You'll note this man is called 'the unjust steward.'"

"Yes, I know. . . ." said Mr Zimmerman, but he still didn't like it.

"And I think you'll find 'unjust' means 'inaccurate,'" said Mr Studley. "There's a difference, you know."

"Well, I don't know about *that*," said Father Urban. "I know there's a difference, yes." Where they were now, Father Urban didn't know. Mr Studley not only made it seem that he and Father Urban were together but that he, Mr Studley, was, of the two of them, the sounder man.

Mr Studley yanked up a nice handful of Mr Zimmerman's grass and threw it away. "Look at it the right way or not at all," he said. "You people are always looking at things from your own view point. You'll *never* get it that way, I can tell you. Look at it from the *employee's* view point. Christ was always on the side of the employee—the little guy. That's what Christianity *means*. That's what all your great religions mean. That's why we fought two major wars. Ask *him*," said Mr Studley, referring to Father Urban.

But before Father Urban could clarify Mr Studley's thought,

he had to clarify his own, and before he was able to do this, Mr Studley was on again, pulling grass. "Zim, if this rich man could look at it like that, why can't you? It's not costing *you*." And with that, Mr Studley lay back on the grass and shut his eyes. "O.K., Zim," he said, when Mr Zimmerman started to say something. Mr Zimmerman started again.

"If somebody in bookkeeping tried something like that on me, I'd prosecute. I'd have to—or set a bad example. See what I mean? *That's* my point," he said, looking to his two friends for support.

"I'll grant it's a difficult text," said Father Urban. "But rightly understood. . . ." he said, and let it go at that. Father Urban had some ideas of his own about this text. Our Lord, in Father Urban's opinion, had been dealing with some pretty rough customers out there in the Middle East, the kind of people who wouldn't have been at all distressed by the steward's conduct —either that or people had been a whole lot brighter in biblical times, able to grasp a distinction then. It had even entered Father Urban's mind that Our Lord, who, after all, knew what people were like, may have been a little tired on the day he spoke this parable. Sometimes, too, when you were trying to get through to a cold congregation, it was a case of any port in a storm. You'd say things that wouldn't stand up very well in print.

The man whose wife had brought the shortcake said, "Father Tom just skips it. 'Every year,' he says, 'I come to it and I just skip it. It does more harm than good,' he says. 'So I just skip it.' "

"Who's Father Tom?" said Father Urban.

"I think I've met him," said Mr Studley, from his prone position.

"Our pastor. He just skips it," said Mr Shortcake.

"What about the fella that's going along with the other fella?" said Mr Zimmerman. "He's just as bad as the other fella."

"Too bad Father Prosperus isn't here. He'd be able to tell us a thing or two, I'll bet." This from Mrs Potato Salad.

"I guess he could at that," said Mrs Zimmerman.

"Who's Father Prosperus?" said Father Urban.

"Our son," said Mrs Zimmerman.

"Your son's a priest?"

"Yes, he's a Dolomite father," said Mrs Zimmerman.

"At St Ludwig's?"

"No, at St Hedwig's. He's chaplain there."

That did it for Father Urban. There hadn't been much reason before to hope that Mr Zimmerman would make a benefactor for the Order of St Clement. Now there was none.

Mr Studley suddenly sat up and said, "C'mon over to my place, and I'll make you a real drink."

"No, thanks," said Father Urban. "But I don't mind if you have one."

"Maybe later," said Mr Studley, and lay down again, this time with a piece of his stomach showing.

All around Father Urban the discussion went on.

"Well now. . . ." he said, trying, in a nice way, to end it, but nobody—nobody, with the possible exception of Mr Studley—was listening to him. Mrs Zimmerman was thoroughly involved now. Employed by Mr Zimmerman for many years as a stewardess, and hearing that she was soon to be let go, she had written off fifty per cent of a debt owing to her master, a matter of fifty barrels, and naturally he was sore about it, and the party Mrs Zimmerman had accommodated—Mrs Shortcake—was also sore, saying *nothing* about her part in the deal. Others were in similar difficulties.

"I say. . . ." said Father Urban, but nobody, unless Mr Studley, heard him. Father Urban glanced at the sky and signed the guest book with a flourish—just signed it. Then there was a tremendous clap of thunder, and the sky, which had been looking more and more like slate, shook, and the wind ran through the oaks, whipping up the green-grey backsides of leaves, and a dozen large raindrops hit the top of the picnic table all at the same time.

Mr Zimmerman ran to the picnic table for his scrapbook in which the carbon copies had been placed for safekeeping, fortunately. Mr Studley rose up in alarm and was last seen running down the beach, heading for his place. And Father Urban—crying, "I'd love to stay, but really I can't," to Mrs Zimmerman and the other women, who, of course, had run for the food on the picnic table—ran to the little Barracuda and raised its little fawn roof. But first he got rid of Frank, who had been sitting on his coat.

Halfway to Ostergothenburg, the rain let up, and then it stopped entirely. On the other side of town, on the highway leading home to the Hill, the Mellon came up behind the little Barracuda at the last stoplight and nudged it. There were girls in the Mellon now, Father Urban saw, and he also saw, as he hadn't before, that the Mellon had no lower teeth—just a dark gap there.

"Drag?" said the driver, in whose face there was a hint of human intelligence, as there is in a shark's.

Father Urban made no reply.

The light changed to green and the Mellon came abreast. *"Chicken!"*

This time Father Urban, though he said nothing, and gave no sign, accepted the challenge. He was ten lengths behind when he made his decision, but slowly and surely, he gained on the Mellon, drew even with it, and still the little Barracuda was full of run. Then he let it all the way out, and shot ahead. Something was happening to the Mellon. Coughing and sneezing and emitting blue smoke, it was pulling over to the side of the road. Father Urban had been winning before this, however, and would've won had the race continued, and, in fact, he had won. The Mellon, though, was about the only thing he'd been able to handle in that diocese. The Mellon, and the guest book at the Zimmermans', which, finally, when nobody would listen to him, he'd signed with a flourish, "Pope John XXIII."

11

Wrens and Starlings

When the history of the Order in the United States came to be written, and Father Urban must have been about the only Clementine who was looking that far ahead and thinking along those lines, would what was now St Clement's Hill go down as one more spot where the good seed of its zeal had fallen and flourished, or as another where the Order had lost out? That was the question in Father Urban's mind, in August, when the Bishop returned from Rome. According to Monsignor Renton, the Bishop was thinking of taking over the Hill for a diocesan seminary. "You guys were all right until you went and built this course," said Monsignor Renton—brown as a berry from playing it.

Over hill and dale, on tee and green, Father Urban pumped the trusty consultor, but although Monsignor Renton talked freely, he couldn't tell Father Urban when or how the Bishop would move against the Clementines—only why. "He's always wanting something." Dear James had wanted one man's choir director, another man's sanctuary lamp, and so on, and what he wanted he got. It had been going on for years. He had seen some wormy statues in London, fingers and whole arms missing, and Monsignor Renton, traveling with him, had done his best to talk him out of these costly purchases, but they were now standing in the Cathedral.

But could the Bishop do such a thing? He could. The Clementines had had it done to them before, most recently at Bolivar Springs, Missouri, where they'd run a minor seminary and boys' boarding school, an indifferent enterprise economically and scholastically, and where the local bishop had wanted first one of his men on the faculty, then two, to which demands the Clementines had gracefully acceded, and thus passed the point of no return. As soon as the Bishop had educated enough men (elsewhere) to operate the institution, the Clementines had been eased out altogether and paid off. To an outsider it might have appeared that this was all to the good—and thus, had the Clementines complained, it would have been made to appear to Rome. Nuns could coo their way out of such difficulties, or, that failing, would often fight, and sometimes cardinals would ride forth in their behalf. But it was almost impossible for a small, unentrenched order of men (whose record might have been better) to defend itself against a bishop and his hordes. What could wrens do against starlings?

"You have to have strong grounds for effecting a transfer of ownership such as the Bishop is contemplating," said Father Urban. He had been making the best of the poor library at the Hill, reading up on the subject of contracts between bishops and religious. "Canon law is quite clear about such things."

"Indeed it is—about any number of things," said Monsignor Renton, in a way that made Father Urban think.

Next year—if there was one—there would have to be a well-defined, enforceable policy on who was entitled to play the course. *Who?* Any man who'd made a retreat at the Hill? His wife? His wife's brother? And *his* wife? What about teenagers with, just possibly, vocations to the priesthood? What about women in shorts? What about ministers of rival faiths? Where did you draw the line? Father Urban didn't know. But sooner or later there would be a scandal of some kind—there were indications that lovers were coming to the course after dark—and voices would be raised against the Clementines.

That wasn't all. A woman in shorts had tittered when the Bishop, teeing off on his first visit to the course, had swung and missed the ball completely. And this after the Bishop had noticed that the new black-and-white sign painted by Brother Harold had been desecrated. The sign had to do with rules of play and was addressed "TO THE FRIENDS AND MEMBERS OF THE ORDER OF SAINT CLEMENT." The "R" had been scratched out of "FRIENDS." That was the public for you.

For some the perfect solution would be to close the course to everybody except the clergy. But Father Urban felt about the course as "a certain eccentric pastor" was said (in one of Father Urban's amusing yet hard-hitting talks to priests) to feel about the Church—that it should exist for the *people's* benefit, too.

Monsignor Renton held that the Bishop was no different from anyone else in wanting his own seminary—"Half the fun for the big frog is having the little ones around him"—but Father Urban wondered if a thing like a woman's laugh might not be at the bottom of the man's desire to seize St Clement's Hill.

In his discussions with Monsignor Renton, Father Urban sometimes clutched at straws. "As I understand it, a bishop needs the consent of his consultors, where this much is at stake. If things get rough, a thousand lire won't even pay for the aspirins," he said, remembering this key figure from his reading. Anything over a thousand lire was considered a big deal.

"I can't recall when we've withheld our consent," said Monsignor Renton. "I don't say we wouldn't, mind you, if our consciences so dictated."

"That's sort of what I had in mind."

"Yes, but suppose one consultor's against something a bishop wants to do, but he knows the other consultors aren't—he knows he's going to be outvoted. In the circumstances, it might not be wise for this consultor to expose himself, nor should he be expected to do so."

"I suppose it would be asking a lot—of this consultor."

"I'm sorry to hear you take that tone," Monsignor Renton said. "I'm doing all I can, within reason, and I'm prepared to go on doing so. In my opinion, you guys have done a pretty fair job here, on the whole."

"Nice of you to say so," said Father Urban, thinking that the course was a godsend to Monsignor Renton, who had let his membership in the Great Plains Country Club expire.

"I can't say better than that, everything considered."

"I know," said Father Urban. The last months didn't quite make up for the time before he arrived at the Hill.

"Here's something that occurred to me," Monsignor Renton said. "I don't know why I haven't mentioned it before. Let's say this place *does* become a diocesan seminary—well, why shouldn't you guys be the ones to run it, or at least staff it? On a thing like that, I'd go down the line for you, and I don't think I'd be alone."

"Whose side are you on, anyway?" asked Father Urban, and then described what had happened to the Clementines at Bolivar Springs.

"Circumstances alter cases," Monsignor Renton said. "It doesn't necessarily follow that you'd get the heave-ho in a few years, or that you couldn't go on giving retreats here."

"Nothing doing—if I have my way." There were moments, though, when Father Urban wished he weren't fighting alone, but no good, he knew, would come from alerting Wilf to the danger—Wilf would just go to pieces. As long as the Bishop didn't declare his intention, Father Urban saw no reason to turn the matter over to less capable hands.

"I advise you to think it over," Monsignor Renton said. "Sometimes, you know, you can't win. Or so I have found."

"Thank God, there's always Rome."

"Rome!" cried Monsignor Renton. "Let's keep Rome out of it. While you're appealing to Rome, how many retreatants do you suppose you'll get from *this* diocese? And what'll happen to all *this?*" The course was lovely in August.

All other remedies should have failed before one resorted to Rome, where, said Monsignor Renton, a judgment might not be rendered until all the principals were safely on the wrong side of the grass. Of such was the wisdom, the terrible wisdom, of the Church. Therefore, one's thoughts inclined not to litigation but to peaceful persuasion. Or should. "It's the only thing," said Monsignor Renton.

"I hadn't thought of *that,*" said Father Urban.

But they had entirely different ideas as to who should be persuaded, and Monsignor Renton was fearful lest Father Urban jump the gun or otherwise betray him to the Bishop. "Watch it," he said, "if you don't want me to lose my job. As it is now, I may be the best club in your bag."

"Let's hope not," said Father Urban. He had little faith in peaceful persuasion as a weapon against the Bishop. Nevertheless, it was one that appealed to him, as it would to anyone with his special gifts.

Father Urban was frankly proud of the little improvements he'd made in the clubhouse since the Bishop's other visit—candy counter, pop machine, pro shop—proud, yes, but far from satisfied. The clubhouse—Mr Hanson's old house—was badly in need of paint. "Green," Father Urban said as he walked to the first tee with the Bishop and Father Feld, the Bishop's

young friend. "I think it should be dark green, with white trim
—unless we get some shutters for the windows, and then it
would be the other way around."

"Wouldn't it be better if you just stuck to white?" said Father Feld. "Easier and cheaper?"

"Dark green," said the Bishop.

"You don't know how glad I am to hear you say that," said
Father Urban, glad that the Bishop agreed with him, glad also
that Father Feld had been cut down. "The farmers around here
seem to have a fixation on the color white. Sometimes when I
look at this old place now, I think I can see dirty white chickens
moving around in the yard. Hard to believe they're not there."

Father Feld, who had a square head, wore a puzzled look,
and the Bishop was not appreciative. Great Plains, after all,
was a rural diocese, and so the Bishop made a point of being
for everything rural—hence the public prayers all summer long
for whatever it was he was told that the farmers wanted in the
way of weather.

"And I'd like to move the front porch away from that dusty
road, around to this side," Father Urban went on, "so our guests
could enjoy a view of the fairways."

"Could you see the lake then?" the Bishop asked.

"You'd catch a glimpse of it, Your Excellency, through the
trees."

The Bishop nodded.

"And, of course, we'll have to put in toilet facilities downstairs," Father Urban said.

"Oh, I don't know," said the Bishop.

"No?"

"Worried about mixed company, aren't you, Father?"

"There's more to it than that." Father Urban was suddenly
at a loss to define his position. To him there was something oddly
disquieting about people—strangers—traipsing upstairs to the

bathroom in the clubhouse. "I guess I was just thinking it
would be a great improvement. That's all. Of course, there's
no *harm* in the way it is now."

"Oh, I understand that, Father, but I was just wondering if
maybe you aren't making things too easy here for *everybody*."

"There'll be some changes here next year, Your Excellency,"
said Father Urban. Himself he had already given up playing
for money, even though what he'd won (always from laymen
well able to lose), every dollar of it, had gone toward the up-
keep of the course.

"Everybody except yourself, that is," said the Bishop.

Father Urban hadn't realized that the Bishop could throw
such a punch. It may have been a little low, too. The Bishop
had made it sound as though Father Urban were advocating lay
investiture. In the ensuing void, Father Urban endeavored to
calm himself. Now he knew what he was up against—puritanism *and* black clericalism.

He hadn't wanted to see the Bishop anywhere near the course
again—not after the last time. But the Bishop had wanted to
come, calling the night before to say that he'd be driving over
with a young friend, and that he might want to snoop around
a bit, too, after playing nine. Father Urban, alarmed, had phoned
the Cathedral. "It figures," Monsignor Renton had said. "His
young friend will be Herman Feld, I imagine. They've been
playing together over here." According to Monsignor Renton,
Father Feld would be just the man to head a seminary. "He's
been over in Europe for three or four years. Louvain. He's
fit for nothing else, now."

If there was to be an ultimatum that day, Father Urban prayed
that it would not be delivered on the golf course, for peaceful
persuasion would be all but impossible there, in the heat of
play. Probably the Bishop would want Wilf, as rector, to be
present for anything like that, and Wilf would be in his office,

where he liked to be discovered hard at work. Somewhere along
the line, though, as they were beating their way around the
course, Father Urban expected to be able to tell whether the
ultimatum was to come.

On the first tee, waiting with the clubs, were three novices
who had been instructed in the niceties of caddying for a prelate.
For one thing, the Bishop would shoot first off the tee unless
he insisted that low man go first—as he certainly hadn't the
last time. The other players would follow always in the same
order, and thus the Bishop would be shown respect in which
there would be no connotation of ineptitude on his part, or un-
due hoggishness. It was the Bishop's ball, therefore, that was
already teed up.

Father Urban was surprised to see that the Bishop, taking a
few practice cuts, was no longer trying to kill the ball. Evidently
Father Feld had been working on the Bishop's swing, tailoring
it to his manifest deficiencies as an athlete. The Bishop had
invested in new clubs, but he obviously hadn't made up his
mind about dressing for the game. He was wearing black ox-
fords to which crepe soles had been applied, black summer-
weight serge trousers, a white dress shirt with its sleeves rolled
up almost to his elbows and with its collar folded down under
—you didn't see that much any more—and an old straw katy.

"Nice one," said Father Urban. The Bishop's drive had gone
up like a balloon and had come down not more than a hundred
and thirty yards out, but it had gone right down the middle
—practically an episcopal pronouncement.

Father Feld went next. He was wearing army-surplus clothing and golf shoes, and he was black from the sun, like Father
Urban. His body was short and bullish, and he was younger
than Father Urban by twenty years. Oh, twenty-five. His clubs
had been used a lot, and they were good ones. He took no
practice swing, so there was no telling about him until he laid

into the ball. His drive stopped rolling about two hundred and fifty yards out.

"Good enough," said Father Urban. He teed up his ball, thinking that he'd somehow have to outplay Father Feld. He removed his stained and floppy panama and waved away some gnats that had suddenly appeared over his ball. He cautioned himself not to try to outdrive the Bishop's young friend. Then he threw his body—medium tall and willowy except for a slight pot—into his foreswing and hit a good long ball that dropped about where he'd hoped it would and kicked, accordingly, to the left. He was short of Father Feld, but in a better position to see the green.

Neither the Bishop nor Father Feld commented on the shot.

The threesome moved off down the fairway, followed by their caddies, nobody talking, until Father Urban said, "Get any golf over there?"

"Some," said Father Feld.

Coming to the Bishop's ball, and seeing that the lie was only fair, Father Urban said, "Winter rules, if you like, Your Excellency. I'm not happy about these fairways yet."

The Bishop shrugged off the suggestion, and, presumably, although he had two hundred yards ahead of him, didn't want to use a wood, anyway. Father Feld was handing the Bishop not a two but a five iron. The Bishop hit the ball cleanly for a distance of about ninety yards and appeared to be well satisfied.

Father Feld went over the green on his second shot, though not into a trap. Father Urban put his second one on the green—only just, but he wanted to putt uphill. The Bishop hit another five iron and was still short. Using the same club, he was finally on. The Feld system seemed to call for the Bishop to use only a spoon, mashie, and putter. Father Urban would have been reluctant to suggest such measures to such a man, but he had to admit that the Bishop's game had improved through simplification, unless he was playing over his head.

Father Feld ran his third shot past the cup. The Bishop moaned. Father Urban and the Bishop both missed long putts. Then Father Feld, who had left himself a twenty-footer, got lucky. "That's more like it, Herman," said the Bishop.

After he'd holed out, the Bishop said, "In the circumstances, I think I'd better be scorekeeper." He was given custody of the pencil and card. "Father Urban?" he asked, after jotting down his own score.

"Four, Your Excellency."

"And four for Herman. Well!"

It was now clear to Father Urban that this was not to be just another round of golf, that the Bishop wished to see done what he could not do himself, and that he had chosen young Father Feld to be the weapon of his will, his champion. Father Urban's defeat was not a necessary part of the Bishop's larger plan of conquest, but Father Urban could understand its appeal—to create an omen, as it were, and then to act in accord with it. In Father Urban's mind, informed as it was by a good deal of solid reading, the match between him and Father Feld took on the appearance of a judicial duel. Victory for Father Urban in the field, however, would not mean victory for his cause. That was the hell of it. Father Urban had read of many ordeals by combat (in the dim past even religious men, unfortunately, had sometimes appealed to the God of Battles for justice), but he doubted that history would reveal a parallel case. He pushed on, with his driver drawn, to the second tee.

Here, if he had come upon a crone crying, "Woe! Woe!", he would not have been more taken aback than he was to see the Reverend Doctor Percy, Hillsop Memorial Presbyterian Church, Minneapolis, who, with his wife, had been staying for some time with friends at a near-by lake. At the request of a mutual acquaintance, a benefactor in a small way, the minister and his wife had been invited out to the course by Father Urban. That was how these things happened. For two weeks now, the Percys had been coming out regularly—she, large, soft, playing with clubs out of his bag, which he pulled on a cart, and he, small but limber for his years, going over fences to retrieve their balls. Doctor Percy seemed to regard it as a test of faith to go on searching for lost balls. Father Urban had told him what he could about golf-course management, before he discovered what the minister had in mind. Doctor Percy assumed that another course, run under Christian auspices, would make the world a better place, and that Father Urban would be all for it. Father Urban had been under the impression that he'd said good-by to Doctor Percy.

"I thought we'd have to go back home if I was *ever* to get those sermons written, Father," said Doctor Percy. "But I find I'm able to think here, after all. That's so seldom happened before, away from my study. Mrs P. and I are simply delighted. She's not feeling well today, however."

"Sorry to hear it," said Father Urban.

Doctor Percy offered to let Father Urban and his party shoot through.

"No, you go right ahead," Father Urban said firmly. He was wishing that the little man would hit his ball well into outer space and be sucked after it. But he topped it.

"Tough," said Father Urban, with feeling.

The Bishop, however, appeared to be gratified by what he'd seen. "Father," he said, "why don't you ask your friend to join us?"

News of the struggle had reached the novices in residence at the Hill, and after the third hole there was a small gallery following the play, creating another problem for Father Urban.

Through his caddy, Father Urban sent word to the gallery that he didn't want a repetition of what happened on the third and fourth holes. On those, the Bishop was attended only by his caddy and Doctor Percy only by his cart. Afterward, the novices began rotating nicely, three or four of them accompanying the Bishop and Doctor Percy at all times, in fairway, field, and stream.

Father Urban had birdied the second hole and won it. On the third green, though, he had missed a five-footer. No. 4 had been the same thing again, only worse, with Father Urban blowing a putt that should have been conceded to him and would have been if the Bishop hadn't overruled Father Feld. On the fifth, a dogleg to the left, Father Urban deliberately hooked his drive, but a gust of wind took it into the woods. Father Feld, in trouble, too, on that hole, recovered brilliantly. Coming to No. 6 tee, Father Urban was two down.

As he saw it, he now had a choice of playing his regular game, hoping that Father Feld, whose irons weren't reliable, and whose powerful drives might suddenly go haywire, would present him with the match. Or he could turn it on—and risk the consequences. This was exactly what Father Urban would have advised somebody else in his position not to do. This, though, he decided to do. He couldn't afford to wait. There just weren't enough holes left.

For the next forty minutes Father Urban, inspired by the gallery, preached a great sermon in golf. In the novices, he saw himself as he had been at the start of his career, and remembered Father Placidus. One of Father Urban's greenest memories was of the great man at games. *Be a winner! Never say die!* These words would ring out from the sidelines, and that day, forty years later, they were still ringing out for one man. *Be a winner!* That was why, for the next three holes, Father Urban's tee shots went off like rifle fire, his approaches soared and dropped like swallows—why even the brass putter turned deadly in his hands.

All this time, the Bishop and Doctor Percy were locked in mortal combat. They halved hole after hole with their sixes, sevens, and eights. Father Urban had never seen anything like it. Doctor Percy appeared to realize that the Bishop dearly wished to do unto him as he dearly wished Father Feld to do unto Father Urban, and boldly the little minister countered the Bishop's praise for his young champion with some of his own for Father Urban. As the matches waxed hotter and the Bishop grew more and more partisan in his looks, language, and gestures, Father Urban found that he was glad to have the plucky little Presbyterian as an ally, and did not deny him words of encouragement and professional advice.

No. 7 decided the match between the duffers. They drove to within a few feet of each other, the Bishop having the better of it. Doctor Percy then put his second shot up into a dense box-elder tree that stood by the green. After knocking around in the foliage for a while, Doctor Percy's ball dropped nicely down onto a corner of the green. The Bishop then drove his ball up into the box-elder tree, and there it stayed. Sticks and stones from the rough were tossed up into the tree, Father Urban directing these exercises. The Bishop, standing off by himself, was approached by novices who doubtless saw this as their opportunity to make His Excellency's acquaintance. Yes, it was certainly odd, the Bishop agreed, and granted them that the ball could be stuck between two branches, and that it could be nesting in a hollow of some kind. When other novices drew near and advanced these same theories, he showed signs of impatience, and did not respond at all when it was suggested to him that a bird or a squirrel had seized upon his ball, mistaking it for an egg or a nut. ("All right, fellas," called Father Urban.) Two novices offered to go up into the tree, which looked un-

climbable, and Father Urban didn't care to discourage them in
the circumstances. When the Bishop saw what they were about,
however, he ordered them down. He then went to his bag and
threw out another ball. But the heart had gone out of him and
his game. He was strangely quiet on the greens. Doctor Percy
went ahead in his match. Coming to the ninth tee, the Bishop
was down two, beaten, and Father Feld was one down.

"If I tie it up, what do we do?" asked Father Feld. "Maybe
we should decide that now."

"Whatever you say," said Father Urban.

"The Bishop wants it to be a sudden-death play-off. He's
tired."

"Sudden death it is, then," Father Urban said, and slipped
over to say a few words to the gallery. He was afraid of a
celebration on the ninth green. "Remember, fellas. No matter
what happens, these people are our guests." He thought of asking the novices to cut down on the applause for him, which was
increasing, but he let it pass. "The guests of the Order," he said,
and wondered if perhaps there hadn't been someone like him,
some elder tribesman hoping for the best, who had spoken thus
to the young braves gathered on the shore a few minutes before the white men landed four hundred years ago.

No. 9, three hundred eighty-five yards, par four, was called
"The Volcano" on the score card. The fairway ran gently
downhill until interrupted by a broad, shallow creek, once the
joy of cattle, and then it ran uphill, for a while gently, then
very steeply, to the green. The creek severed the fairway diagonally, so there were three ways to play the hole. If one
crossed the creek at its nearest point, the hole could be a
dogleg to the left; or it could be a dogleg to the right, if the
second shot was the one over water; but the best way was to

play the hole straight, and to hit a drive that traveled no less than two hundred yards on the fly.

The Bishop and Doctor Percy chose to cross the creek at its nearest point, and both made it to the other side on their drives. Father Feld then took the direct route, and got one of his better tee shots of the day. Finally, Father Urban stepped up, removed his panama, put it back on, assumed his stance —he had twice been mistaken, in years past, for Tommy Armour—and shot. *Bang!* Just nothing for a while and then, in the distance, a jiggling, and then a tiny white hole in the green fairway that hadn't been there before. Then jubilation among the novices. Their grey champion had outdriven Father Feld!

Father Urban handed back his driver for what he hoped would be the last time that day, and called for his seven iron. Then he tried to join the Bishop, who seemed to be in a hurry to have it over. "Be a bridge here next year," Father Urban said, crossing the creek behind the Bishop, on steppingstones. "Maybe just old telephone poles," he added, but he got no response from the Bishop.

Across the creek, the company split up, the Bishop and Doctor Percy going off together—they would be approaching the green from the right—and Father Urban and Father Feld going straight up the hill, followed by everybody else. Once again the Bishop was alone with his caddy, but that, Father Urban believed, was how the Bishop wished it now.

Father Urban watched Father Feld mis-hit his second shot, saw it punch at the rim of the volcano, and roll back down ten yards—into a bad lie, Father Urban would have bet. Father Urban then went on ahead to his own ball, thinking that No. 9 was one of those holes that revealed how much more there was to golf then being able to give the ball a ride. Father Feld's irons had found him out. He was in trouble now.

From where Father Urban took his second shot, it was still

impossible to see the flag, but he knew where the green was, and where the hole was on the green. He swung, taking up a little turf. From what he felt, and then saw, of the shot, there wouldn't be much wrong with it, he thought. Confidently, he called for his putter and continued the ascent to the green, drawing the gallery of novices after him. When they saw where Father Urban's ball lay, they murmured and moved back to the rim of the volcano so as to be in position to see Father Feld hit his next one—on which probably everything, if he had a chance at all, would depend.

Father Urban had kept going toward his ball. It was eight feet away from the cup, and back of it at that. "Close?" he asked Brother Harold, who had come down from the clubhouse in time to hold the pin.

"Well, I was afraid to leave the flag in," said Brother Harold.

"Close enough," said Father Urban, taking off his hat. He saw Monsignor Renton emerge from the clubhouse and waved, watching just that portion of the sky where he expected Father Feld's ball to come into view, and failing to see the ball that came from the right and hit him on the head.

12

God Writes . . .

Father Urban was taken unconscious to the hospital in Great Plains where he was anointed by the chaplain, X-rayed and heavily bandaged about the head by doctors, and put to bed. He regained consciousness during the night. By that time those who could have told him more of what had happened had gone home. All he could find out from the sisters was that he'd been struck in the head by a golf ball. In the morning, his speech was almost normal, and he discovered that he was in the Bishop's suite.

That afternoon, he was permitted to have visitors—Wilf and Brother Harold, Monsignor Renton—but was forbidden to talk to them. Since his head was bandaged down over his eyes, his visitors tended to ignore him after the first few minutes.

However, he learned that it had been the Bishop's ball, and that the Bishop no longer proposed to take over the Hill for a seminary. The Bishop was trying to create the impression that he wasn't entirely influenced by this unfortunate but unavoidable accident, but what else, asked Monsignor Renton, could have made him change his mind? "An act of God, if ever I saw one."

Father Urban regarded this statement as unsound and probably heretical in its implications, since it made short work of him as a responsible instrument of God's will in an orderly universe. Father Urban doubted, however, that he, given the chance, could have wrought the great change that had come about through the wayward action of the Bishop's ball.

"Actually," said Monsignor Renton, "I *didn't* see it. I thought somebody'd opened a bottle of champagne."

"Be that as it may," said Wilf. He was amazed to hear what had been going on right under his nose, and wondered why he hadn't been told.

Thereafter, what could have been an occasion of rejoicing was marred by pettiness. Wilf seemed to think that Father Urban had gone over his head and that anything was preferable to that, and Monsignor Renton seemed to say that what had happened on the ninth green was pretty much what he'd had in mind all along, and that Father Urban, if it had been left to him, would have queered everything by using less peaceful methods of persuasion on the Bishop.

"They're saying he should've kept his hat on, but that's where they're wrong—if you follow me."

"Yes—if what you say is true, Monsignor."

"It's true all right. You guys don't have a thing to worry about now. Just keep your nose clean. I see he's sent flowers."

"What I can't understand, Monsignor, is why Father, here, didn't tell *me*."

"Probably he didn't want you to be worried—needlessly."

"But that's part of my job."

"How's the hay fever, Brother?"

"Better, thanks, Monsignor. I've been getting these new shots."

"Grateful as I am to Father, here, I don't think he should've taken it all on himself."

"I had the misfortune to be looking somewhere else, and I

thought somebody'd opened a bottle of champagne. The chances are it didn't sound like that to him."

"Since I've been getting these new shots, Monsignor, I ran across an article that claims it's all in your head—like seasickness."

"I wouldn't doubt it. It's quite possible he heard nothing at all. We'll have to ask him when he feels more like talking. I'd be interested to know."

"I *know* I've been a lot better since I've been getting these new shots."

"I still think *I* should've been told."

"Frankly, *I* didn't see any way out for you guys."

And Father Urban, lying there, listening with the ears of one blind, wondered greatly at the ways of men.

But when the Bishop himself dropped in and expressed hopes for Father Urban's speedy recovery, and complimented him on his play in the match with Father Feld, the earlier visitors, too, paid tribute to the patient.

"He's one in a million," said Monsignor Renton.

"One of our best men," said Wilf.

"A dazzling performance," said the Bishop, repeating himself.

Father Urban smiled mushily and broke his silence. "Up to a *ploint*," he said.

After three days in the hospital, *it* was all he was really suffering from. His big bandage was gone, the lump on his head was almost gone, and he was feeling fine except for occasional headaches. Plenty of visitors. Two days later, he was released from the hospital but was under orders to take things easy for a while (his headaches still came and went), and so, rather than return to the Hill and perhaps accomplish nothing under such a restriction there, he sought and got Wilf's permission to move out to Lake Lucille. The accident had been kept out of the papers, but Mrs Thwaites had heard of it from her doctor (who was also the Bishop's doctor and therefore Father Urban's), and she had invited Father Urban to convalesce at her home. Katie called for him in Mrs Thwaites's car—a Packard, old but not old enough, one of those postwar models that always made Father Urban ask himself, Who killed Packard?

The house looked and felt better to him in August, and his room faced the lake. Lots of peace and quiet and no outboard motors, for Mrs. Thwaites owned all the land around the lake. In the morning, Katie drove him to town, to the Cathedral, where he said Mass, and then she drove him back to the house. He spent most of the day in his room, in a Morris chair, in the company of the great historians from the library downstairs, but sometimes he could be seen moving slowly about the grounds, under the great oaks, reading his office, and wearing his cassock—he had decided against slopping around in slacks while there. Once he saw Mrs Thwaites watching him from one of her windows, and tried to get a squirrel to take a green acorn out of his hand, but it wouldn't, nor would a dove. In the afternoon, he had tea with Mrs Thwaites in her room, with the sets on. On the first day of his stay, they got on the elevator, and she showed him her bomb shelter, which was well stocked with food and water, games and reading matter, walls and ceiling done in soft pastel colors approved by psychiatrists, and plenty of closet space.

For the next three days, though, he didn't see Mrs Thwaites except at tea, with the sets on. Mrs Thwaites still preferred television to anything else, it seemed, unless it was dominoes with Katie. (Father Urban wasn't asked to play.) They never met at table, but ate all their meals (just so-so) in their rooms, off trays delivered by Katie or by an old woman who said she worked for Mrs Thwaites in the summertime, "when she entertains more." This, though Mrs Thwaites did have some card-playing friends, seemed to mean visits from her daughter Sally and Sally's husband. Dickie, who had wound up his affairs in Ostergothenburg, was living and working at home again but was away just then. His little Porsche wasn't in the coach house, where Father Urban looked for it, and saw a red pony cart, an electric car (on blocks), and a square piano, much like the one his mother had played.

And then the weather warmed up, got hot, in fact, and stayed hot for about a week. Earlier in the season, Father Urban had experienced the heat of summer in Minnesota, but this was worse, like August in Indianapolis or St Louis. At night, tiny bugs that no screen could stop, and large moths that came from nowhere, interfered with his reading. He saw more of Mrs Thwaites during this hot period. There were late-afternoon cruises on "Tilly," the launch, an ancient but sound craft with a faded brown-and-white striped canopy. Mrs Thwaites, in her wheelchair, gazed out at the path of bubbles in the water, and Father Urban stood, or sat, beside her, and Katie, at the helm, kept within easy reach of the shore ("In case of a storm," Mrs Thwaites said). Once around the lake, which was shaped like an egg, and flecked with islands and reef-like rocks, was always enough for the old lady, and took about an hour. They talked against the soft music of the launch's motor—talked mostly of Mrs Thwaites's family.

On the first of these excursions, the old lady spoke (as she hadn't before in Father Urban's presence) of her dead husband. Where was Andrew spending eternity? "Pray for him, ma'am." Andrew had been a great enemy of the Church, like St Paul, but there had been no road to Damascus for Andrew. "Pray for him, ma'am—and I'll do the same." The old lady was also worried about Dickie. Was it well for the boy to be out in the world? "There's much good to be done in the world, ma'am." But wouldn't he be better off in a cloister, a boy like him? "Not necessarily, ma'am. By the way, I had a note from Father Excelsior today. He sends his best. Where is Dickie now, by the way?" The old lady looked unhappy and said that Dickie was away. Away. That was all Mrs Thwaites would say.

This was unfortunate for Father Excelsior who firmly believed that editor and publisher should work together and try to understand each other's problems. One of Father Excelsior's problems was getting out a prospectus for, and not knowing what to expect from, Eight Seasons Editions (under which imprint certain titles of the Millstone Press would be issued, so *Publishers' Weekly* had reported back in May). There had been a certain amount of correspondence between publisher and editor since May, but lately this had ceased on the latter end, and now, far call from the ideal, publisher couldn't even *find* editor. Publisher had last heard from editor in July, and enclosed a copy of the communication received then, a communication to the effect that Father John had agreed, under terms to be arranged later, to prepare a *scholarly* children's edition of *Le Morte d'Arthur*, by Sir Thomas Malory. That was *all* Father Excelsior knew. Could Father Urban help him? No, it seemed not. Dickie was just away.

There was a tower on one of the little islands they passed on their cruises, a battlemented tower of rough red granite, one wall of which, windowless, with iron rungs set into it, and a diving board at the top, rose out of deep water like a cliff. "Sally's castle," Mrs Thwaites said the first time Father Urban saw it. "Andrew had it built for her when she was twelve." The word cut over the door of the tower, "Belleisle," probably came from some romantic tale, Mrs Thwaites said. Sally had been a great reader. Mrs Thwaites, wife and mother, worried a great deal about Andrew and Dickie, but not as she did about Sally and herself.

Father Urban, listening as to a royal complaint, had a vision of life in late medieval times, when nothing and nobody was for sure, when kings and prelates were selling out right and left. They were on a Highland loch, the old queen with her blow-ball of white hair, the rosy-cheeked Irish girl ever true to her queen and Pope (as her queen hadn't always been), and the tall handsome gentleman whose darkness of skin and subtle manner gave him away as Spanish—a traveler lately arrived from the Continent on business of church and state, the success or failure of which would be revealed in the histories, atlases, and stud books of the future. In this vision of Father Urban's, which, of course, derived from his current reading, there were flaws—the putt-putt of the royal barge, the black sunglasses worn by the queen, the Spaniard's cigar—but the conversation rang true.

"I can see myself in her, Father."

"I'm told she favors you, ma'am."

"I was out of the Church myself for a time—does that surprise you, Father?"

It did not, of course, since Monsignor Renton had said as much, and more. "You might say St Peter himself was out of the Church for a time, ma'am. Not a very long time, it's true. The important thing is he came back in and went on to become our first pope."

Mrs Thwaites made no reply. It was the last day of Father Urban's stay, and they'd just sailed past Sally's castle.

"Pray for her, ma'am."

"Father Udovic thinks I should make a pilgrimage."

"You've talked this over with him then?"

"Yes."

"Lourdes?"

"Yes. Father Udovic's leading a tour next summer. When I

was there some years ago, I said I'd never go again, but maybe I will. I understand the accommodations are better now."

"So I understand."

"I'd be grateful, Father, if you'd stay another day or two. Sally and Norris will be here tomorrow afternoon."

"Ah, ma'am, these things are best left to God. But since you ask it, yes, I'll stay."

The next morning, after Mass, Father Urban ran into Monsignor Renton and told him that the Hopwoods would be arriving from Minneapolis that afternoon.

"Sally?" said Monsignor Renton. "She's the best of a bad lot."

Father Urban asked what Mr Hopwood was like.

"Norris? He's a wheat broker. Say, how's the old head?"

"Needs a haircut, as you can see. That's all," said Father Urban, though he was still troubled by headaches. He didn't like the way Monsignor Renton looked at him—at his head, as if there might be something wrong with it.

"I see the girl's still driving you around."

"There's a reason for that, and it's not what you think, I'm afraid." There was no longer any need for Katie to drive him around, Father Urban explained. He let Mrs Thwaites go on thinking there was, though, and thus Katie got a chance to attend daily Mass. There was another reason why Father Urban wasn't driving himself, but this he didn't mention to Monsignor Renton who would have made too much of it. The key to the car had to be checked in and out with Mrs Thwaites, who kept it on her person, pinned to her breast when the car wasn't in use.

"Here's something I've been wanting to ask you," Monsignor Renton said, and then seemed to think better of it.

"Go ahead. Shoot."

"Well, at the time of your accident, when the ball hit you——"

"I thought somebody'd opened a bottle of champagne," said Father Urban, and looked him right in the eye.

Returning to Lake Lucille, Father Urban noticed that Katie was weeping. "Hey, what's the matter?" he said, scooting forward on the back seat. "Pull over to the side."

It took Father Urban a while to find out what was wrong. "All right," he said. "So you're homesick. So why don't you go home for a visit? If you like, I'll speak to Mrs Thwaites about it. Now, how's *that?*" Then it came out that Katie didn't have the fare back to Ireland. During her first months with Mrs Thwaites (Katie had been with her about a year), she had sent most of her earnings home, but she hadn't been doing that for some time. For the last six months, Mrs Thwaites had been winning Katie's wages away from her. "At *dominoes!* I never heard of such a thing. How much?" Katie didn't know how much, all told, but a lot. Katie was broke, and worse than broke. She owed Mrs Thwaites close to seven hundred dollars. "Well, I'll be damned. Look. You leave this to me."

Mrs Thwaites was beginning her day. Father Udovic had brought her communion, she'd had her breakfast, and her sets were on. She turned down the sound.

"I've just met a damsel in distress," Father Urban said, smiling. "Katie. The poor kid thinks you mean to hold onto this money. 'Nonsense,' I said. 'She's just *keeping* it for you. She's just having her little *joke.* Just trying to make it interesting.'" Father Urban was offering the old lady a role that would greatly become her, and before she could reject it, he presented the case for being good to Katie. While he did so—splendid type . . . alone in a strange country . . . very high regard for you, ma'am . . . hard to find another like her . . . could be arranged so there'd be no question of her not coming back to you—while he did so, Mrs Thwaites stared hard at the floor. When Father Urban paused, to give her a chance to speak, she turned up the sound.

So. Even so, Father Urban was serene. There was nothing in his attitude that would hinder Mrs Thwaites should she wish to change her mind and accept the good offices of one who was not only friend to her but to her house and therefore solicitous for its well-being. However, he did step over to the table and examine one of the dominoes. The truth was he thought the old lady must be using a marked deck. He saw nothing suspicious about the domino, though, and dropped it—*plink*—back among its fellows. Then he walked to the door, taking his time, hoping she'd call him back. She didn't. "I'll leave the door open, as I found it, ma'am," he said, which got no response at all, and, so, he left her—hoping she'd see the significance of his last remark.

When Katie brought his breakfast, he said, "Well, I spoke to her, Katie. Don't worry." When Katie brought his tray again, at twelve-thirty, he asked for news from the front.

Katie said that the dominoes had disappeared from the table.

"Oh? And was anything said?"

"No, Father."

"Well, don't worry, Katie. This may take a little time."

But Father Urban wasn't hopeful. *Children, how hard is it for them that trust in riches to enter into the kingdom of God.* And still Father Urban did not despair.

The Hopwoods arrived from Minneapolis in the middle of the afternoon. Their voices, coming from Mrs Thwaites's room across the corridor, reached Father Urban in his room. He heard them before, during, and after tea. For some time after that, he kept listening for a knock on the door, and found it difficult to concentrate on his reading. Finally, as a discipline, he took up his pen and wrote to Billy, intending to describe events leading up to his recent accident, which, apart from his headaches, might be regarded as a means to a good end (as is so often the case with our misfortunes), and to describe the beauty of summer at Lake Lucille, as seen from one man's casement

window, earth, sun, sky, and water, the green, the gold, and the
blue, blue, blue of God's plenty, and all for us, and so on. But,
as it turned out, Father Urban said nothing about his present
surroundings, about summer, or about his accident. His position
in the household was now so odd and uncertain that he didn't
care to dwell on it. He preferred to await developments. And
there was really no way to describe his accident that wouldn't
perhaps lower him in Billy's estimation.

When the knock did come, it was Katie with his evening
meal.

"What's going on around here?" he asked.

"Just the usual, Father." Katie said that Mrs Thwaites had
spent the afternoon talking business with Mr Hopwood—he
helped her with her investments—and that Mrs Hopwood had
gone out with "Tilly."

"Oh?" said Father Urban, though he'd seen Sally doing this
from his window. "Alone?"

"She often does that, Father."

"And now what're they doing?"

"Now they're eating downstairs."

"The Hopwoods."

"And Mrs Thwaites. She sometimes does that when they're
here."

Father Urban thought about this for a moment. "Do they
know I'm here?"

"The Hopwoods? I don't know that they do, Father. Would
you like me to tell them?"

"No, of course not," said Father Urban, and when Katie returned for his tray later, he said nothing.

That evening Father Urban got his things together. He was
downstairs, returning books to the library, when Mr Hopwood
walked in—"to investigate the noise," he said. "Heh, heh." Mr
Hopwood was perhaps forty-five, bespectacled, a neat, smallish

man, with a large head such as illustrators for the old *American Weekly* used to give members of the human race in the not-too-distant future. "Thought you were a ghost," he said. "Heh, heh."

"Afraid not," said Father Urban, and introduced himself. "I had an accident a couple of weeks ago, and I've been recuperating here, but perhaps you knew that."

"No, to tell you the truth, I didn't. We just arrived this afternoon. Nothing serious, I hope."

"The accident? No."

Mr Hopwood, of course, was waiting for more.

And so Father Urban, rather than have it thought that there hadn't been an accident and that he was the kind of clergyman who preyed on rich old women, said, "As a matter of fact, I got hit in the head by a golf ball."

"Sometimes a thing like that can be serious."

"Not with a head like mine," Father Urban said, with a smile.

"Heh, heh. Will you be here long?"

"As a matter of fact, I'm leaving tomorrow."

Early the next morning, Father Urban wrote a brief note— "My thanks for your hospitality, Yours in Christ, Fr Urban"— and stuck it under the old lady's door. Then, carrying his attaché case and bag, he went downstairs to the car. Parked alongside it was the Hopwoods' car, a new Ford convertible, a white one. Presently, Katie, who was usually there first in the morning, came out of the house and told him that Mrs Thwaites had lost the key to the car.

"I see," he said. He saw, too, that Katie had been crying. "Well, in that case, maybe I'd better call a cab."

One afternoon about a month later, late in September, Father Urban was summoned to the office. "Long distance for you," said Wilf, and gave up his swivel chair.

"Hello," said Father Urban. *"Hello!"* It was Billy, calling from Chicago. According to Billy, he had been sitting there in his office, not feeling so hot, when a little voice had said to him, "Hey, let's go fishing." The little voice hadn't succeeded with Billy, though, until it said, "Hey, take Father Urban along." That had done it. Billy was hoping to get in about three days—no more, unless they just couldn't pull themselves away—at a place he liked about a hundred and fifty miles northeast of Duesterhaus, near the Canadian border. "How're you fixed for time, Father?"

"Gee!" said Father Urban. "I'm afraid this is something for Father Wilfrid. I'll see what he says. Fortunately, he's right here." Father Urban explained to Wilf what Billy wanted, making use of Billy's words. Wilf, he knew, would make no objection, but would appreciate being consulted. "Here, Father. Why don't you say hello?"

Wilf took over then. "What's this about a little voice? Yes, this is Father Wilfrid. What's this about a little voice?" Wilf said, getting quite a bang out of himself. Soon he was giving a glowing account of his stewardship at the Hill. He never did say whether it would be all right for Father Urban to go fishing. He was all for it, of course.

The plan was for Father Urban to meet Billy and Paul the next day at the station (they'd be arriving on the Voyageur), and for the three of them to have lunch at the Hill, perhaps play a round of golf, and then drive north. Father Urban was to provide the car.

This was a problem. Father Urban called several laymen, but for one reason or another they all failed him. By bedtime that night, he was down to three possibilities, none of which appealed to him. There was Monsignor Renton, but would he care to lend his black Imperial for a fishing trip? There was a

used-car man in Great Plains who had somehow learned of
Father Urban's need and was offering to rent, sell, or trade a
station wagon that couldn't be trusted if what the man said was
true: "Just the thing for a fishing trip, Father." And there were
the regular car-rental agencies in Great Plains and Olympe—
they wanted a bit more than Father Urban was prepared to pay,
in view of the other possibilities.

There was also Sylvia—the Beans had two cars besides the
little Barracuda—but Father Urban hadn't seen her lately. No
trouble, no. Sylvia had taken him out to see Ray's farm, where,
among other things, Ray raised Morgan horses, and where,
when Sylvia and Father Urban arrived that day, two hired men
were about to breed a mare. Dear God! Father Urban's first
concern was for Sylvia's sensibilities. But, much to his surprise,
Sylvia got right into the act, so to speak. The last Father Urban
heard (for he went off to have a look at the ducks) Sylvia was
crying encouragement to the stallion and being cross with the
mare. Ray, whom Father Urban had been expecting, and then
hoping, to see drive up at any moment, hadn't appeared at all.
Since that day—and this happened shortly after the trouble at
Lake Lucille—Father Urban hadn't asked for the little Barracuda, nor had he seen Sylvia, or Ray.

Wilf, in all seriousness, offered Father Urban the pickup truck
for the trip north. Father Urban, knowing Wilf's admiration for
the vehicle, said solemnly, "I wouldn't want to leave you without transportation."

The next day, as it turned out, Father Urban had to meet
Billy (and Paul) in the pickup truck. He had the promise of
Monsignor Renton's Imperial, but he had to drive to Great
Plains to get it—and the pickup truck simply refused to start
until it was too late for him to do anything but go to the
station. "A comedy of errors!" he cried before Billy (or Paul)

could hear him, and ran up to shake Billy's hand. A smile did
for Paul. Billy was wearing a tan suit of whatever cloth it was
the Army used in warm weather, a primrose shirt, with dotted
navy-blue tie, and a dark straw hat with a dark-red band. Paul
was wearing the pants to his off-black whipcord chauffeur's
suit and a conservative sports shirt. He had on a silly straw cap
that Father Urban disliked intensely.

"I don't see no Indians," Paul said.

"Spoken like a true Chicagoan," Father Urban said, and began
again, "A comedy of errors! I had hoped to meet you in another
car." He looked over at the pickup truck with which Billy and
Paul hadn't yet associated him and told them of his trouble
with it.

Billy and Paul stared at the thing. With its motor running—
Father Urban had been afraid to turn it off—it seemed to
tremble under their gaze.

"What happened to the old job you had when I was here
last spring?" Billy asked, meaning Phil's Plymouth.

"I'm afraid that one didn't belong to us."

"So what do we do?"

Father Urban said that they'd have lunch, which was doubtless
being prepared at that very moment, and then he and Brother
Harold would drive to Great Plains, and he, Father Urban,
would come back in Monsignor Renton's car.

"Good God," Billy said.

"I'm afraid it means a delay of an hour or so."

"I don't like it," Billy said.

"Why not play a little golf? I'll catch you on four or five."

"Not in the mood for golf."

It seemed to Father Urban that Billy was blaming him for a
situation he had done his best to prevent, but he said nothing.
If you failed, as he had, it was better not to seek credit for

trying, and Billy rather liked picking up the pieces anyway. Otherwise, he wouldn't have had anything to do with the Clementines.

"I don't like the idea of a borrowed car," Billy said. "Let's see if we can buy one."

They left Paul with the luggage and walked over to the main street. Father Urban had been impressed by Billy's casual approach to buying a car, but he was afraid that Billy wouldn't be able to bring it off in Duesterhaus, where the dealers sold more farm machinery than cars. The first place looked unpromising, but the other had a station wagon in the window, a Rambler, a brown one—what Father Urban believed was called desert tan.

"That'll do," Billy said.

"I understand the resale value is high."

"Can't you use it around the place?"

Until then, Father Urban hadn't been *sure* that the transportation problem at St Clement's Hill was being solved. "God writes straight with crooked lines," he said.

"Come again."

Father Urban said that they'd had a certain amount of trouble with the pickup truck, and that he had often regretted (and never so much as that morning) having to meet visitors at the station in the old thing.

"What you said before—how's that go again?"

Father Urban repeated the line. "It's an old saying. From the Portuguese, I believe. Anyway, one of my favorites."

"I like it," Billy said, and they entered the establishment. "I'll take the one in the window," he told the man inside.

"You *will?*" said the man.

Unfortunately, however, there was the matter of a license for the car, which had to be procured in Olympe, fourteen miles away. The dealer offered to send his wife for it, but this wasn't

good enough for Billy. He said that he'd been led to believe
that the wagon was ready to roll, and he wasn't going to lose
time because some people didn't know their business. He'd take
delivery at St Clement's Hill in one hour's time or not at all.
Father Urban, who had seen Billy like this before, in restaurants,
followed him out of the place, feeling sorry for the dealer and
hoping for the best. For Father Urban, it was a long one and
three-tenths miles back to St Clement's Hill. On the way, he
tried some small talk on Billy, which was no good, and then on
Paul, which wasn't much better, for Paul did his best to observe
the silence of his master.

At the Hill, they went straight to the refectory, where five
retreatants were eating at the long table, and after Paul had
been introduced to Wilf and Jack, they all sat down at the
round table to beer and hamburgers, frozen sweet corn from
their own garden, and strained conversation. Father Urban
didn't feel like talking, and he didn't feel like eating. (Billy had
removed his watch from his wrist, had put it by his plate, and
was keeping an eye on it.) Oh, to be able to say, "Now, look
here, Billy. What if the man does come a little late? He's *trying*
to do his best, and you have to give him credit for that. God
does, you know. That's really all that counts with Him. Now,
how about it?"

No, it wouldn't do. Father Urban's influence with Billy was
considerable, and growing stronger, but it wasn't up to anything like that. Meanwhile, Billy was doing a certain amount of
tangible good in the world, and this might more than compensate
for his little crimes against humanity, some of which, anyway,
were atoned for right on the spot by Father Urban through his
silent sufferings.

"By the way," Wilf said to Father Urban. "You had a visitor.
A Mr Studley. He was in the neighborhood and thought he'd
stop by."

"I don't really know him," Father Urban said.

"Seems to think we could use an air strip here."

"Bit of a nut on that subject—and others," said Father Urban, thinking if there was one thing Billy hated, it was the airplane.

"He seemed nice enough. Non-Catholic."

Ten minutes later Wilf was still leading the conversation, and it was still going nowhere. He said he'd spoken to the sheriff again about people parking on the golf course at night. The only response came from Jack, who, given more of an opportunity to talk than he usually got, said he understood (from a man he'd met in the Duesterhaus post office) that the trespassers were only looking for nightcrawlers. "They're used for bait," he said, addressing this remark to Billy.

"Well, he made it," Billy said. From where he was sitting, he could see the driveway without turning his head.

"Thank God," said Father Urban.

"You don't blame me, do you, Father?" Billy asked.

"No."

A moment later, the doorbell rang, and Brother Harold answered it.

"Just ask the man how much it is," Billy called after him, taking out his checkbook.

Wilf looked at Father Urban, seeking some clue to what was going on. Brother Harold reappeared, bringing a bill of sale and some other documents. Billy glanced at these and then passed them to Wilf without a word of explanation. That was how Billy gave.

When Wilf had got it all straight, he thanked Billy in the name of the Order, and said he was glad it hadn't been necessary to trade in the pickup truck, which, by and large, had given good service and very likely would continue to do so. "I think this calls for a little celebration, and don't forget *them*," said Wilf, meaning the five retreatants.

Brother Harold brought in another round of beer. Father Urban left the room and led in the dealer. It was Father Urban's intention to make peace between the dealer—a Mr Swanson, who said all his friends called him Swanny—and Billy, who said there used to be a song by that name.

There was a feeling of good fellowship in the refectory now. Mr Swanson, all the better for the bad time Billy had given him earlier, seemed very happy to be present. He took no part in the conversation, but he was enjoying his beer, and when he saw Wilf putting salt in his, was not afraid to ask for the shaker. Paul, not much for beer, he said, went out to look at the station wagon.

"I wanted to serve more of a meal than this," Wilf said to Billy, "but Father Urban, here, said no. He said you'd only want what we usually have. Of course, we don't have beer every day," Wilf said, eying Mr Swanson.

"No," said Mr Swanson.

"I didn't come here to eat, but you don't have to apologize for this," Billy said. Then he addressed Father Urban. "You know Father Gabriel, don't you? The Dalmatian?"

"Oh yes." So Father Gabriel was still buzzing Billy.

"They had me out there for a meal recently," Billy said. "Served three kinds of hock, and then the head man had the nerve to tell me they were a very penitential order."

Father Urban laughed. "I wish we could say the same here—and serve the same."

"They were just spreading themselves on your account, Mr Cosgrove. They're not a wealthy order." This from Jack.

Father Urban could have killed him.

Wilf and Mr Swanson were discussing the pickup truck. "But what if we traded it in—what would you allow us *then?*"

"Hard to say. It would depend on what you had in mind. I might go as high as seventy-five dollars."

"I see. Well, thank you."

Billy had expressed a desire to visit the chapel, and so, when lunch was over, the entire party moved in that direction.

"We'll drive you back to town when we leave," Billy said to Mr Swanson.

Father Urban was gratified to hear this.

As a sacred artist, Brother Harold had done as well as could be expected of a young man whose other occupations—cooking, housekeeping, gardening, and attendance at the golf course—left him little time for church decorating. He had made the most of his deficiencies by painting in the new Byzantine manner. His winged ox, lion, man, and eagle, viewed as a group in that setting, were quite recognizable as the four Evangelists. Father Urban explained who they were, however, in deference to Mr Swanson.

"They're not representational in the photographic sense," said Brother Harold.

"Who's this?" Billy asked.

Father Urban explained that this—a stag drinking from three wiggly lines—was known as "The Living Waters" and symbolized not only baptism but the other sacraments, and therefore, you might say, the Church.

It was apparent to Father Urban that Billy wasn't taken with Brother Harold's iconography. Nevertheless, as they were leaving the chapel, Billy bucked up and said, "You don't have to apologize for any of this, Brother."

After they'd left the chapel, Father Urban said to Billy: "Sure you don't want to play a few holes?"

"Not now," Billy said. "Maybe when we come back."

So they made their way out to the station wagon. Paul had

everything loaded, including Father Urban's bag, and was sitting behind the wheel.

"I'll ride in front with him, and that way I can tell him a few things about the car," Mr Swanson said, as if he hoped thus to work his passage into town.

"Good idea," Billy said.

Father Urban feared that Mr Swanson had been planning for some time to say what he'd just said, and that Billy didn't like it—didn't like having his little friendly gesture of offering Mr Swanson a ride turned to his own advantage.

"And then maybe he can tell you," Mr Swanson said to Father Urban.

"Sounds good to me," Billy said.

Mr Swanson, now confidently addressing Billy, said, "And then *he* can tell the others here when he comes back."

"Let's get going," Billy said.

They paused twice on the way for refreshments, and reached Henn's Haven at sundown. Billy stepped out, with his rod and reel already stripped for action. He introduced Father Urban to Mr Henn who had come out to greet them, and then hurried off toward the dock to try his luck in Bloodsucker Lake. Paul, who knew his way around, drove down a sandy road to their cottages. That left Father Urban alone with Mr Henn, who apparently either hadn't been told that one of Billy's party would be a priest or hadn't expected to see one wearing grey flannel slacks, a white turtleneck sweater, and a crew cap. (You never knew what people were thinking—only that you lost or gained ground fast the moment it was known you were a priest.) Chester, as Billy had called Mr Henn, was in his late fifties and wore an old felt hat. Stuck in the band were three badges: "Keep Minnesota Green"; "Minnesota Centennial 1857–1957"; and "Prevent Fires." Chester had a complaining face and a contented voice. He said he'd run out of the names of game fish native to the region and didn't care to start in on the pan fish, and so he'd taken a doctor friend's advice and named his three new cottages Jolly, Good, and Fun.

"And I suppose I'm stuck with Good," said Father Urban.

"They're all the same," Chester replied. "And if there's anything wrong, I want to know it. If there's nothing wrong, tell your friends."

They walked down to the lake together. Billy was standing at the end of the dock, casting a plug out into the water. He wasn't having any luck, but this didn't appear to bother him. "I just want 'em to know I'm here," he said.

"Doc Strong, he got a nice one off there last month," Chester said. They watched Billy reel in nothing once more. "It's been a lot better in Snowflake this year," Chester said, and led Father Urban up to the main lodge, which was constructed of logs painted dark green, with fresh white chinking. "We'll go out to Snowflake in the morning," Chester said. "And maybe to Strong. That's a lake I named after Doc Strong, who you may have heard me mention."

"Yes."

"Doc helped me when times was hard—like Mr Cosgrove during the war when we got hit by gas rationing. For Mr Cosgrove's sake, I wish we hadn't run out of no-name lakes."

"Say, this is nice," Father Urban said. There was a screened-in porch running clear across the front of the lodge, from which there was a wonderful view of the lake.

"We think so," Chester said.

Inside, the lounge, dining room, kitchen, and lavatories, and on the second floor, Chester said, were living quarters for himself and the missis. The logs were natural-varnished on the inside. The whole place was very well kept up. The stuffed birds

and fur-bearing animals on the walls wore cellophane slipcovers.
That was overdoing it, Father Urban felt.

"Like a cup of coffee?" Chester asked him. "Or we have soft
drinks. Near beer, if you want something a little stronger. Mr
Cosgrove, I guess you know, he brings his own."

"Nothing right now, thanks."

Father Urban knew from signs he'd seen along the way that
the proprietors of Henn's Haven were Dad and Mother Henn,
and from Billy he knew that Chester's first wife had died and
that he had married again. But Father Urban hadn't been prepared to see such a young woman as the second Mrs Henn,
and he didn't know how to take it when Chester introduced her
—she couldn't have been more than twenty-five—as "Mother."

"Hello," she said, and after that she just smiled. She was dark,
perhaps part Indian, and so attractive that Father Urban was
relieved when she left them for the kitchen. Her scent remained, however. Father Urban moved away from it.

"My first wife was an older woman," Chester said.

"I see."

"For business reasons, we go on using the old name. It's a
natural, and in this game all you've got is your name, built up
over the years."

Father Urban nodded. There wasn't much wrong with that.
After all, it would only be a matter of time before Mother
looked the part. As for Dad—"You have children, Mr Henn?"

"Well, no. Neither my first or my second wife—yet. Guess
we just have to keep hoping."

"That's right," said Father Urban, and, in a firm tone, swept
on, "Say, if you don't mind, I'd like to see where I live, before
it gets dark."

"Honey!" Chester called, and his wife returned.

For Father Urban, it had been a rather tiring day, and after
Honey, or Mother, had shown him to his cottage (which *was*

Good), he stretched out on his bed—but not for long, for Billy and Paul dropped in. Billy said he was in Jolly. At his suggestion, they all went over to the lodge for a sandwich and a drink, Paul carrying a piece of Billy's luggage into the kitchen of the lodge. Billy and Father Urban entered the lounge. Billy chose a table near the dead fireplace and shoved it nearer. "Come on," he yelled. "Turn on the heat."

Chester came out of the kitchen. "I didn't know if you'd be over or not," he said. He knelt and set off the logs already arranged in the fireplace.

"This is more like it," Billy said when the logs had blazed up and Paul came in with their drinks. "Hey, where's the piano?"

"You didn't see this, did you?" Chester said, going over to a jukebox and turning on its fiery front. "We didn't have this when you were here in the spring."

"Where's the piano?" Billy asked again.

"I had a chance to sell it, Mr Cosgrove."

"Why, I loved that old piano," Billy said to Father Urban.

"We found out that was where all the moths was coming from," Chester said.

"You must be slipping, Chester," Billy said. "That was the only piano I could ever really play."

"When we found out where all the moths was coming from, I said, 'Honey, we better get rid of this old piano,'" Chester said.

"Those moths were coming from you," Billy said.

To nobody in particular Chester said, "I have to get along with people."

"*Where's* the piano?" Billy asked.

"A fella stopped by that makes a business of buying up these old pianos," Chester told him. "He wasn't from around here."

"I was afraid of that," Billy said. "Well, let's get on the phone and see if we can buy one."

Father Urban looked at the cuckoo clock over the fireplace. "Hadn't we better wait until tomorrow?"

But by the time Father Urban had finished his club-steak sandwich, Paul, on the telephone, had reached the owner of a music store in the nearest town of any size, forty miles away. ("And most of it over gravel roads," Chester said. Father Urban couldn't see why Chester was so sad, if Billy was going to pay for the piano.)

"He don't deal in secondhand jobs," Paul shouted, from the phone. "He says he'll be real glad to sell us a new one."

"Ask him if he'll be real glad to deliver one tonight," Billy said.

Paul reported back. "He says are we kiddin'?"

"Tell him no," Billy said. "You better talk to him, Chester. Tell him who you are and how the hell to get here."

Father Urban finished his drink and declined another. He waited a moment, and then excused himself, saying he was tired. Billy didn't take this very well. He acted as though Father Urban should be willing, and more than willing, to wait up for the piano.

"I've had a long day, Billy."

"We've all had a long day."

"The truth is I have some office to read."

Billy's face softened up entirely. "Oh," he said. "That's different."

13

. . . A Bad Hand

Pity the poor resort operator! At the bottom of his efforts to get
along with people there may be only the base conviction that
it will profit him, but, even so, Father Urban felt sorry for
Chester the next day. Billy and Paul had gone to bed the night
before and left Chester waiting up for the piano. When it had
come, in the wee hours, Chester and the truck driver had had to
move it into the lodge. Early in the morning, Chester had had to
get Billy out of his bed, and minnows for the day's fishing out
of their tank. It was Chester who made breakfast. He said Honey
came down later.

The fishing that morning, as Chester said to a colleague—
another guide in a passing boat—was nothing to brag about.
Father Urban made the only catch, and Billy, who was after
lake trout, had actually wanted him to throw it back—"a lousy
two-pound walleye!" They tried Snowflake and they tried
Strong. They tried trolling, fast and slow, Chester making the
old outboard talk in a whisper. They tried jigging—yanking the
rod up and down when reeling in the line, after a cast. They
tried it shallow. They tried it deep. They tried all kinds of bait
—redheads, daredevils, tezerenos, artificial mice, doctor spoons,
hula dancers, and lazy ikes. Chester went ashore and caught a

frog, and Billy tried that. Billy had one strike, but nothing came of it. "Probably a shoe," he said.

"They're in here," Chester said, and spoke of the wind, the sun, and the moon.

"To think you get paid for this," Billy said.

"They're in here," Chester said.

"Aw, shut up," Billy said, and after that was silent.

They returned to the lodge for lunch. It was Father Urban's feeling that he'd look better to Billy, and that Billy would look better to him, if they spent more time apart, and so, as they were getting up from the table, Father Urban said he wouldn't be going out that afternoon, if Billy didn't mind.

"I don't blame you," Billy said.

Father Urban slept most of the afternoon, but he was on the dock, breviary in hand, when the boat came in. Chester was rowing. Billy appeared to be in good spirits, so Father Urban called across the water, "How was it?"

"Wonderful!" Billy called back.

Paul had driven to town for "supplies" in the morning, but in the afternoon he had taken Father Urban's place in the bow of the boat, and he was the first one to disembark. He was all wet. Chester and Billy were somewhat wet, too, Father Urban saw, but Paul was all wet. "If I could swim, I wouldn't care," he said.

He told Father Urban what had happened. Billy had run the boat full speed through a place where tree stumps stuck up in the water, and he had nearly drowned Paul. Chester had rowed them home because the propeller on the outboard motor had been badly bent. Paul said, "Boss, you won't get me in that thing again."

"Just wonderful," Billy said, jumping out of the boat.

"How was the fishing?" Father Urban asked.

"The *what?*" Billy said.

Chester stayed in the boat, bailing it out with a rusty coffee can, which, scraping the ribbed bottom and swallowing the dirty water, made a melancholy sound. The sun was leaving for the day, and when that happened that far north in September, there wasn't much between you and the night. The lake, a light red wine before, was now black stout, and the air was suddenly dank.

That evening Father Urban went out of his way to be nice to Chester. Two couples, thirty or so, arrived in time for supper, and were asked by Billy to join him and Father Urban in a drink later. They accepted. When the party had gathered, there was dancing to the jukebox, Billy starting it off with Honey, and the couples following. Then they all changed partners. Father Urban and Chester sat together, Father Urban telling him about the Hill.

"You and me got the same problem," Chester said.

"How's that?"

"The cold months. We ought to operate in Florida in the cold months—instead of closing down the way we do."

"You may be right," said Father Urban.

"Mother taught her all she knows about cooking," Chester said a little later, when Honey danced by with Billy.

When Billy sat down to play, Father Urban understood why Chester had sold the old piano, and why he wasn't happy about the new one. Chester had to get along with people.

"Hello, Aloha! How are you?" Billy sang. A line or two was as far as he got into the lyrics, and his accompaniment was like falling planks. He had a glass on the piano, and another by the fireplace, where Father Urban and Chester and the others were sitting at three tables pushed together, for it was no longer possible to dance. Paul, as he must have done on many such occasions, sat on the bench beside Billy and backed him up with noises of his own, all made with his mouth. Paul's "Ahhhhhhhhhahhhhhhhh-ahhhhhhhhh," first heard in "Bye, Bye, Blues," was the full band behind the maestro, and suggested that Paul, like many of his breed, could carry a tune. Paul also did something out of the side of his mouth, with his lips held loosely together, that was rather like a trombone. The sweet trumpet parts he whistled, and whistled well. Unfortunately for Paul, and others, the band featured the leader's piano and voice. "And now, folks"—this, while chording, called out in a genial manner that took Father Urban back to the days of radio, when some of the most important men in the country were the leaders of dance bands—"let's go for a musical stroll down Memory Lane." Billy played and sang "Three O'clock in the Morning," "Diane," and "Dinner for One, Please, James." Then came "Who's Afraid of the Big Bad Wolf?" made famous by little Shirley Temple, "Dardanella," made famous by the immortal Paul Whiteman, "Nola," made famous by Vincent Lopez, and "Got a Date with an Angel," made famous by the late Hal Kemp. "And now, folks, a medley of tunes from *Bitter Sweet*." "Show tunes," he said to one of the women when she crossed the floor—she'd been out of the room when he'd announced the medley. "And now, folks, who'll ever forget this one? Sing along, if you like. 'Here I go singin' low, dodey oh, dodey oh, bye, bye, blackbird!'" One of the men, a fat man, did sing along, but Father Urban could see that Billy didn't like it. "Now here's an instrumental favorite, as played by Glen Gray and the Casa Loma Band—'Smoke Rings.'" Billy went all out on this one, shoulders rolling, feet tramping. He motioned to Paul to rise and face the audience when it was time for his trombone solo, which he did. At the conclusion of this number, the leader played several notes to indicate that the band was taking a break, and rose from the piano. Everybody applauded, including Paul, even Chester and Father Urban.

A little while later, Father Urban heard how Billy had happened to buy the building now occupied by the Clementines on the near North Side. He'd asked the previous tenant, Panache Ltd! to locate some Little Jack Little records for him, scarce items. "'I'm not asking have you got 'em,' I said. 'I'm asking—can you get 'em?' Know what the bastard said?"

"What?" said Father Urban.

"'Wouldn't if I could.' So I bought the building and told him to move. I told him he could and would. He did."

With one of the party, a Mr Inglis, Billy then fell to arguing the merits of shooting wolves from airplanes. In Father Urban's opinion, what Billy really objected to was people having such fun in airplanes and thinking of themselves as noble conservationists. Billy had the heavy stockholder's loyalty to the railroads. "Upsets the balance of nature," he said to Mr Inglis. "We need the wolves. Too damn many deer anyway. Ask the farmers."

"I'll have to do that," said Mr Inglis.

"Go ahead. I'll wait," Billy said.

"What d'ya smoke?" said the other man, the fat one, to Father Urban.

"Usually cigars," said Father Urban, raising the one in his hand.

"Bob," said the man, putting out his hand.

They shook hands, though they'd done so earlier, and since Bob showed no interest in his name, Father Urban didn't repeat it.

"Here. Try one of mine," Bob said, shuffling a cigarette half out of the pack. "They're all new."

"Maybe later," said Father Urban, showing Bob the cigar again.

"Go ahead." Bob shuffled the cigarette farther out of the pack. "They're all new. No filter."

"All right," said Father Urban, taking the cigarette. "I'll smoke it later."

"Smoke it now. Go ahead. Here." Bob struck a match for Father Urban.

"Thanks," Father Urban said, and there he was with a cigar in one hand, a cigarette in the other.

"What d'ya drive?"

"We have a new Rambler station wagon."

"How d'ya like it?"

"Fine."

"What're you doing about parking in your town?"

"No problem."

"No? Where *you* from?"

"For many years I traveled out of Chicago——"

"Chicago! Don't tell me you haven't got a problem there!"

"I now call Minnesota my home. Duesterhaus. Near Duesterhaus. No problem."

"You won't like this, but some of these little towns are worse than the big ones." Bob said he was proud of the facilities in his town, which was second to Rochester in the state. "That's on a parking space-per capita basis."

"Is this your business—parking?"

"Oh hell, no."

"You just feel strongly about it?"

"Oh hell, no. We had this problem in our town, and we licked it. Why can't others do the same? What d'ya drive?"

"Rambler."

"How d'ya like it?"

"Fine," said Father Urban, putting out the cigarette.

Honey brought Bob a steak sandwich.

"Sure you won't have something, Mother?"

"No, thanks," Honey said. She was sober.

"How about you, doc?" Bob said to Father Urban.

"No, thanks."

"Like to have you meet my wife." Bob's wife was dancing with Paul.

"I met her. Very nice." Father Urban turned back to Mrs Inglis and Chester. Earlier he had been discussing the course at the Hill with Mrs Inglis, a golfer, and not a bad-looking woman. She was a southerner who'd had the good fortune to marry a man by the same name ("I've never changed my name!"). Father Urban had pulled out of the conversation with Mrs Inglis after she said she was going to tell him a secret if she wasn't careful. Before that, he had more or less given up on Chester, who had put on a black leather bow tie for the evening and was now talking about the first Mrs Henn. "See anything funny about that sign?" he asked Mrs Inglis and Father Urban.

Father Urban concentrated on the sign, but saw nothing funny about it. It simply said, "WE DON'T KNOW WHERE MOTHER IS, BUT WE HAVE POP ON ICE."

"You never saw one that said 'Mother' before," Chester said. "They all say 'Mom.'"

"He's right!" cried Mrs Inglis.

"That could very well be," said Father Urban.

Billy joined them. "You know that friend of yours, Father Louis? He's not a bad guy, but he's a knocker. And that other friend of yours, Monsignor Whatsit, he's another. All your friends seem to be knockers."

"Oh, I wouldn't say that," said Father Urban.

"Doc Strong had that sign made special for Mother," Chester said.

"His first wife," Billy explained to Mrs Inglis.

"When Mother died, I was going to take it down," Chester said. "But I talked it over with people that knew Mother. Like Doc Strong. Doc knew Mother as well as I did. And Doc said no."

"I still think you should take it down," Billy said.

"Doc said, 'Mother wouldn't want us to take it down.'"

Paul and Bob's wife were still dancing, but everybody else— Mr and Mrs Inglis, Honey and Billy, Bob and Father Urban—

observed a moment of silence. For Father Urban, it was a painful moment.

"*That's* the kind of person she was," Chester said.

After another painful moment, Billy said, "All right, Chester. But should we leave it up when *you* check out?"

Everybody was watching Chester.

Father Urban stood up, saying, "Chester, if I were you I wouldn't try to answer that question now." He let it be seen that he was saying good night. He bowed to Mrs Inglis, shook the hand of Mr Inglis, who was standing, and asked Bob, for whom standing would have been difficult, not to move.

Billy tried to get Father Urban to stay. "Some office to say, Billy." And Billy, who only once before during the evening had shown the company his better side, while at the piano ("And now, folks. . . ."), took it very well. He explained to Mrs Inglis that Father Urban really wanted to stay—to dance and have fun—but couldn't because he belonged to a very penitential order.

Father Urban, looking back as he went out the door, and waving an adieu, was afraid that Billy was developing the penitential theme for the whole company. Well, if so, it couldn't be helped. There were worse things to worry about. Two days and nights of close association with Billy had left Father Urban feeling anything but complacent about their relationship. More had to be done for Billy in a spiritual way than Father Urban had been doing. Fortunately, the sins of the flesh weren't the worst kind. Billy's character, however, wasn't quite what Father Urban had believed it to be. A few spoons seemed to be missing.

Billy, Paul, and Father Urban set forth the next morning, with Billy at the outboard motor—a different and more powerful one. During the night's revels, Billy had decided that Chester was bad luck, and had told him so, which was a hell of a thing to say to a guide, and so Chester wasn't in the boat. As for Paul, he had said the day before that Billy wouldn't get him into the boat again, which probably accounted for his presence there. Father Urban wished that none of this were happening.

Billy ran them around Bloodsucker twice—in the hope, Father Urban guessed, of embarrassing Chester, who was not recommending it that season. Billy then took the boat up a narrow, stumpy stretch of water leading into Snowflake. Chester had warned them to reel in if they went through there, and Father Urban and Paul did so. Billy didn't. He had trolled through there the day before, he said. This time, though, his hook caught on something. He took the boat back and worked for a while to free his line. Then he got mad and broke it. "That didn't feel like twenty-five-pound test to me," he said. Then he had to put on a whole new works—leader, spinner hook, and minnow. "Here," he said to Father Urban, motioning him to take charge of the motor, "you're not doing anything."

No way to address me, Father Urban thought. They changed seats, Father Urban sitting in the stern on one of the two life-preserver cushions in the boat. Before Billy sat down, Paul slipped the other cushion under him, restoring it to its proper place. (Paul, first into the boat that morning, had taken the cushion to his place in the bow, and Father Urban had been quietly doing without it.)

Father Urban took the boat into Snowflake and turned right, as Chester had done the day before. He kept fairly close to the shore. Billy grabbed a minnow from the pail at his feet, took a stitch in its back with the hook, and cast it out behind the boat. It made a little splash.

This roused Paul, who had been dozing, and he now lowered his own minnow, which was quite dead, into the water. Paul

didn't seem to care whether he caught any fish or not. Father
Urban recalled that on the drive north Paul's part in the conversation had consisted mostly of remarks like "I was fishing out of
the same boat when the boss landed this whale in Florida."
Father Urban didn't know how Paul managed not to compete
with Billy in Florida, but in Minnesota he used a dead minnow.

"This isn't what I came up here for," Billy said, addressing
the trees on the shore.

"No," said Father Urban, also to the trees. If this went on,
what would it be like when they finally gave up and rode back
to Henn's Haven? Paul, the non-swimmer, had probably been
thinking of the return voyage when he pinched the life pre-
server. Father Urban had been hoping that wind, sun, and moon
would do whatever had to be done to improve the fishing, but
he was afraid they hadn't. He had been hoping that it would
be possible to go back early, having caught their limit, and get
some sleep, and that when they woke up everything would be
different—so different, in fact, that he would not find it incon-
venient to have a little talk with Billy on the subject of his
personal life.

This was a subject that Father Urban hadn't had to concern
himself with in the past, since he was not Billy's confessor. Until
Father Urban arrived at Henn's Haven and saw Honey—saw
Billy *with* Honey, rather—there had been no reason to suspect
that all was not well enough with Billy. For Father Urban's part,
he wished it were none of his business. Billy, however, was
known to be a big benefactor of the Order, and as such he had
to behave himself in public. What did it mean? Either Billy
thought very little of Father Urban or—what was more likely—
considered him to be very unworldly indeed. This was an idea
that many people had of the clergy, and perhaps the clergy
indulged them in it, as did the major communications media, but

Father Urban didn't see how *he* could have conveyed *that* idea to quite *this* extent.

He was up against a situation that had often confronted the Church, and one that had cost her heavily in lives and property. Father Urban had given a lot of thought to this particular aspect of ecclesiastical history, which, generally speaking, suggested that it is too hard for some people, and all too easy for others, to do the right thing. Father Urban felt that Clement VII had been the wrong pope to deal with Henry VIII, and he wondered what the feeling was in Heaven on this point. Centuries later, Pius IX, who had begun so well, had thrown down his cards in a fit of self-righteousness, and the Church was still trying to get back in the game. A bad mistake, that, since it had left the other players at each other's mercy—and thus had prepared the way for World War I, the Russian Revolution, Mussolini and Hitler, World War II, and now the Bomb.

Father Urban had preached a great many thrilling sermons on saints who had really asked for the martyr's crown, but he believed that there were others from whose lives we might learn more that would serve us better in the daily round. What of those who had remained on the scene and got on with the job? The work of the Church, after all, had to be done for the most part by the living. There was too much emphasis on dying for the faith. How about *living* for the faith? Take Lanfranc and William the Conqueror—of whom it was written (in the Catholic Encyclopedia and Father Urban's notes for a book he might write someday): "He was mild to good men of God and stark beyond all bounds to those who withsaid his will." Lanfranc had recognized the importance of being more than merely right. He must have operated with great finesse, for he had got William and Matilda to found two abbeys by way of penance for their contumacy. Thereafter, the Conqueror was always careful to show himself a considerate and respectful son of the Church.

Call the book "Lambs Who Lay Down with Lions and Lived."
Maybe call it "Conquering Lambs."

"Hold it," Billy whispered.

Father Urban glanced at Billy's line and saw that it wasn't engaged. Then, as the boat turned a rocky corner, he saw what Billy saw—a deer. Its antlers had looked like a floating branch.

Paul saw it last. After watching for a moment, he said, "Hey, how about that?"

Billy was trying to count the points on the antlers. "He'd look all right on your wall, Father."

"Oh, for a camera!" said Father Urban.

"Brother Whatsit could see what a deer really looks like," Billy said. "Go over to him. Want to say hello."

The deer was making for a little peninsula of sand and gravel. Father Urban, mindful of the fishing lines, let the deer get between the boat and the shore before coming alongside. The deer kept going, as if following a narrow path in the water. Billy reached out and touched the antlers. Seizing one, he ducked the deer's head under the water, which was easier done than Father Urban would have imagined. Billy did it again—and Father Urban, who hadn't liked it the first time, said nothing. Then he realized that Billy was trying to drown the deer.

There was power in the deer's neck, but there was no foundation for it. When Billy braced his elbows on the gunwale, he was able to turn the deer by its antlers. When he got the animal squared away from the boat, he pressed down. Father Urban saw the deer's eyes—big black bubbles—watching him, he thought, and he looked away. He *heard* bubbles then, and heard the antlers rubbing against the boat. He was feeling strongly what he'd felt only slightly on several occasions in the last three days. He was feeling cheap. The night before, when Billy had introduced him to the Inglises and the Bobs, Father

Urban had felt like a poor slum kid who was being treated to a few days of "camp."

Father Urban threw the motor into high. The boat stood up in the water. He hadn't counted on that, but he held on, and Paul held on. Billy, holding on to the deer, left the boat on its way up. When it came down, which it did in a loud belly flop, Father Urban reduced speed and circled back. The deer was now swimming for a point farther up the shore. Billy was treading water, apparently in no difficulty, waiting to be picked up.

Father Urban brought the boat slowly alongside Billy and then leaned away while Billy was climbing aboard, with Paul's help.

Father Urban sensed that the next few minutes would be crucial—that his relationship with Billy was going to be a lot better or a lot worse from now on. The situation was so bad that it might be good. That was really looking on the bright side, of course, but this might be one of those times when Billy would decide he ought to pick up the pieces. With God's help, it might be so. Billy might respect Father Urban all the more for acting so boldly, for defying him in a good cause, and he might even thank Father Urban for saving him from himself. What Billy had been up to was not, after all, the sort of thing a self-respecting sportsman could look back upon with pleasure. Father Urban might say, "I know, Billy. You wanted to have it stuffed for us. I don't quarrel with your motives. As a matter of fact, I don't know where *we'd* be without them. . . ." But it probably wouldn't go like that.

"I'm sorry, but I had to do it," Father Urban said. He started to remove his sweater, meaning to give it to Billy.

Billy indicated that he didn't want the sweater, and then that he wished to run the motor.

Father Urban got the impression that Billy wasn't talking to him yet—that the situation was still dangerous, but that Billy was making a tremendous effort to control himself. Getting up to change seats, Father Urban saw Paul slipping back into the bow with the life-preserver cushion, and thought, yes, that would be Billy's way of paying them back—Father Urban for dunking him, Paul for being a witness. They were in for a rough ride, Father Urban was thinking, when Billy pushed him overboard.

Father Urban, an able swimmer, came smiling to the surface, returning good for evil. He stopped this, though, when Billy and Paul, reeling in their lines, drove off without him.

About an hour later, Chester and Honey came along in the boat and found Father Urban sitting on the shore. He waded out to them.

"We heard about it from Paul," Chester said. "But we had to wait until they left."

Father Urban got into the boat. "How did they leave?" he asked.

"Mad."

This didn't answer Father Urban's question. He was thinking about the station wagon.

"And he didn't pay up," Chester said. "Told me I could take it out of the piano. Don't think I won't."

"You can send me my part of the bill."

"I wouldn't think of it," Chester said. "Unless you insist."

"I insist."

"He'll be back," Honey said. She was sitting up in the bow of the boat, facing out like a figurehead. "In the spring, I'll bet. When the trout are up."

Chester thought this over. "I'll sell the piano, and get a good secondhand one," he said. "In case he comes back."

"He'll come back when the trout are up," Honey said.

"Yeah, that's what I'll do," Chester said.

Honey turned toward them. "What will *you* do?" she asked Father Urban.

"I'll think of something," he said.

At four o'clock that afternoon, he was standing in the little park across from the bus station in Great Plains. He was wearing light cotton slacks, a white sports shirt, no hat, damp socks, and wet shoes, having taken only one pair with him on the trip north. So far, though he'd been waiting around the park for about an hour, and though he'd been a familiar figure in Great Plains only a few months before, nobody had recognized him. He was waiting for a Buster Blue bus, this being the line that served Duesterhaus and surrounding trade area, when a woman in a white convertible pulled up to the curb and spoke to him: "Father Urban?"

He smiled back, and, trusting his memory of the car, he took a chance: "Mrs Hopwood?"

14

Belleisle

"You'll be happy to hear Katie got what was coming to her," Sally said.

"I was hoping she would," said Father Urban.

"We've had this kind of trouble before—before Katie. In fact, Norris is getting used to it. I can't say that I am."

Father Urban smiled. "But how'd you know I'd be happy to hear this? For that matter, how'd you know *me?*"

"That morning you left the house—in a taxi—I saw you from my window. And Katie told me how you went to bat for her with Mother."

"And struck out." Or had he? Was it too much to hope that all might yet be well between him and Mrs Thwaites?

"You were trying the impossible, Father, if that's any consolation to you."

"One never knows about these things," he said. Sally could be wrong.

"Norris and I had to pay Katie."

"Oh?" said Father Urban. "Oh, I see."

"Now tell me how you knew *me?*"

"By the car, I confess." Father Urban laughed at himself. "Not entirely, though."

"No?"

"No, there is a certain resemblance. And, yes, I saw you in the distance, when you went out in the launch. From *my* window."

A Buster Blue bus pulled up behind Sally's car. Father Urban signaled that he was a passenger, but the driver was getting out to have a cigarette in the park, and so Father Urban did not say good-by to Sally. She was well preserved for a woman easily thirty-five, possibly forty, small, finely made, attractive. She had a new-old quality that Father Urban had often noticed in children and in other young animals, a fey quality. He could see her in the red pony cart. He liked her as a person and could understand why Monsignor Renton called her the best of the lot. Father Urban felt that she liked him, too, or anyway was curious about him.

"You're going back where you go?" she said.

"That's right. I've been up in the northern part of the state for a few days. On a fishing trip." He was trying to account for his appearance, but he knew it still sounded odd, for although there might be many parts of the world where people went on fishing trips by bus, Minnesota was not one of them. "I saw some beautiful country up there."

"Is someone meeting you in Duesterhaus?"

"I doubt it."

"I could drive you to your door. I couldn't take you there right away, though. Are you in a hurry to get back?"

"Not a-tall," said Father Urban. He was in no hurry to face Wilf without the station wagon, and signaled to the driver that he was not a passenger.

Sally advised him to put his bag in the trunk of the car. "I have to pick up someone," she said.

Just as they were pulling away, Sylvia Bean went by in her little Barracuda. Father Urban waved, but Sylvia cut him dead.

A few blocks away, Sally stopped in front of a run-down apartment building and honked the horn. Presently a woman came out of the building. "This is the person who's taking care of Mother now," Sally said, her tone suggesting that she wished it weren't so.

"Katie's gone then?" said Father Urban. He got out of the car. He didn't want to be sitting between two women.

"Yes, Katie's gone back to Ireland."

Father Urban had advised Katie to get in touch with him if she wished to leave Mrs Thwaites's employment and couldn't for lack of funds, but he really hadn't known what he'd do if it came to transporting her to Ireland—unless, perhaps, Monsignor Renton could have been interested in the underground-railroad aspects of her case.

"This is a friend of the family," Sally said, introducing him to the woman, and not otherwise identifying him—on account of his casual dress, he guessed, and current low rating in Mrs Thwaites's hit parade of priests. "Mrs Leeson's taking care of Mother now."

Mrs Leeson climbed into the car, saying, "We have a lot of fun." Sweet-smelling and made up like a birthday cake, she was a large-boned, muscular brunette somewhere between fifty and seventy-five. "Did you catch the Paar show last night?"

"As a matter of fact, I didn't," Father Urban said, when he realized that Mrs Leeson was talking to him.

"He just got back from a fishing trip up north," Sally said.

"Now don't tell me about the big one that got away," Mrs Leeson said gruffly.

After more of the same, they arrived at Lake Lucille. Mrs Leeson, saying good-by to Father Urban, expressed the hope that they'd meet again someday, and Sally said, "I'll be out in a minute." Father Urban sat in the car, wondering whether Mrs Leeson would mention him to Mrs Thwaites, and, if so, whether the old lady would roll over to a window to see who he might be, this friend of the family, and, if so, whether this was desirable or not. So far as he could tell, though, without staring, he was not observed from above. When Sally came out of the house, she said, "This must be yours," and handed Father Urban one of his collars.

"Thanks. I'm always losing them."

"Can I offer you a drink—or don't you have time for one?"

"It isn't a question of time," Father Urban said, and looked up at Mrs Thwaites's room—and thought he saw a curtain tremble.

Sally smiled. "No, I was thinking of the castle," she said. She gazed away in the direction of the lake and the sun. "I saw Norris a while ago. There. I think I see him. I do, yes."

Father Urban shaded his eyes. "I can't say that I do."

"He's way out."

"What's he doing? Fishing?"

Sally nodded. "Come on, before he moves. Hadn't you better leave that here?"

Father Urban had overlooked the collar in his hand. He deposited it on the seat of the car, and then he followed Sally down to the water. He was still trying to see Norris. They boarded the launch, Sally going to the helm, starting the motor, and Father Urban casting off. They headed straight out into the lake. Soon they were among islands that Father Urban had seen only in the distance, since always before, when he'd sailed under Mrs Thwaites's command, the launch had pursued a coastal course.

"You really think it's safe in here?" he asked. There were rocks all around them.

"No," she said. "Not really. These are the Spice Islands. That's what they were on Dickie's map, when we were kids. This lake was the whole world then."

"What was that big island ahead?"

"Australia. No, he's moved, I guess," Sally said. "If we go around Australia, we may not catch him. No, we'll go back the way we came, and maybe we'll see him when we reach the castle."

Sally worked back through the Spice Islands, and Father Urban was glad when they were gone. When they reached the castle, however, there was no sign of Norris. "He's stopped in some inlet," Sally said. "But he'll see the smoke and come."

"Smoke?"

"You need a fire in the castle these days."

"Don't overdo it," Sally said, coming back from the decanter with their glasses.

"Too much, you think?" said Father Urban, and, with the poker, pushed aside some of the green rushes they'd gathered before entering the castle. The rushes made the fire smoke, and Father Urban felt a certain obligation to keep applying them to the burning logs.

"He won't see the smoke anyway, if he's still out there," Sally said.

Father Urban glanced at the sky darkening in one of the slit windows. "He may not be out there then?"

"No."

"But if he went in, wouldn't he see the launch was gone, and come here?"

"He might not."

"He wouldn't worry?"

"No. I often come here. Sometimes I sleep here."

"You *do?*"

"Is that so odd?"

"No, I guess not," said Father Urban, smiling. Really, it was quite comfortable in the castle, with a fire. It was just a one-room castle with an open iron stairway winding up to a trap

door. There was a bed, or couch, woven of willow and shaped
like a swan, tinted powder blue. In two of the slit windows
there were screens to let in air and keep out insects. No electricity or water (except for the lake, which lapped against one
wall of the castle), but there was firelight, and, on the chimney
piece, if more light were required, there was a lamp. The ashes
and stones of the fireplace had been warm when they arrived.
There was a wind-up phonograph in one corner, and, on the
floor, in front of the fireplace, a polar-bear rug with a number of
burned spots in it. There were tinned snacks—smoked turkey
such as they were having—and there was scotch. "Say, this is
good stuff," Father Urban had said when he tasted it—how good
he hadn't realized until Sally told him it was thirty years old
and a hundred and fourteen proof, which made Father Urban
feel a lot better about mixing it with lake water. He'd hesitated
at that, as he had about eating one of the tiny red berries from
a bush by the castle door. The berry had tasted sweet and then
bitter.

"What'd you say this is?" he asked, raising his glass.

"Old Excellency."

"I'll have to remember that."

"What was your impression of Mrs Leeson?"

"Well, she's nothing like Katie."

"No, I'm afraid not. She's a beautician by trade—a trained
operator."

"That I can believe."

"So Mother's had her hair dyed."

"*What?* I mean—what color?"

"Same as mine."

Sally's hair was mahogany. Father Urban shook his head in
sorrow. Mrs Thwaites must look like hell.

"Father Udovic says it looks just fine."

"Is that what it used to be—the color of yours?"

"No, it was black."

"I don't get it."

"Mrs Leeson and Mother watch for a certain commercial on television—one of those mother-and-daughter soap commercials. When it comes on, Mrs Leeson says, 'My, you two look just like those two.'"

Again Father Urban shook his head in sorrow.

"Young Mrs Oscar Holmgreen and her daughter Debbie, of Fargo, North Dakota."

"What?"

"They're the ones we look like."

Sally seemed to find this amusing, but Father Urban did not find it so. "How *is* your mother, Sally?" He hadn't called her Sally before.

"Happy as a clam."

"Is Dickie still away?"

"Yes."

Father Urban waited for more.

"Dickie and two friends have opened a bookshop in Des Moines."

"*What?* You mean he's gone back to that?"

"I gather it's not like the last one—not Catholic."

"And Dickie's backing it?"

"Oh no. No more than the others. Dickie isn't very well off, you know."

"Is that so?" *Is that so?*

Sally said that Dickie had to get along on the interest from his inheritance, that he'd made over the principal to his mother when he first entered religion. "As he calls it. It was either that or give what he had to them—first it was the Dolomites—or otherwise dispose of it. Naturally, Mother was opposed to that.

She was right, of course, as she has been since—a number of times."

"So Dickie's in Des Moines."

"'A Winter's Tale.'"

"What?"

"That's what they call the place."

"Doesn't sound very good, does it? No wonder his mother's worried." With Dickie not very well off, and with Mrs Thwaites sore at Father Urban, was there *any* hope for Eight Seasons Editions? "Your mother's happy then? No regrets?"

"About Katie?"

"Well, yes," said Father Urban, though he meant more than that.

"None."

Father Urban looked at Sally—her eyes were actually dark brown but appeared black.

"And none where you're concerned. Mother's a hard, hard old woman. You don't want to believe that, do you?"

"Let's just say she's an old woman."

"A hard, hard old woman."

"I wouldn't say she's so hard where you're concerned. You know she worries a lot about you."

Sally picked up their glasses. "I wouldn't count on that, if I were you," she said, and went over to the decanter.

"And what was your impression of Norris?" she asked later on. She had just lit the lamp and placed it on the bookcase, by the phonograph, so the light wouldn't shine in their eyes. They were sitting before the fire in comfortable chairs made of woven willow like the swan but painted a glossy orange that picked up the firelight.

"He seems a very pleasant man," Father Urban said. "The question is what did he think of me?"

"He didn't say. He only said you were someone who'd had an accident. You're all right now, aren't you?"

"Except for occasional headaches."

Father Urban felt that it was time for him to define their relationship. Was it too much to hope that more would come of their meeting than idle conversation and a hangover? "By the way," he said, "would you care to tell me why you're out of the Church?"

"I'm not a religious person."

"You say that as though it were a question of being right- or left-handed."

"Well, isn't it?"

"You could be starving, spiritually, and never know it."

"I know I'm happier out," she said, and offered him another cigarette. His cigars were in his bag.

"Thanks. I'm always curious," he said, lighting her cigarette, and then his, "when I meet somebody who's trying to go it alone. But I'm always disappointed. There's always a skeleton in the closet somewhere—a loved one or a relative back on the shelf. Sometimes people will admit it, but usually they won't. It's hardly ever a matter of faith. There's always more meat for the psychiatrist than the theologian, and it's getting worse, I'd say. In any case, I certainly don't think you're one of those people who lack, or seem to lack, all capacity for God— pillars of the Church, some of 'em. That may cover your mother—*and* brother, for all I know—though, of course, it's not for me to say. But I do say this: if we're going to talk about you and the Church, then we should leave other people out of it."

"Let's not talk about it now." Sally said.

"All right," said Father Urban. He wouldn't push her. He'd made a start. She had said "now" in such a way that it could mean "later."

Sally got up and brought the decanter over to the fire.

"No, I've had enough," Father Urban said. "And whenever you're ready, we'd better go."

She poured a little into her glass. "Sure you wouldn't like to hear the phonograph?" She had suggested this earlier.

"Not particularly."

"I have some lovely old fox trots."

"'Hello, Aloha,'" he said to himself.

"No, not that one. I remember it, though. Is it one of your favorites?"

"No." Father Urban listened to the big trees blowing on the mainland. They were dropping their leaves. On the island, there were only small needle-bearing trees, and they made an indistinct whirring noise. He could hear the water better. He wondered where the station wagon was.

"Then how about a swim?"

Father Urban laughed. "You're psychic, Sally. All right, just a drop," he said, holding out his glass, and then he gave her an account of his fishing trip—suppressing only his suspicions about Billy and Honey, and the part about the station wagon. In the end, though, he told her about the station wagon.

"Then the big one *did* get away?"

"You might say that. But maybe it would've happened anyway—sooner or later. There are some relationships that won't hold up."

"Because they're all wrong."

"This one wasn't *all* wrong. I blame myself, in a way. Billy wasn't ready for anything like that, from me. That was partly my fault. But if he comes around—and that's not *entirely* out of the question—our relationship will be different. Better. From what I know of him, though, I don't think he'll come around."

"And Mother—do you think she'll come around?"

"You know, when you think about it, that was really the same kind of a deal. She wasn't ready. That was partly my fault."

"You didn't enjoy the brute's company, did you? Tell the truth."

"Billy's company? Not particularly. He has a cruel streak."

"Or Mother's company?"

"No, to tell you the truth, I didn't."

"Do you enjoy my company?"

"As a matter of fact, I do."

"But that isn't why you're here, is it?"

"No, not exactly. I don't feel it should be, do you?"

Sally didn't reply to the question. "You say you're always disappointed by people who're trying to go it alone."

"Not by the people themselves but by their reasons."

"Has it occurred to you that people might be disappointed by you and your reasons, and even more by you?"

"I'm not sure I know what you mean," said Father Urban.

"I mean you're an operator—a trained operator like Mrs Leeson, and an operator in your heart—and I don't think you have a friend in the world."

Father Urban smiled. "Now you've gone too far."

"Name *one*."

Father Urban was silent, thinking was there no one he could call his friend? Father Louis? Jack? Monsignor Renton? They were the best he could do, and he could not call one of them his friend—not as Sally was using the word. They all had their shortcomings, though perhaps, as Sally said, the trouble was really in him. He held them off. However, in view of the warnings in Scripture against allowing terrestrial relationships to interfere with one's apostolic work, he wondered if he might not be justified—in not having a friend in the world? "You may be right," he said. "The truth is I've traveled too much, and been too busy, to maintain the kind of friendship you're talking about."

"Busy with Billy, busy with Mother—and busy with me."

"No, this has been fun, but I do think we should be going."

They didn't go, and Father Urban, while Sally played the phonograph, just sat there, sipping scotch and seeing himself as he might have been—in some kind of business you could breathe in, perhaps heavy machinery, much of it going overseas, lots of travel, meeting fellows like Haile Selassie and Farouk's father, whatever his name was, and operating out of a spacious office on Michigan Avenue, high up, with a view of the lake, walnut paneling, Persian carpets, furnished with gifts from potentates and dictators of the better sort, a tree at Christmas, efficient rosy-cheeked girls in white-collared dark dresses, Irish girls hired for the purity of their vocables, and himself hardly ever there. He would have helped the girls with their grave personal problems, and they would be loyal to him and his firm forever, and never marry, and he would have put the crippled son of one of the elevator operators through school. Armour Institute of Technology, which, it occurred to him, was no longer in existence. M.I.T. then, and sent the company plane for him at Christmas. Until his marriage, he'd played around a lot, but he'd never touched waitresses, stewardesses, receptionists, the wives or mistresses of his friends, or anybody who worked for him in the office, in the home office, or in any of his other offices throughout the world. Or—if he had offices, he'd have plants—in any of his plants throughout the world. He had been pretty free and easy with women, it was true, but he'd always been fair. His life hadn't been quite right, though—he'd known it all along—and so he'd fixed that. He'd married late, but not too late. Always partial to mature women, he'd married a widow. Lovely woman. Not beef and not pork but woman. Her throat not as full as it had been, perhaps, but otherwise she was good as new,

nose and mouth finely drawn, arabesque lines, eyes dark, hair
plentiful, tufty (as with some birds), and mahogany, light for
mahogany, expressive hands, holding whatever they held lightly
. . . lovely woman whose first marriage, if you could call it that,
hadn't clicked. In fact, there would have been a divorce if he,
a wheat broker, hadn't been killed in a freak accident. Lost his
footing and fell into a silo—inspecting it for rats—and before help
came, suffocated. Wheat closed over his head. What a way to
go. Same thing—this time a workman—in the news again last
week. Where were the safety engineers? During the football
season, the widow and her new husband came to the Belleisle
Inn, arriving with their golden calf luggage, white stitching, a
night or two before the games. Big Ten. Evanston, Ann Arbor,
or Madison. Nice place, the Belleisle, fireplace in every room.
Out of the night, the orange and black night, the sound of the
wind reached him, and the noise of dating, the squeal of tires
cornering, the rock 'em-sock 'em lineplay in the back seats, and
baa, baa, baa from fraternity houses. No, he hadn't gone East
(his wife's brother was Harvard) because he hadn't had the
dough for it, or even the inclination. Northwestern, Wisconsin,
or Chicago (once a power in the Conference, the Maroons),
one of those places. No table-waiting for him. He went first
class, as a gladiator. A little light by present-day standards, but
who wasn't then? Fleet halfback, and did all the kicking. What
ever happened to the dropkick? Also lettered in basketball and
baseball. No time for track. No hockey, it wasn't played. Not
an athletic bum. History major. Stood him in good stead later
on in life, at dinner tables throughout the world, the old world
anyway. Evening, ma'am. Winston. Aristotle. The wind seems
to be changing. An amateur in the lost sense of the word. His
one book (one's enough), a by-product of road trips with the
varsity, jotted down in hotel lobbies while waiting for the
elevator, but still highly regarded by those who'd spent their
whole lives in the field, and soon to be reissued in a quality

paperback for which there might be a large public, perhaps a very large public. All royalties from *When Saints Were Bold* would go to his wife's charities. Visiting Nurse Association. Junior League. He had no children, so far as he knew, and his wife had none by her first marriage. No regrets. The world was no place for children nowadays. But every summer he sent poor kids to camp, sometimes by station wagon driven by his man Friday, and sometimes on the Empire Builder. Camp Wil-Frid-Bes-Tud-Ik, up in Minnesota, land of sky-blue waters. Non-sectarian camp. Own religious interest? None. Raised a Roman Catholic, he espoused no religion now, but didn't make one of *that*. He had got away, he hadn't fallen away, from the faith of his fathers. Was that *Andrew* Thwaites, Mr Studley? Indeed it was, son, and he likes your style. He could do a lot for you. There's just one thing. . . . But he still went to Mass whenever he was in Rome or Paris, which was a source of consolation and hope to a certain Father Gabriel and a dozen scholarly Jesuits. Some of his best friends were Catholics with a cruel streak in them. He didn't associate with people if he didn't enjoy their company. He wouldn't do business with people he didn't like. He knew people in all walks of life, and was well liked, but too much of a loner to have close friends. He traveled around too much, and was, despite appearances to the contrary, too busy. Oh, high-level stuff. Next week, Ghana. Allis-Chalmers the only danger there. GE in Turkey. Big place, Africa. Room for all, white and black. Egypt, seat of ancient civilization, nicer before Nasser, himself nice enough. Lots of poverty, of course. Europe much the same again. Your best hotels and restaurants are good the world over, and were before Hilton. Tito not a bad guy when you get to know him—his real name's Broz. Communist? Well, it depends what you mean. You have to define your terms. Wonderful food. *Iron* Curtain, Mrs Bean? I didn't find it so. Not a-tall. Sent an old trench coat to the

cleaners and it came back good as new. There right after
Premier Stalin passed away. Malenkov. Too bad. Nice to meet
a Russian doesn't look like a streetcar conductor on the Mil-
waukee Avenue run. Shrapnel Brothers? Never heard of 'em,
but I'll ask my barber about the publication. Recreations:
sports cars, history, golf, people. A bit of fluff, yes, but don't
put that down. Except for occasional headaches, in perfect
health. No, born downstate, land of Lincoln, but consider Chicago my home. New York? All right, if you happen to be a
waiter or a cab driver. I don't. No Michigan Avenue and no
lake and the whole place has a bombed look. Give me Chicago.
The most beautiful sound I know is the sound of whistles on
Michigan Avenue at dusk, especially in the fall. I like to sit in
Grant Park and listen to the cops calling to each other like
nightingales. You know the Chicago whistle? *Wheeeeeeeeeeee-
uhhhhhhhhwheeeeeuhhhh.* I'd say it's a musical instrument, related to the clarinet, piccolo, and oboe, and also related to the
old-time train whistle. It'd scare the hell out of you—rightly
played, that is—if you didn't see the lights and the people and
the Wrigley Building. I like to see Michigan Avenue shining
wet at night. I like to come out of the Blackstone or the Drake
at dusk, especially in the fall, with two or three good ones in
me, and hear those whistles, the mush and the whine of rubber,
the distant roar—it always seems to be centered over LaSalle
Street, to the south, but it's like a haze you can see and never
touch. For many years I traveled out of Chicago, and I'm
proud to call it my home. Expect from life? Only what any
sane person would expect. What I've had from it. I've written
my book, I've married my wife, I've made my pile. No com-
plaints, no regrets. Who could ask for anything more?

Sally closed the phonograph and came away from it, saying,
"Now I'm ready for a swim, if you are."
After a moment, he said, "As a matter of fact, I'm not."

"No swim?"

"If you're serious, no."

She smiled. "It's dark out there, if that's what's worrying you."

"No, if you rented bathing suits—grey cotton ones—I still wouldn't go in, if you follow me."

"No."

"Too cold."

"That's all?"

"That's enough. We've had too much to drink, I don't have to tell you. You could get a cramp, in your condition, and drown."

"Wouldn't you save me?"

He caught the implication, thought it unworthy of her, ignored it. "*I* could get a cramp. You wouldn't be strong enough to save me. We'd both drown. What a way to go. Think it over."

Sally lit a cigarette, and did seem to be thinking it over—as well she might, for the potential for scandal was practically infinite. "I'm going in," she said.

"Could I have one of those?" he said, reaching for her cigarettes. "Thanks." He was in a bad spot, but to act like it would be the worst thing he could do. He recalled the gameness displayed by the keeper of the late Bushman at the Lincoln Park Zoo, man and beast out for their daily walk around the grounds, but out for hours before the gorilla—changed overnight from youngster to monster, knowing his strength and wanting his way—chanced to wander into his cage. Snap! And Bushman had had his last walk. How easy it would've been for the keeper to panic. He had not. He had held on. Father Urban handed Sally her cigarettes and got to his feet, saying in a yawning tone, "Come on, let's go."

"I'm going in."

"Come on. Let's not spoil it."

"Spoil *what?*"

"Come on."

"I'm going in."

"No."

"You wouldn't try to stop me, would you?"

"No," said Father Urban, but seeing that this made her smile, he said, "Yes, if need be. But come on. Let's go. Let's not spoil it."

"Oh, all right."

He got up.

And she got up, but then she changed her mind, and in a matter of moments, she was standing before him, before the fire, back to him, wearing nothing but her shoes. They were high-heeled shoes. Calf. Golden calf. Lovely woman. No doubt of it.

"All right," she said, turning around. "Try and stop me."

"You've got me covered," he said, and took his eyes off her, and kept them off, commending himself. It was like tearing up telephone directories, the hardest part was getting started.

"*Not* going to stop me?"

"No, I'll wait." He moved over to the phonograph. He gazed into the lamplight. If he'd had a cigar, he would've lit it. That would've been something to do. When he heard her heels on the stairway, he moved back to his chair, sat down, and gazed into the fire. He was thinking ahead, wondering how he could make it easier for her later. "Don't be too long," he said. He was playing it down.

The first shoe hit him on the shoulder, a glancing blow, and landed in the dead ashes at the front of the fire, from which he quickly retrieved it, but the second one struck him on the head. "Hey!" he yelled, but did not turn around and look at her. The second shoe had hurt. It might have killed him. What a way to go.

He heard the trap door open and shut. He stood the shoes together, and, looking at them there, felt sorry for Sally. Life here below, no matter how much you might wish it otherwise, was shoes—not champagne, but shoes, and not dirt, but shoes, and this, roughly speaking, was the mind of the Church.

He heard the diving board rumble overhead. Baroomph! said the lake. He heard splashing, and then he heard nothing. She could be climbing the rungs set in the wall of the castle. No, she was still in the water.

Was it too much to hope that she'd return to him chastened in spirit? Water perhaps the best therapy known to man. Listen for sounds of drowning, and hope for the best, and try to make it up to her somehow. Hell hath no fury like a woman scorned. *Not* scorned. Not a-tall. Lovely woman. Tell her so, if need be. Play it down, way down. Oh, I understand. You just wanted to pull up the shrubbery and throw stones at the tigers, but that's all past now. Why, who lives here? The door's open! Say, why don't *you* wait inside while *I* . . . that's it, while I see if I can find some bananas. Snap!

Putt-putt. *No!* Oh yes. Putt-putt-putt. And putt-putt-putt-putt-putt.

"Hey!" yelled Father Urban, shooting out the door, and almost killing himself in the dark. *"Hey!"*

Father Urban stood on the stone pier, where the launch had been berthed, and hoped that Sally would return for him and her clothes, but after a few minutes of this, he went back into the castle, only hoping that she'd manage to slip into the house and up to her room unseen. There was little reason to believe that she'd rescue him later that night, and morning didn't strike him as a very good bet either. In any case, he preferred not to spend the night in the castle. Too much had already happened there. If he had to swim for it sooner or later, the best time was now, in the cover of night.

So he placed the screen in front of the fire, extinguished the lamp, and checked out of the castle. At the end of the stone pier, he sat down and removed his shoes and socks. No stars, only a cloudy half-assed moon, and the lake more or less invisible. It was very definitely there, though, in motion, noisy with waves, waiting for him. After tying his shoes together, and then to his belt, he slipped down into the cold, cold water, and struck out for the mainland. It was perhaps fifty yards away.

He soon discovered that the wind, like everything else that day, was against him. Somewhere between the island and the mainland, when he could see neither very well, and the waves seemed to shove him down, he sensed the beginnings of a cramp, panicked, and, feeling that it was him or them, he got rid of his shoes. He did go along better after that, but when he reached the other shore—when this was no longer his only objective in life—he knew what he'd done. Even as a child, he hadn't liked going barefooted, and what he'd felt then, the innate cruelty of sticks and stones, he felt again. This, though, was nothing now. Wet and woebegone and shivering, he sat on a fallen birch and put on his socks and hid the whiteness of his feet from himself.

He was down the shore about two hundred yards from the Thwaites house. He was tempted to head for the main road, to go on without his bag, and hope that it would somehow reach him later, but this, he realized, could be a bad mistake, the same kind of mistake he'd made when he'd jettisoned his shoes. He would just be letting himself in for more trouble, trouble that could easily be avoided—easily, that is, if all his

instincts weren't for getting off Mrs Thwaites's property before
something worse happened to him.

But he did go to the car and he did get his bag out of the
trunk. Then he thought of his collar, left on the front seat, but
it wasn't there. He felt around on the floor. Not there, either.
So he went on without it. If Sally had taken it, he was afraid
that more was wrong with her than he'd thought.

On the main road, cars passed him by. He didn't blame them.
When he came to a filling station, with a nice warm stove in it,
and a pay telephone, he didn't blame the attendant for looking at
him as he did: Think he'd sell his bag before his shoes. "Use
this one," the attendant said, pointing to the telephone on the
desk. "It won't cost you."

"Well, I must say that's nice of you," said Father Urban.
There was only one person he could call, once he really thought
about it, and fortunately that one was in. "And don't send anybody else," Father Urban said. "Come yourself."

"*Ho*ly Paul!" said Monsignor Renton when he saw what
he'd come for. "You look like you spent the day barking at the
bottom of a well."

15

One of Our Best Men

After a drink at Monsignor Renton's ("Bourbon, Red, and no
ice"), Father Urban was driven back to the Hill in the Imperial.
His bag was heavy with wet clothing—how much Monsignor
Renton didn't know, for Father Urban hadn't mentioned his
earlier mishap. He was wearing his own damp underwear, shirt
and trousers from Monsignor Renton, socks and shoes from
Cox's room (Cox was away, attending a convention of youth
specialists), and a suede jacket from Box, to whom Monsignor
Renton had explained, "It wasn't so cold when Father Urban
left the cloister."

"Well, of course, it was no way for her to act," Monsignor
Renton said, on the way to the Hill, "but if you ask me, she's
still the best of the lot." "You may be right," said Father Urban.
He had told Monsignor Renton that Sally had left the castle in
a huff, and, thinking of her honor as much as his own, he had
let Monsignor Renton assume that Norris had been there at
the time. Monsignor Renton was under the impression that
Norris was still there. "You say there's a place to sleep?" "Oh
yes." "Well, I suppose he'll be all right then. She'll cool off by
morning." "Oh yes." "I wouldn't take it so hard, if I were you.
It may not have been your fault at all. In fact, I'd say it was a

lovers' quarrel, and you got caught in the middle." "You may be right." "If I'd been in your shoes, though, I would've stayed with Norris." "Yes, well, I was in a hurry to get home." "Good shoes, were they?" "Pretty good." "Too bad. Say, I shot one of those Dunlop Maxfli's today. Ever use 'em?" "I have, yes." "Good ball." "Yes." "And how was the fishing up north?" "Not too good." "I'm told you have to go farther north, almost to the Arctic Circle, if you want to catch anything." "You may be right." "Coming back to the other, though, I'd say the moral, if any, is stay away from people."

Father Urban told Wilf that Billy and Paul had left rather suddenly, no more than that, but that was enough for Wilf. According to Wilf, traveling by car was faster than going by train, or even by plane, from remote points. When Wilf asked how the fishing had been, Father Urban said, "Lousy." Wilf said it had been unusually good at home, that Brother Harold had frozen about seventy pounds in the past two days, including one walleye, an eight-pound lunker.

"You should've stayed here," Wilf said.

Father Urban went around with a numb feeling, nursing a cold. He preached when asked, but not too well. He passed up an important funeral in Great Plains. In general, he neglected his contacts. Had there been any occasion to do so, he could not have said "Hello—hello!" with gusto. He wasn't himself. He even stayed away from the course.

Naturally, he wondered what had become of the station wagon, and thought of various heartbreaking ways in which Billy might dispose of it, or render the Order's title to it useless. For two weeks, though, he held Wilf off, with Wilf's help. Traveling (Wilf said) was much faster by car than by train, or even by plane, from remote points, and "business," which had made Billy hurry back to Chicago, was keeping him there and holding him incommunicado. Toward the end of this period, however, Wilf did say it was lucky they hadn't traded in the pickup truck.

And then a notice came from the Minnesota State Highway Department starting that the Wisconsin State Highway Department had reported a station wagon—Rambler, brown, registered in ownership of Order of St Clement, Duesterhaus, Minnesota —parked at Chicago & North Western R.R. Station, Ashland, Wisconsin. Keys, found in car, in possession of Police Department, Ashland, Wisconsin.

"What a man!" said Wilf. "He forgot all about it!"

When Father Urban heard the news, his heart gave a little leap, and a little voice said, "All is *not* lost!" But another little voice said, "Aw, shut up!"

The next morning, Brother Harold was dispatched to Ashland by bus. He was carrying his lunch and a letter for the Chief of Police, a letter in which Wilf explained everything.

And that morning Father Urban joined Jack in the garden where they toiled at getting in the "swedes" and other root crops. Father Urban, who hadn't set foot in the garden since his picture was taken for the brochure, was trying to lick his cold, trying to sweat it away. His cold had hung on, and lately it had descended into his chest from which, from time to time, there now came odd noises, as if he were digesting his lungs. Soon after he began working in the garden, he realized how weak he was, and was ready to quit, but he didn't, and presently he swooned dead away.

When he came to, Jack walked him to his room. Wilf called the doctor. That afternoon, Father Urban was admitted to the hospital in Great Plains and placed in an oxygen tent. That was the last he saw of himself for a while. Crazy dreams—his father raking a sand trap that wouldn't stay raked, his mother playing the square piano by the light of the swan's-head gas jet that had been in the kitchen, over the pump. He spent a great deal of time back in Illinois, in a land of pumps, cisterns, grape arbors, outhouses, lush cemeteries, and rain. The rain went on and on, and then it stopped. When he came to, though, it was there outside his window.

"No," said Monsignor Renton, his first visitor. "We haven't had any rain to speak of until today. Actually, it began late last night. I'd say you missed the best week of the year. You won't see another like it until next year."

"If then," said Father Urban. That was how he felt.

Four days later, he was strong enough to return to the Hill, but he was still pretty weak. His headaches were still with him, and had joined forces with whatever ailed him gastrically, so that they were now *sick* headaches. He had no appetite for food, or anything. Even reading was too much for him. When he was up—he was in and out of bed all day—he just sat in his chair (again on loan to him from the Rec Room) and watched the wind and the rain strip the trees, all but the red oak, and wondered how many old paupers before him had watched the coming of winter from that window.

There hadn't been much mail for him when he got out of the hospital, a bill (forty-two dollars) from Henn's Haven, with a note at the bottom, "Just a friendly hello from the north woods, and that goes double for Mother. Deer season starts Nov. 11 but still time to make reservations if you hurry. Get up a party. Group rates. As always, Dad Henn"; a letter from Father Excelsior saying he'd written, as advised, to the address in Des Moines, but had received no reply—any other suggestions?; and a ballot from the Novitiate.

Father Urban tried to discuss the election with Jack, who, with Rex, visited him in the evening, but it wasn't easy. About all Jack would say was that Wilf seemed to think it would be Father Boniface again. "He would," said Father Urban. "Or," said Jack, "Father Siegfried." "Yeah?" said Father Urban. "I'd say we need more of a change than that. An older man, I'd say. Look at the job Pope John's doing." Father Urban, in a futile gesture, marked his ballot for Father August, and would've advised Jack to do likewise if he hadn't already voted. "I hope you didn't go for Boniface." Jack didn't respond at all to this, and thus adhered to the letter of the Rule. The Holy Founder, who had lived for some years in Rome, and had seen plenty of dirty pool in his day, was very strict on that point—no politicking, fratres.

When the weather turned clear and cold—it was now late in October—Wilf got out his devil's-food coat, Brother Harold put discount-house anti-freeze in the pickup truck and station wagon, and Father Urban plugged in the electric heater. "I'm afraid there's another overshoe down there somewhere," he told Wilf.

"Run it on low, will you?" said Wilf. He was busy with re-treatants these days, and only stopped in to see Father Urban for a few minutes in the evening. If Jack and Rex happened to be there, Wilf, when he left, took Rex with him. "Heat's bad for a dog like this." There was more to it than that, though. Rex had become attached to Jack, and Wilf was jealous. "C'mon, boy!" and "Here, boy!" he'd cry, with a dubious look in his eye. Rex and Wilf would go away together, but Rex soon returned to Father Urban's room and Jack. There wasn't much Wilf could do about it. He'd read about a rabid skunk in the *Farmer*, and didn't care to have the dog out at night, unattended, or to be out very long himself. "You know where that wind's coming from, don't you? Hudson Bay."

Jack brought his manuscript to Father Urban's room in the evening, and worked on it there, in comfort. The first time Father Urban got a look at it, he was alarmed. A huntress, chasing a deer, had shot an arrow into Sir Launcelot by mistake, the arrow going into him past the barb, "in such a place," Jack had written, "that he might not sit in no saddle."

"Hey," said Father Urban. "What kind of English is that?"

"Malory kept the double negative to preserve the spirit of the original French," Jack said. "And that's what Mr Thwaites wants to do—to preserve the spirit of the original English."

"Should be great for children."

"We'll have an explanatory note, of course."

" 'That he might not sit in no saddle'! Let's face it, Jack. It sounds like hell."

"It did to me *at first*."

Father Urban was pretty sure that Jack was wasting his time with Sir Launcelot—as Jack called him. Father Urban called him Lancelot. "Have you heard from Dickie lately?"

"Mr Thwaites? No, not lately."

"Have you done anything with St Adalbert?"

"I still have some way to go with this, and this comes first." Poor Jack!

There were five hundred seven chapters in Malory, and even those dealing directly with Sir Launcelot were too many for the planned edition. It was necessary, too, to treat of such events as the coming of Arthur, and the founding of the Round Table, and such characters as Merlin, Guenever, Morgan le Fay, Sir Gawaine, and Sir Galahad. Jack regarded Sir Galahad as the real hero of the book, and had given him the full treatment. He had wished to do more for Sir Percival and Sir Tristram, whom he rated next to Sir Galahad in holiness, but this was impossible, for reasons of space. The biggest problem for Jack, though, was Sir Launcelot.

"There are times when I don't know where I am with him," Jack told Father Urban. "He's the Hamlet of the book." Jack could find no evidence that Sir Launcelot and Lady Elaine had been married before a priest. Sir Launcelot had been under a spell when he begat the child of their union, but the same could not be said for Lady Elaine. Why hadn't their union been regularized later? With another Elaine, the fair maid of Astolat, Sir Launcelot had been chaste enough—she had literally died as a result. What Sir Launcelot had to say, by way of explanation, was certainly to his credit: "She would none other ways be answered but that she would be my wife, outher else my paramour; and of these two I would not grant her, but I proffered her, for her good love that she showed me, a thousand pounds yearly to her, and to her heirs, and to wed any manner knight that she could find best to love in her heart. . . . I love not to be constrained to love; for love must arise of the heart, and not by no constraint." This, though, was no help where the first Elaine was concerned. Young Galahad, through the negligence of both parents, relatives on both sides, and the clergy, too, it would appear, had been born a bastard.

This was a matter that would not be dealt with in the planned edition, but it did worry Jack. Had he been able to understand it, then he thought he might have understood the relationship between Sir Launcelot and Guenever. This would have to be dealt with somehow, for it was this relationship that had led to war between King Arthur and Sir Launcelot (a war fortunately nipped in the bud by the Pope), to the dissolution of the fellowship of the Round Table, to King Arthur's death, to Sir Gawaine's death, to Guenever's entering a nunnery (as a nun), and to the vocation of Sir (later Father) Launcelot.

"I see what you mean," Father Urban said. "What do they usually do in children's editions?"

"One I have refers to 'sinful love.' "

"You'll have to do better than that."

"I've thought of 'untrue love.' "

"That's better."

"Or 'high treason.' "

"I'd say that's it."

Jack, however, didn't regard Sir Launcelot guilty *as* charged. "Malory seems to be of two minds about the Queen, too." Jack read a couple of passages to Father Urban. "See?" he said.

"Look. I don't know anything about this," Father Urban said. "I've always heard that Sir Lancelot and the Queen were that way, but I don't *know*."

"There's good evidence that Sir Launcelot, *on the night he was surprised by Sir Agravaine and others*, was innocent. I could show you where."

"No, thanks," said Father Urban, and went back to his own reading. He had brought up several volumes from *The Works of Theodore Roosevelt*, one of the few sets in the Hill's library that was all there, and was enjoying a respite from the Dark and Middle ages. It was surprising, though, how often he came across passages that started him thinking on his own life. "Killing a deer from a boat while the poor animal is swimming in the water, or on snowshoes as it flounders helplessly in the deep drifts, can only be justified on the plea of hunger. This is also true of lying in wait at a lick. Whoever indulges in any of these methods, save from necessity, is a butcher pure and simple, and has no business in the company of true sportsmen." And sometimes just a word would start Father Urban thinking: ". . . we are glad to sit by the great fireplace, with its roaring cottonwood logs"; ". . . spangled with brilliant red berry clusters"; "Sometimes we racked, or shacked along at the fox trot, which is the cow-pony's ordinary gait."

A couple of evenings later, though, Father Urban was drawn into the question of Sir Launcelot's guilt or innocence. In the end, after considering the text, he was inclined to agree with Jack. Sir Launcelot's past performances with the Queen were against him, it was true. Yes, even if, as Malory said, "love that time was not as is nowadays," Sir Launcelot had "brast" the iron bars clean out of the window to Guenever's chamber on one occasion, and had taken his "pleasance and liking" until dawn. But on the night he was surprised by Sir Agravaine, Sir Mordred, Sir Colgrevance, and others, Father Urban found him not guilty. "He says he's innocent, and I, for one, believe him," said Father Urban.

"My, I'm glad to hear you say that," Jack said. He had been bogged down in the book, and now went on swiftly, writing that Sir Launcelot and the Queen were "wrongly accused of high treason on this occasion," rushing through the battle scenes, and on to the hermitage where the Archbishop of Canterbury was hermit in residence. There Sir Launcelot died to the world and, after the customary six years of study, took Orders and was instrumental in the vocations of Sir Bors, Sir Galihud, Sir Galihodin, Sir Blamore, Sir Bleoberis, Sir Villiers, Sir Clarras, and Sir Gahalantine. "And there was none of these knights but they read in books," Jack wrote, "and holp for to sing Mass, and rang bells, and did bodily all manner of service. And so their horses went where they would, for they took no regard of no worldly riches. For when they saw Sir Launcelot endure such penance, in prayers, and fastings, they took no force what pain they endured, for to see the noblest knight of the world take such abstinence that he waxed full lean."

"You've lost some weight," said Mr O'Hara, who owned the barber shop in the General Diggles Hotel. Mr O'Hara was a good barber, good enough to hold a chair in the Palmer House, but he wouldn't leave it at that. His real love was medicine, and if you were ignorant of his profession's history, in this respect, he told you about it. He had prescribed "Restorine" for Father Urban's grey hair, and a girdle for Father Urban's pot, "not that you *really* need one." (Father Urban hadn't done anything about these vital matters.) Mr O'Hara also prescribed for the world's ills. Give Arizona more water, and you wouldn't know it from Wisconsin. Heat the Yukon—or even the South Pole, which, unlike the North Pole, had land under it—and evaporate any surplus water atomically, or pipe it up to Arizona in light plastic pipes. Regulate the Gulf Stream. Give the world what it needed, and it would be all right, and do the same for people. Very few of the world's leaders were properly mated, and Great Plains was no different. Ray Bean wasn't good for Sylvia, and Marge, the wife of George, Father Urban's friend in the bank, was bad for him. Mr O'Hara's new shoeshine boy was another who needed help. "Much as I'd like to tell him what to do, I can't. He's a strict Lutheran." For an Irish Catholic, Mr O'Hara was an odd duck. He got a lot out of *Life*, and was so sincerely interested in the physiology of the world and its people, and was so humorless, that Father Urban, when he felt that some objection, or modification, was in order, didn't know how to put it. So he said nothing. Every time he went to Mr O'Hara he thought of going elsewhere for his next haircut, but he always returned to Mr O'Hara—he was such a good barber. Others went to him as they would to a physician. You couldn't quite hear what was being said at Mr O'Hara's chair, which was at the rear of the shop, but you could see Mr O'Hara listening to the patient describe his ailment in his own words. You could see Mr O'Hara nodding and gravely inquiring. Sometimes Mr O'Hara's razor would fall silent on the strop, while he listened, or his scissors would hang open, poised between snips. But then would come the diagnosis, shnip, snip, snip, prognosis, shnip, snip, snip, and cure, if any, and, finally, as the patient left the chair, "Feel free to call me at the house, Bill. Next."

So Mr O'Hara wasn't making idle conversation when he commented on Father Urban's loss of weight, nor when he asked

whether Father Urban's head was still troubling him. At their
last consultation, Mr O'Hara had told him to try standing on it
for fifteen minutes just before retiring. "Did you do what I told
you?"

"I haven't felt up to that. I did try letting it hang down over
the edge of the bed."

"That's better than nothing, but I wish you'd give the other
a try when you feel up to it. Of course, you know what you
should do."

"Yes. I've been thinking of that."

"You really should. Would you like me to make the arrangements? I could give him a ring tonight."

Father Urban thought this over, and then he said: "Would
you?"

"Sure. I won't say it won't cost you something, but I'll ask
him to make it easy on you. I'm taking a little more off the top
than usual."

"Well, I hope it won't come to that," said Father Urban.

Thus his case was referred to Mr O'Hara's son, a big head
specialist in Rochester.

Father Urban went down by train. He stayed a week, and
was given a thorough physical examination. Special attention, of
course, was given to his head, Xrays, electroencephalograms,
and so on—the works. The results were negative.

"Doesn't show a thing," said young Dr O'Hara, holding one
of the Xrays up to the light.

"How do you mean that?" said Father Urban.

Young Dr O'Hara sat down on the desk in Father Urban's
room at the hospital and put his feet on the chair. He didn't
inspire confidence somehow. "Perfectly normal," he said.

Father Urban still felt that something was wrong with his
head. "You'd *tell* me, wouldn't you?"

"Oh, but of course," said young Dr O'Hara, with a big smile.

"That's one thing I believe in. Now let's get this straight. There could be plenty wrong. It just wouldn't show up. You can understand that, can't you?"

"Oh yes."

"When you get a little older, you know, the old machine develops a few knocks. You have to expect these things."

"I suppose you do. I just never had anything like it before."

"First time for everything, you know. Have you tried aspirin?"

"Yes, of course."

"Didn't help?"

"Some. The trouble is I don't know when these attacks are coming, and then it's too late."

"You might try Anacin for faster relief. It won't upset your stomach either."

"That's what you recommend then?"

"Yes, in a case like yours."

"I see."

"Of course, no two cases are alike."

"No, I suppose not. Well, thanks."

"Say hello to Dad," said young Dr O'Hara, after making sure he had Father Urban's correct address.

POWWOW

Present were the Rev. Fathers Wilfrid (Bestudik), John (Kelleher), and Urban (Roche), with Brother Harold (Peters) recording. The Rector called upon Father Urban for a prayer.

RECTOR: Thank you, Father. Once again, I choose this day to meet with you—this day because it marks the Order's second anniversary here. I'm happy to say that the past year was in every way better than the first one, and I thank you for making it so. You, Father Urban, and you, Father John, and you, too, Brother Harold. Without you, well. . . .

FR JOHN: Our thanks to you, Father.

RECTOR: Thank you, Father.

Financially, St Clement's Hill was doing better than ever before, even though expenses were at an all-time high. What had been realized from retreats and weekend work in the past year was no little sum, but was nothing compared with the satisfaction there was in a job well done. Only last week, the Bishop was said to have said, "Those men have become an asset to the diocese." Wasn't that nice? That was how they wanted to keep it, and so they would continue their weekend work as long as it didn't conflict with their obligations at the Hill. In any case, now that they weren't going to St Monica's, there would always be a man on duty at the Hill (Brother Harold would be there, too, of course), and the two men who did go out weren't away as long as in the past, thanks to the station wagon. Nevertheless, there were problems. Several retreatants had complained about the coldness of their rooms. Perhaps more would have done so if they'd spoken their minds freely. Therefore, in the next few days, the Rector would install a blower in the furnace—rather, although this would cost money, would have one installed by local labor. (The blower itself was coming from the discount house in Minneapolis.) Thus the Rector was acting before the Hill got the reputation of being uncomfortable in the winter time. This was what the Rector called staying on top of a situation. He was also doing something about that bad place in the northwest corner of the roof. He had received a number of estimates, and had got the best possible deal, but the job was going to cost $92.50, not counting the cost of materials. It would begin as soon as these arrived from Minneapolis. After that, the attic would be insulated by the same contractor—an *experienced man, presently unemployed, and his son—who would use insulation (Woolite) also on order from Minneapolis. Nobody at the Hill would have anything to do with these jobs, not even Brother Harold.*

RECTOR: Now, as for the holes in the eaves, have you noticed something? The squirrels have disappeared. It's the same all around here. That last frost we had in the spring played hob with the nuts. Hard on the squirrels, of course, but a break for us.

FR JOHN: Where'd they go?

RECTOR: I understand they've migrated to the east of us, but they'll be back next year. House seems awfully quiet at night.

FR URBAN: We still have a mouse.

FR JOHN: Yes, there's one lives in the wall between our rooms.

RECTOR: Does it bother you?

FR JOHN: Oh no.

RECTOR: Does it bother *you*, Father?

FR URBAN: Oh no.

RECTOR: Because if it does, maybe we can get rid of it. You have a mousetrap, Brother? No? Well, better buy one. We can always find use for it. And if there's anything else you need, Brother, let me know. So much for that. Now then.

More than forty religious orders would be represented at the upcoming Vocations Fair at the Catholic high school in Oster-gothenburg. The Rector, after making several inquiries, had been invited to participate, and permission to do so had since been received from Chicago. So the Clementines would have a booth at the Fair. They would display their publications, among them the brochure, and would be ready to talk turkey with likely prospects. Probably most orders would let it go at that, and hope for the best. As always, the small orders would be at a disadvantage. The Clementines would not be favored by the

*location of their booth (between the Jesuits and the Dominicans),
but the Rector and Brother Harold had come up with something that they hoped would not only redress the balance in
their favor but would appeal to youngsters of high school age
—an I. Q. test.*

RECTOR: I don't have to tell you that everybody likes to take
an I.Q. test. Now here are some of the questions. Please listen
carefully. "Who was the Holy Founder of the Order of St
Clement?"—"St Clement of Blois." You realize, of course, that
the questions and answers will be scrambled on the page. "Who
was St Clement of Blois?"—"A Frenchman of noble birth."
Too easy, you think, but wait. "Was St Clement of Blois also
known as Pope Clement?"—"No." "Was St Clement of Blois a
martyr?"—"Yes." You can see it's getting more difficult—and
don't forget these are high school students. "How did St Clement
of Blois die?"—"He was slain by fanatics." "How did fanatics
slay St Clement of Blois?"—"They crushed him under a millstone." Now a lot of 'em will give that answer to the previous
question—"How did St Clement of Blois die?" They'd be right,
of course, but it wouldn't be the right answer. That'll throw a
lot of 'em, and some of the other questions are just as tricky.
Well, that's how it works. There are twenty questions in all.
There are twenty-one answers, however. One of the answers,
H²O, has nothing to do with the questions. Now here's how we
grade the test. First we multiply the number of correct answers
by ten, and then we subtract the number of minutes the student
takes to complete the test. Let's say a student gets eighteen
right, and takes seven minutes. Ten times eighteen is a hundred and eighty. Subtract seven. That gives the student an
I.Q. of 173. Now here's what we'll use to time them. Just an
ordinary kitchen timer. I bought it today. Brother Harold's been
wanting one for some time, and when this is over, I'm going

to let him have it. Well, what do you think? Father Urban?

FR URBAN: Should make for conversation.

RECTOR: That's the idea, exactly—to get these kids talking and thinking about the Order. Even if they don't do anything about it, they'll learn a few facts they ought to know. You'd say it's O.K. then?

FR URBAN: Yes.

RECTOR: Father John?

FR JOHN: Yes.

RECTOR: Good. I was afraid maybe you wouldn't like it. Now then. As you know, since you voted, this was an election year. The outcome I now make known to you, as required by the Rule. Our Holy Founder, you'll remember, was very clear on this point, and so we've never had the kind of situation that he aimed to prevent. Of course, communications are better nowadays. But be that as it may. The honor goes to one of our best men, as it should—and indeed as it always does, thanks be to God. About that I don't think there'll be *much* disagreement here. At least I hope not. I have the honor, then, the special honor, I might add. . . .

The Rector distributed copies of Regula S. Clementis necnon Rituale Ordinis Ejus.*

RECTOR: *Urbanus?*†	Urban?
FR URBAN: *Urbanus sum.*	I am Urban.
RECTOR: *Surge, Urbane.* *Si contigerit (quod Deus* *advertat) te carne esse de-* *pressum, peccato captivum,*	Rise Urban. [Urban does.] In the event (which God for- bid) that you are depressed by the flesh, a prisoner to sin,

* *The Rule of St Clement and the Rites of the Order.*
† From this point on, the Rector and Father Urban spoke Latin.

ignorantia caecum, exteri-
oribus deditum, oremus:
[Orant.]
... *utinam suaviter pur-*
geris, ardenter afficiaris,
misericors fias.

FR URBAN: *Amen.*

RECTOR: *Scisne privatum do-*
minum temerarios servos
nutrire?

FR URBAN: *Scio.*

RECTOR: *Num oportet me*
monere te de periculis in
marsupiis latentibus?

FR URBAN: *Non oportet. De*
marsupiis audivi, atque ea
vitare volo tamquam occa-
siones peccatorum, etsi ipsa
marsupia non sunt mala.

RECTOR: *Quae sunt tria an-*
gula veritatis?

FR URBAN: *Ratio, qua nos*
discutimus. Affectus, quo
aliis miseremur. Puritas, qua
ad invisibilia sublevamur.

RECTOR: *Putas, primo homini*
profuit, licet ipse non lib-
enter peccavit, quod se per

blinded by ignorance, in
bondage to creatures and
things, let us pray. [They
pray.] That you be gently
purged, ardently moved, and
made merciful.

Let it be so.

Do you know that a familiar
master breeds contemptuous
servants?

I do.

Need I speak to you of the
dangers in pockets?

No. Of them I have heard and
will them avoid as occasions
of sin, though in themselves
they are not evil.

What are the three corners
of truth?

Reason, by which we examine
ourselves. Love, by which we
sympathize with others. Purity, by which we are lifted to
invisible heights.

Did it profit the first man
when he said he did not sin
willingly, and advanced his

uxorem, tanquam per carnis infirmitatem, defendit? Aut primi Martyris lapidatores, quoniam aures suas continuerunt, per ignorantiam excusabiles erunt?

FR URBAN: *Non erunt. Qui studio et amore peccandi a veritate se sentiunt alienatos, et infirmitate et ignorantia pressos, studium in gemitum, amorem in moerorem convertant, infirmitatem carnis fervore justitiae vincant, ignorantiam liberalitate repellant.*

RECTOR: *Cur?*

FR URBAN: *Ne si nunc egentem, nudam, infirmam veritatem ignorant, cum potestate magna et virtute venientem, terrentem, arguentem, sero cum rubore cognoscant, frustra cum tremore respondeant:* Quando te vidimus esurientem, aut sitientem, aut hospitem, aut nudum, aut infirmum, aut in carcere, et non ministravimus tibi? *Cognoscetur certe*

wife, that is, the weakness of the flesh, in his defense? Will the stoners of the first martyr, because they would not listen, be pardoned for their ignorance?

Those who are estranged from truth by passion and pleasure in sinning, and who are overcome by weakness and ignorance, must surrender their passion to regret, their pleasure to sorrow, and conquer the infirmities of the flesh with the fire of justice, and meet ignorance with liberality.

Why?

Otherwise, if they fail to recognize truth as it appears now, needy, naked, and weak, they may not know it until it comes with great power and glory, terrible and indicting, and they may then redden and in vain answer in trembling voices: *When did we see thee hungry or thirsty or a stranger or naked or sick or in prison and did not minister to thee?* The Lord shall be

Dominus judicia faciens, qui nunc ignoratur misericordiam quaerens. Denique videbunt in quem transfixerunt: similiter et avari quem contempserunt. Beati enim mundo corde, quoniam ipsi Deum videbunt.

known when he judges, if he is not known when he seeks mercy. Then they shall look on him whom they pierced with a lance, and likewise the avaricious on him whom they despised in their hearts. *Blessed are the pure in heart: for they shall see God.*

RECTOR: *Quomodo?*

How?

FR URBAN: *Per laborem humilitatis, per affectum compassionis, per excessum contemplationis. In primo veritas reperitur severa; in secundo pia; in tertio, pura. Ad primum ratio ducit. Ad secundum affectus perducit. Ad tertium puritas rapit.*

By the toil of humility, by the emotion of compassion, by the ecstasy of contemplation. In the first, truth is found harsh, in the second, loving, in the third, pure. Reason leads us to the first, Love brings us to the second, Purity carries us up to the third.

RECTOR: *Domine, abscondisti haec a sapientibus, et revelasti ea nobis.*

O, Lord, you have hid these things from the sapient and revealed them to us.

FR URBAN: *Amen.*

Verily.

RECTOR: *Num remanet ullum spei refugium, ubi oratio non invenit locum?*

Is there any safe harbor for hope where prayer finds no place?

FR URBAN: *Non remanet. Et si contigerit (quod Deus avertat) aliquem de nostris*

No, and if it should happen (which God forbid) that any of our brethren should die,

fratribus, non in corpore, sed in anima mori; quamdiu adhuc inter nos erit, pulsabo et ego meis qualiscumque peccator, pulsabo et fratrum precibus Salvatorem.

not in body, but in soul, so long as he is still among us I will besiege the Saviour, both with my own prayers, whatever a sinner can avail, and with those of the brethren.

RECTOR: *Visne, pro Dei a-more omni obedientia te subjicere superioribus tuis?*

And will you, for the love of God, with all obedience, submit yourself to your superiors?

FR URBAN: *Volo.*

I will.

RECTOR: *Deinde ego, Wilfridus, voluntate Dei (in quantum cognosci potest a nobis) et voluntate fratrum tuorum constituo te Provincialem Ordinis S. Clementis, Provinciae Chicagiensis.*

Then I, Wilfrid, declare you, Urban, by the will of God (so far as we can know it) and by the will of your brethren, Provincial of the Order of St Clement of the Province of Chicago.

FR URBAN: *Amen.*

So be it.

Dirge

So, late in November, Father Urban returned to the Novitiate as Father Provincial, and discovered what was expected of him there.

Early in October, the Clementines had learned that the building they occupied on the near North Side was up for sale, and that their lease would not be renewed. This, it seemed, had been a big issue in the election, and had had a lot to do with the outcome. Before the new Provincial arrived on the scene, men said, "Wait'll *he* gets here." After he got there, they said, "What's he doing?" Early in December, when the day came to move out (many had doubted that this day would ever come), the Clementines moved out, and not to another location (many had predicted a return to the Loop), but out to the Novitiate. When, later that month, it was rumored that the building hadn't been sold, and that another religious order had been offered the space formerly occupied by the Clementines, men said, "How come?"

Father Louis spoke to the new Provincial about the matter, and spoke as an old friend, pulling no punches, but got no satisfaction, as he told others later, and then, entirely on his own, went to see the owner of the building. After a long evening in town, he returned to the Novitiate none the wiser, empty-handed, and stoned. "What's happened to us wouldn't happen to a first-class outfit, or even to a second-class one," he told the

321

dormitory of first-year men in his charge (most of whom, fortunately, slept on, exhausted as they were by pillow fights), and the next morning he failed to meet his classes in phy ed and moral.

The same day, Father Siegfried called upon a friend of his in the other Order about another matter, and discovered that the Dalmatians—for it was they who were being offered the location —had turned down the proposition: only the owner of the building and Father Gabriel had been sanguine enough to believe that such a thing could get past the Chancery, and *he*, by the way, was being given a well-deserved rest in the country.

Back in November, the Clementines had learned that the radio station on which their weekly program had been heard for so many years no longer wanted them, since it was increasing its coverage of news and music—news on the half hour instead of the hour, the Top 88 Tunes instead of the Top 42. Late in January, after the program had been off the air for a month, the new Provincial came forward with a proposal: fifteen minutes on a smaller station, "Father Clem Answers Your Question" to occupy the time slot between "Civil Service News" and the "Transylvanian Hour," which had already moved from the larger station and gone from a half hour to fifteen minutes. The proposal was received in silence, and voted down. The new Provincial didn't seem to care. Father Siegfried said that they might do well to educate some young men in the field of television, and was praised on all sides for his foresight, but the new Provincial only said, "We'll see."

Men were no longer asking, "What's he doing?" but "What's he done?"

Seldom had a new Provincial so badly disappointed the hopes and calculations of men. Many changes in personnel had been expected, but there had been few, and strangely, the men regarded as most likely to be affected, as almost certain to get the

boot, were spared. Father Wilfrid was still in charge at St
Clement's Hill. Brother Henry, formerly Father Boniface's secretary, was now secretary to the new Provincial. And Father
Boniface himself, whom many had thought destined for Texas
or New Mexico, was still at the Novitiate—teaching Father
Louis's courses. Father Louis was back at the Hill, a two-time
loser, and Father John, who was reported to be writing the life
of St Adalbert in his spare moments, was back on the road.
These were the only major changes, and they made men wonder.

The biggest change was in the physical appearance of the
Novitiate. *Ceratocystis* had reached into the tribe of elm trees
on the grounds, and by order of the new Provincial the infected
members were cut down. For this he was roundly blamed. What
men did not know, and what he did not tell them, was that the
slaughter should have been carried out immediately after the
examination, which had taken place during the previous spring.
Father Boniface, that hard man, had been too soft to order the
job done while the trees were in leaf, it seemed, and later had
feared the effect it might have on his chances for a second term.
And so, besides their prestige address on the near North Side,
and their radio program, the Clementines had lost the Avenue
of Elms. These were the things that came to mind when men
thought of the new Provincial.

About these things, and others, he had little to say, but reading
the speeches of Winston Churchill, and coming to "I have not
become the King's first minister in order to preside over the
liquidation of the British Empire," he thought, "No, nor did
Mr (as he was then) Attlee consider himself so called, but such
was his fate."

By March, "What's he done?" had become "He's not well."

This was true. His head was worse. Standing on it hadn't
helped him either. His severest attacks now came in pairs, the
first one lasting about a minute and a half, the second one about

a minute, with an interval of perhaps forty seconds between them. They arrived and departed like sections of the Twentieth Century Limited—three or four times on some days, a dozen on others—and left him with a dazed and run-over feeling. When somebody was in the office, and he felt the first section coming down the tracks, he swiveled around in his chair, saying, "I'll be with you in a minute, Father," and opened his breviary, and closed his eyes, and waited until both sections had come and gone. Thus he tried to disguise his condition from others, and thus, without wishing to, he gained a reputation for piety he hadn't had before, which, however, was not entirely unwarranted now.

But he did his best to see as few people as possible. Several men were asked not to call at the office except on urgent business (Father Louis, before his transfer, was one of these), and Father Excelsior was asked not to call except on urgent, *new* business. At Christmastime, Father Excelsior had received an imported card from Dickie Thwaites, who had removed from Des Moines (to Greenwich Village), a card on which editor informed publisher that he was going home to be with Mother during the holidays, after which he hoped to write and clarify the situation. By March, he hadn't done either. The MS (as Father Excelsior called it) of *Sir Launcelot and the Catholic Knights of the Round Table* was in the hands of the publisher, but otherwise the marriage between the Millstone Press and Eight Seasons Editions had borne no fruit.

Monsignor Renton had written twice, the first time from the hospital after his prostatectomy, and the second time, some weeks later, to report that he'd had a relapse. This, he wrote, had been brought on by leaving the hospital too soon, and this he'd done because the Bishop had checked in with flu and had wanted his suite. Monsignor Renton, rather than move to a room, had checked out of the hospital. Late in February, on his way back from Florida, Monsignor Renton had phoned from Union Station and invited the new Provincial to have dinner with him in town, but the new Provincial hadn't cared to come in, and Monsignor Renton hadn't cared to come out, and so they'd talked for a while and let it go at that. Monsignor Renton said that he'd advised Father Udovic to put off building a ːw church at St Monica's until spring, or, better yet, summer. The man hadn't listened to him, but now wished he had, because it was costing him fifty dollars a day for oil just to keep the bricklayers warm. The new church would be one of those hatchery affairs, with silo attached.

The new Provincial did entertain one visitor from Minnesota, however. Late one morning, he heard somebody asking for him in the outer office and say he hoped Brother Henry wouldn't mind not being called "Father." Unfortunately, just as the visitor was being shown in, the Provincial had one of his attacks, which, as usual, wiped out what had gone immediately before, so that when he faced the visitor he had no idea who would be there, and did not realize that a minute before, between trains, he'd said, "I'll be with you in a minute, Father."

Mr. Studley, to give him credit, let it pass. He was in Chicago for a reunion of his old squadron, he said, and having got the new Provincial's new address from the folks at the Hill, he'd thought it might be a good idea to stop by and say hello and also to say that Frank had died. Mr. Studley was invited to stay for lunch, did, and had a wonderful couple of hours meeting priests and brothers, faring somewhat better with the latter than with the former. There wasn't much news from home, he said. Zim, and all that crowd, were in Florida. Frank had died.

Father Wilfrid wrote often. In January, the weather was very cold in Minnesota, and also in February. The blower had made a big difference, but the house was a bit chilly just the same. In March, Father Wilfrid said he was grateful for permission to set up a speakers' bureau at the Hill, and, as directed, he and Father Louis would confine themselves to subjects of a religious nature, as would Brother Harold in his chalk talks to teenagers. Rex was fine. In April, Father Wilfrid wrote that the Bishop and Father Feld had been out to the Hill, on a friendly visit.

And the new Provincial, replying at once, said that he was pleased to hear that the Bishop had been out to the Hill, and urged Father Wilfrid to do everything, within reason, to assure continued good relations between Order and Diocese. But the new Provincial was worried. Oddly enough, although for many years he'd traveled out of Chicago, he seemed to think of the Hill as home.

About the Author

JAMES FARL POWERS was born in 1917, in Jacksonville, Illinois. He has contributed regularly to *The New Yorker* and other magazines, and has received fellowships from the Rockefeller Foundation and the Guggenheim Foundation. He is the author of three collections of short fiction, *Prince of Darkness and Other Stories* (1947), *The Presence of Grace* (1956), and *Look How the Fish Live* (1975). *Morte D'Urban* won the National Book Award in 1963; Mr. Powers's second novel, *Wheat That Springeth Green,* was nominated for the National Book Award and the National Book Critics Circle Award in 1988.